Shadows and Splendour
A Diamond of the Ton Regency Mystery
Book 2

Lynn Morrison

Anne Radcliffe

Marketing Chair Press

Cover design by The Killion Group, Inc

Published by

The Marketing Chair Press, Oxford, England

LynnMorrisonWriter.com

ISBN (paperback): 978-1-917361-17-0

Contents

Dedication

"There has to be an insertion point somewhere—"

"That's what she said."

Cast of Characters

- Lady Charity Cresswell (now Duchess Atholl) – Lady-in-waiting to Queen Charlotte
- Lord Peregrine Fitzroy – Former soldier turned spy for the crown

Royal Family and Court:

- Queen Charlotte
- Prince Regent (also referred to as Prinny)
- Princess Charlotte – Prinny's daughter
- Lord Ravenscroft – Gathers intelligence for Prinny
- Prince William VI of Orange – The Dutch prince intended for Princess Charlotte
- Catherine Pavlovna, Grand Duchess of Oldenburg – Sister of the Tsar of Russia

Household Staff:

- Will Hodges – Peregrine's driver and servant
- Antoine – Lord Ravenscroft's valet and lover

- Mr Pritchard – Charity's butler
- Mr Quinn – Peregrine's butler
- Jack Graves and Owen Graves – Peregrine's new footmen
- Mr Croft – Peregrine's valet

Members of the Order and other characters:

- Lady Selina, Marchioness of Normanby - Member of the Order who influences statesmen
- Mr Goldbourne – Member of the Order who runs a bank
- Mr Xavier – Member of the Order with a distinctive six-fingered hand
- Duke Chandros – Member of the Order who influences military figures
- Lord Pembroke – Member of the Order with influence among capitalists and industrialists
- Marian Fitzroy – Peregrine's villainous mother
- Red Hand (also referred to as Red) – A thug known to Peregrine
- Viscount Sidmouth – Home Secretary

Prologue
London, June 1808

"There are many roads to power, none of them paved with virtue."
—Marian Fitzroy

Given the season was still in full swing, Peregrine Fitzroy celebrated the birthday that marked his age of majority quietly. His final exams and farewells at Oxford began a few days after, giving him enough time to join his mother in London for a few last events.

It was to be a brief taste of the adulthood that was now his to become. There were people to meet, places to be seen—and most importantly, legal matters to attend to.

As he rode into London, the world seemed both exciting and full of new responsibilities. By now, the marriage market would have been thoroughly picked over, but the smiles he drew from women walking promised that next season would be... eventful.

His mother and sister greeted him at the door of the estate home. At thirteen, his sister Lark was just beginning to bloom, and Marian looked both lovely and gracious as she welcomed her son.

"Perry," she greeted him, stroking a hand over her son's cheek. "I am so proud of you, my love. Where did the time go? You have become such a handsome, capable man when I was not looking."

Peregrine held his hand over his mother's, leaning into her touch as he looked down at his mama. It still seemed strange to him, to look down at her from the greater height he had sprouted around his eighteenth year. "I think I would owe both to you, *Mama*," he teased her, his heart full as he tweaked a strand of the bright blonde hair that framed her face. Hair so much like his sister's. And his own.

His mother gave him a small, knowing smile. It was a bittersweet moment. At one and twenty, the trust that held the Fitzroy family assets for the last five years needed to be closed and transferred to him. It was the largest part of why he had bothered rushing to London.

The estate had thrived since his father's death. His mother's acumen was far sharper and more canny than the former lord's. Perry had respected his father, but he had to admit the man had no head for investment. Fortunately for him, his mother was still capable and willing to help him learn the ropes.

Perry spent his homecoming enjoying the reunion with his family. His appointment with Grenville was for the following day.

As he set off to meet the old family solicitor, his mother pressed a small bottle into his hands. "A thank you from me to Mr Grenville for assisting you with everything. Plum cordial," she explained. "Mr Grenville adores it. If he offers to share it with you, be sure to decline—we have plenty; he does not need to share his gift."

Peregrine wrinkled his nose. "I would pass in any event. Plum cordial is foul."

Marian laughed. "I agree. But there is no accounting for certain tastes."

He visited the solicitor at his office on Great Ormond Street, carrying his mother's gift, and was greeted by a clerk barely older than himself when he knocked on the blue-painted door. Mr Grenville pulled off his spectacles when Peregrine entered his office.

"My goodness. Little Lord Fitzroy, no longer so little," Mr Grenville laughed as he rose and offered his hand. "Your father would be pleased at the man you've become—but between you and me, it's a good thing you are the spitting image of your mother."

Peregrine chuckled and shook the solicitor's hand warmly, not offended. Robin Fitzroy had been many things, but handsome had not been one of them—nor charming, nor particularly clever. These things Perry had been taught by his mother.

Mr Grenville accepted his gift and spent the next hour generously walking him through the paperwork and some of the details of the Fitzroy holdings. It was painstaking work, and Grenville talked himself dry enough that he helped himself to the cordial, which emanated the sweet, spicy smell of plum mixed with cinnamon and cloves.

Finally, towards the end of their appointment, Grenville closed the ledgers he was about to hand over, running one hand over his chest thoughtfully. "I should let you know, while I was examining the books for closing the trust, I found a few... oddities I could not reconcile. A few regular payments to names not part of the land or household staff. A property that was held under two separate instruments—most likely, a clerical issue."

He lifted his hand in caution, indicating it was a small matter. "I am sure there is a reasonable explanation, but look more closely. If you ever wish to review anything outside these formal meetings, I'm at your disposal, my lord."

"Thank you. Your assistance has been invaluable, Grenville," Perry said honestly. Still, he worried that Grenville had discovered one of his mother's... creative investments.

His mother had taught him years ago that a little bloodless corruption was the way of the aristocracy. Nothing to fuss over. Indeed, it had restored the bankrupt Fitzroy estate, paid for his education, and given his sister clothing. A dowry. The things she would need to live a proper life.

"Mr Grenville... are you unwell?" he asked the solicitor, who was looking peaked.

The man shook that off and stood, his brow dotted with sweat. "I am tired. The joys of advancing age. It was such a pleasure seeing you again, Lord Fitzroy." The man smiled genially at him, patting the back of Perry's hand as he shook it once again.

"Mother, did you know Mr Grenville was looking into your investments?" he asked her quietly when he returned home that evening.

"Of course, Perry," she replied, her voice distant. Unconcerned. "That would be what he was employed to do. Do not worry, love. I am sure things will sort themselves out properly."

Mr Grenville's death was in the paper the very next day.

"The poor man, it must have been his heart," his mother said, shaking her head in regret when he let her know the news.

Peregrine, who at this point was still very innocent—but not at all ignorant—of his mother's shadowy business and ambitious nature, immediately found the timing suspicious. Especially given her words and gift to Grenville the previous eve.

His mother had begun studying the medical aspects of botany, which most physicians treated as country superstition, sometime around the time his father had fallen ill. He had always assumed that she had taken up the hobby to find a cure for her husband.

But a distressing connection formed within his mind: What if the mysterious illness that had put the heavy-handed Robin Fitzroy in bed for so many years had happened after her studies began, not before?

"Tell me you did not have something to do with this," he begged, hoping his logic was faulty.

Marian Fitzroy's face lost its careful animation, and the hair on Peregrine's neck stood on end, sensing something dark and eldritch in her eyes. "*I* did not."

"Mother!" he hissed, concerned by her emphasis. Horrified. Questionable trade and pulling strings for opportunities might have made the law raise an eyebrow, but no harm was done to anyone. "Murder—it could ruin us."

"Yes. It could," she replied calmly. Coldly. "I trust you remember by whose hand he died, and be careful. If you speak, there will be consequences for us all. But mostly for you and your sister. Grow accustomed to the idea you will sometimes have to do distasteful tasks to protect the family, just as I have for all these years."

A threat. She had put the weapon in his hand, very much on purpose, to bind him to her will.

Perry hadn't the first idea who his mother was. He realised he never had. She had picked him up like a tool, and used him without remorse.

God. He had killed an innocent man.

The sense of revulsion and betrayal was so great, Peregrine wanted to vomit. "You *used* me. Without my consent. *You forced me to do this*. And now Grenville's blood is on my hands."

That day, Peregrine got his first close look at the monster that lived beneath Marian Fitzroy's husk. And it would sometimes cause him to wake in the night, sweating and terrified, for years afterwards.

"I held you close, whispered that you were my heart. My joy. You enjoyed every comfort, and it never occurred to you to doubt my will until now. That's the brilliance of using someone's love as a leash, my darling. And now you will be a good boy and remember to obey your mother, because you are mine—body and soul."

1

London, Mid May, 1814

Nocturnis ego somniis
iam captum teneo, iam volucrem sequor
te per gramina Martii
campi, te per aquas, dure, volubilis.
—Horace, Odes, Book IV

On the darkest night of the month, an evening that suitably matched the blackness of his thoughts, Peregrine made a plan to deliberately seat himself in one of the empty armchairs nestled in the bow window at White's.

It was a brassy move, laying claim to what even he still thought of as Beau Brummell's chair. But that was the nature of this game. Establishing one's dominance in these circles required a certain penchant for bluffing—especially when one was on their back foot.

Or flat upon their arse, proverbially speaking.

Since his autonomy had already been used to purchase a truce with the others, Peregrine had decided to first try to run his mother's web of contacts to the ground. Logic dictated prioritizing the enemy who was still actively trying to remove him from the equation.

So far, he was coming up empty-handed.

Perry shoved against the sick, hopeless feeling that threatened to swallow his soul. There was an opportunity here. Tonight. Tonight, he could lay the path to reclaim a little power for himself, and he would do well to remember that.

Brummell's reign had ended. The titleless, parasitic dandy and the Regent had gone from confidants to strangers with excellent posture after Brummell so neatly cut his own throat at the Devonshire ball last year. The chair now was vacant. Sometimes it was occupied by one of a few at the pinnacle of the aristocracy. But tonight they were not here.

So, he sat, and the hum of conversation around the gaming tables stuttered. Men looked at one another, then at him. Even Tremayne, standing near another table, gaped at him like a fish.

Their consternation was amusing. Peregrine affected not to notice, keeping his expression bored. He simply crossed his legs, ignoring the twinge in his side, and sipped his brandy, waiting as though he hadn't a care in the world.

Somewhere out in London, his mother's invisible machine was still at work. McGrath had called it a clockwork. He knew there were still cogs turning, regulated by her plans. But he couldn't find a sign of it.

There were things that he knew, that he couldn't help learning, in the years since his mother showed him what lay beneath her mask. He had tried to remain as ignorant and distant of her unsavoury business as he could, however, and now that was working against him.

Marian had been content to let him stretch the cord as long as he obeyed and was silent. Mr Grenville's particular message had not been repeated, but she had asked him for other things to keep her finger on where his loyalties lay. That was how he had fallen so far that he had become acquainted with the likes of Mr Cameron and McGrath.

So Perry knew of a few other names, other places, other businesses. But only a few, and so far his searching had come up fruitless. Every name he asked for was supposedly gone from London.

And now, Peregrine was feeling sorely pressed. Time was ticking towards the culmination of her design. He could feel an echo of it in his own pulse, like it was counting down to something that would spell disaster for him.

One would think that his mother's threats and machinations should be the foremost weight upon his mind. If his mother was no longer a threat, then he could turn his attention on the *other* three women trying to control his life.

The Queen and Selina were grasping creatures. Their intentions to use him had never been a surprise. It had been the third, the golden-haired duchess, who had been the one to throw him on his beam-ends, sealing him into a pact with a proverbial devil.

Charity, the Duchess Atholl. The one whose kiss still haunted his days and nights. Somehow, he had been blind to the possibility of her betrayal. Failed to anticipate the splitting agony of it.

He had spent years hiding his inconvenient emotions away, but since he had crossed paths with her again, sometimes it felt like he could not close the door on them at all. And that was... dreadful.

The familiar dull ache in his chest made Peregrine swallow bitterly before he caught the expression. He readjusted himself in his chair so people would think it was physical discomfort.

You are three steps behind me, he was reprimanded by the voice inside his head. *You are without friends, without resources.*

And even with the reaper breathing on your neck, you cannot bring your thoughts to the most important tasks.

His personal hell was complete, lacking only a fiddle-playing devil in a corner.

Your man missed, mother, he reminded her.

Her spectre gave a vile, knowing chuckle. McGrath might have missed the killing blow, but the festering wound had been nearly fatal anyway.

It was still far from healed. It itched and ached, and sometimes when he was careless, the outer edges of the wound cracked apart and bled. A heavy layer of tight, wide bandages was mostly keeping him together, physically. Any other broken, bleeding parts were his own damned fault.

A pathetic, wraith-ridden mess, the voice of his mother agreed contemptuously. *No smarter than the farmer who showed pity to the viper half frozen in his fields, putting it in his pocket. Again, you brought the serpent into your arms. You have already taken the actions that will see you dead. You simply have not yet ceased to breathe.*

Do not dare pretend as though you weren't the first venomous creature close to my skin, Mama, he replied lightly, drinking the last of his brandy in one throat-burning swallow.

There was no peace within the confines of his skull. Not when flanked by his predatory mother and the manipulative duchess.

Jerking his attention back to the gentlemen in the room, he watched as shock waned and their minds worked. They were beginning to remember who Perry had been. Before he had been brought down by the events of last year.

Soon, his first petitioner approached. Thomas Crichton, a third son of a baron, who had a favour to ask. Could Perry have a quiet word with Rowland Hill or the undersecretary to aid him in securing a position, he wanted to know?

Of course he'd do what he could. If Hill took Lord Crichton's son, then there would be two people well-positioned to aid him in return. And if he didn't, well at least Thomas would still owe him.

More penitents approached. More small favours granted. An introduction here, begging for a party invitation there. More brandy was consumed. After the last week, it nearly felt like a dereliction of some duty—sitting here, drinking and talking—but it was dangerous to forget that Marian Fitzroy had spent decades cultivating people on both sides of the class divide.

Empire builders understood the value in spanning rivers with bridges.

"The chair seems to suit you," murmured Tremayne, and Peregrine's head jerked up from pondering his empty snifter.

Seeing he finally had Perry's attention, the man smiled somewhat impishly, handing him a full glass. "Oh good, you were only busy gathering wool. I was wondering if you might be cutting me."

"Cutting you? No. My apologies, Tremayne," Peregrine said, taking the proffered drink with a small smile of appreciation, even though his head was growing muzzy after so many similar offerings. "I collected an entire bale."

"I mean it, though. You were always good at... this." Tremayne sat somewhat ungracefully on the edge of the other chair, proving that the chestnut-haired man had also imbibed more than he ought. "Better than Brummell, really. I'm relieved that the prince's experiment in upholstery is over with. You at least have never felt the need to make yourself superior by virtue of pushing others into a ditch."

Perry grinned enough to show his teeth, though it wasn't a real smile. A few years ago, Brummell had told Tremayne that he dressed as though afraid his valet would outshine him, so there was no love lost between him and the former arbiter of taste. "I do admire your loyalty to me, especially when it is so transparently self-serving. What do you want?"

"I want to have a drink with my friend. Why are you accusing me of polishing apples?"

They were on decent terms, but hardly friends. Taking his drink in his hand, Peregrine leaned forward to plant his elbows on his knees, giving Tremayne a scolding look as he did so.

"All right, fine. I did actually have something to ask." The man slouched backwards some, returning Peregrine's frank look. "First... how is your side?"

"Healing well," Perry replied to this non sequitur. It was only barely a lie.

By some miracle, the Crown had managed to conceal the extent of his injury. For all London knew, he had suffered a minor mishap with a housebreaker at his townhouse. A nebulous concern for his safety gave him one excuse to recuperate in a room at White's, and the pedestrian excuses of renovations and tenants at his two other properties had deterred other questions.

You could always leave White's and hide instead behind the lovely duchess's skirts, his mother volunteered.

Never, he shot back at the sly voice.

What an unbearable thought, crawling back to Atholl House and the guards stationed at her home. Not only would he despise himself for such an act of cowardice more than he already did, bringing more danger to the Duchess Atholl's doorstep would completely unman him.

Tremayne let his fingers play on his glass silently, and, irked by his wandering thoughts, Peregrine took another long drink to smother his mama's hateful presence. "What were you going to ask me?" he prompted.

"I have... a friend of limited means searching for a place to hang his hat." Tremayne shaded his mouth with one hand, keeping his voice low. "He has been cut off by his brother. I would not ask if I could think of another option, but the situation has become... well, it is bloody inconvenient, and I cannot put him up myself. He needs somewhere quiet for a week. Your townhouse would do nicely, if you were of a mind to do him a favour."

Curious, Peregrine wondered what scandal he had missed while he had been recovering or nose-down in the stews, trying to locate the few faces he had known to be intimately connected to Marian Fitzroy's underworld operations.

"I assume you mean without asking who he is or what he has done," Perry asked, keeping his words uninflected.

"At least for the moment?"

"I had at least best ask if your friend happens to be prone to Gothic terrors. I cannot swear that my man of business got around to finding someone who could clean up the blood on the floor."

A long pause followed, and as a delicate pink shaded Tremayne's cheekbones at such a lurid statement, Peregrine almost regretted uttering it. But he was also curious as to how desperate the situation might be.

"At the risk of sounding callous, I daresay he would agree that the villain got what he deserved."

The reply was a bit of an evasion. But Tremayne's face didn't flicker with indecision, as it would if he was suddenly thinking better of putting his friend up there.

To Perry, that meant that his friend was in a fine pickle indeed. Probably debt or scandalous indiscretion. Interesting.

"Then of course, he is welcome to stay." Peregrine would write to his man of business—temporarily also acting in capacity as a steward—and let him know that the Neal property was occupied by a guest.

All of the personal possessions he had stored there had already been removed to the main house. Peregrine fully intended to never set foot in it again.

"Thank you," Tremayne said softly. "I can cover a week with my allowance; just name the price."

Perry waved off the offer of money. "He can have the house for as long as he needs it. God knows I am not planning to occupy it. I am sure either you or your friend will be happy to return such a favour to me someday. I will name it when I find myself in need."

"That is… very good of you, Perry. So very good." Lord Tremayne, so very young and credulous, looked relieved rather than troubled by the idea of owing a large, unnamed favour, and Peregrine could feel the corners of his mouth turn down ever so slightly at the man's vulnerability.

"To you, and your health," he added belatedly, toasting Peregrine with his glass.

Perry smiled briefly and drank deeply. It was for the best that Tremayne had asked this favour of him rather than someone else. Peregrine took a perverse sort of pride in being discreet and honourable when finally naming a price. But there were other, much less scrupulous people in the *ton* who wouldn't bat an eye at the idea of extorting Tremayne or his friend.

He continued to play the part of a gentleman, conversing in light banter now that the serious part of the conversation was done. He let Tremayne drag him over to the card tables to be treated to more rounds of drinks. And he silently endured the continued biting mental monologues of his mother, who had something new and cutting to say every time he thought about the duchess's lips, or hair, or—hell, even what she might have to say about the company he kept.

It was time to quit drinking; his fortitude was abysmal. But he didn't get up once he emptied his snifter again. His head swam from too much brandy and too little sleep. He was afraid if he got up before he sobered up a bit, he might tilt over.

"Gentlemen, could I borrow this one from you?" A touch landed on Peregrine's shoulder, and he flinched slightly, giving the owner of the hand upon his superfine coat a baleful look.

Lord Ravenscroft. Prinny's magpie.

The men murmured their assent, and Ravenscroft backed up a step, giving Peregrine the space to slide his chair out from beneath the table. The nattily dressed older man said nothing as he suspiciously watched Peregrine stand carefully, and Peregrine put his hand to his side, pretending it was his injury that had him moving so judiciously.

That caused the magpie to roll his eyes, but Ravenscroft immediately and cheerfully addressed the rest of the table so that they were watching him instead of Peregrine. "Do not wait up for him, lads! I am taking this one out for a night of trouble." Ravenscroft laid a finger alongside his nose and gave an exaggerated wink, earning a few lascivious chuckles in reply. Then he escorted Peregrine from the table as quickly as he could.

"My God, Perry," Ravenscroft muttered in a tone so low only Peregrine could hear him. He waved his hand, encouraging Peregrine to hurry towards the stairs. "You are *beastly* drunk."

"I am not," Perry said shortly. "And I hope you do not take offense to this, but I would rather throw myself from the rooftop if the alternative is to go gallivanting to a bawdy house in your company."

"I would be more inclined to believe in your sobriety if I couldn't smell the fumes emanating from your person. It is a good thing no one next to you decided to light a cigar. But as for a night of illicit passion—do not worry, Canary. I do not have an evening nearly so exciting planned for you."

"Thrilling. Where *are* we bound, then?"

"Never mind that. Can you descend the stairs unaided, or shall I give you my arm as I would to a proper lady?"

Perry glared down at the shorter lord's head, keeping his voice to a note so low that no one would make out his words. "Offer your arm, and I will tell your lover you have been importuning me. Then he will kill you and save me the trouble of doing it myself."

"You should be so lucky." When Ravenscroft still said nothing more, about to reach for the handrail, Perry grabbed the older man by his wrist, hauling him bodily around.

"Ravenscroft—I am deadly serious. I will go nowhere except to my bed without a satisfactory answer as to where you want to take me." Suspicion pinched his features. "You are not trying to take me to a meeting with *her* are you?"

Ravenscroft turned sharply on him, his gaze roving from one side of Peregrine's face to the other, fixated on his eyes. Then he sighed, running a hand through his lightly silvered hair. "I am sorry, of course I should have thought—never mind. No, we are not going to see the duchess, dearest. I pledge to keep you safe from all your enemies. Come along."

He began to descend the stairs, not waiting, and with a small sigh of resignation, Peregrine followed, trying not to grind his teeth. Stairs pulled his flank more than walking did, and he was feeling somewhat green from the pain and the alcohol by the time he joined Ravenscroft at his carriage.

"I say, are you fit to ride like this?" His face was scrutinized again. "I would rather not have you lose the skirmish with your port on my boots. I rather like these ones."

"It was brandy, and I will remind you that you were the one to drag me here. Now that I am down the stairs and outside, you are rethinking the wisdom of it? Because if so, I will vomit on your shoes just to spite you."

Lord Ravenscroft looked like he ate something sour. "If you do not need to have an urgent conversation with the gutter, go ahead and get inside." He made a dismissive shoo-ing gesture towards the step.

Piqued, Perry hauled himself inside of Ravenscroft's

conveyance, taking the forward-facing seat, which Ravenscroft didn't protest.

"Better you there than being ill in my lap," he said with a surly tone. "It is a good thing I hauled you out of there when I did. One more drink, and you might have done something truly undignified."

"My saviour," Peregrine said mockingly, slouching back against the squab.

Now that there was no one to play a part for—except for the magpie, and who cared what he thought?—Perry's exhaustion felt like it was crushing his very bones. "So? Who instructed you to cart me off like a piece of luggage? Prinny, I assume. And for what reason? Is the Queen already impatient? It has been all of what, five days?"

"Since you last appeared publicly? Yes."

"There is still no news to give them," Peregrine said shortly. "I have found and claimed some of the bank accounts my mother created for herself in my name. My solicitor is looking for others. But so far, they are mostly empty. And legitimate."

"I do not care about that!" Ravenscroft made sweeping gestures with his hand. "It was not the Queen or Prinny who sent me to fetch you. It was Antoine, you know."

"I—" Peregrine stopped, frowned and tried again. "Your valet? Whatever for?"

"He was in quite the pucker after I mentioned you were staying at White's. *Alone.* Without so much as a body servant to look after you. I reckon you were unaware of it at the time, but Antoine was responsible for a great deal of your nursing during those days we thought you might expire from fever, you know. He made sure I had not forgotten how recently you rose from your deathbed. At the very top of his lungs, I might add."

The magpie continued dramatically, placing his hand over his chest as he emulated the stronger French accent of his valet. "'*Someone* needs to check on milord Fitzroy. That someone should be you, *mon cœur*. Bring him home from that awful club so that we can make sure he is eating properly and he has someone caring for him.'"

The corner of Peregrine's mouth turned up wryly, but he felt… a strange, forbidding sensation in his chest. Antoine, who was practically a stranger, was concerned for his well being? "Your valet bullied you into kidnapping me?"

"Well actually, he told me this very grim, horrible little story about dying barn cats. Does it amuse you to know that Antoine says you have the personality of one? It made me feel just guilty enough that I decided to kidnap you so I could tell you this appalling little fact myself."

Peregrine's eyes slid towards the old rake, giving him an amused look. "It warms the heart that you felt the need to check I did not expire in some hidden corner like an old Tom."

Ravenscroft looked down his nose at him. "I, of course, told Antoine you were fine. That you were a smart, capable young man who could run circles around the rest of us when it came to your mother's intrigues. I also reminded him that you were a horrible monster who ruined one of my favourite cravats and that you *weren't* alone, you had Hodges acting your nursemaid—"

The smirk fell from Peregrine's face. It wasn't often that he found himself robbed of words. In the silence of his thoughts, his mother laughed aloud at this revelation that he was losing all sense of preservation.

Ravenscroft was giving him a hard look, arms crossed, one hand over his mouth as he digested this. "You… did not know Hodges has been shadowing you."

His lungs would no longer fill with air of their own volition, and Peregrine forced a breath, ignoring a skin-crawling feeling of nervous terror. How had he not seen Hodges following him? "I suppose I am aware now."

"Damn me sideways, Perry. Do you have any idea how many times Antoine is going to tell me that he told me so?"

Peregrine sighed. "You are making a mountain of a molehill, Maggie. My poor sleep has caught up with me, that is all."

"Is it?" Ravenscroft asked in a soft voice. "Shall we pretend that is all?"

Gentian blue eyes, full of secrets and regret, lingered in his mind's eye.

"Pretend anything you like," Peregrine said, voice flat as he rubbed his aching chest absently. "The business between myself and the duchess is not of your concern."

The magpie nodded reluctantly, reaching out to straighten the line of Perry's collar as the carriage stopped. "All I will say then is do not let your good senses be overridden. Don't chew off a limb in your panic to escape a snare, lad; there are other ways to get yourself free. For now, I will hand you over to Antoine's tender mercies. You do need some cosseting. And, I think, a place you might actually feel safe to sleep—unless I've missed the mark."

If his facade was cracking so badly that Ravenscroft and Antoine could read him this clearly, he was in more trouble than he thought.

But oddly, after Ravenscroft's small, slight valet dragged him into a guest room and harangued him for not changing his bandages, sorted him out, and put him to bed like an indignant five year old, Perry did—finally—sleep more deeply than he had in weeks.

2

"His longing eyes, impatient, backward cast / To catch a lover's look, but look'd his last;
For, instant dying, she again descends, / While he to empty air his arms extends."
—Book the Tenth of Ovid's Metamorphoses

The Atholl family carriage rolled forward, nearly at the front of the line. Inside, Charity leaned her head against the carriage seat back and squeezed her eyes shut.

A year ago she had dreamt of attending an opera. She had imagined going with her family, with Grace, or maybe even on the arm of her betrothed. Yet here she sat, entirely alone, in a situation of her own making.

You wanted this.

And she had. This is what she had asked for on the fateful day when she begged the Queen to arrange marriage with a man half in the grave. After having her future ripped away by Lady Fitzroy, any control of her life snatched victory from the jaws of defeat.

Ironic. It was not really control she had gained, but isolation. She was alone on the stage, like a puppet, her strings jerked by the Queen of England. Why else would Charity make an appearance on a night she preferred to hide away in her room?

Stop wasting your time worrying about Peregrine Fitzroy! her mother's imagined voice chastised. If only that were so easy.

Charity had assumed—or maybe just hoped, really—that a few nights of sleep and healing would cool his temper. That she would find another chance to apologise about her deal with the Queen. But from what she had heard, a bed was the farthest thing from his mind. If he was not out carousing at White's, he was nowhere respectable.

His prolonged silence had made it abundantly clear; he was not yet ready to discuss any of it. Maybe it would be a cold day in hell before he forgave her for her betrayal. Which was understandable, as she could not quite find the wherewithal to completely forgive herself either.

After their last bitter conversation, she had spent time imagining how she would have felt in his shoes. The raw conclusion was that she would feel much the same as he did.

Her decision to appeal to the Queen for help when Perry had lain there, gravely injured, was still the only choice she could have made. But her larger mistake was holding her tongue. She should have told him the moment he woke, but she hadn't, and all the wishing in the world could not undo this error.

Charity's vision shrank, the familiar tightness in her chest stealing her breath. With a trembling hand, she reached out and flicked aside the curtain to allow light in, pushing back that feeling of suffocating impotence.

The impressive facade of the Theatre Royal was visible in the lamplight. It had been rebuilt after fire destroyed it five years earlier. Though the evening's production of Orphée et Eurydice was well underway, the line of people waiting to get inside showed no signs of thinning.

Only a fool attended the Royal Opera to watch the performers, despite the voices performing on stage. The real show took place in the boxes lining the cavernous theatre. Lord and ladies, dukes and duchesses, donned their finest attire and raised their opera glasses, not to see the Italian soprano, but to get a closer look at the jewels sparkling in people's ears and around necks.

And on this particular evening, even the Queen was to be there with her diamond. The mouths of the aristocracy must be positively watering.

Eyes turned to watch the Duchess Atholl make her way through the theatre doors. Charity pasted a hint of a smile on her face, willing her beauty to match the famed Atholl sapphire necklace hanging from her neck. Her gown, royal blue silk with hand-stitched Belgian lace covering the bodice and capped sleeves, drew gasps of envy. She imagined herself Venus rising from the frothing seas, personified.

Few would count silk and lace as appropriate gear for battle, but Charity's choice of gown proved worth every pound. Admiring the priceless vision kept them from noticing that her eyes may have lacked their usual sparkle.

No sooner did she set foot in the vestibule than a horde of titled young men stepped forward to surround her.

"Good evening, Your Grace. I hope you will not think me too forward, but I find I cannot contain my words. Tonight, you are more stunning than the fields of bluebells at my country home," one man purred, reaching for her hand.

"Cut line, Mathers," another said, blocking the first. He clasped Charity's gloved hand in his without so much as a by-your-leave and pressed such a sloppy kiss on her knuckles that it left a damp mark on her white gloves. "You will have to excuse young Mathers here, Your Grace, for he does not understand that a woman of your refinement has little use for wildflowers. With your permission, I would be delighted to bring you a bouquet worthy of a diamond. Tomorrow, perhaps? Around four in the afternoon?"

Charity knew the names, titles, and net worth of the men around her. Each of them was in the market for a bride this season. They had given her nothing more than a cursory nod up until tonight, likely assuming her either out of reach or too soon out of mourning.

Yet, somehow, things had changed. For some reason, they seemed to be under the impression that she was in the market and desperate for a new husband.

Charity had far too much on her plate to dally with young bucks, even if she were so inclined. And she most definitely was not. If only someone else were here—Grace, or even Perry—they could have a good laugh over the antics of the spoiled beaus falling at her feet.

But Grace was up in Northumberland, likely with a newborn demanding her attention. And Perry—

Peregrine Fitzroy was not available for her, not even when the Queen herself was the one making the demands.

Charity pulled her hand free of the man's hold, nearly losing her glove in the process, and levelled her haughtiest gaze on the horde. "My social calendar is fully booked, Mr Adams. Now, if you will please make way, Her Majesty is expecting me."

The man's jaw tightened as her cut hit home, but he shifted over to make room for her to go. However, he pitched his voice just loud enough to allow her to hear his passing remark. "I wonder if our good Queen knows about her carriage rides with the traitor's son?"

Her mother's voice hissed for her to hurry off, without a

backward glance. To allow the insult to go unchallenged. But Charity was done turning the other cheek. She swung around, her eyes sparking for the first time in weeks, this time with fury. "What did you say?"

Adams blatantly avoided meeting her gaze, instead smirking at the rest of his group of friends. "My sister spotted them leaving St James's together, if you can believe it. Instead of being grateful that such esteemed gentlemen as ourselves are willing to come calling, she snubs us in favour of a man with a reputation as black as his boots. And even he has thrown her over, it seems."

The voice of Charity's mother begged her to apologise to the young man, if for no other reason than to save the family name from further scandal. But the newer speaker in her head—the calm, collected voice of reason—kept her head held high and her tone sharp. "Mr Adams, I have as little interest in covering your gambling debts as I do in subjecting myself to your juvenile pawing. As for Lord Fitzroy, do not call him a traitor. The only blood on his hands comes from the sacrifices he made at the Nive for our country."

Adams rocked back. The rest of his set found a hundred other places to set their gaze, anywhere but in Charity's direction.

The thrill of victory put a spring into Charity's step. Mr Adams and the rest of the money-hungry ne'er-do-wells would think twice before accosting her in the future. Far too soon, however, triumph faded away, leaving behind a familiar sick churn. Peregrine wanted to break free of his mother's legacy, and incidents like tonight reminded her how difficult that path would be.

She had been eschewing alcohol this season, afraid to cede control to intoxication. But Charity took a glass of champagne from a footman to calm her spirits before she curtseyed to the Queen. She raised the glass, but before her lips touched the rim, someone stepped on the back of her train.

The precious silk ripped under the careless heel, throwing her off balance. Champagne sloshed, spilling down her chin and onto her glove. She pressed the side of her wrist against her mouth to mop up the sticky liquid, heedless of the stain.

"Excuse me, Your Grace, I did not see you there," a woman's voice purred, no hint of apology in her words.

Charity swung around to meet the eyes of Lady Pelham, whose face was lit in unholy delight as she took in the results of her rear attack.

"Far be it for me to question your modiste, but tell her to take greater care when measuring the length of your train. I nearly slipped!" The woman dared to smooth her own skirt and then pat her coiffure, feigning a near injury. "This is your first opera? You will know better next time."

"I will be sure to discuss the issue with the Queen, as soon as I arrive at the royal box." Charity gathered the side of her gown. With a flick of her fingers, the silk folded over, concealing the damage to the train. "Shall I tell the Queen you send your regards?"

At that, the viperous Lady Pelham lost the satisfaction gained from her petty prank. Charity swept off, leaving behind the woman pinch-faced with jealousy.

Despite her bravado, the back-to-back challenges left Charity shaken. She asked the way to the retiring room and begged an attendant to fetch a seamstress from backstage. Ten minutes was lost waiting for the only available costumer to repair her train. The stained glove would have to wait for her lady's maid.

By the time she left, the corridor leading to the royal box was empty. No matter. She could slip into the back of the small room and lean against the wall if necessary. The Queen might not even notice her tardiness.

But unfortunately, all heads turned to glance back when the guard swung open the door. Queen Charlotte's gaze narrowed.

She did not turn Charity away. Worse, she motioned for the man beside her to give up his seat, freeing a place for Charity at her right.

A seat in the front row, where all the people in attendance would be staring at her. Charity smoothed her features into placid acceptance, bobbed a quick curtsey, and then settled onto the wooden chair.

"Apologies, Your Majesty." Charity lowered her gaze, frowning as the candlelight illuminated the yellow stain on her glove. She covered that hand with the other, striving for calm. "I am at your command, ma'am."

You are a duchess now, darling. Untouchable. Charity's mother had voiced those words shortly after the wedding ceremony, her eyes glittering with unshed tears. At that moment, Charity had believed her mother spoke the truth, that a title could shield her from life's horrors.

But now she knew better; a shield was only as strong as the bearer.

The Queen sniffed. "Everyone here is at my command, Your Grace. But you and I both know that some of the bows and curtseys disguise treacherous hearts and minds. I invited you here tonight so that you might be reminded of the size of your challenge. Look around you. Which boxes contain allies? Which ones host my enemies? Can you identify them all?"

Who were the crown's enemies? Charity raised her fan and flipped it open, swaying her hand gently to cool her flushed skin. She arched her neck left and right, and studied those around them through a lidded gaze.

Lady Pelham had returned to her box, and was whispering in the ear of the woman at her side. As if sensing Charity's gaze, the two women glanced her way. Charity inclined her head in a slight nod, like a ruler acknowledging her subjects. Lady Pelham scowled and then swung her head around to look at the stage. She was only fool enough to take Charity on. Not the Queen.

The aristocrats were all happy to squabble amongst themselves, but few would dare to threaten anyone higher. What could they hope to gain?

There were no members of the Order present that evening, or at least none so far as Charity was aware. They were one of the factions determined to stop the royal engagement, but Peregrine had suggested there were others.

Who else wanted to prevent the joining of the English and Dutch thrones? Her eyes stopped on the three couples seated together in Lord Holland's box, on the far end of their level.

She was not well acquainted with the politicians who were not aristocrats. She did, however, know many names and faces. Some of the most vocal complaints against the royal engagement came from the Whigs, and in his younger days, Prinny had counted them among his friends. But once he assumed the regency, he turned on the reformers in favour of the established Tories.

Charity allowed her gaze to roam before returning to the box. Would they do something to prevent Prinny's wedding plans?

"So you are not blind to our challengers," the Queen murmured. "The Whigs are whipping up public sentiment against our future alliance. Prinny refuses to deal with them, so it falls to me. If the men can be brought to heel, it will be by their wives. Go to them as my emissary and see if you can convince them of the benefits of a friendship with the Crown."

"I will do my best," Charity promised.

"You will do nothing less than succeed," the Queen corrected her. "Now, what of our falcon? Where is this list he promised to deliver?"

Peregrine was on the hunt, but not for members of the Order, as the Queen wished him to do first. "He took a few days to recover from his wounds, and has been intent on seeking out signs of his mother's influence. Given all that happened, he judged her the greatest threat."

"To him, or to my dynastic plans?" the Queen asked, not waiting for an answer. "Tell him to adjust his priorities, lest I be forced to do so for him. Our foreign guests are due to arrive in two weeks' time, depending on the winds. Prinny plans to announce the formal betrothal at the welcome event. You and the falcon must ensure nothing stands in our way."

"Understood, Your Majesty."

The Queen shifted position, turning to the soprano gracing the stage. The woman's voice rose higher and higher, her voice filled with so much anguish that it sent chills down Charity's spine. For a rare moment in time, all the whispered conversations stopped.

But then the male lead stepped forward, adding his voice to hers, and shattering the quiet. The Queen lost interest in the theatrical display and again looked Charity's way. "My granddaughter will need your support in the coming days."

The arrival of the foreign guests would necessitate even more pageantry than usual. "I will clear my diary so that I am free to accompany her whenever and wherever needed."

"It is not the public events which have me concerned. I do not believe for one moment that my granddaughter has abandoned her efforts to get out of this engagement."

"Surely the princess learned from her error—" Charity ventured.

The Queen flicked open her fan and covered her mouth, preventing onlookers from reading her lips. "She is young and impressionable. She can be twisted to other people's whims."

Charity could not refute that. However, "I understood that the Prince Regent is keeping his daughter under lock and key. If no one can access her—"

"*Some* people cannot be turned away," the Queen muttered. "The Grand Duchess of Oldenburg has requested permission to pay the princess a visit. If she were anyone other than the sister of the Tsar, we might have declined. I do not trust that woman. She is far too headstrong. She will give my granddaughter ideas. Counter them!"

Everyone wanted to use the princess to their advantage, but few took the time to get to know the girl. Princess Charlotte was caught between two impossible choices. If she married the Prince of Orange, her mother would be banished from England's shores. If she refused the match, the princess would face the wrath of both Prinny and the Queen.

Charity was no longer sure which outcome was best.

The Queen has no interest in your opinion on the royal plans, the logical speaker pointed out.

Charity flipped her fan closed and laid it in her lap. "I will speak with the princess, Your Highness. Is there aught else you wish of me?"

"You speak as though I have asked so little of you. Seeing Prinny's efforts come to fruition is your only focus, Your Grace. You are to ensure that our falcon does his part, and that young Charlotte falls into line. That will cover two of my three greatest concerns.

"Now, paste a smile upon your face so that all may know how grateful you are to have my ear. Orpheus will soon consign his true love to the depths of Hades. I will leave before then. I have no wish to witness a tragedy this evening."

Charity wished she could say the same. The ill-fated lovers struck too close to her reality. Perry had tried to show her a way forward. Instead of keeping her eyes on him, she had looked back to the Queen, snaring him in obligations to the crown.

Finally Charity left the opera, climbing into her carriage and directing the driver to see her home. She was in no mood to venture on to any of the other gatherings to which she had been invited.

She locked herself inside her bedroom. What had seemed a life of privilege and safety now felt like a prison. She grabbed a quill and dipped it into the pot of ink, her hand hovering over the ivory foolscap.

She needed advice, and she knew of only one person who might understand her plight. Her friend Grace, who had suffered under the edicts of the Crown and somehow survived. But when it came to asking for guidance, she drew up short.

What help could Grace truly offer? What if she gathered her child and came running to Charity's side, putting herself in the sights of Lady Fitzroy? Charity could not ask that of Grace, not after all her friend had risked to save her once before.

She dipped her quill again, penning the remainder of the message with a careful hand. Instead of a request for help, she sent a warning.

My dearest friend,

I cannot begin to put into words everything that has transpired in London since I last saw you. But I expect you'll hear this sooner rather than later—there is scandal afoot again. When is there not, you are likely asking? This time, it involves the Prince of Orange and his betrothal to the princess. Or his lack of one, rather.

I wish I dared speak my next words more plainly, but tell your husband to be on guard. I believe there is a possibility that our dear departed enemy, Lady F, has again set her sights on England. To what end her ambition lies, I am not yet certain, but if she decides to take aim against the throne, it would be easy for her to place me in the crosshairs as well.

Do not worry for me; I am taking precautions. But I would not want you and your family to be caught unprepared if she decides to retaliate against you.

Your husband may be particularly interested in the news of Lady F's son, Peregrine. He is back from the front, and he has already found himself in trouble with the Crown once again. Some would think me a fool, but I have my doubts as to his guilt.

Fear not, I will keep you apprised of anything I uncover. Please do the same, should any news pass your way.

All my love, Charity

3

*Men at some time are masters of their fates: The fault, dear
Brutus, is not in our stars, but in ourselves, that we are
underlings.*
—Cassius to Brutus, Julius Caesar

Peregrine slept hard until midafternoon the next day. Antoine
had managed to sneak in and out of his room at least twice.
The fire was burning, his clothes had been retrieved, refreshed,
and laid out. Fresh dressings and a bottle of vinegar to wash the
wound had also been left on top of the nightstand beside him as a
pointed reminder.

Ravenscroft's French valet must have been positioned with his
ear at the door, listening for the first hint of stirring, because he
burst in with a tray even before Peregrine sat upright.

Antoine made straight for a small table set beside the hearth,
carrying the tray with both hands. After he set down the salver,
the valet turned to the windows, parting the drapes to let in more
light. Finally, he straightened, turning directly to Perry and giving

him a pointed but thorough once-over. "My timing is very good. You slept through breakfast, but I would say that was for the best, *monsieur.*"

And then he moved to the bedside, reaching for the coverlet. Peregrine saw his intention and snatched it to his chest.

"You have nothing there I have not already seen before. Let me check your wrapping," the valet scolded him, and reluctantly, Peregrine allowed him to examine the binding he had done himself before falling asleep. Antoine's hands on his flank were deft and gentle, but his face was stern. "Good enough for now, but I will help you do it again after you eat. Such injuries are hard to bind by oneself. Come."

Silently, Perry allowed himself to be helped into a robe and led to the table. Prior to his exile from England, he had employed a fussy valet much like Antoine. But then he had been sent to war, and no one would assign a batman to the son of a traitor. From that moment, he had simply learned to do without. It was strange to be waited upon again so intimately—like old clothing that now hung poorly on his frame.

As he sat, Antoine lifted the cover to reveal a plate of thinly sliced ham, toast, a coddled egg, and stewed apricots. Beside the plate, he could see a folded letter with his name on it.

"A note from Ravenscroft?" Perry asked, lifting it.

Antoine shook his head. "*Non.* It arrived for you this morning, *monsieur.*"

While Antoine poured the tea, Peregrine turned over the letter, seeing that it was sealed with the coat of arms of the Marquess of Normanby. Well, if he had doubts about Ravenscroft's claim he was being shadowed by Hodges, this laid them neatly to rest.

When leaving St James's, he had told the duchess he had been going to Selina, but he had never gone. He didn't believe he would be able to hold a civil discussion with her, either. Selina had let him be for two days, finally ordering him to escort her to

Carlton House and lay to rest some of the rumours swirling about the status of his life and reputation with the Crown.

Gracious behaviour had been quite beyond him that night, especially after he watched Selina flaunt him like a prize in front of the duchess and other peers. He had lingered as short a time as was polite—on the opposite side of every room—and he had left early, leaving behind his carriage to take her home.

"*Tsk*. Eat while it is still warm," Antoine told him briskly, snatching the letter out of his hand and laying it on the table. "Else I shall tell my lord you are fading, and require him to sit beside your bed quoting poetry. I can vouch, the threat of it alone has restorative properties that are quite miraculous."

Inwardly, Perry winced. "That would make me lose the will to live entirely," he replied. "But Antoine—" he said, as the valet went to leave. As the slender man turned back to him, Peregrine considered his words. "Thank you. For *all* your assistance recently."

Antoine only lifted an eyebrow slightly at the unexpected words, but Peregrine could tell that the servant was pleased.

Turning back to his breakfast, Peregrine broke the seal on Selina's letter to read the very brief message it contained as he ate.

Perry, I do hope you accepted your invitation to Cavendish's celebratory soirée at Burlington House tomorrow evening. I have missed having a chance to catch up on all the news.

—S

Drumming his fingers briefly against the back of the letter, Perry deliberated this. He had seriously considered avoiding the event. It was expected that the Queen and Prinny were going to attend, and worse, where they were, the duchess was likely to follow. But on one hand, nursing his bruised ego would only delay an inevitable confrontation. It would also run the risk of worsening his already ailing social influence.

And on the other hand, it would be uncommonly stupid for him to continue pursuing leads in his mother's underworld as one man alone. So, he would go. But he needed to find something to wear.

~

Fashionably late the next evening, and in considerably better shape than he had been days previously, Peregrine made his entrance into the chequered black and white marble foyer of Burlington House. Alone.

He was dressed in one of the brand new outfits that he had commissioned when he first got back to London. The midnight blue superfine of the coat was a touch looser around the middle than when he had done the fitting, but much to Ravenscroft's pique, Antoine had cooed over how well it still clung to his shoulders, and how sharp it looked against the pale shade of his hair.

People took note of his solitary arrival as he joined the party on the first floor, which made a statement of its own. He was not afraid to be seen arriving without an entourage of friends—the option most men would take if they weren't escorting female relatives.

To his right, guests were mingling along the hallway, in the salon, and into the anteroom. Dozens of London's most influential and powerful. And in the midst of the throng, he shoved down every other stray thought as he surveyed the crowd mingling in the space Cavendish's servants had decorated grandly.

Whig politicians were heavily in attendance, the guest list likely influenced by Cavendish's own leanings. But there were still many prominent Tories there, including Bathurst and Lord Liverpool, the Prime Minister. A few high-ranking families also mingled.

Deciding he needed to fortify himself with something other than wine, Peregrine opted to chance his luck looking for brandy or whisky in the gaming room. Before he got there, however, an unusual guest waiting near the hallway caught his eye.

It was clear the man was not there for the party. He was dressed in a grey suit of plain cut and style more appropriate to the professional class. Perhaps a banker, or a clerk.

Or a secretary in the office of a government leader. Because as Peregrine sidled closer, he could see the man was talking with Eldon, the Lord High Chancellor.

Not in his wildest imaginings could Peregrine conceive what circumstances would cause Lord Eldon to be meeting with his secretary at a social event filled with the upper crust. Whatever it was must be unusual enough to be urgent; Peregrine watched Lord Eldon run a hand through his silvered hair, looking harassed.

With a terse oath, Eldon backed up two steps, preparing to return to the party. "I must tell my wife I am leaving. I will meet you there," he said by way of farewell.

The secretary nodded and departed. Peregrine, curiosity piqued, waited as inauspiciously as he could to see if the chancellor's matter involved any others. But Eldon only spoke to his wife before leaving. Liverpool and the other Tories remained behind.

Some personal matter, Peregrine assumed, continuing to survey the guests in attendance. As his eyes passed over the Marchioness of Normanby, easily recognised by her stunning blue-black hair, Peregrine noted that the Order had made a show of strength of their own.

In front of the tall windows, Lord Pembroke was standing next to Selina, and he locked eyes with Peregrine, giving him a polite nod. Chandros was not far away, participating in an animated discussion with the Prince Regent. What *was* surprising to Perry was that he spotted a face that, under normal circumstances, would never have been invited to an event with such an illustrious guest list. He must be mistaken, but...

"Good evening, Lord Fitzroy," a woman's voice said by his elbow, and surprised by her nearness, Peregrine turned to look at who had spoken to him.

"Lord and Lady Barbour," he greeted the couple. He knew the Barbours well enough, and had even been to a few of her salons. "It is good to see you. I heard you went to the continent last year. Did I hear correctly that it was Amsterdam?"

Lady Barbour gave him a serene look. "It was, and it was quite wonderful. I wanted to thank you."

"Thank... me?" Peregrine hesitated, uncertain what he had done to earn thanks for. "Did I recommend the place to Barbour?"

Beside her, her husband looked vaguely uncomfortable, and Lady Barbour gave him an arch look before turning back to Peregrine with a sweet smile. "I learned that a certain wager you provoked with the Duke of Northumberland funded a most pleasant trip," she whispered.

He laughed, feeling genuine surprise. "You laid a wager on Percy? Oh, I hope you told him. That would nettle him."

"I told him at his own wedding, no less." Barbour smiled at his wife and asked after Peregrine's health. "I do hope you are still painting."

"Not recently," he murmured. He hadn't painted in over a year. "I imagine my skill with fruit and landscapes remains abominable."

The Barbours were one of the few couples Peregrine genuinely and unreservedly liked. Most people did. They were gently eccentric, filling their vast circle of acquaintants with artists, authors, and scholars. Barbour, in fact, was the one who introduced him to the Royal Academy and Sir Thomas Lawrence.

"That is because you should be painting people instead," Lady Barbour said matter-of-factly.

Peregrine smiled politely and tried to steer the conversation. "Speaking of people—do my eyes deceive me, or did I spot that banker—what is his name, Rothschild? Amongst the guests?"

Barbour's eyes lit up. "You did. Cavendish put a cat amongst the canaries, inviting the heads of the three largest banks. It is not a very popular topic among the less progressive aristocrats—I am sure you are not surprised by this—but there is much discussion about Britain's economic future, now that the soldiers are home. Manufacturing, trade, the building of the railroad to support it. Cavendish has been optimistic that such modern things can do a great deal to improve society and England's standing in the peace that will follow the talks this fall. But... these things take funding," he whispered, as many of the nearby aristocrats would think the word vulgar. "I have never seen someone try to bring conversations of this sort to a ballroom."

Perry mostly knew Nathan Rothschild by reputation. Many aristocrats had been hotly speculating about how he had made a fortune in the markets. The times were definitely changing. Industrialisation was already causing turbulence in the countryside. On the continent, now that war no longer blockaded the coasts, the face of trade would change. Powerful countries were eager to divide the spoils of France's empire.

Concluding his chat with the Barbours, Peregrine glanced in Selina's direction, but she tapped her fingers idly together in front of her, the gesture that he knew meant *not now*.

So Peregrine decided to step out for air, now that the atmosphere in the room was stifling with so many guests. He made his way to the balcony and eased outside, not realising until the door closed behind him that he was not alone.

The Duchess of Atholl stood by the balcony rail, looking just as surprised to see him as he was to see her.

~

Charity had startled as the door opened, and hastily attempted to marshal her face into something befitting her rank. But then her breath caught in dismay. Since her vision had already adjusted to the dark, she had no difficulty identifying the man who stepped outside before he recognised her in return.

And the moment he did, he froze.

"I am sorry, I did not mean to intrude upon your privacy," Peregrine said stiffly, already turning to leave.

"No. Wait!" Charity cried, her hand flying to her mouth as if astonished that the words had escaped her lips.

He halted his steps, turning back to her. Flushing, she cast about for something to say. "You... need not leave, if you came seeking solitude. I was on my way back inside," she offered at last.

Somehow, even cloaked in shadow, his posture made plain that he knew her words for the lie they were. Even though what he said was, "as you wish," as he stepped away from the door so she could go through it.

She had longed for this moment. Dreaded it. And now that he stood before her, waiting to see what she would do, her courage deserted her.

Charity had thought that his absent silence was the worst torment her mind could devise. But that had paled compared to the agony of watching him circulate on the floor, pointedly not looking in her direction. His cut had been what sent her to the balcony for some measure of peace.

Here, face to face, neither one of them could hide from each other. Especially not as he was appraising her with an expression of flat inscrutability, as he had at Carlton House.

He concealed it well enough, but she had learned to read the signs beneath his mask. She marked the lines of fatigue and tension at the corners of his lips. The way his shoulders rose as his breath came so slightly faster. He wasn't unaffected.

Say something! Her mind hissed as silence stretched. *Fix this! Make him understand!*

"You are looking... better," she began lamely, trying to find an opening for a conversation that would be safe. "I..."

The moment the words slipped from her lips, she knew she had chosen poorly. Peregrine looked out over the gardens and closed his eyes. The night was so quiet that she could hear the long, soft exhale through his nose. Frustrated resignation, not impatience or dismissal.

Abruptly, Charity cut off the apology that had been forming again on her lips, and a different emotion lit within her breast. It wasn't an unfamiliar one, but one that had gone dormant in the face of her guilt.

Anger. And she clutched it to her breast.

It was a better feeling than the rudderless feeling of uncertainty. Anger made her feel strong and capable, not weighed down with a sense of... powerlessness.

She hated the way he looked at her now, as if she were worse than a stranger. And even more, she hated the memory of the way he had watched her before that, when he had studied her like an enemy.

All these unspoken things. All these inconvenient emotions. Bile burned the back of her throat as she thought about the apologies he refused. But perhaps he had refused it because he sensed her words had been... well, if not exactly a lie, neither had they been fully the truth.

Bitterly, she looked out on the night, discarding all her carefully rehearsed speeches stored against this moment, folding her arms over her stomach. "Do you ever wonder if the universe is mocking us?"

"How do you mean?" The words came reluctantly, as if he did not want to encourage conversation.

Charity couldn't help but let her unhappiness stain her voice.

"We find each other, hurt each other. Every time we go away and try to lick our wounds, somehow fate finds a way to put us together just long enough to hurt each other more."

Peregrine's hands dropped to the railing, gripping it just hard enough to make his knuckles stand out sharply beneath the leather of his gloves. Little signs, the only glimpse he'd give her of what he was thinking or feeling. "You, of all people, should know I do not believe in fate, Duchess."

She let out a short laugh. A terrible idea, because she had to pinch her lip with her teeth to keep it from turning into something more humiliating. Like weeping.

"How can you not, Peregrine?" she said tiredly, sweeping her hand wide to indicate the two of them and all that lay between. "Here we are, on a balcony together. *Again*. Forever at odds, the sun and the moon, chasing each other in circles. Can there be such patterns by random chance? Does this not feel like a cruel joke of fate?"

He tipped his head downward, chin to his chest. His forelock fell over his face, a curtain over his expression. *You are being too forward. Too emotional*, her mother chastised. *Any moment now, he is going to get impatient with you and leave again.*

But he did not leave. He stayed.

And finally, he lifted his face to hers, meeting her gaze fully. And she saw, just for an instant, the same soul-deep weariness and pain that had been naked on his face when she had cut him to the quick a week ago.

"If fate alone commands us, we are puppets, performing under the direction of an unseen hand," he said softly, still not looking away. "We are acting stories that are already written. Aping the illusion of choice, living for nothing. All of it, meaningless—what we want, or choose, or think, or feel. How can that possibly bring you comfort?"

It was a fair question, and one Charity had asked herself. But the answer felt so selfish. So small and ugly. "It doesn't. Not really. But at least I have the comfort of knowing some of the misfortunes of my life may not be orchestrated by cruelty."

Peregrine would probably take those words badly, but her thoughts had slipped backwards again, to the suffocating blackness of those helpless nights as the prisoner of his mother. The time she had spent wondering if she would ever be let go. Thinking about what her life would look like after being so thoroughly ruined by Marian Fitzroy.

Trapped in the memories of the past, her breaths grew closer, and Charity abruptly discovered she couldn't draw in enough air. The night was close and smothering, and dizzy, she reached out to put her hand on the railing to steady herself.

Suddenly, Peregrine was in front of her, pushing her away from the balcony's edge and backing her towards the wall where they could not easily be seen out the window. For only the briefest of instants, his face was unguarded. And Charity saw something that resembled concern. Like a spark, it was there and then gone.

"We live mostly in the hells of our own making." His hand was wrapped so tightly around her wrist that her bones nearly squeaked together. As though he was afraid she would fall.

Or maybe he was trading his torment for physical pain. A punishment.

Charity didn't protest. The pinch of muscle and sinew brought her back to the present, grounding her and helping her steady herself. Discomfort of the body was so much easier to endure. So small compared to the vaster world of emotional destruction she now knew was possible.

And he wasn't really harming her, was he? Peregrine could, easily, with his greater strength or with any of her secrets. He could have sliced her to pieces a hundred ways to get his revenge. Instead, he had kept her from stumbling against the railing, reaching out to pull her to safety.

Suddenly she knew, she *knew*, that spark of concern was proof there was something still there to salvage betwixt them. The fractures in his soul showed so clearly under stress, and right now, his nearly glowed, dimmed only by the suppurating sores of her betrayal.

So she dug her fingers into that wound, lancing the infection.

She looked into his eyes. "That is the real reason you do not want to believe in fate, is it not? If there is only a plan, if there is no choice, there can be no justice. And your tally of wrongs done might go unaddressed... like what I did to you."

Charity had expected him to react to such a forceful prodding, but with this, the carefully kept mask shattered. Peregrine boxed her in, one hand planted on the wall on either side of her as he leaned in, furious.

"You talk as though it has only happened once. As if you haven't stuck me every time you found a vulnerable place, every time I gave you the slightest bit of trust. *Then* you gammon me with this trite speech about fate? I watched you do it to me half a dozen times, Charity, beginning from the very moment you spurned me over my insufficient name and title. *You*, not fate."

His words held truth—even if it was only a part of it—and she gave him a small, sad smile. She had mustered her anger to bring a sense of order. To lessen the helplessness of her thoughts. He was using it as a way to protect himself and armour his tender spots—against her.

This was wrong; she had laid him bare, and his anger was the only defence he had left. No wonder he hadn't wanted her apologies. It did nothing to balance the scale between them.

How did she fix this?

That night he had accosted her in her bedroom came to mind with sharp clarity. When she had been at her most powerless, and he had put a knife in her hand, offering her the means to destroy him.

"You are right. I am sorry for certain things," she began slowly, reaching for the hand beside her that had held her wrist so bruisingly. "It was… an act of cowardice to let you believe I was a title chaser. That when I spurned you, the fault lay with you."

He didn't jerk away from her touch, but he stiffened. "Fate or not, we had so little control over what happened last year. I regret that I hurt you when I said no matter what we had chosen then, we wouldn't have found happiness. But that still feels true. Or do you think your mother would have held her tongue?" she murmured.

Standing this close, she could hear his breathing take on a ragged edge, and she knew her time was running short to make her point.

"But this… The bargain I had to strike with the Queen was not the one I went there to make, Perry. I am sorry I was not better at negotiating with Charlotte. Perhaps I can never undo the damage I did. But I will never apologise again for making the choice to accept her bargain, because I believed it was the only way I could save your life."

Even at his worst, when he had her at her most vulnerable, he had responded to her fear. Her helplessness. And in spite of the fact that he had believed she had meant to frame him for treason, he had restored some measure of control to her. It was time she did the same for him.

Trying to control the tremor at such forwardness, she raised his palm and laid it upon her chest, not quite able to meet his gaze.

My heart is here.

With her eyes downcast, she could see his throat working. She knew he understood the gesture for what it was. But when she finally lifted them to his face, his expression was stricken— something she did not expect.

So much of her perception was focused on Peregrine that she

was stunned when suddenly his attentiveness was ripped away. He turned, removing his hand from her, his head cocked as if hearing the strain of some distant battle horn.

"Perry?" she asked, wondering what was wrong.

"Do you hear it?" he asked her.

Hear what, she almost asked, before she, too, let her senses sharpen enough to pick up other sounds. There was an angry susurrus in the distance, which gradually resolved into the voices of many shouting men.

4

"A lady may step to the edge of society, but she must never lose sight of the way back."
—Lady Cresswell, to her daughter

Peregrine turned and looked over the balcony, cocking his head one way, then the other. Then he looked through the windows back at Cavendish's party.

"What is it? What should we do?" Charity asked him.

"The people shouting are outside, and it sounds like they are somewhere out on the street. Probably nothing more than some rowdy drunkards being loud. But let us get you inside, to be sure." He pulled the door open, guiding her through it and back into the anteroom.

She glanced around. It seemed that none of the guests looked like they had noticed anything untoward going on outside. "Should I tell the Queen?"

"It is probably nothing," he murmured. "But—"

A clamour suddenly erupted, this time on the inside of Burlington House. There was a horrific, distant noise of the wooden doors crashing open, and a sound like a roar flooded up the main stairwell, followed by horrified screams.

Peregrine grabbed Charity by both arms, pushing her into the safety of the corner behind him. And just in time, too. Suddenly the anteroom was filled to the brim with hysterical guests pushing into the space, fleeing whatever was behind them. He braced himself, giving Charity space to breathe even though he was being forced up against her.

Finally, the crush eased as people found sanctuary on the balcony and in the dining room. Charity peered out from behind Peregrine's back, trying to figure out what on earth was transpiring. The din began to sift itself into recognisable words, spoken in harsh tones and lower class accents.

"Bread, not banquets!" "Let honest men work without paying bribes to the Crown's lackeys!" "We fought their war, and now there's no bread, no work, and no care for the common man!"

"Protesters!" Charity gasped. "From the lower classes?"

"So it would seem." Peregrine grunted as an elbow took him in the side. "Do you see the Queen or Prinny?"

"No…"

Though the aristocrats kept trying to edge away, the more they did, the more space they left for rioters. People in the rougher garb of shopkeepers and tradesmen began thrusting crude pamphlets at the guests.

Seeing a break in the crowd, Peregrine seized Charity by the wrist and tugged her forward, slipping further away, into the dining room. "Go stand with the royals," he ordered, spotting the Regent and Queen standing together at the same time she did, surrounded by a ring of women and elderly men.

"But—" Charity turned back, but Peregrine had been parted

from her by other women pushing in to seek the relative shelter of the dining space. He joined the barricade of able-bodied men that tried to cordon off the dining room from the mob. So in the end, she did as he told her.

Moving deeper into the room, she peered over her shoulder. She could see rougher looking men than the shopkeepers take up a different kind of chant. *"They mean to sell our princess the same as our grain—foreign and dear!"* one hard looking man intoned, rallying the people around him. *"Tory lords, and royal leeches!"*

"Reform for the people!" another howled. The crowd yelled in agreement. And then the very atmosphere of the group changed, becoming somehow darker and more violent as more and more disparate voices took up the same refrain.

"Lords and leeches!" "Reform!" "Work, not war!"

These were Whig arguments. Party lines and criticisms of both the Tory government and the Crown. Her blood felt abruptly cold. Had Cavendish planned this? Surely he would not do something so foolish.

She scanned faces, seeking the Whigs she knew. Not that she knew many outside of the peerage *well*, but she had at least known the Duke of Bedford and Lord Grey. But then Charity was bumped from behind, and she brushed against someone, trying to catch her balance.

"Lady Holland," Charity gasped, placing the face who turned her way. "I apologise for bumping you."

"I can only forgive you, given the circumstances, Your Grace," Lady Holland murmured, joining elbows with Charity for stability as both women were unsteadied again. "What a terrible evening," she added bitterly. "But then again, perhaps it was an inevitable one."

Whatever did that mean? "Are you saying this riot was orchestrated?"

Lady Holland looked at Charity sharply. "I mean that one cannot spend years stoking the fires and neglecting the cleaning, and then act astonished when the chimney smokes. England is changing," she added ruefully. "And change can be quite terrible. But more so to some than others."

Charity looked out at the crowd, seeing that many of the tradesmen and shopkeepers had shown signs of uncertainty. "Do you believe their cause is just?" Charity asked her.

The Whig wife's eyelids flickered. "I think it takes no great intellect to understand why they would strike out." She pointed with her chin at men in the anteroom who were ignoring the cries about reform, helping themselves instead to the food. "If your belly was empty, would you not resent us for what we have, that you do not?"

That was an uncomfortable thought to Charity. She had never known hunger that couldn't be satisfied. "I suppose I could understand that desire to sate hunger," she said lightly, feeling as though the world were spinning a little bit. "But I do not understand how the princess's marriage hurts or helps them."

"One always hopes a marriage will benefit the nation, but it is a delicate thing—offering an English rose to foreign soil," Lady Holland remarked. "They love the princess because she is a symbol of liberty and she stands in opposition to the systems that hurt them. To her father. If she goes abroad..." The lady's voice trailed off. *Then she would not be able to stand against the Regent.*

Charity glanced back at the clustered royals, looking for the Royal Guard—but she saw none. Ahead, and on the far side of the anteroom, there were only elderly aristocrats in their superfine coats, faces pale with fear above their perfectly knotted cravats. A few ladies had clustered behind the men, most cowering and clutching at each other in terror.

The loudest man of the group of rioters, a broad, burly

specimen who stood a full head above the others, stepped forward and addressed Prinny from behind the line of men standing at the doorway into the dining hall. He pumped his fist in the air as he roared, "Can't turn a blind eye towards us now, can ya, Yer Highness?"

And in front of the brute, she spotted the pale blonde of Peregrine's hair as he blocked the way with his body.

"We fought for you on the Continent, and you repay us with starvation and low wages. Let this be a warning! Turn your eyes on England or we'll bring the fight to your doorstep!"

"This is terrible," Charity whispered, mostly to herself. "How do we stop this?"

Her question had been rhetorical, but Lady Holland heard and answered anyway. "This is not a cluster of people speaking all with one voice. I do not pretend it would work, and you will likely think me indecent for uttering the words, but empathy might soothe wounded dignity, making it harder for the fire of anger to catch hold in their hearts." She made a fierce face. "Although I still believe compassion might have prevented this in the first place."

Charity thought quickly on that, especially as her eyes fell on Sir Thomas Graham standing near the ring of men guarding the way in. Lady Holland was right. These were men with very disparate agendas. Some only wanted their grievances to be heard. Others... they seemed more interested in pushing others towards fighting than to any other cause.

"Thank you, Lady Holland. You have given me something very much worth thinking about. Excuse me for a moment."

Taking her arm from Lady Holland's, Charity began the slow process of pushing her way towards the dining room's entryway, against the flow of bodies trying to push inwards. It was a snail-like effort, and Charity was inadvertently prodded, elbowed, and disheveled as she fought to reach the Lieutenant-General who she knew had been elevated to the title of a baron just a few weeks previously.

"General Graham," she said in a voice just loud enough to carry to his ears. "Things are growing more tense."

The older veteran of the Sixth Coalition looked over his shoulder at her, and Charity met his eyes. "Your Grace, things are not safe here. You really should move towards the wall and bide your time. Some of the servants have gone to seek aid from Whitehall to mount a response to this unrest."

Armed foot guards descending upon Burlington House? The thought was chilling. "I shall move to safety soon, General," she murmured. "But I have a fear that if we cannot somehow calm these men, the mob might become whipped towards bloodshed. If not before the guard arrives, then most certainly after."

"I agree. It would be unfortunate, but it may not be able to be helped, Your Grace."

"Perhaps you are right. Perhaps nothing can be done. But will you try? These men seem frustrated that they are not being heard. If you were to speak... calmly and visibly... perhaps we might find a way to somehow remind them that everyone here is an Englishman first, and not an enemy. That peace sometimes brings opportunities of its own."

Turning further towards her, Graham's mouth turned down. "I cannot promise them bread or reform, Your Grace. I cannot even promise them they will be heard."

"Is there any harm in trying?" she asked him. "If we can fracture the unity joining their causes, some may decide that retreat is the better course of action for now."

"And if the numbers shift, then the chance of violence is reduced. I suppose there is no harm in trying," he replied tersely, running a hand over his jaw as he thought. And then he lifted both hands, bellowing for attention.

The volume of the protestors dropped immediately, and heads

began to turn. This included Peregrine's, who did not look at General Graham. No, he gave Charity a hard, narrow-eyed look instead.

Graham lifted his voice. "Friends! Countrymen! I hear you, and you know who I am. I have fought beside Englishmen in every corner of Europe. Men who asked for nothing but fair treatment and a decent future. You have every right to ask the same.

"But this—this is not the way to be heard. Not with broken glass and shouted threats. You want bread, work, reform? Then we must stand united as Englishmen and look towards the future. Let the men behind these doors see that you are not rabble to be feared—but people to be reckoned with. The men who will help build England as a great nation in peacetime.

"We are not at war here tonight. Do not give anyone reason to treat you like an enemy. Leave civilly, now, before the guard or Bow Street arrives so that there does not need to be any risk of violence. Know that your message has been heard."

Charity smiled thinly as she could see many of the rioters begin to consider how precarious their position was. Dissension began to form, and suddenly groups of people in threes and fours broke ranks to leave before the threatened guardsmen arrived. Mostly it was the peaceful ones... but Charity also noticed some of the very toughest looking men depart.

As if their work was done.

"It may be working," Charity murmured with a fervent prayer of thanks.

"A good idea, Your Grace," the lieutenant general told her. "But things are not over yet. You should take yourself back away from trouble if you can."

"I will, General Graham," she promised him. "Thank you for doing what you could."

Charity slid away, towards the wall. There were still many

unhappy men who were arguing with individual members of the aristocracy, but it was quickly becoming apparent that the full boil of the riot was losing steam. As she waited, she wondered about what had sparked this incident, and whether it was nearly as simple as it appeared.

A riot was hardly likely to convince Prinny to change his position. But Lady Holland also had a point. There were a hundred ways that the mounting pressure might have been eased before it had come to this.

The shopkeepers and the tradesmen—their anger was real. A weapon that someone could harness to their use. And perhaps someone had, but to what end?

Glancing down, Charity spotted a flyer from one of the protestors lying on the floor, and she bent to pick it up, noticing the list of demands upon it and cruel denunciations of the failures being blamed on the Tory party.

She forced her gaze from the flyer and scanned the room, searching for the leaders of Parliament. Plenty of them were present, many clustered about Prinny and his usual entourage. Their faces were red, brows beaded with sweat. But only half of them were looking at the crowd of rioters.

It did seem plausible the Whigs might be involved. However, when Charity followed the direction of those accusatory glares coming from the Tories, the Whig gentlemen being targeted didn't look pleased, as they might if they had orchestrated the riot. Most appeared positively ill. They, too, understood that there would be hell to pay—and that they were likely to be left holding the bill.

Finally, new shouting from the front of the house heralded the arrival of Bow Street and the guards. Immediately, what remained of the malcontents devolved into chaos, and the young men who had been guarding the room shifted their focus to helping corner and hold the uninvited.

Not unexpectedly, Charity could see Peregrine was making

himself useful in restoring order to Burlington House. But this second descent into another kind of violence, however restrained, was proving too much for some. A few women—and even some of the men—swooned and collapsed into nearby chairs. These were being fanned by their near neighbours.

And as people began to filter out, Charity caught sight of Queen Charlotte. The Queen had her back to the wall and her fan in hand, but she was not using it to cool herself. Instead, over the silk fabric, her wise eyes studied the scene with what looked like a curious sense of detachment.

Charity wondered if Queen Charlotte's stillness was strength or something colder—calculation cloaked in calm. After a long moment, the Queen flicked her fan closed and stalked out of the room.

She did not need to see into Charlotte's mind to know what questions she was asking herself. They were the same ones circling through Charity's thoughts. Who had opened the doors to such a bedraggled group? How had they made it so far into Burlington House?

Someone stepped up beside her, a hand brushing her arm, dragging her from her reverie. Charity startled as a whisper in a familiar voice called her name. Lord Ravenscroft stood at her side, his brow creased in concern.

"Your Grace, the royals are summoning us. I presume it is to thrash us for not having clairvoyance about this evening. Where is Lord Fitzroy? I hope he is not starting a second riot somewhere even less fashionable."

"He was…" Charity's voice trailed off as she glanced to where she last saw him, but his blonde hair was nowhere in sight. "I saw him trying to restrain some of the stragglers."

"Well, he is busy then, I suppose," Lord Ravenscroft huffed, but did not waste time going off to search. Instead, he led Charity away from the dining room, in the opposite direction from where the guards had herded the crowd.

"Lord Cavendish offered Prinny use of his private study. Tell me quick now, did you or Fitzroy know this was going to happen?"

"Did I know?" Charity stopped abruptly, right in the middle of the corridor. "What could possibly make you think that?"

"I saw Fitzroy follow you onto the balcony. I wondered if perhaps he was issuing a warning."

With grim clarity, Charity remembered the expression Peregrine had greeted her with when he realised she was there. And the tense discussion that had followed. "Not at all," she said sardonically. "Our interaction was due to happenstance, not design. Had he known I was standing out there, the only reason he would have come out would have been to push me over the rail."

"Nonsense. He seems fiercely protective of you, in spite of everything." Ravenscroft gave her an assaying look. "But I suppose he might have been moved to jump dramatically, to prove some point."

Charity felt her lips twist wryly as she took Ravenscroft's arm. "I do not think the height of the balcony would have suited such needs."

A pair of matching guards stood watch outside the door of Lord Cavendish's study. They must have recognised Lord Ravenscroft, for they allowed them to pass without question. Ravenscroft gave a quick rap on the door, and a footman opened it from inside.

The room was unmistakably masculine—leather, velvet, dark wood, and power. Charity felt like an interloper, an intruder in a den where decisions were made far from women's ears.

The footman must have dragged the chair from behind the desk, for it stood near the fireplace, acting as a throne for the

Queen. Prinny was too full of nervous energy to sit. Instead, he paced a track into the plush carpet.

The room was thick with tension. A handful of Tory figures lingered nearby, chief amongst them Lord Liverpool. They clutched crystal glasses of brandy in their hands while they whispered amongst themselves, waiting for Prinny to determine the next move.

Lord Ravenscroft nudged Charity towards a far corner of the room where they would be out of Prinny's way.

The Prince Regent waved his hands in the air, filling the room with his displeasure. "This is the Whigs. I know it. It can be no one else—for none other would be so damned foolish as to embarrass us all so publicly."

He turned sharply on his heel and paced back the other way. "They have been out to embarrass me since I ascended the throne. This is why I turned my back on them. They want a revolution without understanding the cost."

Lord Liverpool cleared his throat. "Your Highness, as much as I would like to lay the blame at the Whigs' door, I must raise a concern. I know every man in attendance tonight—as do you. Even the most committed Whig would never dare allow a mob into a gathering such as this. We could easily have lost control. We are beyond lucky no blood was shed."

"No blood shed *yet*," Prinny growled, silencing the Prime Minister. "One or two, perhaps. But a mob? Through Burlington House?" His voice rose with each word, flaring like a match to dry tinder. "Are we meant to believe the servants are blind—or complicit?"

At that, Lord Cavendish gave a pained moan. "It was certainly not I, Your Highness, nor any of my staff. I brought only my most loyal retainers from my country estate. I refused to hire unknowns. Still, I shall question them all, rest assured—but I do not believe the answer lies with them."

A knock at the door cut the conversation short. The footman opened it, admitting the butler.

He bowed his head toward Lord Cavendish before explaining why he had interrupted. "The Bow Street Runners have arrived, my lord, and have taken the remaining men into custody. Guards are now stationed at every entrance. Nothing further will occur tonight."

"Bow Street?" Prinny bellowed, "I want them in the Tower—not the local gaol. What is the punishment for such a crime? Surely threatening the Crown with violence must warrant hanging—at least for the ringleaders."

"We would only make martyrs of them, Your Highness," Lord Liverpool replied. "Allow the courts to deal with them. A few nights in the gaol may yield important information."

"The Prime Minister is right, my son," Queen Charlotte said, breaking her silence. "Though I, too, demand answers, we are more likely to get them in time. In particular, the names of whoever put those men up to this. Now, go to the safe confines of St James's, and take the Tory leaders with you. There is the matter of the press. Word will get out, no matter what we do. We must be prepared with a response." She fixed Prinny with an imperious stare.

Though full grown and crowned with titles, Prinny still withered beneath his mother's stare like an errant schoolboy. "Mama, you are right. But I do not like the idea of leaving you here."

"It is late. Have my carriage brought 'round and I will go straight to Buckingham House. We can meet again tomorrow, and you may tell me what has been decided."

Prinny kissed his mother on the cheek—a rare show of filial affection. It was testament to how shaken he truly was. Then, he did as she bade him, guiding all the men from the room.

"You may leave us," the Queen said to the footman still

stationed by the door. He nodded and departed, leaving the women entirely alone.

Under the full weight of Queen Charlotte's fierce gaze, a chill gripped Charity's spine, tighter than even the one caused by the first sight of the invading mob. "Was this the Order? Or is Prinny correct? Was this the Whigs?"

"I cannot say for sure, Your Majesty."

"And *where*," she continued, "is Lord Fitzroy now?"

Charity held her tongue.

The Queen tilted her head, turning her gaze toward the fire. "I dislike the fact that he has been using the slack in his leash to follow his whims. He should have been following my command and bringing the enemy within reach to heel."

"It is not outside the realm of possibility that Lady Fitzroy's hand is behind this," Charity offered, hoping to deflect some of Charlotte's anger.

Instead, it had the opposite effect. "If that is the case, then Lord Fitzroy is doubly worthless to me. He was meant to prevent precisely this sort of thing—not stand beside you, as wrong-footed as everyone else."

Charity's heart pounded, the Queen's disappointment heavier than any rebuke.

Queen Charlotte rose from her chair, a grimace flickering as she placed a hand on her hip, rubbing at her side. "The only reason I have not called for Lord Fitzroy's head on a platter is because no one else can identify the members of the Order."

Charity's breath caught. *No one, perhaps, except for me.*

The elder royal fixed Charity with a final, warning stare. "The clock is ticking, Your Grace. Bring me the names of those responsible, or bring me Lord Fitzroy himself. If he cannot provide me the information I demand—the information I need to hold this country together—then I misjudged him more deeply than I thought. And you."

The Queen flicked her wrist to wave Charity off. Charity bobbed a curtsy and backed from the room, hurrying to do the royal bidding.

Trembling, she worked her way through the crowd. But Perry was nowhere to be found, and Charity couldn't help but note that another person conveniently absent was Selina, the Marchioness of Normanby.

5

"One cannot answer for his courage when he has never been in danger."
—*François de La Rochefoucauld*

The gentlemen who had leapt in to render aid were a bit rumpled from fending off the rioters, but hale. There were no injuries, save minor bumps and bruises. For the most part, the rioters had been loud, not violent.

But the *ton* clung to the walls, weeping and untouched, acting as though they had been dealt a fatal blow. Cavendish fluttered from one place to another, trying to restore order to this madness by rattling off orders to his servants.

Peregrine turned slowly in a circle, thinking. The remaining rioters huddled in a corner, penned in by footmen. All but the drunken ones had fallen quiet. Confidence was easy in the anonymity of a mob, but voicing their beliefs when outnumbered and being held was harder.

For a week, he had been seeking signs of his mother's plans.

Now his gut was telling him that there was no coincidence in what had happened here tonight.

"Perry," a voice hissed in a low voice behind him, and he turned again, seeing the Marchioness of Normanby behind him. "I would like to leave, but I seem to have been left without an escort," she said in a formal tone of voice for the benefit of any listeners. "Might I impose upon you to see me home?"

Selina's face was as serious as he had ever seen it, which was the only reason he didn't refuse her out of hand. Feeling pulled two ways, he glanced back in the direction the royal family had left. Unfortunately, they had also taken Ravenscroft with them, removing the only other person from the party with whom Peregrine would leave a message.

"*Please*," the marchioness added, and finally Perry gave her a sharp nod, trying to keep from gritting his teeth and he offered her his arm as they wound their way to the front door.

Selina didn't have a carriage nearby, but the night was fine, and there would be hacks only a block away. She tugged his arm to get him to walk towards the gates, and kept her reserve until they had gotten into a carriage.

"You look grim," Peregrine finally observed bitingly, "which makes me wonder if you summoned me to this party to witness some new scheme of your little group. Would that be, by any chance, because you and the Order did not succeed in baiting your line with Charity correctly while I lay ill? Or are you planning to accuse me of this to force my will because you no longer have the leverage of Prince William to use against me?"

"None of those things." Selina gave him an irritated look, pressing her full lips together. "I really must say, Perry, I have never thought to meet a man who could be so ungrateful about having his life saved. No wonder Duchess Atholl has been tragically wandering about, looking as though she was publicly barred from Almacks."

He narrowed his eyes. "Do not pretend that you are unaware of my general opinion about being used or *manipulated*."

"The circumstances merited expedience." She inhaled deeply, as if bracing herself. "I don't doubt your ability or your motivations to form your own cabal and protect yourself, but simply put, you do not have an eternity to be so precious about it, *you fool!* If you don't have the resources to protect yourself, your mother will end your life. And that would be a dreadful waste of time—for *all* of us who have spent our efforts in an attempt to keep you breathing."

Cameron would have likely forced him to seek the assistance of either the Crown or the Order anyway. It had been a singularly unpleasant deduction for him to come to, this week. Still, he would have preferred to strike a bargain of his own volition instead of being forced to it by one of his supposed allies.

Working his jaw, Peregrine finally nodded curtly. "Fine. I shall set aside suspicions about your future plans for me. But we are not finished discussing it, Marchioness. You brought me here tonight for a reason. Was it to observe the Order's riot? Because I do not think the Whigs are lacking in all sense."

"I don't think so."

He barked a laugh. "You don't *think* so? As in, you had another reason to invite me to witness the Order staging a riot? Or you do not *know* if it was them?"

"The latter. Never mind that for the moment. Your earlier statement—Perry, when she went to the Queen to negotiate, did your duchess succeed in securing you a pardon for William?"

Peregrine stared open-mouthed at the hard planes of Selina's normally beautiful face. Typically, she played her cards very close to the vest, but she made no effort to conceal her expression from him now. She looked more vexed than he had ever seen her.

"She did," he finally said, grudgingly, not bothering to argue the part about Charity being *his* duchess. "Did you ask her to seek a pardon for me?"

Selina rubbed her arms. "I did not dare ask her to do anything so directly. But this is… good to hear. Our little lamb is learning to wield her wits. Hopefully she is learning it quickly enough."

As she closed her eyes in relief, Peregrine found himself teetering betwixt bewilderment, suspicion, and towering anger. "How, exactly, do you know such details of Duchess Atholl's discussion with the Crown? And what does *any* of this have to do with the Order?" he continued, his voice becoming threatening. "You have five seconds to explain before I stop this carriage and leave."

"It will take considerably longer than that to explain," the marchioness retorted sharply. "So you had best settle yourself comfortably. First, I must begin with a confession that I hope will set a few things to rights. Given how wroth you are with me, I imagine the duchess informed you I threatened to expose you to the Crown for the conspiracy to poison Prince William myself if you did not join the Order."

Peregrine's brows drew down as he began to connect the events that had precipitated Charity's betrayal. "Yes, I am aware you played a part in forcing the duchess to choose between seeking help from yourself or Charlotte."

"Do not misunderstand me," the marchioness said with an edge of exasperation. "It was not my most subtle work, granted, given that I had only moments to decide upon a course of action. But I used my full and considerable influence to try to make sure the Duchess Atholl sought the Queen instead of me. *Us.* I did not want to encourage her to come to the Order or to me to seek aid.

"Whether she realised it or not, there was no choice. We would be the devil with whom there could be no deal. And at the same time, I had to ensure I was driving the duchess—whom I believe, incidentally, has come to care about you to a degree that may be a hazard to her health—into the Queen's hands with all possible speed."

Nostrils flaring in pique, Peregrine considered this quickly, coming to an unpleasant conclusion. "The only reason you would care about my having a pardon…"

"Is because the Order may attempt to use William's poisoning against you. Yes. Not that they had plans to accuse you, so far as I know. But I took the weapon from their hands."

Gritting his teeth, he asked, "Why would I need to worry about the Order attempting to use this against me?"

She ignored him. "To be honest, I knew the Queen would likely salt the bargain, but once the duchess told me about Cameron, it became clear how dangerous the situation had grown for you. You were acutely vulnerable. You *still* are."

Selina gave him a cutting look. "You are reeling, Perry. And granted, you have taken several heavy blows, any one of which would have toppled most other people. But this is not like you, to be swayed by pride and emotion instead of strategy. You were forced to make the alliance you should have done from the outset. So what? It is temporary. All matters change when they have outlived their usefulness. The important thing to heed is that no one person in this world can stand without allies—even when most of us do not have to worry about watching over their shoulders for Marian Fitzroy to stick a knife in their back."

Peregrine looked out the window briefly, stuffing his emotions away. It would be a fatal mistake to let the sharp-eyed marchioness sit in attendance as he re-examined his feelings, especially given how the last two days with Ravenscroft had proven how disturbed his own equilibrium had been. It was likely to get him killed.

Putting a stop to this unproductive line of thought, he reviewed what else she had said.

He pressed his fingers to his lips, giving her a look. "You

should have been leaping with joy at the thought of an opportunity to bind me to you when Charity sought your help. I cannot imagine why else you would push me into the Queen's hands, nor use the duchess to do it when you could so easily do it yourself. Not unless..." his gaze narrowed as he studied her expression, "you had some concern that your allies might no longer be your friends."

This time, it was her gaze that slid away, and she made an expressive moue. "There you are. *Finally.*"

Inhaling through his nose, Peregrine considered this new information. "No wonder you have been so quiet lately. And here I was, believing you were only showing some consideration for my recovery before you dragged me in front of the others to swear an oath, or whatever it is you do. When did you start to feel as though someone was trying to stick a knife into *your* back?" he said, crossing his legs with a nonchalance that he did not feel.

Her eyes flicked back. "Not until the duchess came running to me with the news that your mother's hand was at work, not just her henchman, though the incident had been sticking in my mind. It had been quite the peculiar coincidence, after all. Two plans to poison William just happened to occur on the same day, at the same event."

Peregrine agreed.

"The piece of information that had not seemed relevant to tell you—at least, not until it was too late—was that Pembroke had suggested a poison to me already. They did not know that I had decided to enlist your aid to find something suitable." She gave him a mirthless smile. "I considered you more of an expert on such matters."

Feeling a twinge of premonition, he sat forward. "And that poison was?"

"Henbane." She paused for a moment, studying his face. "Do you know it?"

"I do. I am nearly certain that is what was used to poison William. If you had given him even more…" Perry forced himself to recall his more medical knowledge of his mother's herb lore. "He would probably have gone into fits. Far more likely, he would have died."

Selina rubbed her nails lightly over her temple, her eyes shadowed. "Then it seems I have to be grateful I sought your opinion. And to thank you twice over, this time for keeping me from accidentally assassinating the Dutch prince."

Peregrine could feel his eyelid twitch ever so slightly. "It was nothing."

"There is more you are not saying," she accused him. "Let me guess. That poison has some particular meaning for you—and furthermore, I am guessing that would be somehow related to your mother."

"Such a difficult guess to make," he said, sarcasm heavy. "All things considered equal."

"You know, neither of you did mention to me whose hand Cameron used to do the other poisoning. It would not happen to be someone who lives at the palace, would it?" she commented silkily.

"You are right. We did not." The marchioness was fishing, and he had no intention of rising to her bait. So he changed the topic. "Pembroke made the suggestion of henbane? Rather hamfisted for one of yours, unless he was ignorant or a dupe. But either way, that does make it sound as though he—or possibly another—was in contact with Cameron. Would it be likely for him to know the man?"

"His role within the Tribune might have rubbed up against Cameron's business."

"Explain. And how many of you are there in the Order?"

At the lower levels, he knew the Order was much like any society

—little more than a drinking club with some lofty ideals. Above that, the Order of the Centuriate tried to keep a guiding hand on the reins of Parliament, national prosperity, and commerce. But Peregrine did not know the intricacies of their internal structure beyond knowing that a handful of powerful people sat somewhere near their pinnacle.

"Oh, dozens," she said dismissively. "But the leadership is composed of five of us. The Tribune. We vote upon courses of action together, and an odd number keeps voting decisive," she began. "And each member of the Tribune has a sphere of influence. You already know that I curry with the lords and the politicians. Goldbourne knows the financiers, Chandros with the military men. Pembroke is connected with the industrialists and tradesmen."

Peregrine hadn't known he had both seen and spoken with most or all of the Tribune members of the Order. But Selina was correct; if Pembroke worked with capitalists and men of enterprise, he certainly could cross Cameron's path. "And the fifth man?"

A small smirk. "Do you know Mr Xavier?"

He cast around in his memory for the name, wondering why Selina was amused. "I do not believe so."

"You would remember him if you had. The son of a British East India Company officer, now on the Board of Trade. But his distinctive characteristic is not so much his mother's darker complexion as that he has six fingers on one hand."

"Well, I think I would remember in any case if he had been at your home," Perry said, slouching back slightly. "But it rather sounds like Xavier conducts a great deal of business on the continent." *Where my mother is currently hiding*, he thought to himself.

"I assume there would be easier ways to retire you if they no longer wanted a woman on the Tribune." He gave her a toothy grin. "Or if they wanted simply to vacate your seat for some other toad-eater."

She gave him a shark-like smile in return. "A majority vote could remove me, but this does not feel like an effort of the Tribune. It feels like one hand."

"I concur. Do you believe Pembroke is your enemy? Or did he simply take a suggestion to the Order?"

"Who can be certain? All I know is that he may not be an ally. One of the others might have been using him to speak their words. Or Pembroke might not bother concealing it, believing I would assume an enemy would never do something so blatantly."

"Guessing and second guessing? That way lies madness, Sina."

"Do you think? We excel in playing subtle games." She gave him an ironic look. "I am far more afraid, especially given the way your mother's mind works, that this scheme was contrived to hinder my ability to detect or react to some other course of action. As it stands right now, I cannot trust my allies; the shadow of suspicion has touched every one of my confederates. My hands are tied, my reach curtailed, and my sight obscured. I have been rendered nearly as helpless now as you are."

Peregrine sat forward, letting his face rest in his hands as he thought about the men that had been missing. The businesses that had been sold.

"Cameron's man suggested my mother had more than one pair of hands at work. That concern has merit. Someone is scrubbing every sign of my mother's underworld from existence. For a week, I have been chasing ghosts, and that person is working very hard to stay ahead of me."

The unflappable marchioness actually fidgeted. "Blast it. Then it was no coincidence that Cameron was ready with his trap for you after I reached out to the Tribune, either. The Order is not concealing a dupe. It is concealing an accomplice to your mother.

Cameron's business with Bow Street disappeared so quickly that I knew someone powerful was aiding him. I just never supposed that it might be one of *us*."

The situation was so troubling, Peregrine almost wanted to laugh at the absurdity of it. "You know," he said conversationally, "the deal you had the Duchess Atholl strike with the Queen for my protection? She tasked me to deliver all of your names to her on a platter."

She whitened around the mouth. "You would sacrifice four of us to catch the spy within our midst? After I warned you tonight? And especially after last year, when someone fought me tooth and nail to make sure you met your maker, and I had to stick my neck out so far to save you from a trial that your mother may have asked someone to cut it?"

"You know I would not," he rebuked her mildly, with some amusement. "Which I think is a far better deal than I might have gotten if the role was reversed. Pray, convince me that you would not have decided to let me hang if you had any idea how expensive it might be to fight Vanessa Cresswell's wish for vengeance."

"Of course, I would have—" He got a great deal of satisfaction from seeing Selina's jaw drop. "The *duchess's mother* is the one who arranged for the orders to send you to the front? Are you quite certain?"

"Quite," he said succinctly. "Lady Cresswell wanted her pound of flesh. Destroying Lady Fitzroy's son in return for the harm done to her daughter felt like poetic justice, I am sure. She made certain to crow about it to me herself just before I was shipped out. Just so that I would know to whom I owed my... discomfort. You did not know?"

"Good Lord, Perry. No, I did not know. Now I'm perishing with curiosity to know if the duchess herself played a part in that, or if your two families are even more vicious than the Montagues and Capulets."

"I thought she played a part. At first." In fact, that belief had added much of the fuel to his rage the night he had climbed into Charity's window, when he was prepared to accuse her of poisoning William simply to frame him for the crime. "But... now I am of the opinion that she does not know what her mother did. Is Lady Cresswell likely to pose you a problem?"

"Her? Doubtful. She would most likely have had to prevail upon her brothers for that favour. Not one of them is clever enough to play the game at this level. They wouldn't even know whose board they are standing upon."

She scowled as she considered it further. "That pretentious shrew. Will Hodges was not easy to send along with you. At least now I know with whom that account should be settled."

"Do not bother with Lady Cresswell; she is not our greatest problem right now. We need to figure out what happens next. Do I tell the duchess? The Crown?"

Selina considered that, touching her lip. "I cannot see any way we can tell the Crown yet. Even if you somehow convince them not to fling us all into the Tower, it is likely they will tip our hand. We have but one advantage: whichever one of the Tribune is likely responsible for working with Lady Fitzroy does not yet know we are marking them for a traitor."

"You mean to continue to play your role, hoping that Pembroke—or whoever it is—does not spot you looking for them."

"I do not know if there is any other choice, really. We do not have enough information to guess who it is or what they are about. It could be any one of them; there hasn't been a change in the roster of the Tribune since I joined seven years ago. I will seek the clues within; you should keep looking for other signs on the outside."

Peregrine held his breath for a long moment before exhaling with a nod. "And the duchess?"

"Would you trust her with this?" Selina asked him with frank curiosity. "In spite of the fact that she was manipulated to go to the Queen?"

Yes.

His thoughts nearly had him speaking the word aloud before he clawed them back. When he said nothing, Selina gave a small shrug. "You know what we hazard. I leave it in your hands whether or not you feel she is trustworthy. I believe she would not be compelled to act against your safety. Her own is a different matter entirely."

He lifted his eyes to hers. "And what of your own safety? Even if all of your friends were not conspiring against you, you have likely earned my mother's enmity."

"In for a penny, in for a pound, I suppose. So would you think on that, perhaps, instead of casting off your loyal allies? You already have far too few for my peace of mind. And now, unfortunately, so do I. I would appreciate knowing we can put aside petty differences and be united in our shared time of need."

Peregrine considered that, and nodded. Even if Selina was untrustworthy in the long run, while his mother lived, it seemed they had an enemy in common. "Shall I send you back Will Hodges?"

She laughed shortly. "Keep him. I am not sure he would come, not even if you ordered him to. By the by, when you make the slightest bit of effort, you seem to inspire a most peculiar and stubborn sort of loyalty from people around you, Perry. One you cannot buy with money or threats." The corner of her mouth lifted in a sort of wry grimace. "That *does* make me jealous."

6

*"No one ever remembers who followed the rules. They only
remember who won."*
—Marian Fitzroy

Selina insisted, repeatedly, that she was in no special danger
that her servants couldn't handle. Given that the
marchioness had been the one to somehow find Will Hodges and
employ him to begin with, Peregrine gave up and decided to leave
her to her own devices at her home.

But he was not willing to chance a repeat of the attack at
Atholl House. He entered Selina's foyer, peered around
suspiciously, and then told Selina to wave at him from a window
once she was upstairs to let him know the house was secure.

Once she had, he managed to bribe the hackney driver with
enough coin to head directly on to the Fitzroy estate.

It was well after midnight by the time the conveyance pulled
into the drive, and the house was solidly dark. But only moments
after he alighted from the hack and sent the driver off with

another generous tip, Peregrine heard the sound of boots approaching from the side of the house.

He turned and came face to face with Will Hodges. His man had an open lantern lifted high to cast light in his left hand. A pistol angled towards the ground was held in his right.

"Lord Fitzroy," the older, ex-mercenary said, only the barest trace of surprise in his voice.

"I see you are staying vigilant," Peregrine murmured, and Hodges grunted in response, uncocking the hammer of the pistol and sliding it into his coat pocket. He let out a strange, tuneless whistle as he did so.

When Hodges said nothing further, waiting patiently to let Peregrine speak first, the silence grew awkward. Peregrine studied the man who had been beside him in the firing line at the Nive, wondering at the sort of trouble Selina had gone through to put him there. How much it had cost her, both in money and her political pull.

And how lunatic a man like Hodges might just be. Not only to take her up on such a dangerous position, but then to tell her he was leaving her employment afterwards to work for the man he was hired to guard.

Hodges let Perry look his fill, squinting a bit in the dim light.

Peregrine finally broke the silence. "I need a man."

"You got one."

"A *loyal* one," he added.

Hodges was unruffled. "Aye. And?" As if questions of loyalty had nothing to do with him.

Crossing his arms over his chest, Peregrine wondered if he could dare take the man at face value. "Tell me. Just how *did* you become acquainted with the marchioness?"

"That one you'll have to ask her, sorry."

He opened his mouth to argue, but a strange prickle of presentiment had him turn on his heel. Barely visible in the lamplight, a boy of perhaps thirteen or fourteen watched him casually from the cover of a large hedge near the front door, holding a carbine like he knew exactly what to do with it. The boy kept the rifle ready, but pointed away.

"Oi! Sammy," Hodges hissed. "Mind yer manners in front o' his lordship."

The boy—Sammy, presumably—rested the big rifle upright, against his shoulder. "I weren't gonna shoot him, Uncle Will."

Both eyebrows high, Peregrine turned back to his general hand.

"My sister's whelp," Hodges muttered. "Bloody nuisance most days, but useful now and then."

Peregrine kept his voice light and cutting. "Taking a few liberties in my absence?"

Finally, *finally* Hodges took a stubborn stance. "Took what liberties I had to, my lord. Nothin' that can't be set straight so long as you get more hands in. Place's too bloody big for just me and Dawson."

"Does necessary liberties include continuing to take money from the Marchioness of Normanby?" he asked silkily. "Following me, as well?"

Hodges chuckled, the rough sound like iron striking on cobblestones. "Suppose that's down to you, Lord Fitzroy. Aye, I followed. Aye, I took her coin. Did my job and kept the trouble lookin' the other way. Her ladyship's purse paid for the runner. Just enough to keep your name out o' the scandal sheets. Seemed the polite thing, considerin' all else you had on your plate. Think *you* can cover it now, instead of her?"

Peregrine had assumed he would have to do something to protect his reputation eventually, but right from the start, gossip about him since he returned had been... politely restrained. That oddity had struck him, but he hadn't had the time to delve into that mystery.

Apparently, Hodges had taken the initiative quickly and quietly, using Selina's funds. Which made a certain sense, in hindsight. Asking Peregrine for the money to do such a thing, or even suggesting it, would have been a dead giveaway that his phlegmatic veteran-turned-general hand was a bit more than he appeared to be.

"Of course I can, you cheeky bastard."

"Good," was all Hodges said, shrugging.

Hugely annoyed, because everyone just seemed to assume that Peregrine would forgive Hodges—Hodges included—Peregrine stepped closer. "'*Good*?' That is all you have to say about the whole matter? I am sure you know that neither trust nor forgiveness are among my predilections these days, and you have broken with me."

"Toss me out on my arse if you like," Hodges said mildly. "Won't stop me doin' the job. Just makes it harder, is all."

"You mean to tell me you would stay and do this anyway."

"Always had a soft spot for bad odds. Makes the fight worth turnin' up for."

"What a prize you are. Stubborn *and* foolish." Peregrine arched his eyebrow at Will Hodges. "How do you feel then about going to do something breathtakingly stupid with me?"

The man grunted, turning and heading towards the stable. "Should I bring a gun or a shovel?"

"Both. We need to dig into something that got passed over when we went after Cameron. It is time to see if we can find Red Hand."

Staying in motion, looking forward to the next problems, was the only thing keeping Peregrine's thoughts from drifting into dangerous territory. That, specifically, was the confused muddle of Selina's revelation about her and the duchess. And the way the duchess had laid his hand over the beating heart within her breast.

It was an echo of the way he had shown her where to strike

him when he had given her his blade. Not an offering of her life. But it was an offering of an object he had the power to harm.

That's the brilliance of using someone's love as a leash, my darling.

His breath left him shakily. Not only had he been tricked and shackled by love to his mother and sister, now it was nightmarishly clear how easily he could do the same thing to others. The duchess. Or even Hodges, who had not even questioned where they were bound.

Feelings? Loyalty? It positioned them at his fingertips, like tools to be used for whatever purpose he required. He could collect people and their favours like picking wildflowers into a bouquet.

And likewise, Selina was caught in his web. Her armour was dented, and Peregrine knew too many of her secrets. She would tolerate being bent to his will if it meant she might survive. She would hate him, but she would serve his command, if he issued one.

Selina was his. They all were. Tethered of their own volition. It was a terrifying gift, this power to ensnare, and it left him feeling chilled to the bone.

Tonight, Peregrine stood with both feet upon the path his mother walked. Where she lost her soul, assuming she had ever been born with one.

Tonight, he needed to take the first step, boldly. Hopefully he did not have to walk far.

It was too easy to return to certain old, violent habits. Like putting on an old pair of gloves, really. But it was the only intelligent thing to do, to don the gloves and wear the mask of someone who was both cutthroat and unpredictable.

As sick as it made him, this part of London wasn't any place for gentlemanly behaviour. Only savagery belonged here.

Unlike the other leads he had been following, the Irish bludgeon man who went by the moniker of Red Hand was still keeping his crews busy on the docks and rookeries. But Red Hand was a killer for anyone's hire, and not one of his mother's creatures. Cameron had been her own flash man, typically employing the likes of McGrath for the dirtier business.

Cameron had used Red Hand for the first attack on the bridge, likely knowing that Perry would have made McGrath immediately. Peregrine hoped it cost Cameron a pretty penny to recompense Red Hand for the death of three hired men. And he also hoped that the incident would make the man treat him with a respect borne of caution.

Where it came to his own security, Red Hand clearly felt as bold as brass. He was still at his old haunt, a place so seedy and disreputable that it boasted no sign and only weakly made the attempt to look like a drinking establishment. So he and Hodges took up a position in the alley, behind some crates, to wait for their quarry.

Red for his temper, his hair, and the blood his men spilled. But the man was overconfident on his own turf. Within an hour, Red Hand strolled perhaps ten feet into the alley from the main doorway and dropped his trousers, letting his stream flow against the dirty brick of the shuttered gin shop.

Hodges didn't wait for an introduction. Then again, given his past, it was likely he was already well acquainted with the man. Surging forward from behind the crates, Hodges slammed the thug face-first into the wall, grabbing hold of his collar in one hand and twisting his right arm behind him with the other.

"Good evening, Red," Peregrine said with bravado, stepping carefully over the puddle of urine on the cobblestones.

"You." The bludgeoner made only the briefest attempt to

struggle away from Hodges, but that was more likely an effort to be able to pull his pants up. "Ah, Christ, Fitzroy. Can't even let a man drain hisself without burstin' in like some highborn bastard lookin' to gloat? Now it looks like I've gone an' pissed me fuckin' drawers."

Peregrine smiled wickedly, showing all of his teeth. "By all means, do not worry about stopping on my account. My man has left you a hand free."

Glaring at him, Red Hand made a point of shaking himself left-handed before shoving his parts back into his pants. "Ah, grand. Took yer bleedin' time, didn't ye? Was wondering if you'd grow a spine at last to come to finish it proper."

"You have noticed my mother's associates going missing, then."

Red gave him an incredulous laugh. "I'd have to be blind as a priest in a brothel not to notice the corpses you've been droppin' on me bloody doorstep. That's just rude, Fitzroy. That bridge wasn't personal. Strictly business, so it was. Just a friendly little message, like, with perhaps the exception of that one." He jerked his chin in Hodges' direction. "You're not meant to kill the messengers. And I *don't* like you leaving your trash in my yard."

As he had feared, his mother's web of contacts weren't in hiding. They were being silenced. Thoroughly. Interesting, though, that Red Hand thought he was the one doing it.

He kept his expression bland. "I sent you one of your messengers back."

"As a cripple, oh aye." Red Hand tottered like a drunk for a moment, and then when both men were unbalanced, he spun outward, turning on Hodges, landing a savage left hook unexpectedly on Hodges' jaw.

Perry's man slipped and staggered, losing his grip. And as Red Hand slid a knife from his pocket to gut Hodges like a fish,

Peregrine stepped in quickly, buckling Red Hand's leg with a well placed boot to the back of his knee.

Red Hand fell with a grunt, landing hard with that knee on the cobbles. But Perry didn't wait for him to recover his balance. He pushed in close, and drove his elbow into the base of the brute's skull, felling him like a great, hairy tree.

Shaking the numbness out of his arm, Peregrine sent the knife skittering away with a kick. And then he planted his bootheel on the back of the stunned man's neck to keep him from regaining his feet.

Stirring from her slumber in his thoughts, Marian Fitzroy looked down through his eyes and smiled.

"Trust you to be soddin' left-handed," Hodges snarled, shaking his head as if to reorder his brains after having his bell rung. Quickly, he steadied and drew his pistol, and Peregrine stepped away from the Irishman.

"Ha, hahaha," Red gasped as he lay against the cobbles, shaking with laughter and spitting blood.

"I would appreciate a good joke myself," Perry said, slipping his hand casually into his pocket to withdraw the knife. Just in case.

"You didn't know." Red rolled over onto his side, flopping like a beached fish. "You're not the one who did for your mum's lads. Don't waste breath lyin'. If it'd been you, that two-faced bastard of yours would've slit me feckin' throat, not given me a wee love tap to the skull with a brick wall. And we wouldn't be at this little jig now, would we? You pokin' around to see what I know, tryin' not to show your hand."

At a distance far enough the man couldn't reach, Peregrine squatted down on his haunches to better look Red Hand in the face, resting his elbows on his knees as he lazily spun the knife in his hand.

"That fancy footwork of yours was clever, I'll give ye that.

Had me thinkin' Hodges was the only one who knew how to stir a real scrap. Turns out you've a bit of fire too." Red Hand propped himself up on his elbow, swiping the blood off his chin. "Ah now, don't go bilin' over just 'cause you've had your measure taken. There's worse ways for your night to take a turn. And look. Now I know somethin'. You and me, seems we've got the same problem. And in a place like this? I reckon that is enough to make us friends."

"Then tell me, *friend*, why I should take anything you say as truth instead of a load of bollocks? Especially if you thought I was the one doing the dirty work?"

Red Hand sucked in his breath through his teeth and hocked a bloody gob of spit to one side. "No reason to lie. Death's bad for business. I reckon you'd know that for yourself too."

"Why did you think it was me, instead of someone trying to make their own opportunities?" Peregrine asked him. "Did you think it was just revenge?"

"The number of bodies have been an education, so they have. Properties changin' hands, a few well-placed fires. Clean work, bloody and single-minded. Wipin' out every last trace of her little empire, like it never was. That takes either fierce devotion or deep pockets. And you, well…"

"Would have both."

"Mmm," Red agreed. "But since it's not you? Well, then the pockets. Or some other man so cold he's what others whisper about when the lamps go out."

Camerons' business with Bow Street disappeared so quickly that it could only have been someone powerful aiding him.

Peregrine said nothing, thinking, and Red Hand kept talking to fill the silence.

"I have to say, I always thought yer mum had castrated ye. But seems I was wrong. I rather like this new you, lad. You might just have enough smarts and balls to survive."

Smiling thinly, Peregrine stood, putting his knife away and giving Hodges a comprehensive glance. "Get up," he said to the man on the ground. "You want to be friends, Red?"

"I'd like to think we could form what you guvs call a polite understanding with one another, aye?"

"I am sure, in the interest of friendship, of course, you would let me know then whether or not you still have any contract on me or Duchess Atholl."

"The bridge was the only bit of work that came to me directly. Cameron mostly liked keeping his dirty work personal. Or maybe he was just a cheap bastard." Red wiped his oozing face again with the back of his hand. "But to show you I'm working in good faith, I will let you know that the duchess is still on the black books. The open ones. And there's a large reward for anyone with a mind to take the risk on it. Bounty's already sitting with the bookkeeper."

Perry's blood turned to ice in his veins, and his heart stuttered. Though he struggled to control his expression, his brows drew together before he could halt them.

"I'll tell my men not to try to claim it," Red added thoughtfully, studying Peregrine's face. "But that's the best I can do for your lady friend."

"Generous of you, Red. I… will be in touch."

Inclining his head, Peregrine turned and walked away, towards where he and Hodges had left the horses. Behind him, he could hear Hodges' boots following at a steady pace.

His gorge was rising with every step, and as he reached for the reins of his mount, he pressed his forehead briefly against the horse's neck, swallowing back the acid building in his throat. Just for a moment, a few breaths. Then he shook off the persona of his mother and swung himself into the saddle. Hodges waited, turned, until he was astride.

"I have a task for you that I cannot do myself," he said to

Hodges after they had been riding at a trot back towards Mayfair for a few minutes. "I need you to go to Bow Street. Now. Before I came to you, there was a riot at Burlington House. Find out, if you can, who these men were. They were hired by someone. Whatever information you can talk them out of, bring it to me."

Bless Hodges, who again didn't ask any questions or argue. "Where should I find you when it's done?"

Peregrine considered his options. However much their acquaintanceship had spurs, it felt unkind to repay Lord Ravenscroft and his valet with trouble. And trouble was definitely in the wind. Going back to White's also felt like a poor choice. "I will go back to the estate tonight. Assuming your nephew does not try to shoot me for entering my own home, that is."

"He won't," his man said complacently. "Taught the lad everythin' he knows."

"Your sister must be thrilled with you as an uncle."

Hodges only grunted. And then at the next cross street, he turned off, heading towards Bow Street.

The clocks were striking half past three by the time Peregrine reached Grosvenor Square, and he was beginning to grow weary. But there was one more stop he felt compelled to make before he sought his bed.

Atholl House was dark and silent, save the light cast by the lanterns of the men standing guard, and it reassured him to see that she was still being protected.

7

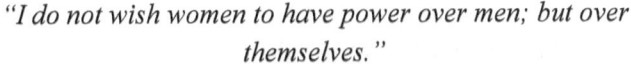

"I do not wish women to have power over men; but over themselves."
—Mary Wollstonecraft, A Vindication of the Rights of Woman

E very time she felt herself begin to drift to sleep, dark and churning thoughts seized Charity with a gnawing sense of agitation. How could Peregrine have disappeared so abruptly from Cavendish's party? And why?

For he had. Sometime during her conference with Prinny and the Queen, while most of the distraught guests made an exodus from Burlington House, both he and the Marchioness of Normanby had slipped away. Together.

A tiny pang of jealousy had raised its head, but it had been quickly stifled by reason. Surely nothing like that lay between him and Selina. But logic opened the door to even more discomposing thoughts than mere jealousy.

I want you to use all of your power to convince Peregrine it is in his best interest to align with mine, the marchioness had told her. Right before she had told Charity that she would expose him for a conspiracy to poison William if she did not.

A plot that he had been involved in, because that had been Selina's price for saving his life. What if the Queen had sent him back to spy upon the Order, and he had gotten himself entangled in another plot on their behalf?

Sickening dread at the possibility, along with the Queen's disapproval, had loomed large in her nightmares. Like the boulder of Sisyphus, just when she thought she had finally managed to approach him and have the conversation so long overdue, things had found a way to roll downhill once more.

Sitting up in her bed, she sifted through her feelings which were overwhelmingly composed of worry and pique. How could he not leave her some message? Why had he not come back to discreetly discuss things with the Queen and Prinny, as she had? And why was *he* taking up so much residence in her thoughts, when clearly he did not give a fig about the state of hers?

It was early. So early she would wake the servants if she called for them, and she couldn't abide the idea of disturbing their rest just because she couldn't find hers. Whipping the covers off her legs, she bathed herself with the cold water left over from last night, punishing herself with the shocking temperatures to send the horrible thoughts scurrying.

And then she lay down again, staring at the canopy of her bed. Seeing not the lovely pink velvet, but the superfine across Peregrine's back, a shade of blue so dark it was nearly black.

Dawn approached. She squeezed her eyes shut, demanding her mind go silent, holding her body with a brutal tension until her very teeth ached. Then she forced them to relax, one by one, from her toes to her jaw. And that is when sleep finally struck her like a mallet, rendering her senseless to the world.

She slept for what felt like all of five minutes when her lady's maid bustled in, pulling the curtains wide to bring sunlight and fresh air into the space. The bright light burned Charity's tired eyes, dragging her into the day. She reached over for the glass of water to wet her bone dry mouth.

"I only just got to bed. Why did you wake me so early?" Charity grumbled when she was finally able to form words.

"It is past noon, Your Grace. Apologies if I overstepped, but I thought you would want to be prepared before people come calling."

The hour galvanised Charity into action better than any prodding might have done. She tossed her covers aside and leapt from her bed. "Bother. I do not have time to read the papers. Do you know what people are saying about the event last night?"

Her maid wrung her hands. "Oh, terrible business, that. Mr Pritchard said there was a riot. He said it were the sort from the stews and the shops, bold as brass, shouting for bread and justice like they expected the *ton* to serve it up to them on silver trays. Lady Elston fainted dead away in the supper room, I heard. Was that really true, Your Grace?"

Lady Elston hadn't been the only one to swoon. "True enough. But what are they *saying* about the men? Were they arrested?"

"I don't know much, Your Grace. Maybe Mr Pritchard can tell you more. It sounded like accounts were a bit confused."

Charity was in desperate need of information. "Then, yes, I would like to see Mr Pritchard and the papers. Have there been... any messages for me this morning?"

"No, Your Grace."

Was this the Order? Or was this the Whigs? And where is Lord Fitzroy now? The Queen's disapproving voice rang in her thoughts.

Going directly to her escritoire, she penned a brief message, interrupting the brushing of her hair to ask the maid to ring for a footman.

Lord Fitzroy, If you have a moment to spare, I would be obliged to speak with you on a matter of some urgency. I trust you will find the time. —C

The seal was pressed and dry when he arrived. "Take this to White's. It is for Lord Fitzroy. You are to await a reply," she instructed him.

Hurrying through her toilette and dressing, Charity ate a hasty breakfast tray in her sitting room. Mr Pritchard had brought her *The Morning Post* and *The Courier*, summarizing the Tory interpretation of the previous night's affair.

"A recruitment of radicals. Men with pamphlets and no proper coats, trying to make mischief among decent folk," her butler had seethed at the danger to his mistress's person. "A ploy, to upset the apple cart and gain attention for their cause with a captive audience of the royal family."

"What about *The Morning Chronicle*? What is the Whig impression of what happened?" she asked, scanning the headlines.

"The *Morning Chronicle*, Your Grace, has decided to romanticise the thing. They call it the voice of the people, suggesting that inaction and policy has come home to roost. As if pelting carriages and frightening ladies is some form of noble expression."

Men had been arrested and taken to gaol, but with so many to deal with and a risk of further unrest, it seemed that the vast majority of the captured rioters had been released with fines or sentenced to short terms in the pillory. Regular men, incentivized by drink and bold words from a handful of agitators that they should force the aristocracy to listen.

Mobilised towards Burlington House by the shouted suggestions of a few who said they knew exactly where to find the Regent and the Prime Minister.

The footman returned with bad news. "He isn't at White's?"

Charity repeated, her voice sharp. "Did the porter say when he left? Or with whom?"

"He only mentioned that Lord Ravenscroft's man came to collect his effects two days ago."

"Charming," she muttered. "Like a guest politely checking out after a pleasant stay."

Vexed, Charity wondered why Ravenscroft had neglected to mention such an odd development. Of all the homes in London, his abode was not where she expected to find Peregrine Fitzroy. Try though she did, she could not imagine a situation when such an invitation would be issued. When had the pair of them become friendly?

"Can you travel to Ravenscroft's then to deliver the note?"

"I did seek him there. Both Lords Ravenscroft and Fitzroy were not there, Your Grace. I could not get an answer as to an expected return time."

"It is of paramount importance that Lord Fitzroy receive the note," Charity said firmly. "Surely if he stepped out, someone in Lord Ravenscroft's household must know where he went. Perhaps if you went back and asked in the stables. Did he call for a horse or did they leave together in a carriage?"

The footman bobbed his head. "I asked the footman who answered the door. He told me that neither Lord Ravenscroft nor Lord Fitzroy returned last night."

Ravenscroft was likely still stuck at St James's, closed in chambers with Prinny and the government leaders. Charity lifted her teacup and took a careful sip of the heavily sweetened brew, considering where Peregrine might have stayed the night.

A man has needs, her mother said bitterly in her thoughts. *Where else might that one find comfort and respite, except in some den of iniquity? Or perhaps the arms of the beautiful marchioness with whom he is so familiar he shortens her name.*

Might he have actually stayed with Selina? He had been an

overnight guest at one unexpected residence lately. Why not another?

Her mind unhelpfully flashed a vague image of splayed limbs and satin sheets, and bile burned her throat. She hated herself for the image that sprang to mind. She, who claimed to be above petty jealousy, now drowning in it. But even knowing it was unworthy didn't make it go away.

It took conscious effort to banish that picture from her mind. *If he stayed there*, she told the spectre of her mother that inhabited her mind, *nothing happened. Peregrine is the sort who bites the owners of the hands holding his leash.*

This, Charity knew from first-hand experience. And right now, the marchioness could be considered as much his jailer as Queen Charlotte.

No, there was some rational explanation. There had to be. Perry had to know that the Queen was looking for him. He had to know that the Order would rise to the top of the royal suspect list. Perhaps he had escorted Selina home with the intention of getting answers. She only hoped he wasn't in hiding because he was somehow complicit in what happened.

The only reasonable course of action was to sit home and wait for him to get in touch. Unfortunately for her, the reasonable course was also the one most likely to enrage the Queen. For both their sakes, she had to find him as soon as possible.

Unfortunately, she could hardly send her footman to the marchioness's home to inquire whether Lord Fitzroy was there. But there was another option. What better way to roost him from the nest than for her to pay the marchioness a visit?

She requested a quill and paper and dashed off a fresh note, entrusting it again to her young servant. An hour passed before the footman returned. At least this time he carried a reply.

However, it was not what she had hoped.

The marchioness had sent a handwritten note of her own,

saying she was unwell and not accepting guests that day. She would be happy to receive the duchess once she had recovered and would send a note in the coming days to arrange a time.

Charity crumpled the letter into a ball and tossed it aside. She was stymied at every turn.

Bring me the names of those responsible—or bring me Lord Fitzroy himself. The memory of the Queen's voice was like the shadow of an axe falling across both of their necks.

Where else could she look for answers? A moment of deep thinking surfaced a possibility. Had not Queen Charlotte charged Charity with discovering what the Princess of Wales truly thought of the pending engagement?

The little spitfire of a princess had caused trouble once before. It was not inconceivable that her hands were still making a mess of the pie, and that was something she could investigate on her own. She wiped toast crumbs from her hands with a linen napkin, then rose from her chair.

Enough. She was tired of waiting. Of chasing whispers and dodging closed doors. If the Queen wanted answers, Charity would find them—starting with the one person who couldn't refuse her entry.

Charity found Princess Charlotte in good humour—and not alone. Her rather infamous guest needed no introduction, though one was made.

"Your Grace, what a delight to see you," said the princess. "Have you met the Grand Duchess of Oldenburg?"

The woman beside her looked up at once. Catherine Pavlovna, who was sister of the Tsar of Russia in addition to her title as Grand Duchess, was a handful of years older than Charity, five and twenty. But she was an unsettling person. Already she carried herself with the calm assurance of someone used to commanding a room and keeping it. Her choice of gown was precise, her jewels deliberate, and her expression absolutely unreadable.

"I have not had the honour to meet Her Imperial Highness," Charity replied with a shallow curtsey, watching Catherine cautiously.

The Grand Duchess gave a small, elegant nod, approval and mischief flashing briefly in her eyes at Charity's cautious appraisal. Something in Catherine's expression gave her a strong impression of someone who might possess a kindred soul with the likes of the Marchioness of Normanby. Wickedly sharp—and in more ways than one, given the stories of how much she was a thorn in the Prince Regent's backside.

No wonder Catherine and Princess Charlotte had struck up a friendship.

"At last, we meet, Your Grace. I have heard of you. One always hears about the interesting women who keep the wheels turning, yes? Even in quiet places."

Charity smiled faintly as she sat beside the princess. "Turning? That seems a far more glorious way than is appropriate to describe someone who is only here to be helpful to Her Majesty."

The Grand Duchess's lips twitched. "Then we shall get on famously. I, too, like to be helpful."

Charity could not decide what to reply to that loaded statement, so she merely smiled.

The princess poured tea to fill the silence. "We were just discussing current events," she said. "It seems I missed quite the scene at Burlington House. But we heard that you were there."

"I should think you were fortunate to have missed it," Charity replied, mildly reproving. Prinny would hate her having this conversation with the princess, and especially in front of the

Grand Duchess. "It was certainly a diversion I could have done without."

"A little shouting is not dangerous. It is the silence that comes after which ought to worry your father," the Grand Duchess said conspiratorially to Charlotte.

"That may be true in St Petersburg, Your Highness," Charity said, flicking her eyes up from her cup to meet Catherine's. The woman's smile widened fractionally at Charity's polite double barb. "But here in London, what they have done is still a crime."

"Of course, Your Grace. But why bother calling something a crime if no one bothers to punish it?" She stirred her tea, idly, as if they were discussing the weather instead of matters of power and sedition. "These 'shouters' were released, yes?"

Dangerous territory. Charity nodded thoughtfully, as if considering the question philosophically. "Not all were released, Your Highness. I favour attempts to be just. Most forms of governance seem to have their benefits and drawbacks," she said slowly. "But most of us have to live within the rules of the courts we inhabit. Flaws and advantages alike."

Catherine gave the princess a look that Charity would have called pouting, had it been worn by a child ten years younger. As if disappointed she could not get Charity to indulge in such a scandalous topic of conversation.

"Speaking of flawed arrangements—Princess, you were saying the Prince of Orange is to call this afternoon?" Charity asked Charlotte to force a turn of conversation.

"I am to walk with him in the garden this afternoon," Charlotte said, sounding anything but pleased. "I suppose one must do what is expected. But I still find the effort of conversation exhausting!"

"The art of great conversation is not important for Prince William to possess," the Grand Duchess said caustically. "You are only marrying him for his title, his bloodline, and his power. And perhaps there may be another benefit or two," she lifted her eyebrow suggestively at Charity, who gave her a vaguely reproving look in return. "Although that can be acquired elsewhere, yes, Your Grace?"

The princess laughed, covering her pinkening cheeks. Charity also felt her face redden.

"I am certain you are right, though I am hardly an expert on the matter," Charity finally replied to the Grand Duchess, once she found her words. "My own marriage lasted all of two weeks."

The Grand Duchess sipped her tea, then added, "I married for diplomacy. I buried my husband without needing to learn to love him. I have travelled since—alone, unwatched, and with a purpose. I speak to whom I please, I go where I will, and I do not ask permission." Her gaze cut sideways to Charlotte. "It is astonishing what becomes possible when one stops waiting to be allowed, Your Royal Highness."

"Do you see why I enjoy her company so much?" the princess whispered to Charity.

Only because she flatters you, encourages your rebellion, and horrifies your family, Charity thought repressively. No wonder the Queen and Prinny were at their wit's end with this one. "It is true, one never knows where life will take them, nor when chance will step in to change someone's fate," she said instead.

"I think I should like that, though," Princess Charlotte said softly. "To stop waiting to be allowed."

Charity looked from one to the other. The princess was too eager, the duchess too polished. There was an understanding between them. "Tell me, Your Highness," she said, her eyes settling on Catherine. "Do you plan to reside in London for long?"

"For now, I go where life takes me, or where my brother needs me to be. I have travelled over much of the continent," she replied without hesitation. "I do not understand the ways of your court. Why must your women be confined by the borders while the men range far and wide?"

"Well, there was a war that made travel more difficult," Charity pointed out wryly.

"Such things are beyond consideration for one of us," the Grand Duchess said, waving aside Charity's concerns. "Do you know that Napoleon wished to marry me? He sent a delegation with a proposal."

"What did you say?" Princess Charlotte asked with bated breath.

Catherine laughed. "I said no, of course! I could hardly accept such an offer. I found the nearest eligible bachelor and hurried to the altar."

Heaven help them all if the princess got it into her head to run off with the nearest bachelor with a title and a pulse. Charity broke into the woman's story, needing to turn the conversation onto safer ground. "If you have traveled so widely, perhaps you can share what the Netherlands are like? I am sure the princess will get the chance to visit soon."

"Oh please, Your Highness. My mind is in a whirl trying to picture it. Tell me—is it true? Are there windmills everywhere?"

"I have passed through, yes," the Grand Duchess replied. "Quiet in parts, prosperous in others. Very orderly. The kind of place that might be dull to rule, unless one were determined to stir it up," she added with a wink.

Charlotte turned to Charity with a grin. "You must come with me when I go. I imagine I will have to visit, sooner or later."

Charity offered a neutral smile, her thoughts already churning. "It would be an honour, of course. Though I can't imagine you staying long. You seem far too fond of London."

"Fondness," said Charlotte, "is not the same as freedom."

The Grand Duchess set her teacup down with a soft clink. "Well, I have imposed long enough. And I suspect I have said more than I ought. But I have always believed a woman should speak plainly to other women. It fosters great understanding and friendship. Do you not agree, Your Grace?"

"Fairly said, Your Highness," Charity nodded.

"Your Highness, you must return soon," Charlotte said warmly. "I do not care what my father says. We shall become the best of friends."

"Perhaps I was wrong to refuse your father on his invitation of lodging," the tsar's sister said in a charming voice, her eyes glinting with devilish humour when Charlotte looked thrilled at the prospect. "Should I abandon the Pulteney and move in with you here at Carlton House? Your father is so *very* entertaining."

Charity nearly choked on her tea at the Grand Duchess's words. In three short sentences, not only had she had referred to her snub of the Prince Regent when she had set up court in a hotel, she implied that she could move into any royal residence she chose as her right. And then insulted the Regent with a compliment.

"It was lovely to meet you, Your Highness," Charity said politely, with a smile. "I do hope we will have a chance to spend more time together."

"You can be sure of it, Your Grace. Perhaps if we strike up a friendship, Her Royal Highness's father will allow the Princess to come visit me in your escort."

The princess's whole face lit up at the prospect of escaping the confines of Carlton House, even if only for a few hours. All Charity could think was that the Queen would need to be informed. Beyond a doubt, the Grand Duchess was a force of nature, a creature of subtlety, and certainly no shrinking violet.

Charity could not help but wonder privately if she might ever have a chance to watch the Grand Duchess go toe-to-toe at an event with the Marchioness of Normanby. Heaven help them all, they might decide to conquer a continent or something.

Once the tsar's sister had taken her leave, Charity let silence sit for a moment before speaking obliquely in a low voice. "I hope you were nowhere near that disaster at Burlington House."

Charlotte looked up at Charity keenly, taking her meaning. "No, I've been under lock and key since Tuesday. Papa seems half convinced I will poison another suitor or lead a revolution. Possibly both."

Charity tilted her head. "And your mother? Is she keeping out of trouble?"

"As much as she ever does. Papa's made it difficult for anyone to see her. Even me." Charlotte's expression shifted subtly. "Not that it is much easier for people to see me right now. My father controls my visitors, my letters... he would have barred the Grand Duchess, too, if he could have done so without offending half of Europe."

"You mean, if the Grand Duchess would let him," Charity said with only faint irony.

The princess's lips curled in amusement. Then she glanced down, as if preparing to broach something difficult. An uneasy feeling in Charity's stomach became a full-blown warning bell.

"You have shown me how to survive a tragedy. I do not wish to be indiscreet, but I have heard the whispers about your debut season. I do not believe my grandmother arranged any sort of knight's quest, and I am not prying. Whatever happened is in the past. What matters is that you have not let it defeat you. That is what I like about you. And I have found a way to respect it in the Grand Duchess."

"Tell me you are not planning anything foolish, like running away."

Charlotte looked at her in horror. "No, not at all. It is my mother, you see. She will never be truly happy here in England, but she is afraid to go off on her own. I worry my father will not give her a choice, once I am not here to lobby on her behalf. The

Grand Duchess… she is woman with no husband, no protector, and no permission, and yet she carves space for herself in the world. It is useful to think about. I want my mother to find the courage to stand apart from my father."

The princess shook her head, brushing aside the deep conversation. "Enough sad talk for one day. Please—tell me where you've been, Your Grace. I am forced to survive on second-hand tales. Tell me everything. Which events have you attended? Who have you seen? Do not leave anything out."

8

"Sometimes even to live is an act of courage."
—Seneca

Though the title and lands had belonged to him since he was twenty-one years of age, Grenville's murder had taught Peregrine the lesson his mother wanted him to hear clearly. Anything he held, he held at her sufferance. And her goodwill was entirely dependent upon whether or not her son remained biddable.

He made the only choice he could. To survive. But that… was complicated.

It began with good intentions. Behave, stay close, and be a restraining influence on the worst impulses. He reasoned away actions he found distasteful, if not sometimes abhorrent. Pretended to still love his mother as though his life depended on it, though real familial affection was impossible.

It wasn't enough. Eventually, he found he was dying a

wasting death like his father's anyway. The only difference was that this rot wasn't physical.

His future was grim, so marriage was out of the question. It wasn't safe to let his mother imagine that she might lose his attention, much less his loyalty. He couldn't sleep or relax his own vigilance when she was nearby. And she was always nearby.

Marian had not given up her rooms after his father's death and Peregrine had not cared enough to attempt to displace her. Indeed, in his mind, the grand Fitzroy estate in London came to represent the seat of his mother's black empire. It certainly could never be a home.

He acquired the Neal Street property to stay at when the fatigue and suspicion drove him to his lowest moments. When he sometimes wondered if perhaps he had made the wrong choice after all.

But the townhouse had been only a shelter, not a sanctuary. And now, that too was tainted with spilled blood.

With his mother and sister gone from England and unlikely to return, there was a need to take up the title and the velvet noose that came with it. After all, there was no one else to do it now. If he let the Fitzroy estate founder, he would lose what little there was left. And though sometimes he had thought about abandoning it… there was a part of him that did not want to yield the last few things that belonged to him.

Peregrine's first order of business upon his return to England had been to dismiss the entire staff. His second order of business was to seek out Mr Archer, Roland Percy's butler. The first reason had been because he did not dare use an agency to find new household staff. The second reason had been because Mr Archer had a military background, and would know others of that persuasion. Serving men who possessed a few extra skills and a stomach that could deal with the risk of violence.

This is how he had come to hire Quinn, his only current live-in domestic. The woman who both cooked and cleaned for Quinn, Hodges, and the stablemen was a charwoman.

Quinn was rather young for a butler, somewhere in his middling 30s, but there was something about his demeanour that had reminded Perry very much of Hodges. Quinn possessed that unflappable attitude of the sort that came from passing familiarity with situations that weren't strictly within bounds.

The butler showed the same reaction to Peregrine's pre-dawn arrival that he had when Peregrine had told him to leave the house closed up. Quinn displayed no outward reaction at all. Not beyond a swift calculation of what needed to be done to deal with such an unexpected development.

There had been no fire laid, of course, but the suite of rooms Quinn took him to had clearly been kept open and fresh for such contingencies. Peregrine only wished he had had the forethought to tell Quinn to make his rooms anywhere other than the family apartments.

Exhausted, Peregrine waved off assistance and comfort. He had stripped himself and crawled into the cold bed, pushing aside the uneasy, goose-walking-on-his-grave sensation that came from sleeping in the room Robin Fitzroy had barely lived and died in. And less than a handful of hours later, he jolted back to wakefulness.

Armed with assistance from Sammy and the charwoman, Quinn had managed creditable breakfast service on such short notice. Not that it would have mattered to him if all they had to serve was bread and cheese.

"Tell me while I eat," Peregrine told his butler. "What is the barest number of people we would have to hire to adequately staff and guard this property?"

Quinn's eyes went distant for a moment as he considered the question. "I assume you do not intend to entertain, and you find young Sammy and Hodges acceptable to stay on."

When Peregrine nodded, Quinn continued, "I would hire, at minimum, two footmen and a valet with… useful skills. A woman who can serve as both housekeeper and cook. Also a gardener and a maid, if you are trying to keep appearances. With the aid of Dawson, Hodges and Sammy, there should be sufficient hands to keep a watch day and night."

Six new people in this house, including a cook who would have access to the many pretty and poisonous plants of the Fitzroy estate. What a lovely thought to entertain. "I do not suppose you have any likely prospects for any of them?"

"As a matter of fact, my lord," Quinn said smoothly, "I do. The charwoman—Mrs Belinda Evers—will suit if you are in agreement. Hodges has already had her background investigated. She left full service as a cook when her husband died in a stable accident five years ago. No children, bad habits, or entanglements. Her references were impeccable, and so far she has been steady, minding the kitchen and her own business."

"All right," Peregrine conceded. "Any others?"

Quinn bit his lip, looking as though he was not certain how to discuss the next recommendation.

"If you are uncertain about him, then the answer is no," Peregrine said bluntly.

"Not about the man himself, my lord," Quinn admitted. "General Hill heard that you were rebuilding your staff, and he sent along an enquiry as to whether you might have a use for Mr Croft. The man who served as his batman during the campaign."

"Ah." Peregrine pushed his half-eaten plate aside, losing his appetite. There would be both tangible risks and benefits to employing Croft.

"If I may be so bold." Quinn slid the plate back with one finger, lifting a scolding eyebrow as he raked his gaze down Peregrine's thinning figure. "He is not young and pretty, but we could make him a footman rather than a valet, if you like. No one would question his suitability, if they thought you were showing generosity to a veteran. Work is scarce."

"Rather a step down for the man," Peregrine picked up his fork again, but only to push food around on his plate. "I expect, though, you would not bother suggesting someone you did not believe we should hire."

"I believe that General Hill's notion of 'spying' consists of little more nefarious than ensuring that the people he considers 'his' are looked after. Officers and batmen alike. We can take steps to test Croft's loyalty and discretion."

And in the meantime, doing the general a favour, of course, would have significant perks. "Fine. He can start as a valet, with minor duties. And no one is to access my bedchamber or study without your observation—not him, or any other." Vaguely irked by the feeling that he was being stared at like a willful child, Peregrine took a bite of his cooling food.

"Very good. I have left the updates from your solicitor on your desk. I shall leave you to your breakfast, if you have no other business for me, my lord."

It was different, so very different, to finally come back into this role as lord of the manor. But it was, after all, a necessary task if he did ever want to reclaim his position in society in full. It felt bizarre. So dull and mundane. And there was so very, very much paper.

Quinn had sorted his desk into neat piles based on the urgency of communication, and Peregrine steadily worked through petitions and documents, trying not to glance at the clock every five minutes. He was biding his time until Hodges returned anyway.

When the most urgent requests had been dealt with, Peregrine cleared a spot on the desk to review the report on the accounts from his new solicitor.

There was more than one way to skin a cat, and while he had taken the direct approach in looking for some of his mother's resources, there was a second avenue of investigation that he had passed to the lawyer. With Cameron's help, Marian Fitzroy had disguised ill-gotten gains that were feeding the estate's coffers by posing them as investments. Over time, as their family's wealth had compounded, many more accounts and investments were added—often perfectly legitimate ones.

Cameron, and perhaps whatever other ally he may have in London, had razed her smuggling and illicit shipping operations. Or at least the part of it that Perry had known about. The building that housed her gambling hell, The Scarlet Jack, had been sold some months after their departure from England. But money was still coming in.

There was a chance that something illicit was still feeding the estate's accounts. A trail he would be able to follow, perhaps to his mother's solicitor, other agents, or another enterprise still working. But unfortunately, the solicitor had no helpful news. He had included a copy of the long list of corporations, marking which ones had been investigated and were legitimate.

The search would continue. But… it would take time.

Peregrine scoured the list himself, hoping to see something that might present a clue. And then checked it against the money coming in. But nothing stood out among the rest.

Just after three o'clock in the afternoon, male voices in the hallway caught his attention, and Peregrine closed the ledger with a thud, looking up just as the knock sounded at the door. "Come," he called, sitting back. Quinn opened the door to let Hodges in.

Peregrine, not caring to stand on ceremony when it was just the two of them, waved at one of the dowdy fabric-covered chairs. But Hodges shook his head. "Covered in horse, still."

"Like I care if you ruin it," Peregrine muttered. Truly, he didn't. His mother's touch permeated every room. It would take a great deal of redecorating—or perhaps fire—to purge her influence.

Hodges stayed standing anyway. "Got news. Took time to chase it all down, bits here and there. Twenty men arrested. Bloody mess gettin' hold of 'em. The Regent and magistrate've been in a state. Sent some runners after the flyer printer, rest've been busy crackin' heads among the rioters."

Perry nodded.

"Plenty o' regular folk. Workers, tradesmen, riled up with ale and sweet talk. But some were brought in special, just to stir it proper."

"Paid instigators." Much as he accused Selina of the Order having done, because the timing and organisation was oddly suspicious. "Probably the ones who brought the flyers too."

"Aye. Managed a word with one o' the hired lot," Hodges continued. "Quiet sort — soft-spoken, looked harmless, so the runners passed him over. I asked who paid him to stir the rest. Didn't ask nice."

"And?"

"Name he gave was Matthew Harrison. Said he worked at the Home Office." Hodges paused to see if the name sparked any recognition, and Peregrine frowned. There was something vaguely familiar about the name, but he couldn't place it.

"So I assume you went looking for Mr Harrison?" Peregrine asked. "With or without Bow Street in tow?"

"Without, o'course. Let 'em do their own bloody work; they've got the tools. Took long enough as it was. By the time I got there, his lot were sayin' he'd put a gun to his own head."

"What timing. A crisis of conscience?" Peregrine was deeply suspicious.

"Or someone gave him a nudge. But who the hell knows? Because I missed the body by twenty bloody minutes."

Peregrine got up from his chair, pacing. "What else? Was there a note?"

"Aye, taken to the palace by the butler himself, or so they say. Bow Street didn't even bother showin'. Called it guilt and justice all tied up neat with a ribbon."

Frissons traveled along Peregrine's spine as he realised he was finally in possession of an actual clue. "Harrison worked for Home Secretary Viscount Sidmouth?"

And then he realised why Matthew Harrison's name was troublingly familiar.

Harrison had been one of Selina's creatures, and he knew that because Sidmouth and Harrison had been one of the strings she had pulled upon to avoid a public trial for Peregrine.

In his thoughts, his mother smiled.

Crossing the room, Peregrine steered Hodges towards the doorway. "We have to go to the marchioness at once."

Quinn sent Sammy running to get the carriage while Peregrine donned his coat and hat.

Swiftly, swiftly. Peregrine attempted to quell a rising sense of urgency and a sense of impending doom. But nothing untoward greeted them when they finally arrived at her home, and Selina's butler looked only mildly surprised to find Hodges arriving with him.

They were escorted to her parlour where Selina was already waiting for callers, dressed in a rich mulberry silk dress with gold braid. "Perry," the marchioness greeted him, flicking a nervous look in Hodges's direction. "I was not expecting you. Is something amiss?"

"I was wondering. Did you, Marchioness, by any chance enjoin a certain young secretary by the name of Matthew Harrison to cause a riot last night?"

"*Matthew*? Do you jest?" Lady Normanby's eyes were wide with surprise. But they quickly narrowed in thought. "Has he been arrested?"

"No, my lady. He is dead," Hodges answered for Peregrine. "Took his own life this afternoon, by what his staff say."

"That rings of falsehood," she said, her voice growing low and angry. "Both that he had anything to do with the riot, and that he killed himself for it."

"Dead men don't argue with the lies folks shove in their mouths," Hodges said succinctly, putting his hands in his pockets. "Or in their letters."

Selina's head turned to Peregrine, who added, "Hodges says they found a confession addressed to Sidmouth, but he does not know the contents of the letter."

"That poor man!" Selina exclaimed, putting a hand to her lips. But her thoughts were clearly running ahead, no longer sparing any tender sympathies for the dead secretary. "Murder to cover up... what? Coercion? Blackmail?"

Suddenly, it seemed very much likely that that infiltrator might be making a play for the marchioness. Either to bind her ability to see and interfere with his work, or to remove her from the chessboard entirely for vengeance's sake, and kill two birds with one stone.

He knew the Duchess Atholl's mother, Lady Cresswell, was willing to come after him. But he doubted Lady Cresswell knew much of anything about Selina besides her name. The lady had practically crowed in his face about him being sent to the front. No, this was beyond Charity's mother's capacity in spite and subtlety.

Beyond hers... but not his own mother's. Nor the leaders of the Order, who would likely know exactly which people were in Selina's pocket.

"Selina," Peregrine said, striving for patience. "I am rather concerned this bodes ill for you."

She gave that the moment of consideration it was due. "No, I cannot possibly be the target of this scheme. Or at least... if it poses danger to me, I would not be the only one to fall. This is too elaborate, to foment a riot to bring me down with a whisper when there are a hundred simpler ways to do it. Not when a man could have been hired at the riot to push me down the stairs or stab me with a knife."

Her gaze flicked apologetically to his wounded middle.

"If not you... Sidmouth?" Peregrine asked.

No sooner had he asked the question, however, than a great racket sounded in the front hall of the marchioness's home. An urgent fist, upon the main entrance, and a muffled shout for admittance.

Peregrine and Hodges strode swiftly towards the door of the parlour, standing in the entryway to listen as Selina's butler hurried to open the front door. The tromping of boots indicated the presence of a goodly number of men, and an imperious voice announced, "We come by order of the Crown for the Marchioness of Normanby. She is required to attend at St James's. Immediately."

Required, not invited.

Selina lay a hand upon Peregrine's shoulder, gently moving him from her path. "I will be fine," she murmured to him. "But this is starting to have the smell of a planned scandal. And like a brush fire, it may burn wild, heedless of what is in its path."

Stepping past him, she looked over the balcony rail to the men below. Three men stood on the threshold, cloaked in the crisp navy of the Royal Guard. No flamboyant parade gear—just the cut of authority and the sheen of polished boots. One stepped forward and removed his hat with stiff formality, holding a letter sealed with red wax.

She glanced at it and gave a faint smile. "Well then, I suppose I should not keep His Highness or Her Majesty waiting."

Descending the staircase, she did not look back as she passed through the front door, her skirts whispering over the marble. Two of the guards fell in around her, not touching her, not rushing her —only escorting her, as though the threat lay not in her defiance, but in her compliance.

The third leveled a very sour, very suspicious look upwards at Peregrine Fitzroy from below.

"Lord Fitzroy," the guard greeted him, his voice only a shade below civil. "Imagine my surprise to find you here."

Of course, it would happen to be the same guard who had arrested him at his townhouse. Of course it would.

"Is it a surprise? I was here about the Queen's business, after all," he responded coolly, leaning over the bannister.

"Is that so, my lord? You should be careful. I suspect that a man in your position already stands in a precarious situation without deliberately consorting with people complicit in encouraging seditious assembly."

"She is standing accused of the riot?"

The head of the guard gave a thin, professional smile. "She is to be questioned about her associations with it, yes. For now. Good evening, Lord Fitzroy."

Hodges, who had been waiting out of sight behind the doorway, crept forward as the door shut behind the guard. "Bloody hells," the man grumbled. "What now, then?"

Peregrine took a breath, letting it out in a slow exhale. He hadn't found his mother's trail in time; Marian Fitzroy had reached out and torn away yet another of his dwindling list of allies first.

And his mother chuckled softly in agreement.

"We visit the Duchess Atholl. It seems I am badly in need of her help."

107

9

"Seven years would be insufficient to make some people acquainted with each other, and seven days are more than enough for others."
—Jane Austen, Sense and Sensibility

By the time Charity returned to Atholl House, she was in a foul mood. The visit with the princess had been interesting, but yielded little information regarding the events of the prior evening. Charity had ventured on to pay a call on Lady Elizabeth, with whom she had debuted. Lady Elizabeth also happened to be a keen hoarder of gossip about the *ton*. Today, however, the only person she wanted to discuss was herself. Her parents had just announced her engagement to Lord Dunstan, a man whose blandness was only outweighed by his bank balance.

"He has promised to take me to Venice for our wedding trip," Lady Elizabeth had gushed, while Charity pretended to enthuse delight. Everyone, it seemed, was destined for parts unknown, while Charity was left chasing shadows around London.

Charity stomped through the front door of her house, barely taking notice of her butler waiting for her wrap and gloves. She handed them over without so much as glancing his way. "Do I have any messages?"

"One, Your Grace," Mr Pritchard replied. "A missive from your mother, I believe."

Charity swung around, giving him her undivided attention. "She is not in town, is she?"

"No, ma'am. It arrived via post, and based on the sheer volume of fingerprints, I would think at least three people handled it along the way."

She eyed the letter with suspicion, hesitant to pick it up. Her mother's swirly penmanship was marred by a splotch of ink and sharp lines. This was no casual note, but a frantic missive. What word had reached the countryside? The attack on her home? Her carriage rides with Peregrine? What did it say that Charity was more concerned her mother had learned of the former and not the latter?

Pritchard inched his hand forward, proffering the silver tray holding the letter.

"Leave it in the study," Charity said, already turning away from it. "I will answer it later."

"Is aught amiss, Your Grace?" Pritchard asked, venturing past his normal reticence. He had been fiercely protective of her from the moment she arrived in London, and recent events had made him worse than a mother hen. Even now, he surveyed her for any signs that she might have been in trouble.

"All is well," she assured him, even if that was far from the truth. She was well, for now anyway.

"Excellent, Your Grace. Miller is waiting upstairs in your bedroom. I believe she wishes to get your opinion on which gown you'd like to wear to dinner this evening."

Her choice of gown hardly mattered. Right now, everything

about dress choices and evening plans with nattering ladies seemed so… pointless.

Charity shook her head, trying to dislodge the worries that clung to her thoughts. Dinner parties were her battleground, the clothes and jewels her only weapons beyond her wits.

Mr Pritchard was still standing patiently, awaiting her next command. "Could you ask Cook to prepare a small tray to be sent up in an hour or so? Lady Grantham's suppers always begin intolerably late, and it would be mortifying to swoon from hunger before the first course arrives."

"Of course, Your Grace. If there's nothing else, I'll go speak with her now."

Charity gave him a nod of approval and swept past him towards the main staircase leading to the upper floor and the family rooms. She opened the door to her suite, and like a thief, her eyes snuck towards her pink chaise lounge by the window. But it was empty.

Empty, lacking a single trace that Peregrine had ever sat there. The dust from his boots had long since been cleaned.

Good God. How foolish was she, getting sentimental that her maids had managed to remove the dirt from it?

Pushing that thought to the side, Charity made a note to ask a footman to go looking for Peregrine again and finally deliver the request that they meet. If she didn't get some answers from him or the marchioness soon, the Queen was going to do something drastic.

Miller, her lady's maid, managed to dress her despite her unenthusiastic aid in selecting the gown and jewellery. Charity tried to focus on the routine instead of the gnawing at her nerves, but she met with little success. She was dabbing on drops of perfume when a knock sounded at the bedroom door.

Mr Pritchard opened the door and stepped inside, bowing

slightly in apology for the interruption. "You have a visitor, Your Grace."

Whoever could be calling at this hour? "Someone from the palace?" she asked him.

"No, Your Grace. It is Lord Fitzroy." Her butler's face was a study. "Shall I tell him you are unavailable?"

Charity stood so quickly that her chair nearly toppled. Peregrine was here? And he had come through the front door? Relief that she did not have to track him down warred with both hope and cross feelings from his abrupt abandonment at Burlington House.

Do not *do anything so unseemly as rush down to meet him,* she ordered herself. Her mother's voice only added a hiss of disapproval.

"Please, offer him a drink and tell him I shall be down shortly," she told her butler. Ten minutes. That was all she would allow herself—not to gather thoughts, but to pretend she didn't care.

However, as she approached the drawing room where he waited, she caught herself nervously twisting the ruby ring on her finger. Then, she entered the room exactly as her mother had taught her—head high, shoulders back, and with a faint, unreadable expression on her lips.

Peregrine was... he was standing, but well out of view of the windows. Dressed as if he was expecting to go see the Regent. And his face was as unreadable as hers.

What did he want? Charity glanced down at her evening gown and then back up at him. "It is well past the social hour, Peregrine. I am on my way out the door."

"I need to ask you a question."

Something about his request, so baldly put, chilled her. It was only then that she noticed he was fairly thrumming with tension, from his hands clenched at his side to his shoulders tight, as if preparing for a blow. He was distressed. And for some impossible reason, he seemed to think that she was capable of helping him.

Taken aback, she began twisting the ring on her finger again. And then she turned, dismissing the footman from the room to wait in the hallway. "What is it?" she asked him carefully.

He was watching her face so intently that she wished she had skipped eating. "Why did you not tell the Queen about who Selina was?" he asked, his voice barely louder than a breath.

"*That* is why you are here, delaying my evening plans?" The words sounded more hurt and confused than Charity wanted them to. *What does it even matter that I didn't tell the Queen Selina was in the Order?* She wanted to hurl at him.

But that was a childish question, borne of those injured sensibilities. Of course, it mattered. She could see it in the line of his body. This was a test of trust. Blinking, she tried to reorder her thoughts and bury her feelings while being held pinned by his silent gaze. In the end, she delivered the kernel of truth that lay at the very bottom of it all in a low, clipped voice.

"I was trying to do as little harm as I could. To you. To her. Not so much because she is something of a friend to you as because…" This was too near the bone. "Though I may not be a player at your level, I also know better than to reveal more than is absolutely necessary. I look at who will pay the price, because I was the one forced to settle the debt between our mothers. If I thought only the marchioness would bear the cost of that revelation, I would truly be as foolish as both you and she think I am."

His shoulders eased a fraction, as if it wasn't exactly the answer he expected, but it would do. "Would you happen to be willing to abandon your plans for the evening? I… need your help. Please."

Charity stared blankly back at him. Peregrine Fitzroy, asking her for help? She narrowed her gaze, searching him for any hint that this was a cruel joke. But, no, the way his face still pinched suggested something was afoot, and with dread, she wondered what had gone wrong now. But she merely nodded. "I assume this is something you need me to ask of the Queen? I will need a few minutes to change."

"Of course," he agreed.

And Charity went back to her rooms, calling for Miller, trying not to let a single breath of what she was feeling show upon her face.

Two of her guards followed them to Peregrine's carriage waiting outside, climbing onto the footboard at the rear. The familiar but stern face of Hodges sat in the driver's seat, and Charity's eyes flickered over both him and the lord whose arm she held. Peregrine had gone back to the estate, she realised. And had somehow made up with Selina's spy in his house in the bargain.

Peregrine stopped, pulling her to a halt midway along the path to the carriage, where his low voice might not be overheard. "Selina is being falsely accused of the riot at Burlington House and has been taken by the Crown, and I fear only an intervention on your part will save her."

Surprised, Charity clutched his arm hard to keep her balance. Selina, Marchioness of Normanby, the woman who had outmanoeuvred Charity at every turn and set in motion the final events that had splintered the two of them apart. Suddenly his question made far more sense. But he wanted her to *save* Selina from the wrath of the Queen?

He waited in silence, as if he expected her to change her mind about leaving with him.

"The Queen will be at home this evening. Her hip was paining her yesterday." Charity let go of his arm and walked toward the carriage. "We should hurry. If I am to change her mind, I will need to do it before she decides Selina's fate without us."

"You will help?" Perry asked from behind her, surprised.

Charity glanced at him over her shoulder. "Would you prefer I argue?"

He swiftly caught up and she let him hand her up into the carriage. Sitting opposite her on the rear-facing bench, Peregrine carefully angled his legs so that they did not touch hers. And as the carriage jerked into motion, he settled his hands on his knees, the corner of his lip showing the barest trace of a sardonic curl. "I admit, I thought you would have more questions."

"Oh, I have *plenty* of questions, Peregrine Fitzroy," she said, a note of exasperation colouring her voice as she stared out the window, unable to meet his eyes when they were so close. A hot flush crept up her chest towards her collarbones as she thought about her words on the balcony. Perhaps she should have never said anything at all.

"I thought I might let you explain first. Beginning with where you so suddenly disappeared to while I was being questioned about the Order's possible involvement by the Queen. Or perhaps you should go back even further and let me know what you have been doing for the entirety of this past week."

When he held onto his silence, she finally glanced back his way—and then wished she hadn't. Like the hawk he was named for, he was still watching her with an unnerving, steady attention.

"What?" she asked sharply. "Is it your intent to shame me further, or is your staring just idle curiosity?"

"She asked me if I trusted you."

"...Did she? I suppose I can guess what your answer was."

He took a patient breath. "Then I suppose you might be surprised. Because however angry I am—was—I have been forced to reconcile with the fact that, in a way, your hands were as tied as mine."

Whatever that meant. Charity wrapped her arms around her middle to still the butterflies. "I do not understand."

He told her, then, how he had taken Selina home, and how the Marchioness of Normanby had confessed that her 'offer' to Charity had been nothing of the sort.

Charity's mouth hung open. "She *played* me for a fool. And I was. I went right to the Queen and offered you up, exactly the way she wanted me to."

"It is an uncomfortable feeling, is it not?" Peregrine asked, his voice gentle and ever so slightly amused. "Being used."

Uncomfortable? She felt positively ill, digging her nails into her thighs to reduce the nauseating, terrible sense of wrongness. She hadn't thought it was possible to feel worse about her deal with the Queen.

Suddenly, warm pressure captured both her hands. Peregrine was holding them tightly, letting her fingers bite into his, even as he stroked her knuckles with his thumbs. "Stop," he told her. "It is not your fault, Charity."

Isn't it? If she had half of Peregrine and Selina's experience with these sorts of dealings, perhaps she would not have been nearly so easy to dupe.

"What I cannot seem to understand," she said, her words high and strained, "is why you want me to help her. Despite this very wretched way she went about everything, when she could have just *told* me—"

"I would not have cooperated." There was no give; it was a statement of simple fact. "At least, not easily. Persuasion takes time, and when it comes to submitting to other people's governance over my actions, I have... strong feelings about it, to say the least. Selina needed me to be able to investigate the Order, and to not be spending my time fighting the Crown and my mother all at once. She *wanted you to get that pardon.*"

He squeezed her hands to emphasise those last words, and Charity swallowed, trying to generate moisture in her suddenly very dry mouth. Investigate the Order? Why would Selina want Peregrine to dig into her own organisation—

"Marian Fitzroy has another man in the Order, and Selina does not know who it is. Tell me I am wrong."

The faintest, ironic smile touched his lips. "I cannot. We met three of the four other leaders of the Order of the Centuriate the morning I took you to Selina's home. One of them appears to be in contact with her, at the very least."

Suddenly self-conscious about the fact that he was still touching her hands, she returned her arms around her middle, unable to think of a single word to say. Cameron had nearly killed them both. Would they survive dealing with another one of his mother's men?

Peregrine let her sit in thoughtful silence for the remainder of the trip to Buckingham House. Of course, if the Order was compromised, they would need Selina to help unearth the villain, Charity's mind reasoned, filling in the gaps. She shivered, trying to imagine if one of the three men who had smiled at her so politely was far more sinister than he had appeared.

At Buckingham House's front drive, he descended first from the carriage and then turned around to help her down. When he stepped aside to walk her to the door, Charity saw the Queen's butler striding down the front steps at a hurried pace to intercept them.

"My Lord, Your Grace, Her Majesty is not available to receive you this evening," the older man said the moment he was within speaking distance.

The Queen must have been aching worse than she let on. Charity rushed to reassure the butler of their intentions. "We do not need long. If she can spare us but a few minutes of her valuable time—"

The butler cleared his throat, interrupting her. "I am afraid you misunderstand. Her Majesty will not be receiving *you*, this evening. She left word in case you came by, to tell you that the Marchioness of Normanby is her guest for tonight and she is busy entertaining. Her Majesty will send for you when she has further need of you, and otherwise wishes you both a fine evening."

Charity blanched at the terse message, which though politely phrased, landed like a slap across the face. For all her loyalty, all her sacrifices, she'd been reduced to a message delivered by a butler.

Should she protest? She cast a look from the side of her eye at Peregrine and saw him shake his head sternly. Perplexed at the fact that he was willing to give up so quickly, she turned back to the butler. "Yes, well, thank you for letting us know. Please send the Queen my regards and let her know that we—I am, as ever, at her service."

"Of course, Your Grace," the butler said, his voice breathy with relief that the two of them did not plan to argue. He bowed once and then retraced his steps back to the door.

Her knees shaking slightly, Charity did not wait for any help to climb back into Peregrine's carriage. She slid onto the seat, hunching close to the wall, with less than her usual grace and then pinched the bridge of her nose. The bench shifted as Peregrine sat, this time slouching into the seat beside her. She startled at the sharp rap he gave the roof, but did not look at him.

"A penny for your thoughts?" he asked her lightly, as though her world was not falling down around her head.

Was this the end of her social circuit? Was she about to be banished from London, doomed to live out a quiet life in the distant reaches of Scotland?

She shook her head, her eyes still closed while she tried to keep her breathing steady. "I am starting to think you don't just invite calamity into your life, you also introduce it to everyone you know."

He chuckled ruefully. "The good thing about being acquainted with calamity is you become very adept at surviving it, at least."

"But Selina—"

"If Selina is a guest at Buckingham House, she will, no doubt, be cooling her heels in the Garden View Chamber. It is not ideal, but at least it sounds as though she is not under any formal arrest. There should be time to persuade Her Majesty to hear us. The Queen will not commit to any rash manoeuvres while she thinks she is holding all the cards."

"That is assuming I will have any standing among the peers by tomorrow," she said sourly.

"It will be all right, Sparkles."

That stupid nickname, Charity thought desperately. But at the same time, it felt as though some piece of the world had been restored to balance. How unbelievable was her life these days, that his contemptuous irreverence for her title was an unexpected source of comfort? A furtive happiness began to unfold in her stomach, and Charity shook her head in disbelief.

After a little silence, he added, "It seems I owe you two apologies, and the first is for ruining your evening plans for nothing. Though you were generous in coming without question."

"Please," she interrupted. "I owed you that much at least after the way things fell out between us."

"Well, that does not excuse my behaviour," he continued, his voice muted. "I was... rather beastly to you, and I am sorry for that."

"You were speaking the voice of your worst fears." Charity hadn't put the words together in her head before, but as she spoke them now, it felt true. "The idea of being manipulated—being *used*—" she said, employing his own specific turn of phrase, "it is a nightmare for you, isn't it?"

"...Yes."

It was as though, little by little, finer details were emerging in the portrait of the man. The way he wore armour to protect his vulnerabilities from the world at large, much as she did. His was a shell built with a stand-offish attitude, isolation, and the secrets he collected but only rarely employed.

"I do not want your penny," Charity said impulsively, seeing a rare opportunity. The question was whether she had the courage to take it. Finally she turned to face him, though she could barely make out his face in the little light afforded by the crescent moon and the gas lamps. "I want a secret."

She could feel his appraisal from the shadows.

"I seem to be a bad influence on you, Charity."

"Or a better one than you think. Besides, you owe me at least one answer. I have already answered several of your questions tonight."

She could hear the soft snort of amusement. "Shall we play a different game than Question or Command, then? One where we are trading in information? Best pose your question carefully. Because you know there are some I cannot answer. And if you refuse to answer any of mine, then the game is done."

Carefully, she considered that. "I agree to your terms."

"Then, pose your question." He bent his head towards her, waiting as though it were a dare.

What questions from the past would she answer, given this power? She considered their history, stretching back to their mamas before either of them had been born. "What did my mother really do to start such a rivalry between our families? Do you know the truth?"

10

"Friendship and enmity have the same source: interest."
—Baltasar Gracián, The Art of Worldly Wisdom

Peregrine was both surprised by her choice, and also not. Given free rein to ask a single question, it would not have been the one he would have chosen in her place. But Charity had been buffeted by some of the same winds that had shaped his own life. Of course, she would want to know why Marian Fitzroy would seek to punish her over ancient history.

He, however, had some experience in knowing how little comfort the truth could bring.

"Yes, I know it," he told her softly. "But I ask you if you are sure you want to know? No amount of quiet can stuff the truth back in once it is out, and it is not an answer likely to bring you any peace."

He could just see the bare outline of a wry smile as they passed another lamp. "How fortunate for us that I am not seeking peace. Gaining an understanding is my aim. I already know our mamas sought the same man during their season. But this goes beyond jealousy, and I never got a satisfactory answer from my mother. Especially... afterwards."

Peregrine knew the story that anyone else would tell her: that when Lady Vanessa made her debut, she had turned every head, including the young Lord Cresswell's. Choosing Lady Vanessa over Lady Marian, in the context of the *ton's* usual criteria for marriage, made perfect sense.

"Your father was, I have been told, the catch of the season," he began. "He had everything. Youth. Virility. Independence, with no need to marry for a position or purse. A distant connection to the throne itself. Despite the fact your mama had been declared incomparable by the Queen, by all accounts, it was my mother that Lord Cresswell preferred. They suited one another. Lord Cresswell and my grandfather were deep in negotiations to arrange their engagement, and it had been all but concluded. And then... your mama and grandmother conspired together to trap Lord Cresswell in marriage."

"I suspected there was something more sinister to it than spite." She wrapped her arms around her middle again. "And so your mother was forced to make a different match to an older man."

"With the season nearly over, Grandfather decided to... encourage her to settle with my father, Robin, Lord Fitzroy, yes. As marriages went, it was... not a very happy one."

There was a long silence as she thought that over. "Such terrible consequences from a single choice."

And she knew not a tenth of it. But why spoil what remained of her blissful ignorance with tales of his father's murder? And if they were going to bring old grievances to air...

"If you did not know any of this, then *I* want to know the real reason why you spurned me the night you learned my name."

He could practically feel the regret emanating off of her, that she had agreed to this game and was now caught out. As far as subtlety went, this was not his finest hour. But time until they arrived back at her home was short, and there would never be a better opportunity to demand this answer.

"There is not something else you would rather ask me?" she evaded, bringing her fingers up to pinch her brow again.

The barest trace of annoyance crossed him. "At the moment, no. You say it was not about my title, but my curiosity is unsatisfied."

"It is a humiliating story, Perry," she beseeched him in a small voice. "Must I tell it?"

If he was a nicer man, perhaps he would have relented. But he had endured his own dose of humiliation when she had practically cut him in front of others following their introduction, and that had flayed him raw. "Only if you want to be able to ask me other questions, both now and in the future," he said casually, as if it made no difference to him what she decided to do.

She heaved a great sigh, her chin dropping. "Fine." Charity was silent for a long moment, thinking. "Your mother was not the only one who ended up unhappy with her marriage. When I was —I do not know, ten years of age or so?—there were... several bad years where my father could barely speak a word to my mother. He drank a great deal, and only then would they talk. If one could call shouting speaking. *In vino, veritas*."

Lost for the moment in her memories, she let her fingers twist in her skirts, headless of the wrinkles she might leave. "He was... so *angry* with her because it was clear she would not be able to produce him any more children. There would be no heir. No son to carry on the title with his bloodline. There was only me and my younger sister. Useless *girls*."

The bitterness in those words spoke of far more than a man shouting at his wife while drunk. Peregrine would lay a wager that Charity had borne the brunt of Earl Cresswell's anger directly, and suddenly he felt the urge to pay the man a call to have a few ungentlemanly words with him himself. And perhaps to adjust the tightness of his cravat. "Charity—"

"I am getting to the point," she waved him off. "When he was at his utter worst, he told me he should have married your mother instead of mine, because then he would have ended up with you. The son he *deserved* to have."

God. Well, now he did feel quite wretched about pressing her on the question. He disentangled her hands from her skirts again, letting them grip his fiercely instead.

"So... I knew your name long before I knew your face, Perry. Years before my debut. Both my mother and I knew you were the standard to which my father held me up against and found me lacking. My mother had warned me away from your family. We met on the balcony as strangers, and I liked you. But then... when I suddenly realised I was face to face with *you*, I—" Her voice broke. "I nearly wept in front of everyone. It was the most mortifying moment of my life. As though I was a child all over again, being told I would never be enough."

"Oh, Sparkles," he said softly, pulling her into his lap to give her what little comfort he could.

Her chest hitched twice, and then she collapsed against him, burrowing her face in the crook of his neck. Peregrine closed his eyes, nearly overcome by the smell of her beneath the fading florals of her perfume. By the feel of her breath against his throat. By the sense of how perfectly she fit against him, as if they were two broken parts that somehow fit together to make a whole.

He let his thumb graze possessively along the curve of her shoulder, tracing what he had no right to claim. She was so fragile, made for finer things. Deserving of a proper match to someone who would give her a family, standing, and security.

And no matter how many cautions he had been served, he could not seem to force himself to remember that he was the son of a monster.

He was tainted.

Opening his eyes with regret, he glanced outside the window and saw they were nearly back at Atholl House. Charity, feeling the change in tension in him, pulled back to her side of the bench, straightening her clothes.

"You are not going home yet, are you?" Her words were more of an accusation than a question. "What will you do now? Is there anything I can do to help?"

"Formulate some plan to get yourself back into the graces of Her Majesty. If you must throw me to the wolves to do so, I will trust your judgement. I am going to see if I can find Prinny at one of his usual haunts," he told her, brushing a fallen lock of her hair behind her ear. "Perhaps we can get him to reason with the Queen. At least long enough to be heard. If you plan to go back out tonight…"

Peregrine did not want to have to tell her about the contract. Not tonight. "Until things are sorted with my mother, it would help me to know you will not go out without your guards."

Do not worry, Perry. I am not nearly done with you yet, his mother whispered into his thoughts.

Hodges brought the carriage to a halt in front of Atholl House, and Peregrine alighted to help her out, walking her to the front door.

"I will cancel my plans. It seems I feel a headache coming on," she murmured with a slight quirk of her lip. But it faded as quickly as it showed, and she turned her head away as if embarrassed by her earlier confession. "Perry… keep yourself safe."

∽

With time to kill, Peregrine swapped his court wear for something more fashionably careless. A bottle green velvet coat and a jewelled pin in his cravat would put him in good company with the sotted nobles and gentry. And just after midnight, he set out on his hunt to find a regent.

Not that Prinny was difficult to locate. One of the loose-lipped footmen at Carlton House gave Peregrine that information practically for free, though he tossed the man a guinea anyway. It seemed that the Prince Regent still routinely favoured the den of iniquity known by the name of the Scarlet Jack. Despite its history.

The prince was apparently undeterred by the fact that he had been there the night last year that it had been set on fire by an arsonist and nearly burned to the ground. It had been rebuilt, newer and better, taking over the space beside it and bringing its reputation and clientele back to bare.

What was a heavy piece of irony about Prinny's preference for it was that this particular establishment had been one of the more lucrative businesses Cameron had run for Marian Fitzroy. And Peregrine wondered if the Regent had any idea that he had been feeding the Fitzroy coffers for years, drinking French liquor acquired by her smuggling operations, plowing her whores, and racking up small mountains of gambling debts at her card and dicing tables.

Cameron had sold it shortly after the Fitzroy family left for the continent, which was a small relief. The Jack would not be his problem to deal with. That had been the other half of the task Peregrine had set the solicitor to—finding and burning out any remaining investments in ill business, which he would not tolerate.

The Scarlet Jack was busy, and Peregrine had to weave around bodies as he strolled into the establishment casually, trying to spot the Regent before he could be spotted in turn. There—in a side room with the Faro table—he could see a crowd of gentlemen pressed shoulder to shoulder as they watched the banker turn the next draw.

Prinny's eyes were fully fixed on the cards, but Lord Ravenscroft beside him noted the movement at the doorway, and locked eyes with Peregrine. The expression on the man's face warned him against coming any closer, and Perry turned on his heel, heading back towards the bar.

In less than a minute, the magpie was beside him. "What are you *doing here*, Canary? You are not made for discretion. Certainly not with that hair of yours," Ravenscroft flicked the back of Peregrine's head.

"Touch me again like that and I will do worse than ruin your cravat, *Maggie*. You know why I am here. I have come to speak with a man about a woman."

"No." There was no give in Ravenscroft's clipped word. "This way lies only trouble."

Peregrine gave him a sidelong look. "Do you even know what woman I am referring to?"

"You incorrigible blockhead. Upstairs parlour, behind the blue curtain. Knock thrice," Ravenscroft said shortly as he went back to the Faro room.

Peregrine idled long enough to finish his own drink before heading up the stairs, checking cautiously to make sure the Regent was nowhere near the door. In his distraction, he nearly bumped into a dusky-skinned man in dark clothes as he glanced over his shoulder, but fortunately that collision was neatly avoided when the other backed out of his way.

Did Ravenscroft actually dare to have a conversation upstairs? The brothel and gambling tables had been the 'legitimate' business of the Jack. It was profitable enough, to be certain. But profits were even better when all the men and women who had been employed by Marian and Cameron were also taught how to mark patrons who could be blackmailed. A new owner or not, certain business 'tricks' would likely persist.

The madame didn't blink an eye when she opened the door to find Peregrine standing there, and she graciously invited him into the parlour where a cluster of women lounged like ornaments. The air was thick with the scents of hedonistic pleasure, and he resisted the urge to wrinkle his nose in distaste.

Taking another drink in the quietest corner, Peregrine smiled neutrally at the women who invited him to sample their wares, demurring. Fortunately, he only had to fend off two direct advances before Ravenscroft arrived, enthusiastically greeting a pretty, petite woman with dark hair and limpid eyes, dragging her with him over to where Peregrine sat.

"This is Kitty," he introduced her. Kitty smiled at Peregrine hopefully, but obediently snuggled up to Ravenscroft, who nuzzled her neck and ear with great affection. "Let us retire."

Peregrine schooled his expression, showing nothing as Ravenscroft herded both of them into a room at the far corner. Inside, the older rake smiled slightly, cupping Kitty's jaw in his hand so that she was looking at Peregrine. He nipped at her earlobe. "Would you like to enjoy Peregrine's company, Kitty?" he murmured in her ear, just loud enough for Perry to hear.

Any courtesan who understood Ravenscroft would have shown some sort of agreement, no matter how feigned. But Kitty, Peregrine saw immediately, showed no sign of even hearing his words, much less understanding them.

Perry tipped his chin in acknowledgement. Kitty was stone deaf, by all appearances. Ravenscroft had bought them a modicum of privacy from the other women, but Peregrine hoped the other man knew why a madame would prize someone like Kitty in her business.

"You cannot leave well enough alone, can you?" the magpie

continued to murmur in a low voice, standing behind the girl. "You pursuing questions about your marchioness is only going to prove to the throne that they are right in believing she is indeed tangled up in this riot business. And you in it as well."

"I only seek to inquire about her welfare, of course," Peregrine drawled in a vague way, bored.

Unfortunately, he must have looked too bored, because Kitty made an inquisitive gesture in his direction.

"No, pet," Ravenscroft turned her and told her kindly, with a smile. And indeed, Peregrine watched her trace the words on his lips with her eyes. "My friend is saving himself for marriage, like a good girl."

The prostitute's eyes shot in his direction, and Peregrine sighed. "He thinks he is amusing."

Kitty smiled sweetly, and Ravenscroft planted a kiss on her forehead, leading her to a stool set in the corner. Kitty let Ravenscroft seat her facing the wall. Clearly, he had used Kitty for such clandestine meetings before, and she was familiar with his routine. She helped herself to the plate of sweets and carafe of wine put there for customers, likely appreciating a break from her usual obligations.

"*She* is still being questioned about her associations," Ravenscroft finally answered the question in a low voice. "A guest of Her Majesty—but you and the duchess already know that."

So the magpie knew they had inquired at Buckingham House. Which meant Prinny and the Queen did as well. "Since you do not seem to be inclined to share details, let me take a guess that she was implicated in Harrison's confession," Peregrine whispered irritably, looking to make sure that Kitty was still looking away. "Something to the effect of payment?"

Ravenscroft scowled at him. "How, exactly, did you come by

the knowledge of the association between the riot and Mr Harrison?" he asked in a low hiss. "And the fact that there was a note?"

"Maggie, you disappoint me," Peregrine drawled as he leaned against the wall. "You are well aware of the resources I have. In this case, the *he* in question drives my carriage. He followed the path of the rioters from gaol to Harrison's home."

Ravenscroft stepped closer, 'til he was standing inches away from Peregrine, allowing him to keep his voice quiet. "Take care where you speak of this matter. The butler says he found the note first and brought it straight to His Highness for a reason. Everyone is busy trying to keep Mr Harrison's confession within the palace walls."

Peregrine scoffed. "That will never happen. Their walls are infested with more rats than men at the best of times. And these are not the best of times. *You* are going to tell me everything because I believe you have some idea of where my loyalties lie. If you do not, I am going to keep whatever I know about the matter to myself, and when the Crown discovers they have ignored the brush fire in their backyard until it has become a conflagration, they will have nobody to blame but themselves."

Closing his eyes, the rake let out a long growl. "Does your share of information include whether or not Lady Normanby is a member of the Order? Because if you are confronted by the Queen, that will be the first thing she will ask you. She rather suspects that to be the case."

Peregrine kept his face perplexed. "Why would you ask me that instead of her?"

"Not only does the confession say she gave Mr Harrison the funds and letter of instruction to pass along to someone to plan the riot, he claimed the marchioness also had a habit of asking others for favours as well. He meant no harm in taking her money,

Harrison claimed! Well, not until he learned the nefarious purpose she had set him to."

Ravenscroft gave him a sardonic look. "I know the marchioness well enough to believe it of her. And she is just evasive enough in replying to her questions that the Queen suspects she has caught one of the troublemakers you have refused to give her. Why else would Lady Normanby bribe people, if she was not one of the Order?"

"Hell and damnation," Peregrine breathed, his spine going stiff and his eyes unfocused as he considered the magpie's words. "Selina is not the target—or at least, not the larger one. Viscount Sidmouth is."

"Explain your meaning," Ravenscroft demanded. "Sidmouth was not accused of anything."

"This is not the Order." The Order would not foul their own nest like this. "Harrison worked as secretary for Sidmouth in the Home Office. What do you suppose a public accusation of several members of the Home Office accepting bribes from Selina would do?" he growled.

The magpie's lips flattened. "The scandal would damn near empty the Home Office, Sidmouth included. They would crucify him for being oblivious to the activities happening under his roof, if nothing else."

"And can you think of anyone else who would be interested in damaging a leader like Sidmouth? A man who just happens to have been interested in trying her publicly as a traitor? Perhaps someone more interested in striking at me, as well?"

Ravenscroft grimaced. "You think your dear mama's hand is behind this?"

"It is as likely as any other explanation. And if it is her, she will not limit herself to putting Selina's head in the noose. There will be more to this plan. Think, Maggie. What if Harrison's death was a murder, and that note forged? In that case, what hope have you of containing it? I assume Prinny and the Queen are so overconfident, no one has checked to ensure that something has not been given to the papers. Because if I am correct, the connection to Sidmouth will be at the top of the columns today. How much would *you* trust my mother to bide her time?"

"I wouldn't."

"Shall I leave you to it, then?" Peregrine pointed with his chin at Kitty. "*Or*, shall we leave right now and go to The Morning Chronicle, to find out if I am right about a story being given to them while there is still time to do something about it?"

Ravenscroft balled his hands into fists as Peregrine named the paper that printed society news. "And what do you plan to do if you are right? What story do we give them to deter them from printing what they have? Because a rumour or bribe will be insufficient."

"What if you gave them a different scandal?" Peregrine suggested slowly.

Ravenscroft looked sidelong at Peregrine, his face pale. "You are an absolute lunatic, if you are proposing what I think you are. Especially after everything it took to keep the other one quiet."

"If given a carefully contrived version of the facts, the news story will involve no one who is not already motivated to remain silent. But you will need to obtain Prinny's approval to release the story. And the royal stamp on it will certainly trump anything from Harrison's written confession."

Peregrine only wished he could be a fly upon the wall when Sidmouth had a chance to learn who pulled his arse out of the fire. It would stick in his craw until the end of days.

To his credit, Ravenscroft didn't dismiss this out of hand. "It is a good thing that the Prince Regent is well in his cups tonight. He will be easy to convince to go along with this madness."

"Do you think he will remember enough of tonight to also protect us from the Queen's wrath?"

"I wouldn't count on it, Canary," Ravenscroft barked a laugh. "I hope you can do without your beauty rest. We will have a great deal to do very quickly, and there will be even more explaining to do afterwards—to a great many people."

11

"Falsehood flies, and truth comes limping after it, so that, when men come to be undeceived, it is too late; the jest is over, and the tale hath had its effect."
—Jonathan Swift

The advantage to skipping out on her evening activities was that Charity had plenty of time to consider what she would say to the Queen—if and when Her Majesty deigned to receive them. Unfortunately, she spent much of that time steeping in thoughts of other matters.

Given Queen Charlotte had been ill-tempered enough to bar them entry the night before, Charity had no illusions their next meeting would go pleasantly. She would have to tread carefully, trying to find out how much of Selina's connection to the Order was known. Giving up Selina as a member of the secret organization would have terrifying consequences for the marchioness, if not Peregrine. And the Queen might not care that

Selina was the only person who might be able to spot which of the others was working for Marian Fitzroy.

Responsibility weighed heavily on her, especially since Peregrine was leaving the choice in her hands. He trusted her. It still amazed her that he had said those words aloud. And it terrified her. And what had happened with Peregrine had been what had preoccupied her for the largest part of the night.

At least, she thought with a slightly hysterical tinge, *we are no longer cutting each other dead.*

But where life would take them was still very much in question. It seemed impossible to imagine any real future together. Not now, or even soon, given everything that was stacked against them.

For that reason, Charity avoided her mother's letter. She had enough of her mama's voice screeching inside her head to keep her on as straight a path as possible. She did not need to read a letter demanding she retreat to the countryside or chastising her for doing the best she could given the circumstances. When all was said and done, when the princess's engagement was announced and the current challenges were behind her, Charity would pen a long note of explanation to her family.

And at least, for now, there was a semblance of peace between her and the tethered falcon.

She drifted off to a dreamless sleep, the exhaustion of the previous days taking its toll. However, when her maid, Miller, shook her awake again, it was still dark in the room. Only the barest hint of a glow lit the edge of her curtains.

"Your Grace, you must wake up. It is urgent," the maid said, her voice rough with sleep. "Lord Fitzroy is here and he said we must rouse you."

"And you listened?" Charity asked, rubbing the sleep from her eyes.

"He threatened to come up here himself if we did not. Even so, Pritchard was of the mind to turn him away, until his lordship showed him the morning paper."

It was far too early for the newspaper to be in circulation. For Peregrine to have a copy, something truly terrible must have happened.

"Give me my wrapper." Charity tucked the loose strands of hair framing her face behind her ears and smoothed her braid with her hands. She belted her wrap, slid her feet into her slippers, and hurried down the stairs.

Peregrine was in the parlour, pacing in front of the cold fireplace. His coat was rumpled, his cravat pin drooping from a loose knot. His stark blond hair nearly glowed under the light of the chandelier, but it was the shadows on his face that stopped her in her tracks.

"Have you slept at all?" Charity gasped, and then hurried over to him. "Egads, you reek of alcohol. What has happened?"

"Please, can we sit? I have been run off my feet, and there is a great deal I have to warn you about."

She nodded, and Peregrine collapsed onto a settee, rubbing his bleary eyes as he looked sidelong at the footman pointedly stationed in the room with them. "Ravenscroft and I conceived of a plan to prevent a disaster, Your Grace," he said vaguely. "The unfortunate news is that we were obliged to part with something else to pay for that plan. It, er... I expected you would be unpleasantly surprised if I did not rouse you."

Peregrine opened his coat, pulled a folded broadsheet from the inside pocket, and held it out to her. She took it from him, ignoring the newsprint staining her hands, and unfolded it.

The first word she spotted was poison. The second she spotted was her name. Her breath caught in her chest as she struggled to make sense of the story swimming in front of her eyes.

"Queen's Diamond Averts Royal Tragedy! - Duchess Atholl proved she had wits to match her beauty when she warned the Home Office and foiled an attempt to poison Charlotte, the beloved Princess of Wales. His Royal Highness the Prince Regent confirmed the story..."

The rest of the article disappeared as black spots filled her vision.

"Breathe, Charity," Perry hissed.

She sucked in air without thinking and then coughed, nearly choking on it. The paper crumpled in her hand as she tightened her fists. When her vision cleared, she glanced down at the wadded ball in her lap. It hardly resembled a broadsheet any longer.

It had to be some kind of a joke, an idea he had that she could still stop. The morning papers were not due to arrive for at least another couple of hours.

"Say you are not serious," she finally uttered, looking at him. "You cannot possibly be thinking of going through with this."

"It is already done. With Prinny's approval." Peregrine held her gaze, but he let his eyes flicker towards the footman again.

Rage began to heat her skin from beneath. Charity stood up and faced the servant, struggling to keep her face and voice stony. "Leave us."

The man retreated hastily, seeing something Charity evidently hadn't concealed well enough. Charity began to pace in front of the window, uncertain what else to do with the terrifying feelings coursing with her. Scream? Cry? Throw things at him?

Peregrine stood and crossed the room, forcing her to stop in front of him. She speared him with a blistering glare.

"Tell me you did not set me up to fall in order to save your friend," she shot at him.

"I know this is an unwelcome revelation. But after everything, you *cannot* possibly believe I would trade your welfare for hers," he replied, his voice dry.

"I do not know what to think! But we cannot go through with this," she insisted, trying to remain in control of her faculties. "The two of you have as good as told the whole world I thwarted your mother's plot. There will be a line of people forming outside of my house who will want to kill me for this, and both your mother and the Queen of England will be fighting for the first spot in the procession!"

As she ranted, the lines of tension eased on his face. Now, the pale blonde devil actually *smiled* at her, and Charity's vision swam with red.

"You think this is *amusing*?" she asked, poking him hard in the chest. "You must leave now and make the paper print something else!"

He wisely did not answer, but his smile increased fractionally. "It will be all right. I daresay you will be a hero, the woman who foiled a plot to assassinate the heir to the throne. Just think of the invitations that will flood your doorstep."

"How dare you patronise me!" She poked him again, harder, only barely resisting the urge to do greater violence. He captured her hand, trapping it. Charity yanked, but he did not release her.

"Let me go," she growled.

"So you can continue to poke me so rudely? You should remember how I feel about *doing unto others* as they do to me, Duchess." He gave her a hooded look and her face flamed.

"I mean it! Release me at once."

"Say please," he teased her, his voice a low purr that was both playful and dangerously wicked.

Flustered by the sudden heat between them, Charity's eyes dropped to the cravat hanging loose on his neck, and for a moment she considered the merits of grabbing it with her other hand and throttling him with it.

Or… perhaps kissing him would be the better choice.

"I can see you thinking something dangerous, Sparkles. I wouldn't, were I you," he warned her, his voice light. When she jerked her attention back to his face, his eyes held something hot and dark. And then they dropped to her lips.

Desire, she named the expression on his face suddenly, also identifying the feeling growing within the pit of her belly. Her racing heart somehow picked up more speed, and she tensed, steeling herself against the urge to provoke him further. To see what would happen.

Reluctantly, he let her hand go, moving back a half step. "I know you are worried. But I would not have done this if I thought it would put you in more danger. If anything, this will better ensure your safety. The Queen will not dare take away the guards now."

Shakily, Charity ran her freed fingers over her face. The air felt cooler with him no longer so near, and she shivered. "But Cameron is dead."

"But he was not the only one working for my mother. Charity, listen to me. I discovered yesterday there is a bounty on your head —paid in full, waiting only to be claimed. This news changes you from diamond to national treasure, someone to be protected at all costs. You cannot be left unguarded."

And where will you be? her thoughts shouted at him. *What of the threats to you?* She inhaled through her nose and banished her nightmares back to the darkness.

Stand tall. Be fearless, she ordered herself. Even though she was anything but.

"We are not done discussing this, but what's done is done," is all she said instead. "So we must focus our minds on what comes next. And that is an audience with the Queen."

~

Charity's words proved to be fortuitous, for the pair had barely finished their breakfast before the summons arrived. Her Majesty required them to present themselves within the hour. The missive did not include any hint of what would happen should they choose to ignore it. Explicit warning was not needed, given the amount of wailing Charity's mama was doing in her head.

A footman had been dispatched to Fitzroy House to collect a change of clothes. Pritchard unbent enough to offer to act as valet. "It would not do for someone in disarray to accompany Her Grace," he stated, making clear his motives.

Charity and Peregrine arrived at Buckingham House with five minutes to spare. As opposed to their last attempt to see the Queen, this time they were ushered straight into a vast drawing room.

Queen Charlotte sat upon a seat that more resembled a throne than an armchair. Her most loyal retainers fanned out at her sides, standing at attention. Two guards followed Charity and Peregrine into the room, taking up positions only a few short steps behind them. Though it was impossible, Charity felt their hot breath on the back of her neck. One false move and that tension heating up her spine would turn into the sharp cut of a blade.

Charity dropped into a deep curtsey, noting Peregrine executing a similar bow of obeisance. Like her, he remained bent over until a sharp word from the Queen bid them to rise.

The royal aide-de-camp stepped forward and unrolled a broadsheet, flourishing it in the air. Charlotte gave it a slashing glance before turning her furious force on the pair of them.

"Did you know of this before the story went out?" she asked.

"I did not," Charity replied. Peregrine remained mute, leaving Charity to take the lead as they had agreed. She continued. "When I learned of the matter, I was less than pleased, particularly once I heard that Your Majesty had not been consulted. However, Lord Fitzroy has convinced me of the necessity of the actions undertaken by himself and Lord Ravenscroft, with the Prince Regent's permission, of course."

"An action taken in the wee hours of the morning, when my dear son was likely deep in his cups. That he has not sent me any word suggests he may not even recollect his part in the matter. So, do not wave Prinny's so-called permission as though it is an excuse for what you have done. Your marchioness funded the riot that embarrassed all of us. The clerk she bribed felt so guilty for his part that he could not continue on."

"The marchioness did not stage the riot," Peregrine said with as much conviction as he could muster. "She has nothing to gain by publicly embarrassing the Crown. She is a convenient scapegoat, to keep us all distracted from seeing who is truly to blame."

"And who might that be, pray tell?" the Queen demanded.

"My mother, Your Majesty."

"Your mother, who is not here in England," she said scornfully. "And not this Order I told you to investigate?"

"I know why you would be skeptical, Your Majesty," Peregrine took a deep breath. "It would be far easier to control events from close at hand than at such a remove. But I will explain my logic."

"My patience is thin this morning, thanks in no small part to your own actions," Queen Charlotte replied. "I will grant you some leeway, but if you hope to use charm to distract me, think again."

The apple does not fall far from the tree, Charity's mother hissed from the recesses of her mind. *The Queen must not heed his lies.*

He speaks only the truth, Charity replied, willing her mother to retreat again to the shadows.

It seemed that Charity was not the only one suffering from

memories of a mother. Peregrine shifted his stance, his shoulders tight.

"You must understand a few things about my mother. First, she craves power the way we are born to crave air. And second, matters of conscience do not trouble her in the way it would for the rest of us. She believes she has the right to whatever she has the ruthlessness and the wit to seize, and she will play a game so patient that it spans years." He let his eyes slide to Charity. "She built an empire on the backs of dark dealings that I have been trying to trace, to rip it from London by the roots."

"Much good you have done, if she is truly behind the riot, as you claim," the Queen pointed out.

"And that should tell you something, Your Majesty. My mother remains a step ahead of us. For the past weeks, I have chased after every thread I knew, and at every turn been foiled. Cameron is dead, but there is still some agent of my mother at work here, selling her businesses and silencing her past associates."

The Queen steepled her fingers over her lap. "It seems your mother is in retreat, Lord Fitzroy."

"A retreat is not the same as a surrender. And just because they are cutting off the avenues of investigation I might know enough to follow does not mean that there is more I do not."

"I would be willing to entertain that your mother is petty and vicious, but it is a much further step to see her hand at work."

"It becomes clearer when you understand her motivations. Her targets are her enemies, but the manner of their demise is also meant to serve her larger purposes. She has struck at me and her old accomplices, because we might be able to stop her. The poisoning and the riot are because it suits her to cause this trouble for the Crown. And Harrison's death because..." Peregrine made a helpless gesture with his hands. "We believe that Viscount Sidmouth or the Home Office was the target—a suspicion

Ravenscroft and I were able to confirm when we arrived at the office of the Morning Post."

The Queen's face grew more displeased as he described the article they had found the paper about to print, rife with suggestions that its clerks could be bought and sold under the viscount's own nose. And his suspicions that Mr Harrison's death was far more likely a murder designed to facilitate the lie.

"You have convinced me there is some conspiracy at work, Lord Fitzroy." Charlotte made this admission as though it pained her; her face was hard. "I am curious, however, to know one thing. I would like to know what Viscount Sidmouth and the marchioness did to earn a place on your mother's black books."

Peregrine's hesitation was ever so slight, Charity knew he was struggling to find a way not to reveal the truth—that the marchioness was, after a fashion, guilty of exactly what the paper was going to imply. That she had used her influence to keep the Home Office from pursuing a charge of treason against Marian's son.

"The marchioness has, several times over, proved herself a loyal friend to both Lord Fitzroy and me," Charity answered for him. "Mr Hodges was a man in her employ before she sent him to work for Lord Fitzroy. And she helped me after the attack on Atholl House."

Peregrine tipped his chin towards her, a slight loosening in his shoulders indicating his gratitude.

"Hmm," the Queen said sourly, unsatisfied but unable to refute this. "Fine. It is a compelling tale, and I am willing to entertain that it may be your mother's plot and not the Order's. But I fail to understand why you and Ravenscroft chose to drag my granddaughter into the limelight. Thank God you at least had enough wisdom to alter the story and leave Prince William's name out of it."

Charity cleared her throat. "Lady Fitzroy is not the only one who can kill two birds with one stone, ma'am. With that story, both the princess and the viscount are afforded some protection. Now, more than ever, the princess needs the support of the nation. With this article, all of society—high and low—will rally to her cause. Who can question the Prince Regent's haste to see his daughter wed and off to safety? And Lord Sidmouth is afforded credit."

"And what of the benefit to yourself?" the Queen fired back.

"I seek no glory," Charity said softly, "beyond what grace Your Majesty has shown me. However, Lord Fitzroy believed this notoriety would help protect me as well. His mother's agent set a bounty on my head."

Queen Charlotte speared him with a look, and Peregrine gave a grim nod in confirmation. "I greatly dislike all of this," she hissed. "Disorder at home makes us look weak at a time where we should be celebrating our triumph over France. Whether it is the Order or your mother, the result is the same. You must discover the shape of their ambition!"

Peregrine looked haunted, and Charity somehow knew he was regretting that Cameron died before they could question him. "I will continue to do what I can."

"It is not enough. Our royal guests are already enroute for our shores. I do not want you to wait for the next move, and time is not a luxury we can afford."

Peregrine flattened his lips. After a long moment, he replied, "Then we must go on the offensive. What better way to provoke her agent into making a mistake than by flaunting Cameron's failure to murder us? They might stumble when they change their plans. Leave some clue. Or perhaps even come directly after us, giving us someone we might be able to question."

"You mean to make appearances and set every tongue in London to wagging by having my diamond on your arm." The

Queen stroked her chin thoughtfully, as though the idea bore a certain amount of merit, but it was too foolish to entertain.

"Only if both you and the duchess consent to it. I will have to bait a trap with myself as best I can if she is not minded to take such a risk."

Charity bit her tongue to avoid protesting. The Queen bore him no love and would not take any steps to ensure his safety if he set out on his own.

To flirt with society together? It was a desperate plan, and possibly a disastrous one for both of them. Rumours of a courtship would drive his mother mad and encourage her persecution. And… there was also her own family's reaction to consider. She thought of the unread missive lying on her desk.

What on earth would her mother say about this?

You know exactly what she would say. But on the other hand, a farce will likely be the only way you will ever get to court Peregrine Fitzroy.

She met Peregrine's gaze and nodded her head in permission. The corner of his mouth curled slightly, like he was anticipating trouble. And welcomed it.

"This plan is foolhardy," the Queen said, gripping the edge of her armrests as she stared down the pair. "But I suppose it is better than doing nothing. Very well, make your plans, Lord Fitzroy. But wait a day before making your debut. Prinny and I must agree on what is and is not to be said about the matter of the poisoning. I will send word to you, my diamond, when we have reached an agreement."

"Of course, Your Majesty," Charity replied, bobbing a curtsey. She could hardly believe that they had survived their encounter with the Queen. Time to depart before Charlotte's temper made another appearance.

Unfortunately, Peregrine was not of the same mind.

"Your Majesty, there is the matter of the marchioness. She could prove useful—"

"Oh no, Lord Fitzroy. I shall entertain the notion that she may be a victim of your mother's schemes, but I cannot help but notice that Lady Normanby is a very canny, resourceful, and well connected woman who appeared on your arm after I sent you to hunt the Order. And despite all evasions, I cannot help but wonder if perhaps I have a prize in hand after all. For the moment, she will remain my guest, Lord Fitzroy, until I decide otherwise. Or do you have further objections?"

"No, Your Majesty," Peregrine said, his voice without any inflection whatsoever.

She lifted a hand and flicked her wrist to shoo them out. The guards standing behind them moved closer, giving Charity and Peregrine no choice but to leave. They curtseyed and bowed in turn and then beat a hasty retreat.

Charity waited until they were outside Buckingham House before speaking. "I am sorry we could not free Selina."

"She is capable of fending for herself," Peregrine replied. "And also, while she is a guest of the Queen, she will be safe from harm. Come, let us get you home before we cross paths with anyone else."

Hodges drove them back to Atholl House. "What will you do now?" she asked him in the carriage. "Have you had any luck determining who in the Order might be working for your mother?"

Peregrine looked as harassed as Charity had ever seen him, but at least his irritation did not seem to be for her. "I have barely had a chance to begin looking. But it is on my list of tasks now."

She controlled her voice carefully. "And... this other plan of yours? I am to pretend... what, exactly?"

"You do not have to pretend to be enamoured of me. But

perhaps we should pretend to be... contemplating the possibility?" That slight smile again, like a challenge.

She gave him a cool look. "I suppose I could. Pretend, that is. And where, exactly, do you plan on making our debut?"

"Do you trust me, Sparkles?" He lifted his chin, daring her to bring some inevitable argument, and she felt her pulse race at the idea that she did not want to argue.

"I might have to trust you with my life, Perry. But I do not know yet if you can be trusted with a guest list."

His answering chuckle was wicked.

12

"Love and warre are all one."
—Don Quixote

Peregrine wished he could split himself into three. There was a great deal to accomplish in a very short amount of time.

Following the interrogation by the Queen, Peregrine had set Hodges's runner—the man who had been conducting investigations on the new staff and managing Perry's appearances in the paper—into collecting information on Duke Chandros and Lord Pembroke. Hodges, he had assigned to looking into Mr Xavier and Mr Goldbourne.

Xavier and Goldbourne were the two members of the Order with whom he was most unfamiliar, and also the two who he had the most ready alibi for investigating, since neither was a peer. Given Goldbourne's position as the head of a bank and Xavier's on the Board of Trade, should Hodges be caught, he could simply tell them he was performing a routine inquiry on behalf of a financial concern.

He was less sanguine about keeping his hand hidden from Chandros and Pembroke, if the runner was caught. But Hodges assured him the man could give an excuse about checking their affiliations for a committee seat or some such.

Idling at the estate, doing paperwork so that Hodges was free to make his inquiries, was made harder by a sneaking sense of guilt. It ate at his soul to consider the danger he was exposing Charity to. Flaunting her in society on his arm like a bullfighter waving a muleta should have been an action borne of desperation, an action of last resort.

Hoping he could spur his mother's agent into some action that would reveal his identity was risky. But he was afraid that if they waited too long to try to anticipate his mother's henchman, they would forever be on the defensive, unable to see a looming disaster before it struck.

But there were other means. He was mad to suggest they present as a couple.

His conscience was bleeding raw knowing a treacherous part of him *wanted* this. He desired to keep Charity close and safe, to be sure. But the unreasoning, animal part of his brain also wanted the *ton* to see—that she was his.

Peregrine took a steadying breath in the middle of composing a letter to Charity, up to his wrists in ink.

Dearest Duchess, Lady Barbour was delighted to be asked to arrange a small gathering tomorrow evening in your honour. I can think of no finer host to recognise your recent admirable service to England. It would give me the greatest satisfaction if you would allow me the honour of escorting you. If you are agreeable, I shall call for you at half past seven.

—P. Fitzroy

Sealing it with wax, he dispatched it with one of the two new footmen Quinn had managed to acquire over the past two days, along with the cook, Mrs Evers, and Mr Croft to serve as valet.

Jack and Owen Graves were brothers, both standing a few inches over six feet, and when they planted themselves side by side in livery, they looked rather like a yoke of oxen dressed for court.

They hadn't served as soldiers in the war, but apparently they had been part of a local militia in Norfolk before drifting towards service. Peregrine intended to have both men riding on the back of the carriage tomorrow, to make a not-so-subtle point.

He was grateful that Lady Barbour had been so accommodating for this favour. Her salons were considered quite *de rigueur,* and it would give him a respectable place to be seen and incite speculation.

The next day felt a hundred long. The initial reports on the four other members of the Tribune were little more than a loose collection of facts—addresses, personal information, and some bits of gossip.

In addition to his position on the Board of Trade, Xavier was paid for advising several firms. All considered him to be politically neutral. Chandros's reputation and financial standing was so perfect as to be impeccable; almost too clean. Goldbourne managed his bank with a partner by the name of Hartwell, and invested heavily in speculative ventures. His wealth was second only to his nearest banking rival, Nathan Rothschild. And Pembroke had old family coffers and standing, but was publicly progressive.

Skimming those details occupied too little time, leaving Peregrine to pace the hallways of the estate until Quinn and Mr Croft conspired to get him washed, shaved, and dressed for his evening out. At half past six, he departed in a deep blue tailcoat, pantaloons, and a cream waistcoat a couple of shades darker than his hair.

It was time to pretend, for all of London's upper society, that he and Duchess Atholl were soft on one another.

The duchess's footman admitted him at once, vanishing into

the house to fetch his mistress. Peregrine waited in the dim glow of the lanterns, staring out the window as one gloved hand idly tapped against his thigh. Then he halted the gesture abruptly. Nerves like this? He was a man nearly seven and twenty, not a green lad.

Soft footsteps on the marble drew his attention, and he turned, his lips parting as he watched Charity descend the stairs with the slow, deliberate grace of a woman accustomed to being observed. She wore sapphires and a gown of ivory silk that caught the candlelight, the colors echoing his own attire.

Her neutral smile of greeting widened slightly in satisfaction as she took in his appearance. "Lord Fitzroy. I hope you do not mind that I took the liberty of consulting with your Mr Croft on your outfit."

Clever of her. He offered his arm with faint amusement, lowering his voice for her ear alone. "I would be a fool to object, Your Grace. You wear my colors far better than I do. Shall we go?"

She set her hand to his arm, and the smell of orange blossom stirred in the air. Like a club to the back of the skull, the perfume struck him with a suddenness that left him stunned and gasping. This new scent was a more complex one than she had worn last year, but one that spoke its message clearly nonetheless.

Orange blossom is for joy.

Despite the thousand reasons she should keep her distance, their trials and tribulations… she had brought a fond memory of their past into the present.

She had done it for him. And he was so lost.

"Perry? Are you feeling unwell?" she asked him softly, her gentian blue eyes creased with mischief.

Scraping together his wits, he forced his feet back into motion and led her to his carriage. "I am perfectly fine," he said, his voice rough with a twist of emotions he couldn't quite contain.

She made a slight scoffing noise, dropping his arm to allow Owen to hand her into the carriage. She sat in the forward facing seat, leaving him enough space that he could sit beside her. When the carriage door shut, she glanced at him with an arched eyebrow. "I remind you this was a battlefield of your own choosing."

"True. But I did not prepare an adequate defence against your weapons," he replied, giving her a faint grin to soften his words. "I commend you on their effectiveness, but perhaps you might save your artillery for our enemies."

"Oh, are we supposed to be allies in this conflict?" She batted her eyelashes at him.

Now he barked a laugh. "Do behave yourself, Sparkles. I am but a mortal man."

She gave him one more searching look and subsided. The carriage ride to the Barbours' residence was far too short, and she behaved. Peregrine couldn't quite decide whether that was a fortunate happenstance or an unfortunate one.

Lord and Lady Barbours' other guests were ensconced and enjoying their wine by the time Charity and Peregrine arrived. Lady Barbour rose with a quick, beatific smile as they approached, extending her hands to Charity. "Your Grace! It is so wonderful that you have come! We are long overdue for getting to know one another better."

"I shall try not to take my position among the furnishings personally," Peregrine teased Lady Barbour, who wrinkled her nose in an impishly charming fashion at him.

"I was planning on coming around to you. Eventually. Your Excellency, Countess." Lady Barbour turned to a couple with a faintly exotic look seated on a settee. "This is Her Grace, the Duchess of Atholl. And this charming wastrel beside her is Lord Fitzroy, who was among the defenders at Burlington House.

"Your Grace, My Lord, His Excellency Count von Lieven

and the Countess von Lieven," Lady Barbour continued, introducing the Russian ambassador to London and his wife. Peregrine and Charity exchanged nods of greetings with the pair. That left still two others, both men who were vaguely familiar, though Peregrine drew a blank when searching for their names.

"Our remaining guests have agreed to set their differences aside long enough to share space on the sofa. Mr Carew, MP for Abingdon, is a silent, but strong-willed presence within the Whig party. Mr Godwin, representing the people of Liverpool, may sit on the back bench, but do not underestimate his power as a Tory," Lady Barbour explained.

"It is an honour to make your acquaintance," Mr Godwin said, rising from his seat. He was tall and gaunt, but his voice was firm. "Your Grace, I understand we have you to thank for our princess's good health."

"I did only what any loyal servant to the Crown would have done," Charity demurred, following the Queen's instructions to remain mum on all details.

"Please, have a seat, the both of you." Lady Barbour pointed them toward a narrow settee.

Peregrine eyed it as they approached. Trust Lady Barbour to play the patron saint of meddling matchmakers; it would be nearly impossible to keep his distance from Charity. Indeed, as soon as he lowered himself to her side, he found their legs pressing together.

Charity was in fine form, keenly aware of what she was doing to him and delighting in it. She shifted, but it was no more than a feint for the other attendees. Really, she smoothed her skirts, sending her perfume floating through the air, and did nothing to move away.

It was a peculiar, enjoyable kind of torment—this slow burn to exquisite ruin, done by the smallest of degrees. The temptation was strong to embrace destruction. To allow himself, for just a moment, to indulge.

To forget.

Try to forget, his mother whispered in his ear, *but I think you will remember you belong to me.*

Do I, though, Mother? After all, you cast me aside. His gaze drifted across the room, catching the Barbours in a moment of quiet affection. He envied it.

Tell me, dearest, she murmured from the dark corners of memory. *Do you truly believe she won't do the same, once she learns what you really are?*

Of course, he didn't. If Charity peeled back the dust cloths on the last five years of his life, she would be horrified. A woman like her could never knowingly choose a man like him. Not unless he lied. And hoped the past stayed locked behind shuttered doors.

But that was the future. Tonight was different.

Tonight, he was playing the role of *Cinderella*, full well knowing the magic would break with the final stroke of midnight.

So he took a glass of wine from the passing footman and offered it to Charity, ensuring their fingers brushed as he passed it to her. The faint flush that coloured her cheeks told him he wasn't the only one clinging to whatever pleasure they could draw from the illusion.

Lord Barbour, ever deft, steered the conversation into deeper waters. Though he fancied himself an artist and a poet, both he and his wife had the instincts of tacticians.

"Loyalty," Barbour said, voice smooth and genial, "is an interesting question, is it not? Her Grace speaks of duty to the Crown—commendable, of course—but others of us must balance competing claims: ideals, the people we represent... and in the case of His Excellency, the delicate waltz between the master you serve and the master of this land. Anyone who believes it simple is naïve at best."

"You forgot the heart, Lord Barbour, and I must confess, I am disappointed," Peregrine said, his grin tempering the reproof. "For if a poet who married for love does not place it foremost among consideration, who else might?"

Barbour tipped his glass in salute. "Ah, but as Shakespeare wrote in *Love's Labour's Lost*, 'And when love speaks, the voice of all the gods make heaven drowsy with the harmony.' But love speaks so rarely, Lord Fitzroy, that we are apt to forget it speaks at all."

"Or its voice is drowned out by reason," Mr Godwin interjected, his tone bearing the weight of Tory caution. "As in the case of Prinny's insistence on seeing his daughter wed. Peace in Europe is as delicate as a butterfly's wings. We must do all we can to preserve it. To that end, forging alliances with like-minded powers is paramount, would you not agree, Your Excellency?"

"Europe breathes easily for the moment, Mr Godwin. One hopes England, Russia, and others will recognise the wisdom of cautious stewardship," the Russian count replied with diplomatic poise. "As for the prospective marriage of the Princess of Wales, I am not, I think, the most qualified here to comment on the matter."

"Qualifications—or the good sense to choose the proper time and place—rarely prevent some from offering their opinions," Mr Godwin said pointedly, his gaze flicking toward the Whig beside him, his nostrils flaring with disdain.

"Come now," Lord Barbour interjected smoothly, "we mustn't go laying blame upon doorsteps without first establishing who owns the house."

"Indeed," Mr Carew agreed languidly. His thick moustache twitched over a deepening frown. "Lord Cavendish was so horrified that he fled to his country seat. Whoever opened the gates to those protesters did no favours to my party. Are you quite certain your hands are clean, Mr Godwin? I noticed Lord Eldon departed early. Did he, perhaps, leave the door ajar behind him?"

The Tory flushed a dark shade of crimson, lifting a hand as if to jab a finger in his opponent's face. But before he could utter a word, to Peregrine's surprise it was Charity who spoke.

"Ultimately, it will be the princess who decides whether the alliance proceeds. And who among us can speak with authority on what lies in her heart?" Charity said calmly. "I have spent many hours in her company and do not envy her. She must live each day with the consequences. Matters would be far simpler were she even half so fortunate as our gracious hosts, to find abiding love that transcends all else."

"Well said," murmured the Russian countess, speaking for the first time. She proved her diplomatic finesse by deftly steering the conversation away from dangerous waters and toward safer territory.

Talk moved to the latest production in the West End, and whether it was worthy of its playwright's former triumphs. Peregrine only added the occasional remark, playing the role of genial observer with the easy charm he had spent years perfecting. But to say he followed the conversation closely would be a lie. Time and again, his thoughts drifted to the woman seated at his side.

He tossed back the last of his wine, forcing his mind back into the present. The Whig's jab at Lord Eldon had stirred a memory he'd let slip in the chaos of the past days—the meeting at Burlington House, and Eldon's abrupt departure just afterward.

When Mr Carew eventually rose and stepped outside for a cigar, Peregrine followed. He declined the offer of one with a shake of the head, murmuring about needing only a breath of fresh air to clear his thoughts.

"Were I seated beside such a glorious creature, I daresay I, too, would require assistance clearing my thoughts," Carew said, with more than a hint of envy.

Peregrine smiled briefly. "I was speaking with Her Grace when the rioters breached Cavendish's gathering, and I would far rather face down the French again than endure that a second time. We were deuced lucky the outcome was not worse."

He paused for a moment and then added, "I happened to see Lord Eldon speaking with someone before he left. A clerk of his, if I'm not mistaken. From his expression, I assumed the news was unwelcome."

Mr Carew cast a quick glance toward the salon door to ensure it was shut, then leaned in slightly, voice dropping. "His office was burgled. The Tories are keeping quiet about what was taken, but I doubt it was anything minor. Why else bury it? Mark me—I suspect whatever occurred that night was of greater consequence than raised voices in a ballroom. But then, Tories have always excelled at keeping their scandals off the front page."

Perry chuckled dryly. That he helped bury the latest scandal made the irony sharper. "Such discipline is why they remain in power."

The salon ended soon after, and as Peregrine escorted Charity out to the carriage, he noted a look of disappointment on her face. "You look rather forlorn for a woman who held the room in her palm all evening," he teased her gently. "Did you not enjoy yourself?"

"I did," she said, looking up at him. "I only wish the night was not so eager to be done with us."

He felt very much the same. "Well... if you are inclined to suffer my poor company a little longer, I daresay we might find some mischief to occupy us."

"Goodness, my lord," she said archly, the ripple of a laugh in her voice. "If I did not know better, I would think you were trying to lead me astray."

"Of course not. I would never be so naughty." He leaned just a little closer, and her perfume drowned his better senses. "Though if I were… would you trust me not to get us into trouble?"

A fierce blush stained her cheekbones adorably. He was the worst sort of cad, to enjoy provoking her this way. But as he watched Charity's lips parting, her breath picking up speed, he knew her body was also thrilling in this illicit dance along the edges of impropriety.

"I trust you," she whispered, letting the footmen hand her into the carriage.

God help him, she shouldn't. Because for all the suggestion in his words, his intentions had been chaste. And now Peregrine was left choking on the taste of his own provocation, the joke half-dead in his throat. He bought himself a moment to compose himself, whispering their next destination to Hodges before he joined her in the carriage.

As the carriage slowed, Charity brushed aside the curtain to peer out, then drew back, startled. "Vauxhall Gardens? Half of London will be there!"

"Was that not the point?" Peregrine replied, reaching past her to flick the curtain back into place. He gave her a look that was part challenge, part devilry. "Second thoughts about our little charade? We can go home instead."

She lifted her chin stubbornly, her eyes sparking. "No. You wanted them to whisper. Well, then, let them."

Indeed, tongues began wagging the moment Peregrine helped Charity descend from the carriage. She tucked her hand into the crook of his arm, took a steadying breath, and stepped forward through the gates.

It was a new experience for both of them—not merely the sort of public outing associated with courtship, which Peregrine had avoided since coming into his majority, but something far more disarming: the fact that they were enjoying it.

He did not miss the way Charity's gaze sought his when conversation pulled them in separate directions. And though he told himself he watched her only out of concern for her safety, he knew, in his heart, the lie of that excuse.

The moonlight made her ivory gown gleam like silk poured from the stars, and the flickering gaslight turned her hair to molten gold. Only a blind man, or an utter fool, could ignore her. And truly, there were no blind men that evening in Vauxhall.

They flocked around Charity, working to entice her away from Peregrine's side. As he watched them natter at her inanely, a surge of jealous possession finally drove him to reclaim his spot. *Mine*, Peregrine thought, rudely cutting off the man mid-word as he offered her his arm. "We are late for an appointment," he told her.

Charity raised her brows in confusion, but did not contradict his statement. "A third stop, Peregrine? Surely you jest?"

But he did not lead her to the gate. Instead, he guided her onto the swept stones that served as a dance floor beneath the stars. The orchestra struck up the opening notes of a waltz.

There were titters from the crowd. The couples on the floor began to drift away, leaving only the married—and those openly courting. But she followed, instead of pulling away.

Peregrine slid his arm around Charity's waist, wishing not for the first time that he could remove his gloves and feel the satin of her gown beneath his palm. That she would take hers off, and lay her palms to his cheek again, as when he had lain fevered. But perhaps her skin would be hot to the touch instead of the comforting coolness this time, because it felt like his shoulder burned where her fingers lay.

They moved as though they had danced together a hundred times before. Neither spoke. Their eyes said more than words could manage.

This was the dance he should have had with her, last year, at his ball. Where she would have ended her night with a pleasant memory instead of fractured nightmares. At least now he could give her a dance she would remember the way he did.

And then midnight struck.

A burst of fireworks overhead scattered colour across the night sky and drew delighted gasps from the crowd, shattering the spell. The evening was drawing to its end; the entertainments had run their course.

Peregrine felt the familiar weight returning. Reality waited beyond the garden's glow.

Charity must have felt it too. As guests turned to make their departures, she lingered and said softly, "Do we have time for a walk? It is only... I have never been before, and I have heard so much—"

As excuses went, it was flimsy. But he didn't care.

He offered his arm with gratitude for the warm night, and she slipped hers through it with a closeness that made him ache. Once they entered the Long Walk, she went so far as to rest her head lightly on his shoulder.

The gas lamps dwindled, leaving long stretches of darkness between the pools of light—perfect for couples in search of shadows and seclusion.

Peregrine slowed their pace, letting the couple ahead of them fade into the distance. It was sheer folly, but he no longer cared. Her perfume clung to him, twining with his scent of cloves. It fogged his thoughts, turning every rational argument to smoke.

Where the darkness pooled, deep enough for a person to vanish, that was where he meant to stop. But before he could draw her close, before he could press his lips to the delicate pulse at her throat, Charity gave a sharp, shocked gasp—and was pulled sideways from his grasp.

13

"The heart has its reasons of which reason knows nothing."
—Blaise Pascal, Pensées

C harity barely had time to understand what was happening. A squat, meaty man had seized her upper arm and yanked her away from Peregrine with brutal force, dragging her deeper along the path. Another heavyset figure surged forward, cutting Peregrine off before he could so much as reach for her.

"Perry!" she cried, heart pounding. He was still recovering, and facing down a man of that size was hardly fair odds.

But she had no time to see more. Her captor set off at a rapid march, his grip vice-like on her arm, forcing her into an awkward half-trot to keep up. She twisted in his grasp, trying to look back, heels digging into the path, but he was far too strong.

The darkness of Vauxhall Gardens closed in around her, thick and oppressive. The few scattered lanterns flickered wildly, casting restless shadows. Even the gravel beneath her feet felt treacherous, shifting maliciously with every hurried step.

Behind her came the dull sounds of a struggle—grunts, the thud of blows—and her stomach threatened to rise into her throat. Distracted and off balance, she lost her footing on the loose surface. Pain flared as her ankle turned sharply beneath her, sending her stumbling.

As they jerked to a halt, Charity flung her head backwards, glimpsing flashes of movement. Peregrine was battling furiously, but she could not tell who had the upper hand. Her captor gave her a vicious jerk forward to make her move, and agony ripped through her shoulder as well.

The pain made her shriek, and behind her, Peregrine shouted her name.

The brute hauled her upright and shoved her into the arms of a third man. Taller, foul-smelling, reeking of beer and unwashed skin. Her new abductor wrapped one thick arm around her waist and half-carried, half-dragged her deeper into the Long Walk.

Pinned awkwardly against his chest, Charity twisted enough to look back. She caught a glimpse of Peregrine breaking free from the man who had intercepted him. He was sprinting toward her, despite his pursuer still at his heels.

And behind them all, barely visible in the shifting lamplight, she thought she saw a fourth figure moving. Fast, silent. A ghost sliding through the dark.

It was not the man he had been fighting. Someone else?

Between the stench of the man holding her, the jolting grip, and her rising fear, Charity could scarcely draw breath. Her heart galloped, each frantic beat tightening the invisible bands wound around her chest. The night pressed in on all sides, thick and airless, and a lightheaded dizziness began to overtake her.

Peregrine paid no heed to the beefy man who had passed her off. That man had melted into the shadows, waiting for Peregrine to come closer, tightening his hand on a stout branch he held like a club.

"Come out, then, milord," he said in a quiet, mocking voice that she only barely caught.

Charity opened her mouth to call a warning to Peregrine, but nothing emerged from her lips.

Her lungs refused to draw air. Cold, suffocating panic surged up her throat. Her limbs trembled; her chest burned. Darkness crowded her vision, and she began to list sideways, consciousness slipping like water through her fingers.

The tall man cursed and shoved her away in disgust. She fell hard into a shallow niche along the path, landing against a wooden bench with a jolt that stole what little air remained in her chest.

But the hard landing broke the spell, forcing her to suck her breath in from surprise. She gasped, and the gardens began to waver back into focus. From her position at the tall man's feet, she looked up to see him glancing from her to Peregrine, uncertain whether he would be needed.

Move away, her mind screamed at her. *Move now!*

And then Peregrine rounded the corner at full tilt.

"Watch out!" came a shout from a man she did not recognise.

The thug with the branch swung hard, but the warning came in time. Peregrine twisted mid-stride, the heavy blow slicing past him through empty air. He barely broke pace, pivoting at once and throwing himself into a desperate fight against the armed thug and the man who had caught back up with him.

Shaking so violently she could scarcely move, Charity began to crawl, dragging herself away from the flurry of limbs and weapons crashing around her. The memory of that windowless room and the feel of airless walls closing in threatened to seize her entirely. Her body refused her, sluggish and insensible, even as she tried to force it to stand. To be useful.

If only she were brave, like Grace.

Just a few feet away, chaos reigned. Peregrine was now being forced back on the defensive. Trying to get to her, he had been careless of his own safety.

Everyone knows how they can harm me. I finally have a fatal weakness, Charity—and it's you.

Grief swelled sharp in her throat, bitter and choking, as she understood at last the fury behind the words he had thrown at her. He had not lied. And now she was going to watch him fall for it.

Not like this, she begged silently. *Please—not like this.*

The one who smelled of beer and unwashed flesh spotted her dragging herself backward and lunged, hauling her bodily away from the fray. She did not struggle. There was no point. She let him take her, watching Peregrine with grim finality, her emotions lodged somewhere betwixt terror and despair.

Then her captor jolted, a strangled noise escaping his throat. His grip slackened. And in the next instant, she was torn from his arms.

She found herself held fast, pressed against someone else. Turning her face upward, she saw a man she did not recognise: dusky-skinned, black-haired, his features half-swallowed by the shadows.

But this stranger wasn't looking at her. He was watching the tall brute collapse.

In one swift motion, the stranger spun with her pressed tightly to his side as he scanned the remaining fight. Peregrine was still locked in bloody combat. The stranger did not hesitate. He raised the knife in his hand and let it fly... straight into the back of one of the thugs.

Charity squeaked in horror as the man crumpled, just as Peregrine's fist cracked against the jaw of the final attacker, felling him brutally.

Peregrine whipped his attention towards the stranger holding her, wearing an expression that made him look like Death itself.

"Please," she murmured, as Peregrine ripped the stranger's dagger free and strode towards them.

Every line of his body was coiled, ready to kill. It was only the three of them now—Charity, Peregrine, and this unknown man. But the stillness crackled with potential violence, and Charity feared it might soon be only two.

The stranger didn't flinch. He waited until Peregrine was almost upon him.

Then, without a word, he thrust her forward.

She stumbled into Peregrine, and both his arms closed around her in an instant. The dagger slipped from his hand, striking the gravel with a faint metallic clink. For a breathless moment, there was only silence, broken only by the sound of their ragged breathing.

"I've got you. I've got you," Peregrine whispered into her hair, his voice rough with spent fury and relief.

Still unsteady, Charity buried her face against Peregrine's chest, drawing in the familiar scent of him and the hard staccato rhythm of his heartbeat beneath her cheek. She remained there a moment, catching her breath, then forced herself to lift her head in time to see a silent battle of wills playing out between him and their unlikely saviour.

Peregrine eased her behind him with deliberate care. His gaze never left the other man's. The two regarded one another with the stillness of predators, each measuring the other, weighing friend against threat. Charity, her hands resting lightly against Peregrine's back, could feel the tension simmering beneath his skin like a storm held barely in check.

"I shall leave you in peace, Lord Fitzroy," the stranger said at last, his tone faintly amused. "But I should like my dagger returned. It is a good blade, you understand."

His accent was nearly flawless. Only the faintest Hindustani lilt curled through his words.

At the sound of it, something clicked into place. He had been the one to call out the warning that saved Peregrine from the blow. Peregrine must have come to the same conclusion, for his posture shifted, some tautness easing from his frame. Without a word, he nudged the fallen dagger forward with the toe of his boot.

Peeking past Peregrine's shoulder, Charity studied the stranger more closely as he stooped to retrieve the weapon. He was of middling height, perhaps in his forties, dressed in a suit of decent but unremarkable cut. With quiet precision, he wiped the blade on his handkerchief, slid it back into its sheath, and then placed one hand against his chest in a small, graceful bow.

It was the deliberateness of the gesture that caught her eye. His left hand, splayed across the lighter fabric of his shirt. She could see it bore six fingers.

"Mr Xavier, I presume," Peregrine rumbled. "The Order's spy."

Xavier met Peregrine's gaze evenly, his lips parting in a thin crescent of white teeth. "So. Lady Normanby did indeed share more than she ought to with an outsider. I suspected as much the moment I glimpsed you at the Scarlet Jack following her... detainment."

Charity felt Peregrine's arm shift, his hand sliding back to grip her hip, pressing her more firmly behind him.

"I had nothing to do with the marchioness's situation," he said flatly.

"That, I believe. Now." Xavier folded his hands before him, his manner almost courteous. "After I saw you leave with the Regent's little magpie to redirect the tide of scandal."

Charity's breath caught. He knew—about the newspaper, the story, the diversion. Peregrine's grip told her he knew it too.

"I have been watching the wrong front," Xavier said, voice

tight with self-reproach. "Too much attention to matters abroad. And now, a rat has made its nest in my walls, fouling my shelter."

Peregrine's fingers stopped biting into her side. "So it seems," he murmured.

"These few," Xavier continued, nudging one of the sprawled bodies with the toe of his boot, "sought to claim the bounty on Her Grace. You should take her home."

His tone had softened, but it was not warm.

"There are weapons of every sort," he added as he turned. "But it seems coin is our adversary's preference."

Then he inclined his head in a brief, almost mocking bow, and turned on his heel, vanishing into the trees without another word. The gloom swallowed him whole.

Charity clutched Perry's coat, scarcely believing it was over. They were both alive. Somehow, against all odds, they were both still alive.

Peregrine turned to her, taking her trembling hand in his. "Come now, we must go."

Charity nodded silently, taking only a single step. A sharp pain lanced up her leg from the ankle she had twisted earlier. As she faltered, Peregrine caught her, sweeping her up without hesitation.

"Put your arms about my neck," he told her, striding towards the entrance to Vauxhall.

After that, neither dared speak. The urgency of their escape quickened his steps and sharpened every sound in the dark. Charity's heart thudded against her ribs, and she kept casting glances over his shoulder, half-expecting more figures to emerge from the shadows.

At last, the welcome sight of the gates came into view. Only a handful of stragglers remained, but no one she recognised, thank God. Most of the *ton* had already departed.

Perry seemed to have the same thought. "Keep your head down. The carriage is close."

Though it was only a short distance, Charity let out a soft breath of relief when she saw it: his carriage, lanterns burning like beacons in the dark. Hodges and the footmen leapt down the moment they saw Peregrine carrying her, hurrying forward to assist.

"I've got her," Peregrine said, his arms tightening around her. Jack opened the door for him, and Peregrine lifted her in, all but bundling her into the safety of the carriage.

Climbing in after her, he took the opposite bench and lifted her foot, running his hands carefully over her ankle. And as the carriage lurched into motion, Charity bit her lip and struggled not to unravel.

Could fate not let them even have just one perfect night?

"Am I hurting you?" he asked her softly, mistaking the cause of her stiff silence. And she saw something there, then, that she had never seen so clearly on his face before. Not when he usually clothed himself in mockery and charm.

There was a naked vulnerability. She turned her face away, feeling shame at seeing it exposed, as if she were a peeper. "No, Perry," she said, feeling bitter. "Not you."

Peregrine let her leg slide down to rest upon the floor, and then he let his face rest in his hands instead, breathing steadily.

He is blaming himself. The thought compelled her to move, crossing to the other bench.

She pulled on his shoulder, forcing him to return upright. And then she wrapped her arms around his neck again, this time to offer him comfort instead of taking it. "I am all right," she whispered, kissing his brow as if he were a bruised child. "You protected me, just as you said you would."

His breath shuddered against her neck, and he wrapped his hands around her waist. For a moment, he clung to her fiercely.

But then he transferred her gently back to the far bench and pulled the curtains shut completely.

Charity swallowed, feeling the hurt of it even as she understood why he did it. He was trying to build the wall between them again, to keep the boundaries that others would enforce. The veils began to fall over his eyes once more, and a part of her hated herself for saying nothing to try to stop it.

"Xavier is not my mother's man. I would stake my life on it," he said distantly, and Charity could barely make out the movement of his arm as he raked his fingers over his forelock, pinning it back. "I suppose I staked both of our lives on it."

"Don't hog all the blame," she told him tartly, trying to lift his mood. "I should like some for myself. Well if there is one boon from this, it is that we are only stuck guessing from among Chandros, Pembroke, and Goldbourne now. Do you think he might be trustworthy enough to help us?"

Peregrine shook his head firmly. "I would not dare to. But I think Xavier may have trusted us. At least, he trusted us enough to provide us with one other clue."

Reviewing her memory, Charity was dismayed by how badly her wits had been scattered by the attack. "I am afraid I did not understand it."

"For days, I have been wracking my brain, trying to make sense of the pieces. There is a line that can be traced, from my mother to you and myself, to Selina, the Crown, and even to Sidmouth. But I could not connect Cavendish and the riot unless one dismissed him as only a victim of convenience—the easiest way to get to the others."

"But, would that not be true?"

"Yes," he admitted. "It would, and perhaps that should have been enough. But—have you ever had a word on the tip of your tongue? It is like that. I have been so certain there was something else. Something I couldn't see. Eldon was the same. It did not quite make sense. Not until Xavier said that he thought our foe was using money as his weapon."

"The paid rioters. The printed bills," Charity began, her forehead creasing. "My bounty."

"The people who worked for my mother, disappearing," he added. "Whoever does this has access to their own money, or my mother's funds."

"Like a banker?"

"Or someone like Lord Pembroke. With a generous old income, and money from industrialists besides," he agreed.

"Would Duke Chandros not have the money?"

"He might have access to my mother's funds," Peregrine admitted after a moment to consider. "But Chandros consorts with mostly military men. He is the Order's strategist, and he would never encounter someone like Mr Cameron as easily as Lord Pembroke, who works with the tradesmen."

"That seems to make sense then. It would be hard to imagine that a man I have met could be that callous to murder us, but…"

She imagined his lip was curled now, because she could hear the amused resignation in his voice when he answered. "But you *have* met my mother."

14

"Can we become other than what we are?"
—Marquis de Sade

Moving the duchess bodily back to the other bench had been a harrowing experience in more ways than one. Peregrine gritted his teeth, ignoring the wet warmth seeping at his waist, trying to decide which member of the Tribune was the traitor.

Charity had subsided into a grim silence. In the occasional light that filtered through the crack in the curtains, he could see she had wrapped both her arms around her middle again. From what he could hear, there was no distress or tears. She seemed merely... thoughtful and unhappy.

The leash becomes a trap rather quickly, does it not? his mother asked, the shadows giving her a greater freedom to haunt him.

Peregrine could almost feel her drawing a phantom finger along his bleeding side, increasing the pain. *You have become so soft. No longer the creature you used to be—that hard one with the strength to defy me because he felt so little fear of my retribution. But he is gone now, isn't he?*

Peregrine closed his eyes briefly, drawing in a ragged breath. He could feel Charity's attention on him in the darkness, drawn by his soft noise.

Life was so much simpler when you did not care, wasn't it? his mother murmured. *You have to care about something to feel fear. I thought you had taken my warnings to heart. But now it will be so easy to break you completely.*

But before Charity could speak, a change in the gait of the horses warned them that they were nearly to their destination. Peregrine twitched back the drape, seeing that Atholl House had been lit in anticipation of the duchess's return. By the time Hodges brought the carriage to a halt, the front door was standing open, light spilling out across the front steps.

Quickly, one of the Graves brothers opened the door, and Peregrine squinted into the shadows to make out the figure of Jack. "Help Her Grace inside. She cannot walk."

"Really, Perry, I can probably walk—" she demurred.

"Take her." Peregrine moved out of the way, letting Jack reach in so he could lift Charity into his arms.

The carriage rocked as Owen dismounted as well, but Peregrine got out on his own. Flustered footsteps at the front of Atholl House sounded as her servants stationed inside quickly realised that this was no ordinary return and hurried to assist.

Peregrine made himself keep within a few paces of Jack, following into the foyer. So he heard, clearly, when the maid clattered down the stairs and gave a shocked cry at the appearance of her mistress.

"Your Grace! You're hurt!"

"I turned my ankle, Miller. And really, I am sure I can walk by now. Please put me down," Charity asked his footman.

Jack lowered her feet carefully to the floor. Miller's face was aghast, and she pushed to Charity's side, her hands snatching at Charity's skirt. "But—there is blood on your dress."

Charity twisted in the footman's hands, looking at the dark stain on the hip of her gown. And then she looked up sharply at Peregrine, her eyes both somehow fearful and accusing. "*I* am not bleeding."

"No," he said wearily, caught. "I suppose that is me."

"Fetch bandages," Miller said sharply to one of the under-footmen. "And hot water—Mrs Temple may already be abed, but wake her if you must—"

"There is no need to trouble yourselves," Peregrine told them, trying not to be curt to Charity's servants. "Take care of the duchess. I will take myself home to be bandaged."

"Do not be ridiculous," Charity snapped at him, pulling off her gloves. "Take him upstairs. We can let him stay in the Duke's room again for the night and see him properly tended—"

"No, Your Grace," he interrupted, his voice a shade sterner than he intended. But he would not let her keep him at Atholl House this night. At once, she gave him a hurt look, and he had to steel himself against it. "It would not be proper of me to impose on you that way."

Charity's jaw tightened, but she nodded. "Fine. Take Lord Fitzroy then to the drawing room. I would at least like to ensure he is bandaged and in no danger of bleeding to death all over my front hall before he tries to go home."

Peregrine felt the corner of his mouth turn up. But he allowed himself to be led by a limping duchess to the drawing room, which was quickly being set up as an impromptu infirmary. Miller bustled, bringing her sewing kit, hot water, linen, and vinegar with which to bathe the wound.

"Thank you," he told her, trying to send her with Miller. "I am sure Jack and I can tend to this."

"I want to help you," she said, reaching for the buttons of his coat.

He blocked her hands and tucked a lock of her hair behind her ear to soften his rejection. "I have already brought too much blood and violence into your life, Charity. You shouldn't have to endure this horror too."

She paused, studying his face with troubled eyes. "Caring for you is not a horror." Then she smiled a little ruefully. "A difficult endeavour? That I might agree to."

"Not caring—me." He saw her confusion, and it made him feel hollow inside. "You should cast me from your house. You should be terrified of me. Disgusted. I might have killed a man in front of you tonight. This... this was not even the first time I have hurt people in front of you."

Charity looked down for a moment, and then she looked up at him again. "The violence in your world shocks and horrifies me," she said softly. "But not you. I cannot pretend to be afraid of you any longer, Perry. I don't know how to. Not when I have seen over and over that you only do what you must to survive."

His fingers felt nerveless, and Charity tugged her wrists away, continuing to unbutton his jacket and waistcoat briskly. Behind him, Jack helped him out of each coat, Charity carefully peeling each layer away from where it clung to his side.

When he was down to just the linen shirt, she could see how it had begun to dry in places, sticking to the bandaged wound in his flank. She pushed him into a chair, using the wet cloth to loosen it as carefully as she could. Jack helped her unwind the old bandages to reveal the wound.

Since he was put to work holding up the cloth of his shirt, he could not see the injury. But he knew how it had looked before— ugly, angry, and red, bumps of raised flesh forming where the stitches had been placed, had torn around the scar tissue, and been stitched again.

Apparently, the damage was not improved by this latest fight. Charity gave it a long look. And then she poured vinegar over the wound with the grim resoluteness of someone who had tended it before, cruelly ignoring his hiss of pain.

"Fortunately, the tearing is shallow, and it's still trying to heal clean. But it is turning into a terrible scar because you keep disturbing it." She avoided looking into his face. "Are you still determined to go home?"

"Yes. We do not know who else saw us tonight. I have to look further into our two most likely suspects. At least, I have to try."

"And you are sure we should not give both of them up to the Crown instead?"

"I can't. I can't send people who might be innocent to gaol... or worse. Our charade did what we needed it to do, Sparkles. We wanted to stir the *ton*. Well, you can be sure they will be talking tomorrow. We should not waste that effort."

He let the fingers of his unbloodied left hand lightly trace along the line of her jaw. Tipping her chin up to face him, he gave her a gentle look. "Your guards will keep you safer than I can tonight. All I can do by staying is cause you harm."

She hesitated for a moment, pressing a cloth to the seeping wound. "I know. But... I almost cannot bring myself to care." Her eyes flickered briefly to Jack.

He was struck harder by the words than he should have been, unable to muster any sense of gratitude for her understanding. Her defiance. Instead, he felt a kind of grief because of what she could lose by loving a man like him.

"To think, just a few short weeks ago you cared so much about your reputation," he teased her, falling back on the only defence he had left. "And I was the prig who didn't care if I left a little dirt on it."

"Yes. You *are* rather lucky my servants kept your annoying tendency to housebreak silent," she said tartly. "If you keep soiling my furniture with blood and dirt, however, I cannot promise they won't decide to toss you in the gutter."

"I consider myself warned," he said, standing up at her direction so that Jack could help her wind fresh bandages around his waist. And when she was done, he tested the bindings, lifting his shoulders slightly. "Thank you, Your Grace."

"Think nothing of it," she said absently, bundling up what was left, busying her hands and turning to go. "I am quite exhausted. I hope you will not object if I retire. I will stay here, I suppose... and you can call upon me if you need me later."

Before he even realised his own intention, he caught her wrist, halting her retreat. She turned to him in surprise, her eyes wide. Meeting her eyes, he lifted her hand, slow and deliberate, to press a soft kiss to her knuckles, ignoring the spots of his blood marking her skin. "I enjoyed your company this evening," he murmured against her hand. "And I'm sorry I ruined your dress. You looked beautiful tonight."

The darkness in her eyes eased, and she gave him a breathtaking smile that made him as dizzy as her perfume did. But she only pulled her hand from his after a moment, leaving him in her drawing room alone.

It was nearly three in the morning again by the time Hodges got them back to the Fitzroy estate. The lanterns in the front hall had been dimmed for the night, but one was still burning low by the servants' stairs. Peregrine stepped inside the front door, filthy and weary.

He'd intended to go straight to bed, or at least to the bottle of brandy. However, he had only just set his hand on the stair rail when suddenly both Croft and Quinn emerged together from a side passage, hurrying towards him.

"My lord," Quinn said urgently. "A problem arrived on our doorstep while you were out—"

Croft had reached for Peregrine's jacket and helped him remove it in the dim light of the foyer. But in just his lighter waistcoat, the dark stain on the front was visible. Quinn halted his train of thought, his face inscrutable. "Do we need to call a physician?"

"It has already been tended," Peregrine told both men as Croft began to prod at his waistcoat. Then his valet turned and hurried upstairs. "What is the problem?"

Quinn hesitated only a second more before continuing, his voice lower. "One of the former servants came to the door while you were out, begging to be sheltered. He is afraid—" Quinn cut off his words, looking to see that Croft was out of the room before continuing in a much lower voice. "He is worried your mother has marked him for death, and he says he has nowhere else to go."

Peregrine's shoulders tightened as a curious rush of exhilaration and dread filled his veins. His mother was going so far as to strike down the pensioned former house staff? "Who is here?"

His butler's face remained neutral, but the pause said everything. "He would not give his name. I ensured he was unarmed and shut him in my office."

Perry trusted Quinn wouldn't have admitted a person without at least a strong suspicion of the truth. Looking down at himself, he sighed. "I suppose I should change first."

"No need, sir," Croft said, returning with a new waistcoat and linen shirt in his hands. "Best not confront someone from the past looking like you have already lost a fight."

Peregrine gave his new valet a sidelong look. Croft might certainly be put to a test of loyalty tonight. "Thank you, Mr Croft. And let me remind you that if a single word of what you see or hear reaches the general—or anyone else—you will be out by morning."

Croft, to his credit, didn't argue or even look dismayed. "Understood, my lord. Not my first secret."

"Thank you. Wait for me upstairs. I expect this will not take long."

Quinn led the way toward the steward's office. At the door, he stepped aside and lowered his voice. "He wouldn't give a name— but I believe it's your former butler."

Peregrine's gaze narrowed, disbelieving.

Quinn offered him the handle without ceremony, and Peregrine pushed the door open. Locking eyes with the ageing man waiting in Quinn's office, Peregrine halted abruptly, his hands balling into fists at his side. "Quinn was right. It *is* you."

Edmunds, his mother's butler of nearly thirty years, stared back at him, his jowls wobbling as he trembled beneath Peregrine's sudden fury.

"How *dare* you set foot back here," Peregrine shouted, prowling forward when Edmunds said nothing.

The man looked like he had aged ten years in the last twelve months, but Peregrine couldn't find it in himself at all to pity the old butler. Not after he had found out Edmunds had been the one to ensure Charity had been drugged and put in a carriage, kidnapping her from his ball that evening.

This was the man who had helped concoct the scheme and overseen her captivity for the week she had been missing, ensuring she was kept compliant and helpless. No wonder Edmunds had refused to give his name to Quinn. Peregrine would have ordered him tossed out of the house without ever laying eyes on him. Or worse.

"*I had to,*" Edmunds whispered in a plea, lifting his hands pathetically as he cowered in front of Peregrine. "You, of all people, know that I had to do what she ordered me to do, my lord. If I hadn't…"

Peregrine knew. Marian might have chosen a different path to gain her revenge on her nemesis, Vanessa Cresswell. Perhaps a slow poison like belladonna to give her fits of erratic behaviour, getting Charity consigned to an asylum. Or arsenic, which gave Robin Fitzroy his wasting illness. Or foxglove, which had caused Grenville's heart to seize.

Edmunds may have felt he was choosing the lesser evil. Unfortunately, that did little to relieve Peregrine's urge to smash his fist into a wall. He closed his eyes and inhaled deeply, shaking. After Vauxhall, violence was already too close to the surface.

Fortunately, Quinn saw him struggling and became the voice of reason. "We may have been handed a gift, my lord. We should interrogate him to see if he knows anything useful."

It was the break in tension Perry needed to regain his senses. He flicked his eyes to Quinn, grateful. Then looked down at the pathetic man in front of him, hating Edmunds nearly as much as he loathed himself.

He was no better than this man. For years, he had done the devil's work, pretending to himself it was better that way. That by making himself complicit, he might be able to control his mother, steering her away from the paths of greater evil.

It was a lie he had told himself, over and over, so naively wanting to believe it.

"Tell me why you came here tonight," Peregrine said, gritting his teeth.

"She's housekeeping, my lord," Edmunds let out a half sob. "You wouldn't know, not after you sacked us. Some of them wrote to me. Mrs Patch was the first to let me know there was trouble two weeks ago. She was working in the stillroom at Blackdown and sharing a room with Mary at a boarding house.

She told me Mary didn't come home from work one night. And then Mrs Patch disappeared too."

Two weeks ago, Cameron was dead. If Peregrine needed more proof that another hand was doing his mother's bidding, he had it. Not that it was required. Both he and Red Hand had seen the path of destruction this new agent had been leaving in the rookeries and on the docks.

But he had assumed that the attacks had targeted her illegal business. He hadn't known that the killer had been targeting the former domestic staff. Mrs Patch had been one of the servants holding Charity that week, too—a sour, tight-lipped stillroom woman with a taste for power and a deep fear of Marian Fitzroy.

Edmunds swallowed nervously. "After Mrs Patch, then others began to vanish. I wrote the others I heard from, told them to leave London if they could. Some of them did, I think. The rest are dead."

"And you thought someone was about to put an end to you, too." Peregrine cocked his head. "Why are you here, instead of somewhere else?"

"For sanctuary. Someone was in my place," the old man whispered, shuddering. "I didn't know where else to go. Who else I could tell. Please. I'll give you anything I can. I don't want to die like a dog."

Peregrine bit his tongue on the words that perhaps Edmunds deserved to. Perhaps they all did, in the end. But he couldn't make himself say it, because he, too, was a coward who had wanted to live before he realised it hadn't been worth the price paid.

But that had been before. The memory of Charity against his shoulder tonight, bringing him peace and filling his lungs with the smell of joy... now he wanted that, too.

Even if he could get it only in small, stolen moments, he wanted to feed his heart on whatever meagre crumbs of happiness he could seize before the Reaper came to collect his debts and he was consigned to the hell that he had earned.

Quinn was a silent, reassuring presence at his left side, letting Peregrine order his thoughts.

Coin is our adversary's preference.

"Quinn," Peregrine said slowly. "Write a note to the solicitor, to go out first thing in the morning. I do not care if he has not yet finished. I want him to give us everything he has accumulated so far on the accounts and the investments at his earliest convenience. And find a room for Edmunds, will you? Something with a locked door, if you don't mind."

15

"Man proposes, but God disposes."
—Thomas à Kempis, The Imitation of Christ

C harity rose from her bed with great care, concern for her ankle foremost in her mind. It gave a twinge of complaint, but no longer pained her fiercely. She took a few tentative steps over to the pull to ring for her maid. But before she could tug the cord, the bedroom door swung open and her maid bustled in.

"I will take a tray in here—presuming, that is, that there is not someone downstairs demanding my attention."

"Not this morning, Your Grace," Miller assured her. She studied her mistress with a critical eye, noting Charity's hesitant steps, and then offered her an arm. "You must keep your foot elevated, ma'am. I will ask Cook to prepare a poultice."

"Nothing odorous," Charity requested. "I intend to receive callers this afternoon, and I cannot be surrounded by a cloud of camphor."

Miller returned in short order, holding a bundle-filled basket in her hands, and trailed by a footman bearing a tray. The footman deposited the tray on a side table and then shifted it to be within easy reach of Charity, removing the metal cover to reveal a plate of eggs and toast, along with a fresh pot of tea.

Meanwhile, Miller knelt down, sorting out the contents of her basket. She had a ceramic pot filled with some kind of pale paste and thin bandages. "This bread and milk poultice will draw out the swelling," she explained as she smoothed it onto Charity's foot. "Cook added a bit of rosemary in the mix, just for the healing—and no sharp smell, I promise."

No sooner did she finish her breakfast than Pritchard rapped on her door. "Letters for you, Your Grace," he said, holding out a silver tray covered in folded parchment. "They began arriving first thing this morning, and there is no sign of them stopping."

You are the most sought-after guest in London, her mother's voice purred from the recesses of her mind. *Finally, society is giving you your due.*

Though her mother might have been right, Charity was not foolish enough to believe it was her charms alone people sought. The first pile of messages consisted of probing notes from society's most notorious gossips. Implied was that the polite twenty-minute call would be insufficient for their needs.

"Set these on my desk," Charity said, passing the stack to her lady's maid. After all was said and done, such contacts would be useful in clarifying her future plans. For now, she had little desire to submit to their inquisition.

Next came the embossed cards inviting Duchess Atholl, *plus guest*, to other public events. These Charity reviewed with greater care, considering which events would serve their needs. She focused specifically on events where the guest list was likely to be wider than the *ton*. Lord Cavendish was not the only person in town who was willing to dance in the grey area that separated the aristocrats and the wealthy. Rubbing elbows with the men and women of means might be useful in their investigations.

The morning passed in a rush, penning the appropriate responses. Twice she had to stop and rub her wrist as it grew stiff from all the writing. Luncheon was again a cold tray in her room, and then Miller helped her to dress. There was only the slightest twinge of pain in her ankle. Tightly laced boots were sufficient to protect against further harm.

"I suppose I should descend to the drawing room now," she said, checking her reflection in the mirror. Her day dress was a pale rose, bordered with ribbon in a deeper shade. When Miller had suggested it, Charity had half feared it would make her look like a debutante. Now, however, she noted how the colour lent warmth to her cheeks.

The pink on her cheeks deepened to a deep scarlet as she recalled some of the more dizzying moments from the previous evening. Like how Peregrine had swept her into his arms and carried her. Or how he had made sly jokes that filled her head with ideas and put her pulse to racing.

"Is aught amiss, You Grace?" Miller asked, coming out of the dressing room with a necklace in her hands. "Are you feverish?"

"No, no," Charity stuttered. "I stood up too fast, that is all. Too many hours spent sitting this morning."

"If you say so," Miller said. Her narrow gaze confirmed Charity had done little to dispel her suspicion. By the time she finished closing the clasps to Charity's favourite string of pearls, Charity's flush had faded. "Do you require help descending the stairs, ma'am?

Charity refused, instructing her maid to see if anything could be done to save her gown from the night before. Between the bloodstains and the tears, it was likely an impossible task. But so long as Miller was occupied with it, she would not be around to notice any further emotional foibles.

Truthfully, the boots provided enough support for Charity's ankle, and she made it to the front drawing room with a minimum of pain. A footman positioned a footrest in front of her preferred chair, and then retrieved her sewing basket from the cupboard. Thus ensconced, Charity waited to see who would visit first. A friend of her mother's? Someone from Charity's own circle of acquaintances? Or would it be one of the *ton*'s battleaxes, coming to warn Charity off any thoughts of misbehaviour?

It was not, however, a woman who showed up on her doorstep. Instead, a half-French dandy strode into her drawing room without waiting to be announced. Charity tucked her sewing into the side of the chair and shifted her feet back onto the floor.

Lord Ravenscroft dropped into a deep bow, an obeisance he usually reserved for the royal family. "Your Grace. I hope that you have had a chance to take out your anger on the canary. I am here now to humbly beg for your forgiveness."

Charity did not roll her eyes but it was a close thing. Logic dictated that she should forgive him immediately, given how things had worked out. But for once, she decided to give her mother's voice free rein.

"You do not know the meaning of the word humble, my lord, and your delay speaks volumes about concern for my forgiveness," she said with a sniff.

Ravenscroft remained bent over, but dared to lift his head to check her expression. "My time is not my own, Your Grace. Prinny has dictated my every action and provided me not even a moment of spare time until now."

"And yet, the elaborate knot in your cravat suggests you had time enough to spend with your valet," she pointed out drolly. Her face remained a mask of composure, though a single measured blink conveyed just enough displeasure to make the man falter in his words.

"Well. I could hardly present myself here in a state of dishevelment—"

"Had you rushed here in the early morning hours like Lord Fitzroy did—"

"Then I would have interrupted what was *clearly* a private time," Ravenscroft countered, straightening up with a wink. He smoothed the lines of his purple coat and added, "All of London is ablaze with talk of your courtship, Your Grace. Perhaps instead of offering apologies, I should be asking for thanks for providing an excuse to mend your *relationship*."

"You are quite daring!" she stuttered, her eyes narrowed.

"It is my role. To dare where others fall short." Despite his words, he clasped his hands, the picture of supplication. "Come now, I acted with the most honourable intentions. You are a valued ally and I will be utterly bereft if you cannot find it in your heart to forgive me."

Charity drummed her fingers on the armrest, her eyes narrowed in the Queen's own heavy-lidded stare. Her impersonation was so precise, Ravenscroft shuddered.

"*Mon dieu*, you are nearly as terrifying as *she* is," he moaned.

"Then you have some inkling of what I experienced when you and Prinny left it to me to explain that article to Queen Charlotte. I will forgive you, but on two conditions. The first is that if you ever put me in that position again, and do not bother to even send a note of regret for doing so, I will have your head on a platter. The second is that you owe me a boon."

"Make it two," Ravenscroft replied. He collapsed into the nearest chair and covered his face with his hands. "Or three. In fact, you may have all the future favours you like if you will agree to assist me now."

The man was a picture of dramatic misery. Charity could not find it in her heart to make him suffer further. "Oh, what is it?"

Ravenscroft wiped his hands across his face and then lifted his head to meet her gaze. "It is the Grand Duchess of Oldenburg. She has driven Prinny to the brink."

"She has? What has she done now?" Charity asked.

"She took exception to his choice of orchestra and demanded they cease at once, claiming the violins were giving her a megrim. This, mind you, after she forced him to plead—on bended knee, I suspect—for permission to have the national anthem sung at the ambassador's dinner."

Charity goggled, unable to believe her ears. "Why does he not refuse?"

"Because she collapses in a dramatic swoon the instant anyone contradicts her. It's rather like dueling with a chaise lounge. And as the room inevitably fills with ministers and matrons flapping like hens, the poor man caves every time. If anyone can coax Her Imperial Hysteria into sparing what remains of the Prince Regent's hairline, it is you. Now let us go to her hotel, before he starts tearing it out in tufts."

Charity had plenty of reasons to refuse his request, not the least because it was a fool's errand. But the thought of sitting at home, subjecting herself to incessant questions from curious visitors brought no joy. Besides, had the Queen herself not assigned Charity the task of determining the Grand Duchess's motives with regard to the princess?

"I will come along, but only if I can bring along my guards. *Someone* drew a target on my back and now I cannot leave home unescorted."

"Bring an entire regiment if it pleases you, Your Grace," Ravenscroft replied. "At this point, I'd welcome a battalion if it meant she stops threatening to set the drapes on fire."

The lobby of The Pulteney exuded an air of understated grandeur. Its marble floors gleamed under the muted glow of gilt sconces, and a long, Persian-carpeted runner softened the footfalls of guests who swept in and out beneath the towering columns. The light from dozens of candles flickered over the polished mahogany reception desk where a pair of clerks moved with precise, measured grace.

Lord Ravenscroft had sent a footman upstairs to request permission to pay a call, but it seemed the Grand Duchess was not in any rush. When several minutes turned into more than ten, Ravenscroft suggested they take a seat on a damask-upholstered settee.

Charity let her eyes drift across the room as she waited, acutely aware of each tick of the longcase clock in the corner. Gentlemen in well-tailored coats strode past, murmuring to liveried footmen. A matronly Frenchwoman argued with a bellboy over the handling of her trunk, her gloved hands flitting with impatience. Further off, a young woman in a maid's black dress sat perched on the edge of a chair, nervously twisting a handkerchief as she waited for a summons.

Charity noted the clipped voices in German, French, and Russian. The Pulteney was a crossroads of Europe's elite, each guest layered in intrigue and ambition. At the height of its social pyramid sat the Grand Duchess. Given her exalted position in society, none dared to contradict her, not even the Prince Regent. Yet, now that very task fell to Charity and Lord Ravenscroft.

"Tell me you have a plan," Charity whispered from behind her raised fan.

Ravenscroft grimaced. "Naturally. But I would rather not brandish my sharper implements unless absolutely necessary. If your dulcet tones can soothe the storm, I see no reason to unleash the full horrors of diplomacy."

Charity had little hope of such an outcome, but just then the footman arrived to show them upstairs. He led them up the grand staircase at a measured pace, and guided them to the door of the hotel's state suite. A maid opened the door to let them inside.

The Grand Duchess rose, gliding over to kiss Charity's cheeks. Despite her effusive greeting, Charity harboured no illusions. The woman was every bit as skilled at wielding social graces as weapons. Was that not why she had left them waiting?

Lord Ravenscroft bowed low over the outstretched hand, brushing his lips against her knuckles with theatrical reverence. "Your Imperial Highness," he murmured, accent thickened to a decadent French drawl. "How magnanimous of you to spare us a sliver of your precious time. We crave but a quiet moment—"

"I am enchanted by your visit," she interrupted smoothly, her smile wide. "Do sit. Both of you. I have already rung for tea and a variety of cakes. The pastry chef here trained in Paris and Rome, you know, though I find he lacks the melancholy of true Italian baking. Still, his *mille-feuille* is passable."

"We do not wish to intrude," Ravenscroft said smoothly.

"Nonsense," she replied, slicing the air with one jeweled hand. "Sit, my lord. I insist. And you as well, Your Grace." Her gaze flicked to Charity with warmth that somehow still felt like a challenge. "I so enjoyed our last little exchange. It is a pleasure to resume it."

With a sweep of her silks, the Grand Duchess led them to an intimate sitting area near a bowed window, the sunlight pooling like gold on polished wood. "It is a glorious day, yes?" she declared. "Such sunshine is a rare luxury in your country, I'm told. Tell me—shall it remain so when my beloved brother arrives? Or will the clouds return to match your politics?"

"June is often warm, Your Highness," Charity answered, wondering where the woman was going with inane conversation.

"We are to go to Ascot, yes? And then Oxford?" the Grand Duchess continued, her tone light but relentless, as if dictating a schedule to underlings. "My brother is most eager to see the university—he has such romantic notions about English education." She gave a tinkling laugh, entirely at odds with the glint in her eye.

As she spoke, a maid entered with steaming tea and delicate cakes arranged with military precision. Without missing a beat, the Grand Duchess observed the service like a general inspecting troops. "Ah, *finally*. Do try the lavender honey sponge. I find it almost distracts from the lack of real coffee in this country."

Even after the maid excused herself, the Grand Duchess kept the topics firmly on the social niceties. A wave of disappointment flowed over Charity as she wondered what had happened to the opinionated woman she had met a few days before. Lord Ravenscroft, too, made several failed attempts to twist the conversation in a new direction.

She is manipulating you, the cool voice of logic explained.

Lord Ravenscroft cast a desperate glance her way, silently pleading for her to intervene. Charity took a sip of her tea, buying herself a moment to consider the best way forward. The Grand Duchess was clever, forthright, and unashamed. She was also sympathetic to the young English princess's plight.

That gave Charity an idea.

"Have you visited Princess Charlotte again, Your Highness?" Charity asked, pure sweetness and smiles.

"I have summoned her here several times," the Grand Duchess replied with a regal pout. "But Prinny guards her like a treasure he neither understands nor intends to share. As if confinement will temper that girl's spirit. He only fans the flames of her discontent. And in so doing, his own misfortune."

"The princess is chafing at her constraints, on this we are in agreement. But do you not agree that she must learn to fight her own battles?"

"What do you mean?" the Grand Duchess said, fluttering her lashes in innocence.

Charity lifted her shoulders in an artful shrug, and then studied the duchess from under her own lashes. "There are many ways to express discontent with the Prince Regent. Some speak with loud voices, while others choose more subtle ploys. Your Highness prefers the second, if I am not mistaken."

The Grand Duchess stilled, her porcelain teacup poised halfway to her lips. For a long moment, her eyes remained fixed on the delicate rim, the smile at her mouth holding steady—but the skin around her eyes tightened, a flicker of calculation ghosting across her expression. With exquisite care, she set the cup down on its saucer with a soft clink and folded her hands in her lap.

When she looked up, her gaze was cooler, sharper. The playful socialite had receded, revealing the steel-spined strategist beneath. She tilted her head a fraction, studying Charity with the detached interest of a woman examining the set of a chessboard. One brow arched with delicate amusement, but her posture was the lean of one predator acknowledging another.

"My dear duchess," the tsar's sister murmured, her voice silk over steel, "you do me too much credit." Her smile was small and deliberate now, stripped of warmth and laced instead with challenge. "But surely you know—I do not retreat simply because someone asks me to." Her fingers toyed idly with the heavy ring on her right hand, a glint of satisfaction in her eyes. "How very dull it would be, do you not think, if we all played by the same rules?"

Charity's smile cooled, her fingers tightening slightly around the fragile teacup. "And yet, Your Imperial Highness, it is the princess who pays the price." She leaned forward, her voice calm but edged with quiet urgency. "Prinny does not lash out at you.

He vents his frustration on his daughter, curtailing her freedoms as he pushes her ever harder toward a marriage she dreads."

She saw the Grand Duchess's eyes narrow, just slightly, though her smile remained in place.

"There are far more powerful voices than mine at work. They are the ones driving Prinny's actions. Perhaps if he spent more time organising more pleasant events, I would not need to take him to task." That said, the Grand Duchess helped herself to an iced bun.

Charity cast a desperate glance at Lord Ravenscroft, who had played the silent observer during their exchange. He stared into his cup, avoiding her gaze, until she narrowed her eyes in a glare. She had no other avenues short of outright imploring the Grand Duchess to behave, and only a fool failed to recognise that road led to a dead end.

Ravenscroft took a measured sip of tea, as though steeling himself for battle, then set the cup aside with practiced elegance. "Speaking of matrimonial bliss," he said lightly, "I hear whispers that Your Highness is contemplating an escape from widowhood. Tell me—have you a particular victim in mind?" He smiled, all courtly mischief. "You may confide in us. We are frightfully good at keeping secrets... especially the scandalous ones."

"Should the right opportunity arise, I would consider the possibility," the Grand Duchess murmured, her voice light as air.

"Or one might engineer the opportunity, might one not?" Ravenscroft countered, his tone still playful. But a glint of tempered steel shone beneath the surface. "A barren wife, a mismatched union... patience wears thin, even among the nobly born. Some have been known to test Parliament's limits when properly motivated." His smile curved, elegant and razor-edged. "Divorce may not be fashionable, but as Your Highness so wisely observed, the world would be dreadfully dull if we all played by the same rules."

The words landed like a blow. Even Charity, who thought herself prepared, caught her breath. Secret liaisons were one thing. They threaded through the *ton's* whispered scandals, half-expected behind closed doors. But to seduce a married man into seeking divorce? That was a powder keg. Parliamentary divorce shattered reputations, marked all involved, and came at a public, searing cost. Even royalty approached it with caution.

The Grand Duchess, however, only gave a delicate flick of her gloved wrist. "Dear Lord Ravenscroft, you mistake the wedding for the victory." Her smile sharpened as she lifted her teacup. "A wedding only sets the ship upon the water. Even beneath the fairest skies, there's no telling when the vessel may strike the rocks."

And then, she bade them farewell, with a carefree wave.

16

"Three may keep a secret, if two of them are dead."
—Benjamin Franklin, Poor Richard's Almanack

The solicitor arrived promptly at half past nine, a leather case of papers tucked under one arm. He was an unremarkable man, about Peregrine's age, with a fondness for drab brown suits that matched the colour of his hair and the ability to vanish in any crowded room. That was fine; Peregrine had no use for peacocks.

Lincoln Frank had first caught his attention back at Oxford, during a seminar. He'd argued a tutor into a full retreat with line after line of obscure precedent and legal commentary delivered in a way that would make even absurdity sound irrefutable. He wasn't merely pedantic. He was compulsively correct and not above digging through metaphorical—or literal—muck to arrive at the truth.

Peregrine waved him into the study from behind his desk, gesturing to the seat. "Thank you for coming on such short notice."

"Your note left little room to do otherwise," Lincoln remarked. His voice was mild, but the twitch of a wry smile softened the edge. "If I were in your shoes, I'd be dragging in a tribunal and a priest. Fortunately, I travel lighter."

Peregrine cleared the desk, watching as Lincoln opened the case and began sorting its contents into neat, methodical piles.

Once satisfied with the arrangement, the solicitor lifted the first stack. "As you requested, I have been reviewing your family's investments. Some proved straightforward—your interests in the mines and farmland, for example. It is this larger stack that has required the greater share of my attention."

Peregrine regarded the papers. "What makes them unusual?"

"Primarily their scale. These are minor holdings. A trading company with no more than two ships, a lone warehouse near the docks. Despite that, they are producing substantial dividends on a monthly basis."

Peregrine's expression darkened. "That bears every mark of one of my mother's ventures."

"Indeed," Lincoln agreed. "With your approval, I will proceed with divesting your interest in those holdings. The final category is little more than names on paper, with no discernible assets beyond a long chain of subsidiaries beneath. The money passes through layer upon layer, making it nearly impossible to determine the true source of their earnings."

Peregrine leaned back, gesturing for him to continue. "Nearly impossible for anyone except *you*, you mean."

"I have sent inquiries to capital cities across the continent and am awaiting replies. These accounts are paying into various banks around London, which makes the process of uncovering them all the more difficult." Lincoln selected a list from his pile and handed it across the desk.

Peregrine scanned the column of names, running his finger

along the edge of the page until it stopped. "Hartwell & Goldbourne? I have two accounts at that bank?"

"The second account was opened three years ago. I discovered it only because I requested a full accounting of the primary one, and a clerk included a note regarding the newer entry. I followed up, but thus far, they have not replied."

A second account at Goldbourne's bank. As evidence, it was tenuous at best. For all Peregrine knew, both accounts could be entirely aboveboard. It was not enough to take to the Crown. Not yet.

He asked Lincoln to wait, then rang for Quinn. "Would you be so good as to fetch Mr Edmunds? I have found an opportunity for him to earn his keep."

A night under the Fitzroy roof had done the old butler no favours. He looked no less haggard than he had the day before, the shadows beneath his eyes like bruises pressed into parchment. But he came at once, executing a polite bow before stepping into the study.

"You offered to assist me. Well, now is your chance. Look through this list of companies and tell me if anything stands out."

Edmunds drew a quizzing glass from his coat pocket and affixed it to one eye. He read the first page, then the second, before returning them with a slight incline of his head. "There is one queer one—Florey & Sons. I suspect your mother had a hand in its creation."

Peregrine narrowed his gaze. "And why is that?"

"Mrs Florey was your father's housekeeper when he and her ladyship married. Your mother pensioned her off shortly before his lordship took ill. She kept a close eye on him, if you take my meaning, sir."

It did not surprise him. His mother would have considered it a nuisance to share the household with a woman loyal to her husband, particularly one who might have noticed too much. That she would then use the woman's name for an illicit business venture—that sounded precisely like the sort of joke his mother found amusing.

The solicitor checked the name against another of his lists, then looked up. "Quarterly dividends into the new account at Hartwell & Goldbourne, my lord."

Peregrine steepled his fingers together, thinking.

"Thank you, Lincoln. That will be all for today," he said after a moment. "Quinn, see Mr Edmunds returned to his quarters, and ask Hodges to bring the carriage around. I find myself in need of some pocket change."

Hartwell & Goldbourne gave no outward impression of impropriety. Quite the opposite, in fact. Located in a respectable part of the city, the bank spoke of its clientele in restrained displays of wealth. The carpets were thick enough to muffle footsteps, and the wood panelling had the soft, matte gleam of careful maintenance.

It was the sort of establishment where clients arrived by private conveyance and spoke only to clerks who already knew their name. As Peregrine stepped down from the carriage, he noted the narrow frontage. A deliberate choice, he suspected, to keep casual foot traffic out.

Hodges had the same thought. "Front ain't no spot to linger. Circle 'round or wait?" he asked. "There's a wider street just ahead."

"Go ahead to the next block," Peregrine told him. "I do not expect to take long."

Peregrine stepped through the double doors alone. The air smelled of old paper, sealing wax, and beeswax polish. Behind the counter, clerks bent over ledgers in silence. A bank porter glanced up, offered a shallow nod, and returned to polishing the brass handle.

A younger man approached deferentially from a side desk. Ink stains marked his cuffs, and his eyes flicked over Peregrine's coat, gloves, and bearing with practised subtlety. "Good afternoon," the man greeted him. "Have you an appointment, sir, or shall I direct you to one of the senior clerks?"

Peregrine gave him a polite, empty smile. "There is no need to trouble anyone who may be engaged. I am conducting a small inquiry. While reviewing some of my late father's ledgers, I came across a reference to this bank. It seems there may be one or two accounts here held in my name, or loosely connected to it. I should like to confirm the particulars, if you would be so good."

"I would be delighted to assist! It is no trouble at all. What is your name, sir?"

"Peregrine Fitzroy."

The clerk's eyes widened fractionally. "*Lord* Fitzroy? Oh, dear."

"Is there a problem with my request?" Peregrine asked mildly. "I ought to have sent word ahead, perhaps?"

"Oh, no trouble, my lord. None at all," the man said quickly, though his fingers twitched against the edge of his ledger. "It is simply that—well, we were not informed you would be attending in person. Most gentlemen of your rank handle such matters through their solicitors."

Peregrine's gaze narrowed. The man was unsettled, and the awkward explanation only deepened his suspicion. Perhaps the clerk had some inkling of the account's true nature. Or if not the specific irregularities, then at least that it was not meant to draw attention.

Certainly not this kind of attention. Not until the businesses feeding the investment had been quietly folded, sold off, and erased.

A pulse of fierce satisfaction rose in him. For once, he was no longer three steps behind his mother's creature. He had caught the scent, closed the distance, and now stood near enough to watch one of her accomplices begin to sweat.

He kept his expression carefully neutral, offering a small nod as if the excuse had sufficed.

"I take it, then, that the accounts do exist. Especially given that you recognise my name. That was the larger part of my curiosity, really. And I thought, since I happened to be in the area, I might take the opportunity to see the bank and inquire," he lied smoothly. "I understand if Mr Goldbourne is unavailable, as I did not make an appointment—"

That seemed to reassure the clerk. His shoulders eased, though his chin took on a faintly grim set. "Yes, Mr Goldbourne is not in at the moment," he said regretfully. "But his partner, Mr Hartwell, will be happy to spare you a few minutes, I am certain."

Peregrine did not particularly want to meet Mr Hartwell, a man who most likely had nothing to do with anything Goldbourne was up to. But he nodded politely.

"This way, sir."

The clerk led him past the front counter and into a narrow hallway lined with filing cabinets and closed doors. They passed a stairwell leading upward, but the clerk continued past it, stopping instead at a side door near the rear.

The moment the door opened, Peregrine knew something was wrong.

The light changed first—dim and grey, with the washed-out cast of an overcast afternoon. Then came the smell: coal smoke, sour refuse, the acrid tang of damp brick. Beyond the threshold lay a narrow passage, barely wide enough for two men abreast, wedged between the bank and the building beside it.

This was no office. It was an alley. A way to eject him quickly from the premises while Goldbourne slipped out the front?

Peregrine tried to turn on his heel, but the clerk shoved him forward and slammed the door shut behind him. He spun at once back towards the heavy door, but there was no handle on this side. Just solid wood and the muffled sounds of the banking hall beyond.

As his eyes struggled to adjust to the dim, narrow space, a man's arm unexpectedly snaked around his neck from behind and began to tighten, like a noose.

Before the arm could close the loop, Peregrine thrust his left hand upward, catching his attacker's wrist in a desperate grip. But with the man's left hand pressing his neck hard into the crook of his elbow, Peregrine had no leverage to strike the ribs. There was no room, no angle.

Anger and fear gave him the desperate strength to keep the man's forearm from crushing his windpipe, but the pressure was enough to constrict the flow of blood. Peregrine's ears began to ring, and sparkles began to appear at the edges of his vision. With a great heave, he shoved backwards with all his might. With any luck, he would crack his attacker's skull against the brick wall, or at least knock the wind out of him.

He failed to land the blow, but that capricious witch, Fate, decided to spare him all the same. The attacker's elbow cracked against the brick, and the hold loosened just enough for Peregrine to twist free.

Peregrine staggered forward, collapsing to his hands and knees, dragging in air with harsh, ragged gasps. He tried to crawl, just far enough to recover, out of reach.

Behind him, the thug moved, silent and sure. He was wiry and strong, with the muscle of a man accustomed to labour. Peregrine spared only one glance over his shoulder, certain he had the pleasure now of dancing with Edmunds' bogeyman. A killer who —if he was responsible for his mother's housekeeping—might have a rather fearsome body count.

That glance did nothing to solve any mystery. The man was perhaps an inch shorter than Peregrine stood, and more thickly built. But little else could he tell. He was dressed in a heavy brown cloak with a deep hood, only a darkly stubbled chin and nose protruding from the shadows.

And he calmly he stepped forward, gloved hands outstretched, to wrap his fingers around Peregrine's neck to finish the job. Peregrine clawed at his attacker's grip, but there was no give this time. The fingers were like iron.

"I have got you now," the man said, his gravelly voice rasping through the cotton that dulled Peregrine's ears. "Ought to thank me, really. This is kinder than what the boss had in mind. But I have others to see to, y'know? Already behind schedule. And June will be here soon."

Peregrine was going to die. And unfortunately, his last coherent imaginings were not actually about the duchess or even about his mother.

No, he was currently occupied by the thought that he was a stupid, stupid man, assuming that there would be no harm to be found in a bank.

His vision narrowed to the point of blackness, and Peregrine felt himself begin to swoon. From a great distance, sound reached him. Boots striking cobbles, and what sounded like a muzzy shout.

With a snarl, the killer shoved him, choking, to the ground, and Peregrine lay face down with his cheek in the wet muck for a long moment, trying to suck enough air through his bruised throat to make the sparkling darkness recede again.

"My lord!"

Owen? Peregrine's mouth shaped the name, but he couldn't seem to make his voice work quite right.

The footman hauled Peregrine onto his back and began

patting his shoulders and cheeks with nervous urgency. "My God. Are you all right, my lord?"

Peregrine blinked. It took too long to make his eyes focus on Owen's face.

A shouted command cracked along the walls of the narrow alley. Familiar. Furious. Running steps preceded Hodges's arrival, too.

"What the hell happened!" Hodges barked, looking between Owen and Peregrine.

"I was circling the building like you said," Owen answered, pale and shaken. "Found a man in a cloak trying to strangle Lord Fitzroy. Damned lucky you told me to go 'round. Wish I had got there a little sooner."

Hodges dropped to one knee beside Peregrine, offering him a hand to help him into a sitting position. "Christ alive. You breathin'?"

"Bare-ly." Peregrine's voice rasped, and Hodges gripped his shoulder, steadying him.

"That wasn't a bloody pickpocket," Owen said, still rattled. "Didn't even take your watch."

"Mother's... bogey... man." His throat ached like fury, but if he spoke slowly, he could get the words out. And so he related the story of the clerk as briefly as possible.

Hodges cursed more. "'Course I can't get him."

Peregrine said nothing. He agreed. There was no action they could take now that would not cost more than it gained. The bank would have security. Trying to question the clerk—or drag him out—would create more problems than it solved, not least of which would be exposing the account tied to Peregrine's name.

"It's Goldbourne," he said shortly. "I have... to let people know."

"Aye. Her Grace, if nothin' else," Hodges added, eyeing the red welts already blooming beneath Peregrine's cravat. "Let's scarper before the bastard comes back with a proper weapon and starts shootin' fish in a barrel."

How had the clerk known to expect him? He did not imagine that the cloaked man had lingered there for days on end on the off chance Peregrine showed up. It must have been Lincoln's request for more information that had caught Goldbourne's attention.

Or Edmunds knew which of us is more fearsome to cross and decided to lure you into a trap, his mother's voice offered.

If there was only some way to be sure.

Hodges gripped one arm and Owens the other, helping Peregrine to his feet. Fortunately, by the time he was standing, his legs were steady enough that he could walk his own way to the carriage. But he clapped Owens on the shoulder in the privacy of the alley nonetheless, in silent thanks.

And as he let Hodges drive them back to the estate at a fast trot, he reviewed the list of correspondence to send immediately. Charity, of course—she had to stay within the safety of Atholl House. Just in case his attempted murderer decided to get revenge on him another way.

But he also badly needed to talk with Selina. To let her know about Goldbourne. And given that the Queen had been disinclined to do him any favours while being accompanied by Charity suggested that this card wouldn't be well-played thrice.

Who else could make Her Majesty capitulate? The sole person who had any hope of it was her son, the Regent.

He would have to write to Ravenscroft. If he was lucky, the magpie would do this favour for him as recompense for saving his arse about Sidmouth. But Peregrine had a sneaking feeling that he was going to end up in deep debt at this rate.

17

"One life is all we have and we live it as we believe in living it."
—Joan of Arc

Charity returned home to find three carriages lining the pavement in front of Atholl House, each bearing society women desiring to pay her a call. She was in no mood to play host.

Pritchard led the visitors in and out of the drawing room, with Charity raising and lowering from her chair like a marionette on a wooden stage. Her expression remained placid, but there was no heart in her conversation.

"What of the Dorset ball?" Lady Stephens asked. "Will Your Grace be in attendance? Perhaps with a *certain debonair gent* at your side?"

"We have yet to coordinate our social calendars," Charity demurred.

"Of course he will attend!" Lady Stephens carried on,

ignoring Charity. "It is a highlight of the season. What could be more important than escorting you?"

Answers sprang to mind, but Charity could hardly voice them. Instead, she asked what Lady Stephens planned to wear to the event.

When the last guest left, Charity collapsed into her favourite chair, massaging away the ache at her temples. Daylight still streamed through the open drapes, but the atmosphere in the room was dark and heavy. The desire to escape her responsibilities grew.

But where could she go?

Your place is here, my darling, her mama's voice reminded her, *would you leave it behind after all you sacrificed?*

"Pardon me, Your Grace," Pritchard interrupted her musings, holding his silver tray in his left hand. "Both Lords Fitzroy and Ravenscroft have sent messages. I thought it best to bring them straight in."

Charity looked keenly at her butler, appreciating that the man had divined that there was more to her discussions with both men than the usual frippery. She took the folded notes from the tray, reading Peregrine's first.

Your Grace—I have news both good and bad. The good is that I believe I have indeed identified a certain banker as the source of our problems. The bad is that now he knows that I know who he is, too.

Tonight proves ill-suited for outings, so a quiet night might be for the best. I'll call another time. —P

Dropping the letter in her lap, Charity puzzled over the vague tone of his written words. But the message was clear enough. Things had become more dangerous now that he had tipped his hand to Goldbourne. He wanted her to stay home.

Ravenscroft's letter sat folded still, and Charity wondered what Prinny's magpie wanted. She hoped that it wasn't another complaint about the Grand Duchess. Peregrine's letter would make it difficult to help him. Carefully, she unfolded his, too.

Your Grace, a little yellow bird has petitioned me urgently to get him access to Lady Normanby, by any means necessary. To judge by his poor penmanship, I believe something upsetting has transpired and I am hoping he has sent some sort of explanation —and perhaps a warning—to you. Be safe. —Ravenscroft

An ill-feeling was growing in the pit of her stomach, and she picked up Peregrine's letter again. His words had been rather terse, but his handwriting seemed more or less as even. That, and the arrival of Ravenscroft's letter at roughly the same time, suggested that he had written to her later.

"Is there bad news?" Pritchard asked.

"It seems Lord Fitzroy may have had some sort of incident."

"Again! Trouble has developed a fondness for Lord Fitzroy's company," her butler said sharply, no doubt thinking about their bloodied appearance in the wee hours of this very morning. "For your sake, I hope his problem isn't... infectious."

Poor Pritchard. He had no idea that she had already caught the plague. She had only advised her senior servants to take greater precautions, mostly to explain the presence of her guards.

At least she *had* guards. Trust Peregrine to understate the matter if he was in trouble.

"Have the unmarked carriage brought out and alert the guards. If Lord Fitzroy will not seek protection, I shall take some protection to him," she said in a tone that brooked no argument.

She was on her way to the Fitzroy estate within the hour.

The footman who greeted her at the door was not Jack, the one who had carried her. But she did recognise him as the other one who had ridden on the back of the carriage. And as she looked at him discreetly, she marked the lines of tension in the footman's jaw and body. He was clearly in a state of considerable strain, made suddenly worse by her arrival.

"Your Grace," he said stiffly, glancing at her and the guards. "Lord Fitzroy is not presently receiving callers."

Whatever could have happened?

"I am not a caller," she said, adopting the imperious tone that got the Queen her way. "I am here to see him."

The footman was clearly torn in two directions. Finally he led her to the morning room. "Please wait. I will see if he's fit for company."

For Perry, that sounded decidedly sinister, and her suspicion was borne out when Charity waited longer than she expected for him to show. The minutes passed—first ten, then twenty. With every glance at the large clock on the mantle, her nerves got worse. His house clearly wasn't prepared for her arrival, to judge by the lack of hospitality. She wasn't upset for her own sake. It was for his. If the house was this unready, how well protected was he?

She had just begun considering the idea that she might be refused and how she would respond to that when hard steps sounded on the stairs. Charity turned and was confronted by a freshly dressed but clearly irate Peregrine Fitzroy who swept into the room, fists clenched.

Relief swamped her immediately. He wasn't broken or bleeding—or at least not too much to see her.

Really, how strange your life has become, she thought.

"I know," she cut him off before he could open his mouth and snarl at her for leaving Atholl House. "I know you are wroth with me because you wanted me to stay safe at home. But before you shout at me, Ravenscroft wrote to me and said you might be in trouble. I wanted to make sure you had protection, too."

In a rare state, Peregrine lifted both hands to his temples, snatching fistfuls of his hair. But she smiled at him sadly, because she had seen this expression before. When he realised she had brought him while unconscious to her house and invited all the danger of his life to her doorstep.

So she was unsurprised when he grabbed her by the shoulders, giving her a shaking. "Not at your expense! *Never* at your expense!"

There was a hoarseness to his words that gave her pause. And something... unusual about his cravat, which was wrapped all the way to his chin in a deviation from his usual style.

Suspicious, she reached for it, and he flinched away. "What has happened!" she barked crossly, when he retreated from her reach.

"Goldbourne's hired killer happened," he said shortly, his words gruff and brutally honest. "But only because I allowed myself to be caught out at the bank. There is no need for concern; as you can see, I survived. You need to go home, Charity. Lock your doors and put a guard outside your balcony. Two of them. I can plan a trap to catch the bastard if he thinks I have inadequate protection. If he thinks I will be an easier target than *you*."

His words felt like a slap, and Charity's head snapped back. But she had his measure now, and rather than be hurt by his words, they only made her furious. "Perry," she began slowly, as if speaking to a dimwit, "if you think it would grieve me one whit less to have something happen to you because I let myself leave you too unprotected, you are a very stupid man."

A small, bitter smile curled his lip. "Well, Sparkles, that would make two of us who think so. And both in the same day."

His voice—something was broken and hoarse about it. Charity stomped back to face Peregrine, lifting both hands to the knot of his cravat with an expression that dared him to argue with her.

But Peregrine simply inhaled softly, resigned, and let her start to unwind the loosely tied neck cloth. As she got down to the bottom, and the darkening bruises the exact size and shape of fingers wrapped around Peregrine's neck were revealed, she stared blankly, dumbly horrified.

Finally, she let her eyes sweep up to his wary, closed expression. And to her mortification, the moment their eyes met, her composure cracked entirely. Its suddenness was shocking. Barely, she managed to spin away in time as hot tears burned and overflowed onto her cheeks. The ache in her own throat was robbing her of the ability to breathe.

"Charity." Peregrine rested his palm lightly on her waist, trying to turn her back to him, but she resisted, struggling for control.

Abruptly, the world revolved, and she stumbled against him as he forcefully turned her by the shoulders this time. But though his movements were rough, his expression was… gentle.

He let his hands run down her arms and drop to her waist, tracing her shape before he pulled her to his chest. "Don't. Don't cry. Not for me," he murmured, letting his lips skim her brow and wet cheekbones.

When she lifted her face, astonished, he captured her mouth with his.

This was a kiss very different from the one Peregrine had let her take before. She had been clumsy, having exchanged only chaste kisses in her marriage, and Perry had held back to let her make her own explorations. This time was—

He was firmly in command and showing her all the difference that experience could make. His tongue prodded her lips open and swept between them, plundering her mouth with a skill that undid her entirely. She hung in his arms, helpless to do anything other than thread her fingers through his white blond hair, pulling him closer. Uncertain what she wanted from him, but still demanding *more*.

The taste and smell of him overwhelmed her, rich with the dark warmth of brandy, laced with the spice of his cologne. He lifted his mouth, stopping, and the sound of frustration that snuck from her parted lips sounded... embarrassingly wanton.

Peregrine pulled back enough to meet her gaze, his eyes half-lidded like a cat basking in the sunshine. Seeing her dazed, flushed expression, he chuckled softly, rubbing the last of the tears from her cheeks with his thumbs. "I meant to distract you with a kiss, but I wasn't quite expecting you to look that surprised."

She had to clear her throat to find her voice. "I, er, wasn't expecting you to distract me so thoroughly," she said wryly. "Or so pleasantly."

"Consider it retribution for the state you had me in last night," he murmured teasingly, pressing his nose again briefly to her throat in search of the scent at her pulse point. "You played such an unfair game that stealing this kiss was almost all I could think about."

This last was said with a smile that took her breath away. Not because he was beautiful to her—even though right now, he was. But because that smile felt like she had won the rarest of prizes. She could not remember ever having seen such a look of genuine, contented happiness on his face. And it was directed at her.

In spite of everything, her thoughts whispered, turning sad, *this was the Peregrine he always should have been.*

He pressed a kiss to the furrow of worry forming between her brows. Feeling shockingly daring, Charity grabbed his hair to pull him back to her mouth, wanting to feel the sensation again. Peregrine let out a low groan as he complied. Then his lips wandered a taunting path of devastation to her ear, where he nipped at the delicate skin with his teeth and sucked gently on the lobe.

She shivered, awed by the sheer pleasure such a touch could

engender. Was this what it could really be like when two people were fond of one another? She never imagined it could be this... consuming.

But then he released her ear with a sigh of resignation, stiffening beneath her hands with resolution. "We should stop this now, before it goes any further," his voice was quiet.

Charity didn't want to. "But why?"

His eyes closed. "Because you deserve better than what I am. Perhaps you were right, Charity. We are cursed and have been from the very start. Things are not nearly done between my mother and me. It is my fault that you've been caught on the battlefield, and I will do whatever is in my power to see that you survive it." He pressed his forehead to hers. "I do not want to be one of the things you look back on one day with regret."

Madness. She could not imagine regretting this. "You won't be," she whispered. "I would never."

"You can't be certain," he said softly. "Not when you don't know the truth of what I really am."

His breath hitched. "I am not a good man, Sparkles. You may forgive that my mother's business made me hurt people. But I have done so much worse."

She studied him, unflinching. He may have hurt others, but he was the one who had suffered for it. And suddenly she guessed what Marian Fitzroy might have done to clip the falcon's wings. "She made you kill someone innocent. Is that it?"

His throat bobbed. "Oh, yes. She put the poison in my hand and sent me to her enemy, ignorant and unaware. And after I discovered what had happened, I did nothing. I didn't go to the authorities and name her for what she was. Because she told me if I did, she would ruin Lark, and me, too."

Marian had yoked him into doing terrible things by threatening his sister. And suddenly, all of Perry's attempts to push Charity away, the things he said and did, made a perfect, tragic sort of sense. His feelings made him exploitable by someone like his mother, who likely didn't feel anything at all, and he had learned this lesson the hardest way.

But he couldn't help wanting to feel something, sometime, even when it wasn't safe to.

"She is the one who did something monstrous, Perry," Charity said evenly. "Do not hold yourself in such contempt when she is the one who put you and your sister into an unbearable position."

Peregrine gave her a chiding look. "No. It was the wrong decision."

"You believe the right decision would've been to sacrifice yourself and admit to murder." Her eyes burned. "And what then? Lark was a child. You are not a man who would condemn his sister to a lifetime of ruin. She would pay a price, and you would have gone to prison. Perhaps to hang."

He gave her a small, ironic smile. "There was always a blood price that would have had to be paid, and it should have been paid by my family only. She would have been ruined, yes. But she'd be safer. It is not a perfect solution, but my mother's evil would have been stopped. No one else would have had to bleed. That would have been the right choice, in retrospect, and not the coward's one."

Now he carried the guilt for that choice. For every act that his mother had committed since, he felt the blame was on his head.

But Charity could see clearly where his hindsight did not. Peregrine didn't know for certain that he would have been able to stop his mother's depredations. Marian might have eluded justice by throwing the blame on him. Or perhaps she would simply have killed him, the way she was trying now.

"Maybe others would condemn you. But I cannot. You survived," she said, slowly. "You endured something impossible, and you chose to keep your sister safe. That isn't cowardice. It's... love."

Something about that word broke him, and he glanced away, blinking moisture from the corners of his eyes. "It astonishes me that you can look at me and still see something respectable. It makes me wish I were a better man."

"You already are." She laid her hand upon his chest, trying to bring comfort. "You want to set things right, and that is worth everything to me. Oh, sometimes you are vexing and obnoxious, and you refuse to give me the respect I am due as a woman of superior station," she said archly, unable to keep her face entirely straight.

"But you have also shown me your courage and integrity so many times. And—" her voice broke off at what she saw in his eyes. A bottomless hunger for… something she couldn't quite name. Reassurance, perhaps, that there was something worthy in him. It nearly broke her heart. "And you haven't broken into my bedroom in weeks," she continued lightly. "Surely that is worth something."

As she hoped, that made him laugh, though it sounded a little pained. He lifted his hand to rest on top of hers, letting their fingers twine together, and the expression on his face was both wicked and soft. "I want you so badly, Charity. And it feels like I have so little to offer you—except chaos. That I seem to have in abundance."

She felt a smile growing on her face. "I will own, when we were at odds, my life seemed very dull without your chaos. Perhaps…" Her face warmed as she tried to figure out how to ask for what she wanted. "Perhaps you might be able to teach me how to enjoy… it?"

His free arm wrapped around her waist, pulling her tight against him, his breath coming faster. "Be certain, Charity. Nothing will destroy me more than you waking up tomorrow wishing it had never happened."

"I want this," she told him, her voice barely louder than a

whisper. "I want *you*. And no further promises are required than that."

She was shocked at her audacity, but Charity was tired of regretting her lack of bravery. Of regretting her fear of speaking up, or choosing a different path. Peregrine regretted the things he had done; Charity had so many regrets for the things she hadn't. If this was the only moment she could have with him, she did not want to waste it.

"Please, Perry," she whispered, letting her body yield against him.

It was her quiet plea that broke through the final barriers. He brought her hand to his mouth, kissing her knuckles with parted lips and a teasing tongue, and then turning it over to brush his lips over her wrist. She shivered, filled with wonder at how such a soft touch could seem so intimate.

Encouraged, he nipped at the sensitive skin, his eyes holding hers with a question.

"More," she answered again.

He tugged her fully against him, pinning her to his chest as his hands began to explore, sliding from the nape of her neck down the curve of her spine, and then to grip her hips as he captured her mouth in another deep kiss. Moaning her encouragement into his mouth, she let her own palms sweep the planes of his shoulders and chest.

Abruptly, he pulled back from the kiss, but the smile on his face told her he was not finished. Lifting his hands, he quickly began to pluck her hair pins out, tossing each one to rain upon the floor around them. She laughed, because she already knew how much he adored her hair, and then sighed as his fingers plunged into the loosened fall, massaging the small bones of her neck and skull in a way that felt sinfully decadent.

"That look, yes, *that one*," he informed her as she looked up at him through her lashes, letting him support her weight as he continued his devastating ministrations, "is going to haunt my dreams, Sparkles."

As if she was going to be able to forget this herself. Especially when his hands returned to knead at her hips, pooling fabric around her waist and causing the hem of her skirts to slide upwards, baring her legs to the air.

Her brief, ceremonial wedding night hadn't even been a shadow of what she now felt burning through her veins. Obligation, not desire. Duty, not fire. She had thought herself incapable of wanting, of craving, of *aching* for touch. She had thought herself beyond such things.

But here, now, with Peregrine Fitzroy—the man she had once believed forever out of reach, too sharp, too *dangerous*—she was falling to pieces. Every whispered breath, every grazing brush of his lips sent tremors through her, as if her body were awakening to something it had been denied and would leave her forever starving for another taste of it.

He waited, his breath ragged, his eyes darkened with desire. For a moment they hovered there, trembling on the edge, neither quite daring to cross.

She saw the question flicker again in his eyes. *Shall I stop?*

Her hand slid up along the line of his jaw, thumb brushing the faint stubble at his cheek. "Don't stop, Perry," she whispered.

He exhaled sharply, as if that single word broke whatever tether had held him in check. With a soft groan, he enclosed her in his arms, holding her so tightly she could scarcely breathe. A startled laugh bubbled in her throat, half-sob, half-joy, as she buried her face against his neck, feeling his pulse race beneath her lips.

She could not believe this was happening. That it was *real*. That in this moment, after everything, they had found their way to each other.

"Tell me what you want, Sparkles," he whispered, trailing his fingers down her spine.

"I—I don't know. I don't even know the words to ask," she stuttered, a lifetime of propriety tying her tongue in knots.

"If you trust me, I will teach you how to ask. Whatever you want. This night, I give to you."

"I trust you," she whispered. "Teach me how I should have had the courage to make a different choice a year ago."

Without a word, he swooped her up against his chest. He carried her from the firelit room, his footfalls steady and sure, and very quickly, the rest of the world fell away.

18

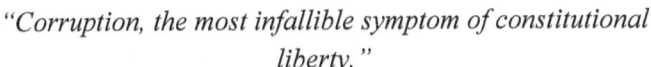

"Corruption, the most infallible symptom of constitutional liberty."
—Edward Gibbon, The History of the Decline and Fall of the Roman Empire

Peregrine watched the light creep in behind the curtain. The pair of breeches he had refused to shuck had rucked uncomfortably sometime in the night. His left arm had gone completely numb. The duchess was sleeping hard in the crook of his shoulder—and she might be drooling on him again, if the small drop of wetness he could feel on his chest was any indication.

But in all, it was… rather nice, actually. Peaceful in a way that felt strange. Curiously domestic, to steal a phrase from the woman beside him. One who had so ardently responded to his tutelage last night, and then decided to repay his generosity with torment by purposefully shrouding him in a blanket of her long, loose hair instead of tying it back when she went to sleep.

It was amusing that she had decided to punish him so. He had been willing to teach her many of the pleasures of the flesh, but he would not let her cross that final threshold with him yet. She had no idea how unnecessary her torture was.

Little witch. He would show her how sensual such torture could become, next time—if there was one. Keeping himself from making presumptions was hard. It felt like tempting Charity's cruel mistress fate to intervene once more.

The night had been a sleepless one for many reasons, and exposing some of his worst secrets even marginally to Charity had left him feeling rather raw. But it was part of a conversation long overdue.

It had been painful to put the burden of knowledge on someone else. And he couldn't imagine ever accepting the words she said without reservation. Still, it had given him a small sense of hope. Perhaps not all was entirely unforgivable.

Charity rolled over at almost nine, after the barest tap sounded at the bedroom door. His hearth was cold. Quinn had kept any staff from disturbing him, but most likely was leaving supplies. Freed, he used his fingers to gently comb her hair into a mass less likely to snarl, and pulled the covers over her more securely before he rose, finding his housecoat, and opening the door to his sitting area.

Someone had left a generously laden cold tray, along with a wrapped pitcher of hot water and a teapot. Beside the door was a coal scuttle, giving him the option to build the fire.

But what caught his attention was the way that the morning papers had been laid out, with the headline of the front page of the Morning Post visible to see. *"Whispers In Whitehall? Eldon Buries Bad Debt!"*

To actually name Eldon, the papers must have had some proof. Leaning over the table, Peregrine lifted the Morning Post to see the Times beneath it. It also sported the story, although in a briefer, less sensational way. Both papers suggested that an inquiry and Eldon's dismissal as Chancellor was simply a matter of time.

Setting the Morning Post back down on top, he scanned the rest of the gossip column's version. The column speculated on something that the Times would not.

"Could it be that Eldon's shame has something to do with the brother of Lord V— and Lord S—? Mr V— had reputedly left for the countryside on the 18th of May. One cannot help but notice, the same day Lord S— reputedly expired from wounds sustained in an unfortunate hunting incident."

Peregrine considered that, and his time spent in the bay window of White's the next evening sprang to mind. Tremayne had made his request for a favour, asking him for the loan of his townhouse.

That now felt like something other than random chance.

Before he could speculate further, the door exiting to the hall cracked open, and Quinn entered. "Good morning, my lord. Is there aught that you need?"

Peregrine felt the corner of his mouth turn up slyly. "I believe you have already done an exemplary job of anticipating my needs and wants this morning."

His butler allowed himself a brief, self-satisfied expression, seeing Peregrine's hand on the paper. "I thought you might find it interesting, my lord. Seems that the men of government can't go a week without causing a stir."

"Indeed," Peregrine mulled that over, deciding that introducing himself to his unnamed guest might be a wise course of action this day. Assuming, that was, that the townhouse was still being occupied. Neither Tremayne nor his solicitor mentioned whether or not the person had moved on.

"It is chilly this morning," Quinn observed, no inflection in his voice whatsoever. "The adjoining rooms have been freshened and a fire has been laid in them. As have some other effects for Her Grace."

Startled, Peregrine straightened, and Quinn gave him a studied look. "Perhaps I have overstepped."

"No. Not at all. I just—" Peregrine trailed off, feeling foolish. Admitting to a crawling sense of unease about putting Charity in the room that Marian Fitzroy had called hers made him sound like a child with an overactive imagination. It would be only for the morning, and it was not like Charity was moving into the vacated chambers that traditionally belonged to the lady of the house.

But he needed to say something. "Just a brief feeling of superstition."

"Ah." Quinn said, as if this explained everything. And perhaps it did. Quinn was quickly becoming privy to some of the darkest secrets of the Fitzroy estate, especially with Edmunds staying under his roof.

"Most of the dowager Lady Fitzroy's personal effects were already stored, and I thought it would be convenient since the adjoining room was empty. But I can set Her Grace up in another room, if you like," he offered.

"Do not trouble yourself, Quinn. What you did was considerate and logical. How does our *other* guest fare?"

"Edmunds is quiet, at least," his butler said dryly. "And for now, content to be kept locked in his room. But we will have to figure out a more permanent solution soon."

Peregrine silently scratched the back of his head, uncertain what that solution would be.

Quinn nodded. "Do ring when you are ready for Mr Croft."

His butler left, and Peregrine peeked back into his bedroom. The duchess had wound herself up in the coverlet like a person-sized croissant planted smack in the middle of his bed. Amusement flared, and he was suddenly possessed by the completely inappropriate itch to paint her that way and present it to her as a gift.

Immortal proof that the lovely, untouchable ice queen had her moments of flawed humanity.

He hadn't felt like painting anything in over a year. It was astonishing how quickly he could almost see the strokes of white and yellow ochre building on canvas, blending it with blacks, cobalt, and a hint of burnt sienna. The contrast of warm light and cooler blue shadows on the sheets and her skin, where thick locks of her hair lay over it as she basked in the morning light.

But it would be deeply wrong to paint it without permission, he admonished himself. And then the urge was further tempered by contrition. Soundly asleep or not, she was cold. So he unlocked the door to the adjoining suite—which was toasty warm —and picked up the awkward bundle of covers.

"Perry?" Charity asked sleepily. "Should I get up?"

"You may sleep in, but I am getting up. *Someone* robbed me of all my covers," he teased her, and Charity made a rude face at him, blinking as they entered the adjoining suite. "It is warmer in here, and you've been given everything you can possibly desire, including ink and paper so you can write your household for a change of clothing."

"I should have Miller come by, yes," she admitted, wincing as she lifted her hand to her messy hair.

He refused to feel sympathy for her on that score, and dropped her playfully into the center of the bed. "I would say take your time. But, don't take too much time. Things… appear to be afoot involving Lord Eldon."

"Oh?" That got Charity moving, and she struggled out of the bedding and over to the desk to jot down a quick note. She had appropriated his linen shirt again as a kind of night rail, and Peregrine had to stifle a quick thought that it was a bit of a shame it was not just a little shorter.

He retrieved the papers and a second banyan, draping it over her shoulders as Charity handed over the sealed message. "For Atholl House—if someone can be persuaded to deliver it?" she asked.

When he poked his head into the corridor, Owen and one of Charity's guards blinked at him.

"Er. Which of you gallant souls would care to run a note to Her Grace's residence?" he asked them, holding up her missive. The guard, predictably, bristled at him, so he gave the letter to Owen.

When he returned, Charity was looking at the papers, reading both headlines. "Covering up debt for members of the Tory party! And concerns of embezzlement? Rather serious."

"Especially since they apparently have proof enough to print. What do you think the odds are of the Morning Post having a second delicious scandal involving a high-level government figure? And so soon after Ravenscroft and I managed to convince them not to print the one that would implicate Sidmouth?"

Her lips pressed together. "Someone seems to be making subtle trouble for the purpose of ensuring the stories are leaked to the press. Goldbourne has to be working for your mother, if he is behind all of these," she murmured, looking between the two papers. "But what does he have to gain from it? I cannot imagine why else a banker would be involved or care that these men are brought down by scandals."

"Goldbourne does not exactly have to be a willing accomplice," Peregrine reminded her grimly. "Blackmail was always one of Marian Fitzroy's favourite tools. But we would be mistaken to assume there is no financial gain for him."

"Lord Eldon's Treasury has obvious benefits, but in the Home Office?" she asked dubiously.

"Oh yes," Peregrine said mildly. "There's information in the Home Office both my mother and Goldbourne would find…

profitable. Secrets to sell, pressure points to exploit. Evidence that might conveniently vanish or reappear in altered form. And then there's the matter of embezzlement."

He gave the paper a flick. "A few obliging clerks, a forged signature or two, and suddenly funds are flowing uphill. Loyalty, as ever, is a question of price. Or pressure."

"Your point is made," she sighed. "But finding his work, just the two of us, sounds like a needle in a haystack."

He inclined his head. "It isn't quite as dire as all that. I am wearing the proof that what we are doing is causing annoyance. Enough that he has hired a rather expensive paid blade," he said dryly, tracing a fingertip lightly over one of the darkening bruises on his neck.

"If we keep up the pressure on Goldbourne, we will either find what we are looking for or cause him to stumble. But we are short on hands. That's part of why I have been leaning on Ravenscroft to help recover Selina. She knows the game, its rules, and how to cheat them. More importantly, she has a personal interest in seeing Goldbourne brought to heel," he added.

Charity glanced over. "And what about Ravenscroft?"

Peregrine's mouth twitched. "Don't tell the magpie I said so, but I suspect he might just be able to hold his own against the marchioness. God help him. We will see him later this afternoon and we can ask him how he feels about joining this misbegotten effort then, before we use him to twist Prinny's arm."

"Later? What else are we doing before?" Was it his imagination that her coolly curious voice sounded a trifle hopeful?

"No rest for the wicked, Sparkles. How would you feel about a trip to the Seven Dials?"

Blinking at him, she tried to follow this non sequitur. "Your townhouse?" she guessed, and he nodded. "What does that have to do with the chancellor? Or Goldbourne."

"Just last week, an acquaintance of mine at White's begged a favour, since he knew I was not staying in my townhouse. He asked if I might be willing to rent it to a nameless guest. I am now half possessed of the notion that it just might be our missing Mr V—."

~

When Charity and Peregrine arrived at his townhouse, they did indeed find that Tremayne's favour had bought Mr Vesey refuge in Peregrine's property.

He was the youngest brother of a viscount who sat in the cabinet. Despite counting fewer years than Peregrine, his hair was already thinning, and his face was already beginning to show the signs of a dissipated lifestyle. He had occasionally mingled at *ton* events, but more often, he could be found spending a great deal of his time ingratiating himself with Prinny's usual circle of gamblers.

Gambling was how Vesey had first gotten himself into trouble.

"I lost almost five hundred quid to Lord Shedford playing cards. I was late, but I paid the debt." Mr Vesey bit the tips of his fingers and paced the floor. It was difficult to watch him since he was rather twitchy, and Peregrine wondered whether the man's vices also ran to things like opium.

Peregrine waved Charity backwards, to stand nearer her guards, and used his body to physically herd Vesey farther away.

"What happened after you paid your gambling debt?" Peregrine asked him in a low voice.

"Shedford accused me of paying with counterfeit funds. I thought he was being a weasel—trying to get me to pay more—and I told him so."

"*Were* they counterfeit?"

"No!" he exclaimed, offended. But then his face fell. "At least, I don't think so. They shouldn't have been. I had some of it, and my brother went to the bank himself to get me what I lacked. Hartwell & Goldbourne, I think. The one my father used to use. They're reputable enough."

Peregrine kept his face expressionless. "So, you told him you thought he was trying to extort you for more money. Then what happened?"

The man's face went through a sea change of emotions. "We... fought. He threatened to tell everyone about me being a cheat. It would ruin my brother. I... challenged him to a duel. I meant to miss. But..."

"But you didn't. You aimed his way instead of into the air. And now he's dead, and your brother cut you off, and you have no means of escaping the law. That's why you're hiding here in my house. Is that about the size of it?"

Vesey pressed both hands to his mouth and nodded. Glancing over his shoulder to see what Charity seemed to think, Peregrine saw her lips pressed together into a line. A furrow was forming between her brows.

"And Eldon? What does he have to do with the mess?" she asked.

Cringing into himself, Vesey uttered his words in a whisper. "He did pay off the runners to stop the news. I told him everything that had happened. I know it looks bad. But I was being set up, I'm sure of it. I would never do something so despicable. If any of what I paid was counterfeit, it was an accident. I would never do such a thing on purpose."

But a banker interested in causing scandals for a lord sitting in the cabinet might—a thought which clearly hadn't crossed Vesey's mind. "I assume you will be remaining here for the near future," Peregrine said dryly. "I have another appointment to keep, but I may think of more things I want to ask you later."

The man nodded, hanging his head.

Offering his arm to Charity, Perry swept her back out the door, handing her into the carriage quickly before anybody could get too close a look at her. "To St James's, Hodges," he told his driver as the guards hopped onto the rail.

"What are you thinking?" Charity asked him.

"That *Lord* Vesey was the intended target, and not his useless brother. Eldon, Vesey, Sidmouth, Cavendish," he murmured. "All politicians, all scandals."

"Political enemies?" she guessed.

Peregrine shrugged a shoulder, frustrated. "Perhaps. Every time we find a new piece of information, this becomes wider and deeper. I need Selina's insights. Some of these are her people. She might also have some sense of the larger plan afoot."

"We will figure out the pattern," Charity told him firmly. "We also need Selina's help at the very least to determine whether Goldbourne is a willing participant in your mother's schemes or someone she has had to blackmail into taking part."

19

"For still I prophesy, though still unheard."
—Dryden, Fables, Ancient and Modern

S t James's Palace bustled with activity, even at midday.
Carriages lined the road in a restless queue, surrendering
passengers slowly. Their own unmarked carriage jolted forward.
Charity leaned closer to the window. For all its bustle, the palace
seemed to her less a seat of grandeur than a fortress.

Perhaps that was why the Tories were currently flocking to its
grounds—both for a degree of protection, and in the hopes that
they might reassure the crown enough to save them from
catastrophe. With the press having wind of the Lord Chancellor's
actions, Prinny would be furious and want an explanation. They
would badly need the Regent's royal backing in order to contain
things.

As she peered out of the window, Viscount Sidmouth passed
by, apparently having abandoned his carriage in his rush to get
inside. The tightness around his mouth and the twitch in his

temple gave him the bearing of a man who had found himself, unexpectedly, knee-deep in filth.

"There goes a man who is about to have a thoroughly unpleasant day. I do not envy him in the slightest," Peregrine said, watching the seasoned peer go by. "Scandal within a party is bad enough, but to have a senior minister accused of misdeeds must have the party leaders reeling. Given his late arrival time, my guess is that Lord Sidmouth has been out gauging public sentiment to report to the Regent."

"His news does not appear to be positive," Charity replied. "Come, it is our turn."

Their carriage rolled to a halt, its wheels grinding softly over gravel. Jack sprang down from the back and came swiftly to open the door. Peregrine stepped out first, then turned to offer his hand. Charity accepted, more for steadiness than protection. A reminder that she did not face this alone.

The possibility of a future between them? She could not say; there was still so much to overcome. But this accord, and his readiness to keep her close, kindled the fragile hope that maybe they might make a true attempt... someday. If they survived his mother's efforts. If they could keep their duties with the Crown and Atholl from intervening between them.

If, if.

For now, they had a nebulous something she would hold with all her power. Even if it was not nearly enough. She wanted more. But she also did not want to let these moments together go to waste because she was too impatient. Too demanding.

She would not force the issue. Not right now.

She smoothed a hand over the pale green muslin of her gown, acutely aware it was not quite up to palace standards. But time had been pressing. She trusted the Prince Regent would forgive her wardrobe under the circumstances. With luck, she would not have to see him at all, assuming Ravenscroft had been able to follow his instructions.

Inside, the palace felt like the eye of a storm. Suited men filled every shadowed corner, their faces flushed. The Tories hissed accusations and pointed fingers; the Whigs, by contrast, looked positively jubilant.

Several turned to stare as she and Peregrine entered, their curiosity thinly veiled. Peregrine acknowledged a few with brief nods but did not pause until they crossed paths with a passing footman. He hailed the man and inquired after Lord Ravenscroft's whereabouts.

"He is waiting outside the throne room, my lord. Shall I fetch him for you?"

"No, we will make our own way," Peregrine replied. After the footman continued on, Peregrine whispered to Charity, "Let us hope he can get us in to speak with Prinny."

Ravenscroft did not look pleased to see them. He was deep in conversation with a member of the Dutch delegation when Peregrine and Charity drifted past, catching his eye. Peregrine gave a slight nod to suggest that he join them when he could, and they moved on without interrupting.

The door to the throne room opened now and then, revealing gray-haired men in heated murmurs, their faces grim beneath powdered wigs. Beyond them, Charity glimpsed the Prince Regent slumped in his chair, hands folded over his expansive waistcoat. He looked thoroughly disheveled, though it was hard to tell whether that owed more to the day's events or to his usual excesses.

She and Peregrine retreated into an alcove. It was hardly private, but at least it was less exposed. Neither spoke, finding no use for idle words while the palace seethed around them.

It was ten full minutes before Ravenscroft managed to break away. He blew a hair out of his eyes, took a breath to reassemble his dignity, and crossed to join them at last. "What in God's name are you doing here?" he asked, dispensing with any form of greeting. "Did I not make myself painfully clear in the note?"

Peregrine lifted a hand to forestall further protest. "We did not get your note. The duchess and I have been out conducting other investigations this morning. So am I to assume then, based on your temper, you have had no luck in getting us a private word with our mutual acquaintance?"

Ravenscroft huffed a laugh. "I have not even been able to get a private word with *Prinny*. He spent the wee hours cosseted up with Lady Vivienne, and then the Tories practically dragged him out of bed the moment the papers hit the doorstep. I came straight here the instant I heard, but every foreign dignitary in London seems determined to pin me to a wall and demand answers I do not have."

"What have you told them?" Charity asked.

"Given my general state of ignorance, nothing of consequence, I assure you," he muttered. His expression soured into a glower as he stared past them, jaw working. Then he blinked, visibly reining himself in, and turned back. "I do not suppose either you or the canary has anything enlightening to offer?"

"For Heaven's sake. Not here, Maggie," Peregrine said under his breath, casting a glance toward the knot of people only steps away. "And not until I have confirmed a few details with our friend. Are you quite sure there's no way to get a message in?"

Ravenscroft's glare said more than words ever could. After a beat, he smoothed his expression back into something resembling his usual insouciance and turned to Charity, ignoring Peregrine. "You will have to take the *direct route*, if you take my meaning. I would wish you luck, but as we have all discovered, that is rather thin on the ground today. So instead, I will simply urge you to be quick about getting to the bottom of things, preferably before I am driven around the bend."

Charity laid a gloved hand on Ravenscroft's arm and gave it a gentle squeeze. He sighed then, some of the tension leaching out of him, and gave her a half smile of thanks for the momentary reminder that he, too, was not dealing with things alone. If no one else, she understood the challenges associated with the role he played at court.

"I suppose we must throw ourselves on the Queen's capacity for reason," she breathed, looking for a footman to find out whether Her Majesty was in the palace grounds.

Peregrine sighed slightly. "Marvelous."

Queen Charlotte was not in her presence chamber, but as luck would have it, she was there, still hidden away in her private apartments. Charity followed the footman down the long gallery, her slippers silent against the thick carpet, while Peregrine's boots thudded faintly beside her.

She had walked this way before, many times, in fact, but never with such a weight pressing on her chest. The corridor felt narrower than she remembered, the portraits of long dead queens along the walls crowding inward, their painted eyes tracking her progress.

She stole a glance at Peregrine. His expression was unreadable, but she could feel the tension in him. They were both aware how much they were risking by coming here unbidden, to beg a favour they had not earned.

The footman paused before the door to the Queen's apartments and bade them to wait while he went to find out if Charlotte would see them. Charity swallowed hard and nodded.

"She will want to know why we are asking for Selina. Do we tell her about the spy within the Order?" Charity said in the quietest voice she could.

"Tell her about others no more than you must," Peregrine

murmured beside her, his voice pitched just as low. "Goldbourne must be the focus. Otherwise he will slip the net."

The door creaked open behind them. Charity turned, smoothing her skirts, lifting her chin, preparing her words. Whatever they had been before, they would have to be something sharper now. Steadier. Smarter.

"Her Majesty will see you now," the footman said in a hushed tone.

Be brave, darling, her mama whispered. *You are about to step into the lioness's den.*

Charity led the way, Peregrine close behind, as they entered Her Majesty's private audience chamber. Despite the pale shades of the decor, of the delicate, feminine furniture filling the space, the Queen's dour expression cast a pall that not even the brightest sun could defeat.

She sent her retainers out with a flick of her wrist, but did not invite Charity and Peregrine to take the now vacant chairs. She had eschewed her preference for cushioned armchairs in favour of a small settee upholstered in lavender. Beside her sat abandoned a wooden embroidery frame with a half-completed picture of a clutch of yellow daffodils.

Charity could not imagine Queen Charlotte doing anything so domestic as sewing. But it was a useful reminder. The Queen had been raised much like herself, to occupy the woman's place in the household. And it had not diminished her power.

Queen Charlotte brushed a strand of grey hair from her temple and surveyed the pair with cool detachment. "My diamond and the falcon—together again before me, and again, not by summons. How rare. How ominous. Especially after what the sheets have been whispering about the both of you at Vauxhall. I hope I am not about to hear about the need for a special license."

She flicked an eye in the direction of Peregrine, who stood

and inclined his head. "No, Your Majesty. You wanted us to ignite a firestorm of talk, and that is what we did."

"Then I am hoping that that stunt of yours bore fruit, Duchess?"

"We have a new avenue to explore, yes. Lord Fitzroy was attacked outside of a bank while investigating what appears to be one of Marian Fitzroy's accounts, Your Majesty," Charity said smoothly as she rose from her curtsey. "There is the possibility that one of the bankers might be aiding our enemy, either by choice or as the result of blackmail."

The Queen's bosom heaved once in annoyance. "I see."

These vagaries, they had decided, were safe enough to tell Prinny, as there was nothing he could do that would not exceed his authority. Not without calling on the Home Secretary's help. Queen Charlotte would be similarly bound, compelled to ask Sidmouth to investigate with the assistance of a magistrate or runners. And Sidmouth, now, was conveniently... busy. Which meant the Queen would also have to continue using indirect assistance.

"We were hoping to speak with the marchioness because of her connections amongst the *ton*. She may know the reputation of the bankers enough to speculate without the risk of needing to set foot inside of it," Charity explained further.

"No." The Queen's flat reply stunned Charity into another round of silence.

She had expected to face difficulties, but the sharp edge to Charlotte's voice offered no quarter. "But, Your Majesty, it is the truth—"

"No," Queen Charlotte intoned again, "I will not be put off. I am nobody's fool, Duchess Atholl. I am most certainly not yours. I find your repeated attempts to seek out Lady Normanby quite suspicious, especially since my guards reported that a certain falcon was present when she was *invited* to visit."

She raked a quick look over Peregrine. "I do believe you, that Lord Fitzroy was attacked. But if you think you can appease me with half truths, you are quite mistaken. You see, I rather think you both know more than you are letting on, especially about the disaster currently playing out in the main hallway. You will explain everything to me. Now. Consider it an order. If I agree that the marchioness's insight is warranted, I will call for her to join us."

Charity forced her fingers to let loose of the muslin of her skirt, from where they had latched on in the face of the Queen's anger. She shifted her weight onto her heels, subtly ceding the floor to Peregrine, whose eyes flickered slightly as he considered what information he would have to give away.

"Your Majesty tasked me to find both my mother and the Order. You were clever to suspect Lady Normanby of being more than she seemed. But the marchioness was my key to reaching the others, and I could not lose that connection. What became apparent only after the riot was that Lady Normanby also wanted my help, as she suspected my mother of planting one of her accomplices within the Order's ranks. That is what made following my mother's trail so important."

The Queen's face clouded as he recounted events from the riot onward, explaining how he had seen the chancellor's hasty departure from Cavendish's ball, the effort to cast blame on Selina and Sidmouth, the incident at Goldbourne's bank, and Mr Vesey's story about the debt and Eldon's efforts.

Charity noted Peregrine said nothing that involved the remaining three members of the Tribune. He didn't bring up the attack in the gardens, nor any of the details about how exactly he had found a connection to Goldbourne. He also, for obvious reasons, said nothing of their private conversations nor her overnight stay.

When Peregrine finished, Charity waited for Charlotte to call them on their further omissions. But instead, the Queen seemed nearly lost in thought.

"There were bankers there that night, at Burlington House," the Queen said instead, casting backwards in her memories. "I remember snide whispers about it—though that scandal was quite forgotten after the riot."

Peregrine nodded. "Goldbourne was among them."

"Tell me, Lord Fitzroy." The Queen suddenly fixed him with a look that was for once absent of her usual casual discontent. "Do you have a theory concerning the men she has chosen as targets? Why these, and not others?"

"Just the notion that they were enemies of my mother. And the marchioness was caught up in it, I suspect, because she was best in a position to catch Goldbourne's activities. She has many friends in Parliament."

Peregrine's eyes narrowed slightly. He believed Charlotte had a theory; Charity knew it. "I will admit, I was also hoping to speak with Lady Normanby because she might see the shape of my mother's pattern, now that Goldbourne has been exposed. Does Your Majesty suspect something?"

Charlotte shifted restlessly. "I would not be surprised that these men are also conveniently your mother's enemies. But yes, I have a different suspicion. They may all be considered an attack on the Tory party."

"But Cavendish—" Charity began, and then stopped. Cavendish was not the intended target. "The Whig points would be embarrassing to the Tories, if it looked like there was civil unrest and not even the aristocracy was safe from it."

Peregrine was looking down at the floor, his eyes flickering rapidly as he thought the Queen's words through. "One scandal might only displace a man. And the plan might fail. But if you take out the Lord Chancellor, and the Home Secretary, the Home Office, and cause civil unrest…"

"You have a government at risk of dissolving," Queen Charlotte said grimly. "Falling like a stout tree after several swings of an axe."

"And even as we speak, the Tories are trying to stave off such an occurrence," Charity said, awed by the audacity of Goldbourne's and Lady Fitzroy's plan. "But—even if Parliament were to dissolve, there would be new elections."

"Yes, Duchess," Charlotte agreed, her breathing coming faster as she began to quietly seethe. "But for those months until those elections are concluded, England will be in a position of great diplomatic weakness. Which might be a prodigious boon for an enemy of our country as we squabble over Europe's remains in Vienna. Instead of spending time preparing for the negotiations over the spoils of the war, the government ministers will be running ragged, campaigning for their seats."

"And the royal visits!" Charity said with a gasp. "The world's leaders will have a front row seat to the fall of the British government."

Beside Charity, Peregrine's head snapped up. "The flyers whose presses couldn't be tracked after the riots. The counterfeiting. Even if Prinny is convinced to back the current government and we lay Eldon's scandal to rest, a new crisis involving currency would be a death blow to the Tory party. That will be the knife thrust that will be coordinated to happen within the week, once the sovereigns arrive. I am sure of it."

"Creating that disaster would be spitting in the face of the monarchy, if my son averts this disgrace. And it could be an economic disaster for our nation. Both of which, Lord Fitzroy, I believe would suit your mother's perverse sense of revenge."

"It would indeed, ma'am," he agreed grimly. "Please, Your Majesty. We *need* the marchioness. The best we can hope for is that Mr Goldbourne forged a few bills to stir the pot. But where my mother is concerned, I am no longer of the opinion that she would think small. Lady Normanby is our best source of information on Mr Goldbourne. She may have some clue that helps us find the presses before it is too late."

The Queen's lips were pinched so hard, they were white. But she nodded curtly. "You have made a believer of me, Lord Fitzroy. And let me say, you were correct; your mother was most certainly the more dangerous threat. While I do not consider the marchioness absolved of being my rival—not in the least—this will provide her a chance to prove that she is not a traitor to England. We may question her, together."

She lifted a bell from a side table and gave it a ring.

The outer door swung open and a footman came in. At Queen Charlotte's instruction, he brought over her writing desk and then waited patiently while she inked a note onto a scrap of paper. She sanded it, folded it, and sealed it with her stamp.

"Deliver this to General Billingham at Whitehall immediately," she ordered, dismissing the servant to do her bidding. "Sit, the both of you. My neck grows tired from staring up at you."

Charity eyed the pair of gilded antique chairs opposite the Queen as though they might swallow them whole rather than offer them a place to rest. She circled around and perched carefully on the edge, not daring to grow comfortable enough to rest her back against the wooden frame.

"Is the marchioness being held at Whitehall?" Charity said. Whitehall was but a few minutes away from the palace.

Queen Charlotte grimaced. "No. The Marchioness is not at Whitehall, nor any of my London properties. I did not want to risk *someone* getting the idea of attempting a rescue," she said mildly, giving Peregrine a sideways glance. "So I put her out of all reach."

Peregrine gave the Queen a slightly jaunty bow. "There was going to be no rescue, ma'am. I considered Lady Normanby to be safer in your hands while we were still trying to get a sense of who my mother's agent was than she could be in mine."

"Hmm," Charlotte said noncommittally, though she looked mollified. "The general knows where she is. While we wait for his reply, I will ring for refreshments. I do not want you to grow parched." She rang her bell again and ordered a pair of trays brought 'round.

"Do you think Her Majesty is becoming fond of me?" Peregrine whispered to Charity while the Queen was issuing orders. His eyes sparkled wickedly, amused by the sudden show of civility.

Charity coughed lightly into her fist, stifling a laugh. "Please do not put yourself right back into her black book by commenting on it."

Two footmen, twins of above average height and black hair, brought a tray each, one with a steaming silver teapot and porcelain cups, the other with plates of sandwiches, their ends free of crusts. Her Majesty gave a nod of encouragement, all but demanding Charity and Peregrine help themselves.

For the second time in as many days, Charity found herself with a steaming cup of tea as her only shield against a formidable opponent. Considering the fearsomeness of Lady Fitzroy's plan cast a pall over the room. The meetings taking place at the other end of the palace were testament to the seriousness of the situation.

"There is still time," the Queen murmured as if hearing their thoughts. "I want this Goldbourne here. Right now. We cannot afford to delay. I assume you know what the man looks like, Lord Fitzroy? I cannot send guards to *search*, but if you were to go to his bank, acting in capacity as my *representative*, I believe I should feel compelled to send men to guard your safety."

Peregrine nodded, a slight smile on his face. Her Majesty

would use the excuse of protecting him to discreetly exceed her authority and aid in the search.

A light tap on the door interrupted them from further discussion. The Queen called for the person to enter. It proved to be the original footman she had sent off with the message for General Billingham.

"He has ordered his carriage prepared, Your Majesty. He will be going to fetch her. But he says the marchioness was moved to a house outside of London, so it will take some time to retrieve her."

"We are losing time," the Queen said with a glower at the messenger. "Duchess Atholl, go with the general's carriage and fetch the marchioness directly. You may use the ride back here to apprise her of the situation and gain her thoughts."

Charity gathered her skirts and bobbed a curtsey, determined to be on her way. She retraced her steps to the courtyard outside the palace. As promised, a tall black carriage with bright blue trim was waiting. General Billingham himself helped her inside and then gave the directions to the carriage driver.

The carriage lurched into motion, the turn of the wheels matching the roiling in Charity's stomach. They had an inkling of what Lady Fitzroy intended, but it remained far from clear whether they had a chance of stopping it.

Traffic had not abated during her time inside the palace. The carriage's slow progress only added to her woes. She closed her eyes, focusing on her breath.

She did not hear the latch of the carriage door slide open, and knew nothing was afoot until a strange man in a brown cloak climbed in and pushed into the space beside her, his weight rocking the stopped carriage.

"Who—?" Charity said, so shocked she did not scream. Instead, she looked into the heavily-stubbled face, most of which was hidden beneath a hood.

The man smiled at her. A pitying one—not predatory. "Hallo, Your Grace," he said. "Now I'd ask you not to scream, seein' as I've no wish to hurt a lady. But if you do, I'll have to shut you up sharp. Just business, yeah? You understand."

She felt faint. This was the man who had tried to strangle Peregrine. She was certain of it. "Are you going to murder me?"

"No, sweetheart," he said offhandedly, reaching into his pocket for a flask. "Ain't here for that. Not today, anyhow. Be a good girl and drink this, would you?"

"I will not," Charity breathed. "It might be poison."

The man's mouth kicked up in a smirk, and he uncapped it, wafting it under her nose. It was bitter smelling, like alcohol and something earthy. "Laudanum, Your Grace. I'm afraid I've got to insist. Can't have you knowin' where we're goin'. And if you won't drink—" he shrugged.

He'll hit you, her mother finished, and Charity shivered.

"For what it's worth, it'd be a damn sight easier to cut your throat than to talk you into poisonin' yourself, sweetheart. So let's not make it ugly."

"You promise I will wake up from this?" she asked, her hand shaking as she took the flask.

"On my black heart, I swear it. Drink up."

Charity put the flask to her lips, recognising the same familiar, acrid taste that she had been dosed with again and again during the week she had been held against her will.

The man watched her steadily, waiting. And finally, she took her courage in both hands, downing it. Her last clear thought was that this time, neither Peregrine nor anyone else was going to get there in time to save her.

20

"In all great undertakings, there is usually a trace of madness."
—Tacitus

After Charity departed, Peregrine collected the guards and found his carriage. Quickly, he explained their destination while the six guards who had been sent with him mounted horses to ride in escort.

Hodges looked unimpressed by the pageantry. "Six bloody guards? You really think Goldbourne's just sittin' there like some daft duck paddlin' in circles?" Hodges scoffed. "Even if he was, he'd spot this a mile off."

"That would require far more luck than I've enjoyed lately," Peregrine admitted. "No, I don't expect we'll find Goldbourne himself. But if we can uncover more about his counterfeiting operation, that will be the next best thing to finding him. We have to try. And if Her Majesty's guards can both watch the doors and give me the consequence to overawe the officious little oafs who would keep me out of his office, I will take it gladly."

Hodges grumbled. "About time Her Majesty gave a damn someone's out to kill you." He pulled his cap snug around his ears as Perry climbed into the carriage.

The procession was enough to draw the eyes of passersby, especially after the guards split into two groups, a pair clearing the way up front while the others followed behind. Their loud voices called for all to make way for business of the Crown, and Peregrine fancied he could hear Hodges's eyes rolling all the way from inside of the carriage at their utter lack of discretion.

After the disaster at the bank the day before, Peregrine had little hope that Goldbourne would still be lingering. The man would have gone to ground. But hurried departures left traces— and that, Peregrine intended to exploit.

Outside the bank, he gathered the guards close. "There's a rear entrance off the alley," he said. "Hodges knows the way. Two of you, go with him and ensure that no one goes in or out that way. The rest will come in with me. Quietly, if you please. We are here to find loose threads, not cause a scene."

The guard captain echoed his agreement and then divided the men as directed. Hodges gave Peregrine a look that said plainly without words to make sure someone was watching his back.

The reception area was just as it had been the day before, and the clerks were studiously uninterested, no hint that any of them expected trouble. Peregrine scanned the room, eyes narrowing in search of the clerk with the ink-stained cuffs who had so helpfully escorted him into an ambush. No sign of him.

In his place sat an older man at the side desk, plain-faced and heavy in the jowls. But the moment the booted tread of Peregrine and the guards crossed the threshold, the man's salt-and-pepper head jerked up. He scrambled around the desk with the brisk, strained energy of someone determined to be useful.

"I am Clark Timmons. May I be of service?" he asked, his eyes flicking from face to face, fingers twitching at his sides.

"We're here for Mr Goldbourne," Peregrine said flatly—loud enough for every clerk and customer to hear. "Take us to his office. Now."

The man got flustered. "Mr Goldbourne is not in—"

"That's immaterial," the guard captain cut in from behind, stepping forward and gesturing sharply. "You." He pointed to a nearby clerk. "Show Sergeant Ives the back entrance. Sergeant —station one man at the rear and begin a full sweep. Every room."

Sergeant Ives saluted crisply and moved without hesitation. Another guard took position at the front entrance, and the remaining men began to spread through the building.

"Now, Mr Timmons," Peregrine said coolly, "if you would be so good as to lead us to Mr Goldbourne's office so I can finish conducting Her Majesty's business?"

Timmons swallowed hard. Colour drained from his face, and sweat bloomed along his temples, but he obeyed. Unlike Peregrine's last visit, this time the clerk took him to a narrow interior staircase and led the way up two flights. At the top, he paused before a broad door overlooking the street. Exactly the sort of office a banking partner would occupy—and exactly the sort of place where men who thought themselves untouchable liked to hide.

The thick carpets and gleaming wood panelling from the lobby continued into Goldbourne's office, all polished oak and quiet wealth. A massive desk dominated the space, backed by a wall of built-in shelves. Sunlight poured through the open shades, catching on the scattered papers strewn across the desk.

"Does he normally leave his office in this state?" Peregrine asked as he stepped inside.

Mr Timmons hesitated. "Not quite this bad, but yes, sir. He hasn't been in for two days."

Not since Peregrine's solicitor had started digging. And at that point, Goldbourne had chosen to put his efforts towards silencing the inquiry rather than covering his tracks.

Before he could press further, a gruff voice echoed from the corridor. "What's this about?"

"Crown business, sir. Step aside," the captain said curtly.

"That will be the other partner, Mr Hartwell," Timmons whispered, just loud enough to reach Peregrine.

"Keep an eye on him," Peregrine called to the nearest guard. Then, without waiting, he moved to the desk and began sorting through the mess. "Timmons, if you value your freedom, you will answer every question I ask. Sit there. Speak when spoken to."

Timmons obeyed, dropping onto a secretary's chair in the corner. He gripped the edges of the seat like a man expecting to faint and hoping to hold himself in place.

Despite the disorder of the papers, the desk held nothing more than what one might expect. Mostly ledgers, staff records, asset lists. Peregrine thumbed through quickly, setting aside anything bearing the names of Tory donors or political clients for later scrutiny. The scribbled notes he handed to Timmons one by one, forcing him to decipher Goldbourne's handwriting.

Nothing. No link to his mother. No hint of criminality. Just immaculate records and the faint stink of evasiveness. Despair scratched at his spine. And then he cast his eyes around the room. "Can you think of anywhere else in here where Goldbourne might have kept information? Perhaps a safe?"

"No, my lord." Timmons wiped nervous sweat from his brow and cast Peregrine a pleading look. "If you have no other need of me, may I go?"

"Join the others downstairs until the guards decide what to do with you all."

Timmons dropped the papers he had studied back into a pile on the desk and scurried out of the room without so much as a backwards glance. Peregrine half-wished he could follow, leaving this mess to someone else, but there was nothing for him but to continue his search.

There had to be something more here. Goldbourne would have needed some way to keep track of his illegal activities. It was simply a matter of finding his records.

"I need Hodges," he said, and then he ordered one of the guards to fetch him from the back alley.

When Hodges showed up, Peregrine waved the man in. "Help me. I need to search every nook and cranny of this place for any sign of something hidden. Some hidey hole."

He barely had time to start searching before Ives leaned through the doorway. "My lord," he said, voice low and grim, "there's something you'll want to see."

The tone alone raised Peregrine's hackles. "Trouble?" He followed Sergeant Ives down the corridor.

The guard's hand rested firmly on his sword hilt. "Yes, my lord—but not the sort we expected. Best if you see it for yourself."

Sergeant Ives led Peregrine down to the ground floor, then around a narrow corridor and onto a staircase that descended into the basement. The air grew colder with each step. "We found him in a supply cupboard," Ives explained.

Peregrine saw the open door ahead and braced himself, expecting ink-stained cuffs and the smug face of the junior clerk who'd lured him into an alley. What he did not expect was exactly what they found instead.

"Goldbourne," Peregrine muttered, lowering into a crouch. The banker had been propped upright against the inside, but his head lolled to the side. His mouth was slack, eyes open and glassy.

"He's cold," Sergeant Ives said. "Been here since yesterday at least. Possibly longer."

Peregrine didn't reply. He only stared, heart pounding dully behind his ribs. Goldbourne hadn't run. He'd been silenced. Which meant that however much he might have been entrusted to do, Goldbourne had not been the one to take Cameron's place.

Someone else was his mother's new right hand, and whatever information Goldbourne had possessed died with him.

I did warn you. Goldbourne had his uses, but I knew from the beginning he would be far too easy to find, his mother purred.

Hell and damnation.

Scrubbing his eyes with the heels of his hands, Peregrine stood, trying to think quickly. Who else might have enough power to be Marian Fitzroy's puppet? If one man in the Order could be corrupted, it was possible that there were two.

"Unfortunate." Peregrine could find no other word to describe the situation that wouldn't betray how close he was to losing his temper. "Search his pockets, just in case he has anything useful on him, and send someone to check his home. I will go back upstairs to the office to see if Hodges has uncovered any other surprises."

But he was growing more pessimistic. If Goldbourne had been betrayed by what he thought had been a friend, everything here might be lost.

He was back to guessing.

Was Chandros or Pembroke more likely to benefit from this play? Or had Xavier staged everything, down to the encounter in Vauxhall, to remove himself from suspicion? Frustration ripped at him. Maybe Charity had been right after all. Perhaps they should have given all of the men to the Queen.

In the end, Selina was his last hope for insight. The sooner he returned to the palace and connected with the marchioness, the better for all involved. But any thoughts of a quick departure fled when he marched back upstairs and saw Hodges holding a leather-bound book in his hand.

"Found this tucked behind a false back on the bottom shelf.

Well made. Near missed it myself." Hodges passed the book over to Peregrine.

A hidden ledger? Peregrine sent a hope to the heavens that Goldbourne was exactly the sort of little toad one might expect—a man who would keep enough track of his dirty dealings that he could ensure his own protection. Together they went to Goldbourne's desk to examine it.

Peregrine shoved aside the remaining papers, clearing space at the center of the desk. The book opened easily, revealing pages filled with records of transactions. He ran a finger down one page, spotting a few lines that he thought might be some of the private companies from his own investment list. He would have to ask his solicitor to be certain.

Why hide a ledger of investments? Such things would be common in a bank. There had to be something else contained with the pages. He flipped past the rows of incomings and outgoings until he stumbled across something different.

"What's that?" Hodges asked, looking over Peregrine's shoulder.

"A list of names with numbers next to them." Peregrine leaned closer. "All members of the Tory party. What do you think these numbers represent?"

The numbers were all three digits long. Some names had one number beside them, others had as many as five numbered items assigned to their name. One name leapt out at him from the page.

Lord Vesey, the older brother of the man currently hiding in Peregrine's townhouse.

"Could these be the numbers for counterfeit bills?" he asked Hodges.

Hodges scratched his chin. "Bill numbers run longer, but if they printed 'em in batches, guess they wouldn't need the whole thing writ down."

Peregrine checked the rest of the ledger, but the final pages were blank. He flipped it shut and moved to the window.

Below, the street carried on—carriages crawling past, wagons trundling forward, pedestrians darting through every gap like practiced machinery. A system, moving parts. Just like the funds in Goldbourne's ledgers.

How many people were receiving dividends from fake companies in the ledger? And those numbers, did that mean even more Tories were holding counterfeit funds? Whatever the truth, he had to unmask it, because the fate of the nation might well depend upon it.

And there it was again. *Fate.*

Charity's cruel mistress seemed to be mocking him for his disbelief. No matter how he tried to deny her power, she visited him again and again, claws outstretched.

It was a behaviour not unlike the Queen's. Despite their current truce, Peregrine knew he was going to have to tempt her ire again. He was not going to hand the ledger over to anyone else. Not until he was certain what those names and numbers meant. Especially not if he, too, was going to be implicated, simply because he had ended up listed as an investor in the fake companies.

He did not trust Charlotte's amiability to not be fickle, especially if she needed a convenient person to blame. It was wise to be prepared to defend himself, in case she turned on him.

"Take this back to the estate and put it somewhere safe," he said, handing the ledger to Hodges.

"What about you?" Hodges asked.

"I will return to the palace. Selina needs to know that Goldbourne's dead. She is best positioned to suggest where we look next."

Hodges shoved the ledger inside his coat, gave Peregrine a nod in goodbye, and left him there.

Perry gave the room a final glance, then stepped out into the corridor just as the guard captain was coming up the stairs. "We've rounded up the staff and are taking statements. Mr Hartwell—the other partner—is en route to Whitehall for questioning, under escort."

"Can you spare a horse? I need to return to the palace."

"Of course, my lord. Sergeant Ives's mount is yours. He'll accompany the body to the coroner."

The sergeant's gelding was steady enough, though he danced a bit as Peregrine swung into the saddle. Perry tugged the reins firmly, clicked his tongue, and pressed his heels lightly to the horse's flanks. The animal surged forward into a clean canter, weaving neatly around carts and slower riders.

He was a good mount, however spirited. It made for better time than a carriage, but even so, the sight of St James's columned façade brought relief. That relief soured quickly when he spotted Ravenscroft in the courtyard, shouting orders at a trio of footmen.

Ravenscroft could be rather sensational, but Peregrine had never seen the man lose his composure so thoroughly. Whatever had happened was worse than expected, and a surge of misgiving chilled the pit of his stomach.

He reined in the horse sharply and swung down, his boots crunching on the pebbled drive. Without breaking stride, he marched up to Ravenscroft. "What happened?"

Lord Ravenscroft spun to Peregrine, his face pale. And that's when Peregrine knew.

"*What happened*? Where is she?" he asked again. A tightness squeezed around his lungs, and his ears began ringing.

"I do not know. The duchess, she is gone."

Peregrine moved forward without a conscious thought, his long legs taking him to the carriage parked further ahead. The door hung open like an entrance to a nightmare. Streaks of blood painted the walls and floor of the carriage. The rear seat was scored by a terrible rent, its stuffing bursting free.

"Perry. Perry. Are you all right?" Lord Ravenscroft shook him by the shoulder lightly as they stared into the damaged carriage.

Peregrine's throat ached so fiercely, he wasn't sure whether or not he had held back the urge to scream his rage at the sight of it. Fisting his hands, he held onto his senses by sheer force of will. And he made himself look at it, taking note of everything that this carriage both said—and didn't say.

The blood was horrifying, but there was not that much. It might not even be hers. And the ruination of the cushions was theatrical. Like a message. A gauntlet thrown.

He was certain Charity was still alive... at least for now. But right now he could take little comfort from that fact. The bounty on her head was there, waiting for someone to claim it. And their other enemies had a reason to toy with them both.

Peregrine was supposed to protect her. He had promised her that she would be safe. And not since Grenville had he felt this keenly that he had failed someone so utterly. It was worse than standing in the fields of the dead, waiting for a bullet to catch him at the Nive. Worse than discovering that he had been blind to his mother's evil for the first twenty years of his life.

Because now it was Charity. And he deserved the blame for oh, so many reasons. But the most damning one was that he had let her go alone, trusting another's escort when he knew that no one else should be trusted.

And what will you choose to do now, I wonder?

That traitorous harpy, Fate, mocked him now in his mother's voice, already knowing the answer. It did not matter what it cost him. He was going to convince Red Hand to do him a favour.

He spun, nearly knocking over Ravenscroft. The magpie stumbled out of his way, but then grabbed his arm to keep him from leaving.

"Perry? Wait. Where are you going? Are you not going to speak with the Queen?"

"Back to my estate. To get Hodges. I have a new *friend* who might be able to help us, but time is of the essence." Peregrine shook himself free of Ravenscroft and sprinted over to the sergeant's horse, galloping out of the palace gates without so much as a backwards glance.

21

God setteth the solitary in families:
he bringeth out those which are bound with chains:
but the rebellious dwell in a dry land.
—Psalm 68:6

I n her dreams, Charity was trapped in the belly of a carriage that was alive. The walls expanded and contracted, like the bellows of lungs. The velvet curtains fluttered, trying to keep out the light. And Peregrine was sitting on the seat across from her, his face pale except for the dark hand-shaped bruises that slid upwards from beneath his cravat to mark his face, like dappled shadows.

"You are late," the Queen said beside her, and Charity jerked her head that way, finding Her Majesty dressed in mourning blacks. "They have already opened the door."

The carriage door? Charity reached for the handle, but her fingers began to turn to dust, floating away. Her legs were twisted in something, and the inability to move made the old familiar terror grip her fiercely, sparking nausea. She couldn't breathe—she was going to choke—

Horror struck her hard, wrenching her stomach, and in a sickening haze, Charity wrenched herself to semi-consciousness, trying to turn her head to vomit.

A chamber pot appeared beside her, and hands helped lift her upright enough that she could disgorge the last of the laudanum-laced drink from her belly without being sick on herself.

The sickness gripped her, leaving no room for anything but gasping breaths between the violent spasms of her stomach. But she could not take advantage of it, because in those brief moments of reprieve, the little bit of air she took in rushed right back out as she sobbed.

Because she was back in Lady Fitzroy's grasp. She was back, trapped, in the little house, uncertain of the time or the place, dizzy and lost because they kept forcing her to drink more laudanum to keep her quiet.

This time, no one would come looking. Roland was far away and in love with Grace. And Perry—

The world greyed at the edges, and the terror melted into confused despair as she tried to pull her fractured senses back into order. Was Peregrine alive? Or dead? He had been dead in the carriage. But now... now she couldn't remember whether or not that was real.

Charity began to list forward, too wrung out to keep herself upright on her trembling arms, and the chamber pot vanished. Her bones had been hollowed out and filled with cold water, and her mouth tasted like death.

She lay there on the stone, weak, confused, and shivering, trying to throw off the final effects of the drug. The light hurt. Someone was rubbing her back, she realised, and she turned her head, squinting to make out a familiar face that looked very, very different.

"Selina?" Charity asked her in a raspy voice, shocked. Then a terrible sense of betrayal clenched her now, as she wondered if this kidnapping had been orchestrated by the marchioness.

The raven-haired woman frowned down at her, holding Charity's face in her hands as she studied Charity's eyes. "He gave you too much. It is a good thing you purged some of it."

"You kidnapped me!" Charity demanded, and Selina's face shuttered, her shoulders hunching in abject misery.

"You're still confused. I didn't kidnap you, Duchess," she informed Charity. "And if you think I did, well… then I suppose that confirms my fear that no one was even aware I have been missing."

Charity put a hand to the side of her head, now angry about her muddled state. Nothing was making any sense. "I don't understand!"

A sigh. "I know. Be easy, Your Grace. If you are awake now, the rest of the dose will wear off soon, and then things will become much clearer."

The marchioness brought her knees up to her chest, wrapping her arms around them, and Charity rolled over, eventually finding enough strength to pull herself up against the nearby filthy wall.

Her vision wavered. Patches of darkness crawled like a living thing along the walls and floor, spreading like ink, and Charity whimpered, cringing back from them, disoriented. "Where are we?"

"A cellar in a little house, Your Grace," Selina told her patiently, reciting facts in a steady voice to keep Charity moored as the delusions and the drug wore off. "I would guess that we are not too far from London. It was still daylight when you were brought in, and it has been dark for a few hours now. You have been asleep for a long time."

Charity nodded, eyes shut, trying to hold tight to that. And then she began to take in the details around her, even though her eyes ached fiercely and watered in pain despite the dim light. She was sitting on a patchy layer of straw that was far too skimpy to protect her from the damp dirt of the stone floor. The only windows in this place were small, near the ceiling, too high and too small for a person to fit through.

Selina's elegant black hair was plaited in a simple braid, tied with what looked like a scrap of linen torn from her shift. Her dress was badly wrinkled, and stained in places with black smudges and sweat.

The marchioness met Charity's appraisal steadily, turning her head. Charity could see a blue-green smudge running across Selina's cheek. The fading remnants of a bruise.

Then the meaning of the marchioness's earlier words sank in. *That confirms my fear that no one was even aware I have been missing.*

Charity's breath hitched again. "How long have you been here? How *did* you get here? The Queen said she put you under house arrest with General Billingham."

Selina hitched her shoulder. "I don't know. Four days? Maybe more?" She glanced up at the dirty windows that let in some light. "Suffice to say, when she decided to put me in Billingham's care, that is when I learned who Peregrine's mother managed to turn. A little too late for me."

"Yes, we figured out Goldbourne as well," Charity agreed. And then she halted, because Selina was giving her the queerest look. "What is it?"

"Billingham is one of Chandros' creatures," Selina said bluntly. "In the Tribune, Goldbourne's sphere of influence is the banks. Mine is the lords and members of Parliament. Duke Chandros is our strategist. The one whose influence is with the military."

Charity blinked, dizzy, feeling slow to comprehend this new information. "Chandros is the one who took you?"

"For certain. Billingham stopped his carriage just outside of London and handed me over to some butcher like a sack of potatoes! The general would do no such thing unless he was instructed to, and only Chandros has the means of controlling Billingham so thoroughly. Chandros is the only reason that lump of flesh exists in his current role. What were you saying about Goldbourne?" Selina demanded in return.

Pressing her hand again to her stomach, Charity fought down a new wave of nausea. "Goldbourne and his bank have been the purse behind almost everything. The riot, Eldon, Sidmouth—"

"What has happened to Viscount Sidmouth?" Selina interrupted, and Charity realised then that Queen Charlotte must have restricted information to the marchioness even before Billingham arranged for her disappearance. The marchioness thrust her fingers into her hair, vexed. "I have no idea what has been happening! This is *utterly* intolerable."

Charity began explaining all that had happened since the marchioness had been taken into custody, laying out the pieces in order as best she could. Her tongue and wits felt slow, but this exercise helped her create a new sense of order. And it kept her from thinking about their situation. As long as she didn't have to think about what was happening to them, then she could keep herself from tilting into panic.

"So there was not one turncoat working for Marian Fitzroy, but two," Selina said bitterly, when she began to tally up what Charity explained. "The Order is well and truly rotten to the core, because our ideals were always meant to steer England towards prosperity. Not our own pockets. And we should have *never* espoused such conscienceless tactics such as those favoured by Marian."

Grimacing, Charity didn't voice her disagreement. She felt some amount of sympathy for the marchioness's disillusionment, but from where she stood, some of the differences between the

Order and Marian Fitzroy were only a matter of degree. "I wonder how long both Chandros and Goldbourne have been her lackeys," she said instead.

"Impossible to say. Goldbourne could have been helping Perry's mother conduct her illicit banking for at least twenty years. If managing her empire is how he earned his wealth and power, he could have always been in her pocket, feeding our information back to her. That would be very much like what I know of Marian. Chandros... well, I would have thought that man had more spine. But then again, he could have slipped into her thrall more slowly. Goldbourne might have even recruited him to the cause. I've never liked that sanctimonious little slug."

Charity mimicked Selina's posture, bringing her knees to her chest, both for comfort and for warmth. They were being held in the small room of a basement—she could make it out now that the light wasn't giving her head pains—and it was damp and cold.

"What do you think they're going to do with us?" Charity asked next, trying to keep her breathing even. But Selina seemed to sense that Charity's sense of calm was beginning to fracture again.

"Best not to think too much about it. Clearly, they have some purpose in mind," Selina said, trying to find some point to reassure her on. "Killing me to prevent me from noticing the attacks happening on the Tory party and my allies would certainly have been easier than arranging this."

"I cannot *not* think about it," Charity snarled. "I worry, because Perry doesn't know about Chandros."

"*Don't* panic. Perry has a knack for cheating death that rivals a cat, Duchess."

Charity shivered, sniffling. "I hope you are right because he has used up at least six lives already."

Selina slid closer to Charity, letting their shoulders press together. "You need to control your fear. I will not ask you if you are all right, because you are. You are alive. You are breathing. You can move, and you can reason."

"I—I cannot stand the feeling of being trapped in small spaces. Not since Lady Fitzroy had me kidnapped last year."

"You can," Selina said mercilessly. "You indulged your moment of doubt. Anyone would. But now it is time to move on. You cannot think if you are afraid. And if you cannot think, you cannot make a plan to act. Don't be afraid. You are not a little lamb. Don't be their prey. Be cold and *angry*, like a dragon. Hoard that feeling to yourself as you coil up and wait for your turn to strike."

Charity could do that. Had she not done that for most of these last months, imagining how she would destroy the Fitzroy family? All she had to do was hold her temper a little bit looser instead of pushing it down.

Temper is for tradesmen, her mother said disapprovingly. *A lady endures.*

Shut up, *mother!* She shouted back in her thoughts. *You and grandmama didn't 'endure' when my father did not want to marry you! And was enduring his cruelty when he was so upset about your treachery worth what it did to us? To all of us?*

"Feeling better?" the marchioness asked, her voice amused.

She realised that she was. Her breathing was unfettered by the tight bands of hysteria, and her mind surprisingly clear. "It helps that I am making a list of people who I want to destroy. Starting with Lady Fitzroy."

Selina chuckled briefly. "I can see why Peregrine is fond of you."

"It might be better for him if he wasn't fond of me—either of us," Charity said hastily, tucking a lock of her hair behind her ear. "Although I am glad that you have cared enough for him to do so much to protect him. Even when the results were… unpleasant to experience."

"Are you attempting to thank me for my nasty manipulations, Your Grace?" the older woman asked Charity archly, but the slightest of smiles was hovering at the corner of her mouth.

"I do believe I am, Lady Normanby. As well as your excellent advice about pickpockets."

"What passes for Marian's affection left her son with sharp edges," the marchioness said darkly. "But don't wish that he did not have feelings for you. Given his bloodline, it is a mercy that he has found love."

"You don't—" Charity stuttered and gave a short, disbelieving laugh, her heart seizing in her chest. "Affection, yes. But… it has been such a short time. You think he might actually love me?"

Selina tilted her head to give Charity a stern look. "Do you jest? You haven't said the words, but the two of you are both so utterly gone on one another, it's as obvious as the sun." Her eyes sparkled once with mischief, before growing solemn again. "Not that recognising this fact will smooth the way entirely. If you think Marian hates you now, imagine what she will do to you if she learns you threaten to usurp her title and become the new Lady Fitzroy."

Charity's lips parted, her mouth hanging open in horror.

"You cannot tell me that thought hasn't crossed your mind, truly," Selina said, astonished.

"Not in such words, no." Her voice was strangled. Both the title of duchess and the obligation of caring for the duke's young heir had been cemented into her thoughts, since that had been the arrangement. But guardianship didn't necessarily preclude the possibility of remarriage.

And then she thought about their society debut. "We went to Vauxhall. To deliberately provoke whoever Marian's agent was with rumours that we were courting."

Despite the grim reality of their situation, Selina actually laughed in a sharp, short bark. "When we get out of this—and mark my words, we will because I *will* be the one to throttle Chandros and Goldbourne with my own two hands even if I have to sell my soul to the devil to do it—you and I will need to go off for a little feminine confidence."

"You may interrogate me to your heart's content if we manage to escape in time to warn Perry that Chandros is also our enemy," Charity told her.

"Well then, Your Grace," Selina said thoughtfully, examining the room, "I suppose we should bend our wits to this end."

Charity joined her in examining their surroundings, still feeling dizzy from the aftereffects of the laudanum, but the crawling shadows had stopped moving for now. The door was forbiddingly sturdy looking, and the only other possible means of egress was a coal chute high on the wall above a rather depleted coal pile.

"Is there someone guarding the house?" Charity asked her. "I was taken by a dark-haired man in a hooded cloak. He got into the carriage with me and forced me to drink the laudanum. Is he here?"

The marchioness shook her head. "I know the fellow you mean. He's the one who brought you in. But he's not the one who has been tending to me these last few days. There's another little tyrant serving as our guard. Godfrey Bellrose is the sort of pompous little man who likes to prove his manhood on someone even softer than he is." She pointed to the bruise on her cheek. "I got this when I slapped him for taking liberties. He took it as an invitation to slap me back."

Selina was blithe about it, but Charity blinked at her, horrified. "You *know* him?"

"Vaguely. He is a deputy in the treasury. Or he was. *Perhaps* he was dismissed from his posting."

Charity considered that, frowning. "A man from the treasury as our guard? How… strange."

"It is not so strange now that you have told me about Goldbourne and the counterfeiting," Selina murmured. "He is clearly complicit in this scheme, somehow. If I had to guess, he likely thinks the blame for what is to happen will fall on his superiors, and hoping that his absence will absolve him."

Unsteadily, Charity resolved to have a look at this Mr Bellrose herself. The door was locked. So Charity began to pound on the wood with her fists, wondering if the man would hear them.

Selina watched Charity, but did not argue. "Be meek and ignorant, Duchess," she suggested.

It took a long time—at least by the reckoning of Charity's aching hands—but finally a man's voice sounded through the wood. "Stop rattling the bloody walls, or I will make you silent!"

"I just want to talk," Charity told him softly, and after a long moment, the rattle of a key in the lock sounded.

She stepped back just in time to avoid being clipped by the door when Bellrose flung it open. After a quick glance at the marchioness to make sure she wasn't waiting to escape, Bellrose took a longer, contemptuous look at Charity, his eyes lingering inappropriately on her bosom.

Charity felt her face flame, but she followed Selina's advice, cowering slightly. And as she did so, she studied the man in return. He was pale, fussy looking, and unremarkable. Perhaps thirty or thirty five, but his thinning brown hair combed flat against his skull made him look older than his face suggested. The only interesting thing about him was a pointed chin that might have been permanently lifted in petty condescension. That, and the way his lips pinched peevishly.

Bellrose sneered at her, his eyes cold. "What do you want, Your Grace?"

"I want to know what I might be able to offer you to let us go," she said softly. "Money? I can get you money. My father can get you more. Connections, perhaps?"

"I don't need your pathetic offerings, Your Grace. Money and power are already at hand. All I have to do is ensure that you and the Order's bitch are fed and watered for a handful of days more."

Charity watched as the man dismissed her, and then the way his eyes flared contemptuously when he looked Selina's way again. He hated the marchioness, and it was clearly more than her standing that was the cause of his resentment. There had been entitlement in his possessive gaze as it had lingered on Charity's chest, but her passivity had mollified him.

Selina was off to one side, but she stood with a hip canted, her arms crossed over her chest. And the marchioness's unbowed stance provoked him into a smouldering anger. Charity marked it well. That was why Selina had told her to be meek—so she would not draw his ire.

"You are better than the people you are working for," Charity tried again, but Bellrose ignored her.

"You are *filthy*," he scolded the marchioness, raking a look over her.

"I apologise, sir. There is a great deal of coal dust down here, and you have given us no water for washing."

His nostrils flared as he picked up on Selina's sarcasm, though her voice had been neutral. And then he slammed the door in Charity's face. There was click of a padlock closing, and then the sound of boots stomping away, up the stairs.

"Well," the marchioness murmured. "You see what we are up against. He is not much to look at, but he has a strength in his violence."

"He seems to despise you."

"He does, rather. I tried to prevent his appointment, and he knows it. Chandros seems to have promised me to him as a reward for his work, and it raises Bellrose's passions to envision how he will work the kick from my gallop. If I present the greater threat to his masculinity, hopefully he will not develop such imaginings about doing the same to you."

Charity slid down the wall again, exhausted and nauseated.

"Sleep for a while," the marchioness ordered her, pushing the straw into a sorry pile with her hands. "We cannot escape anyway while you are fainting and plagued with visions, and we need time to come up with the bones of a plan."

Shivering, Charity curled up on one side of the pile, wrapping her arms around her, and the marchioness lay behind her, their backs touching. It was far more comforting than Charity expected, and the warmth of Selina pressed against her helped her tumble quickly back into vivid dreaming.

22

"Grief hath no lullaby."
—Unknown

Inside his head, Peregrine was raging with frustration. A furious, silent litany hurled itself at every obstacle in his path. He had already wasted too much time going to the estate to retrieve Hodges and his weapons. Every second scraped at his nerves like grit under the skin.

Nearly two hours had passed since he'd learned of Charity's disappearance, and who knows how much longer it had been since she had been grabbed. Now, at least, on his return to London, Hodges riding at his side, Peregrine felt some of the pressure loosening its hold on his lungs. Hooves pounded the dry road in a dull, rapid tattoo as clumps of earth scattered in its wake, matching the pace of his racing heart.

Traffic picked up as they re-entered London. Their steeds slowed their gait, winding around the slower moving wagons and carriages at every opportunity. Hodges shouted for Peregrine to slow down, but Peregrine could not hear him over the roaring in his head.

A sudden blur darted across the cobbled lane. Small. Fast. Unmistakably a child. Peregrine sawed at the reins, instinct taking over, hauling the bit hard against the horse's mouth. The animal reared slightly, hooves striking sparks off the stones as it checked mid-stride. With a wrench of his weight and a tight pull to the left, he swung the mount wide, narrowly avoiding the child. The horse skidded, muscles bunching as it fought for balance, but it stayed upright.

The near accident was enough to jerk Peregrine free of his inner turmoil, shaking him. His inattention had nearly consigned another to their death.

Just as you may have consigned the duchess, his mother observed coldly.

No. She was alive. He *had* to believe it. Even if she was kidnapped again, this time he would save her. There was no price he was not willing to pay to right this wrong.

That was why he was racing to the slums of London to find Red Hand. The criminal cared for little more than indulging his greed and ensuring his own continued existence. So if Peregrine lacked a better currency… well, there was always the option of dire threats.

Peregrine and Hodges did not bother with subterfuge this time. Peregrine tossed a coin at a street urchin and bade him to keep watch over their horses while they went inside Red's favourite haunt.

The dirty pub was busy, the barstools and tables filled with gruff men in sweat-stained clothing, enjoying a watered-down ale after a long day of work. Peregrine tossed another coin at the bartender and called for two pints and then made his way toward the redheaded man tucked away at the table in the far back corner.

To give him credit, Red did not bolt out the back door when

he laid eyes on Peregrine's stony countenance. His left hand slid from the table, disappearing from view. Likely to ready whatever weapon he had available. Peregrine prevented him from taking any further action by tossing a coin-filled velvet bag onto the table and then settling onto the seat opposite him. Hodges remained standing, putting his back to the wall where he could keep an eye on both Peregrine and the rest of the room.

"I would like to engage your services," Peregrine said, his voice cool.

Red squinted at the bag as though it might contain a spitting viper. "Ah now, *engage my services*, is it? That's a pretty turn o' phrase, comin' from a man who once held some loftier ideals o' morality." He leaned back, fingers steepled. "If it's blood you're after, Lord Fitzroy, you'll find my prices steep. You sure you can stomach what you're buyin'?"

Peregrine lifted his chin. "You do not know what services of yours I am seeking. I had hoped, as a *friend* with a vested interest in the power now changing hands, you might be persuaded to offer something not among your… usual dealings."

"Well now. Colour me intrigued—and just a touch suspicious." He tipped his head. "Go on then, Fitzroy. Let's hear what flavour o' madness you're after."

"Information, for the most part." Peregrine tugged his cravat down just enough to reveal the bruises ringing his neck, and Red let out a low whistle. "I believe I have encountered the person leaving his work in your 'yard.' An assassin with dark hair, skill, and a long list of people to see."

"One man's doin' all that? Och, I'd say you've met the Maker," Red breathed, glancing at Peregrine's neck now with something that looked like respect. "He's not cheap, that one— and he don't take just any job."

Wonderful. "I don't suppose you have heard anything about who he might be working for, or where he might be found?"

Red Hand snorted, putting his hand on the coin purse. "The Maker's a free agent. His contracts don't pass through any books."

Peregrine laid his hand over Red's, stopping him. "I have more questions. What do you know about counterfeiting banknotes?"

"That it'll put a rope round your neck." When Peregrine didn't lift his hand, Red added, "I don't touch it, and not just 'cause it'll get you hanged. Takes coin, connections, a press, steady supplies, and a forger who don't drink or talk. That's rarer than hen's teeth, that is. Killing's a simpler business."

"Yes, you are too principled by half for doing such things." Peregrine grinned at Red Hand, showing his teeth. "But as you say, people talk. And I want to know if you might know who would do such things. I'm looking for a certain illegal press printing bills."

"One in particular? Good luck wi' that. You can't swing a dead cat in this city without hittin' someone trying to forge bills."

"I imagine it narrows the field somewhat if we're looking for a press in the slums with ties to my mother—and a banker named Goldbourne. Established. Organised. And, I suspect, recently relocated. Within the last few months, perhaps."

To his credit, Red Hand looked thoughtful. "Aye, well. I could put my ear to the ground, see what slithers out. And if I do find it, what's in it for me?"

Peregrine lifted his hand, freeing the purse.

Red picked up the purse and gave it a testing heft. "Money's a fine thing, sure. But knowin' what you usually deal in, I'd rather have a favour, Fitzroy. Somethin' I can call in later, when it suits me."

"Information in kind?"

"Maybe that. Maybe somethin' else. We'll see."

Peregrine did not like the idea of owing *anyone* an unnamed favour, much less one of London's bludgeon men. He leaned across the table, holding the man's eyes. "I warn you now. I am *not* my mother."

"An' thank Christ for that. Do we have a bargain?"

"For a price like this, I want every rat of yours scurrying along the streets, looking. And not only do I want them looking for that printer, I want them also looking for the duchess. I believe she may have also been taken by the Maker."

Red whistled softly through his teeth again, this time regretfully. "Your lady's been taken. That's a bloody shame. Why not let the proper authorities chase ghosts for you? Or are they not so proper when one of yours goes missin'?"

"They are still looking, but probably in all the wrong places. And you can help me find out whether anyone has claimed her reward."

"Well now, seein' as I'm properly motivated, I'll send my boys to do what I can. And I'll check with Nibs while I'm at it. He's the one keeping the black book she's on. If the bounty's been paid?"

"Then someone's made a very short-sighted decision," Peregrine said, the cold beginning to bleed through. "I'll bury them with it."

Red looked at him sidelong. "You might not be your ma, Fitzroy, but you've still got a bit o' her nasty in you, when you feel like bringin' it out to play."

To that, Peregrine had no reply. Right now, he had no desire to be nice.

Not in a world where Charity was lost to him.

～

The bounty remained unclaimed. That, at least, was something. It was the only scrap of encouragement to be found in a night that had otherwise yielded nothing. When dawn broke without so much as a strand of Charity's golden hair to show for their efforts, Hodges put his foot down.

"Let Red's lot do the heavy liftin'." He said firmly, steering Peregrine back toward his mount. "You're no good if your head's turned to mush."

It said everything about his condition that Peregrine did not protest harder. A few hours' rest, a change of clothes, and a shave did just enough to bring his thoughts back into order. One thing was certain: he would not stay here, cloistered at a remove from the action.

He considered returning to the palace but discarded the notion just as quickly. He had no appetite for courtiers, and even less for the demands of royalty.

The arrival of a note from Ravenscroft resolved the matter. Peregrine could hear the man's voice ringing in his ears as he skimmed the page. Ravenscroft harangued him for disappearing all night and insisted he come to Atholl House to assist with the search for the duchess.

Quinn—likely playing nursemaid at Hodges's behest—insisted Peregrine eat something first. Not the worst suggestion, considering he couldn't recall his last proper meal. While the staff assembled a plate, he requested Goldbourne's ledger be brought to the study.

Once there, he swept aside the usual clutter. Letters, invitations, neatly stacked insignia of a life he barely inhabited. None of it mattered now. Not his reputation. Not some overstuffed drawing room. What mattered was stopping whatever it was his mother had set in motion.

A knock at the door. "The ledger," Hodges said, holding it out. "You want me to hang about?"

"No. Saddle the horses. We will leave for Atholl House as soon as I finish making a copy of this list."

Peregrine grabbed a fresh scrap of foolscap, a quill, and ink and opened the ledger to the list of names and numbers. He jotted them down, then dusted sand over the paper. When he was certain the ink was dry, he put the note in his pocket and stored the ledger in the wall safe he'd had freshly installed after his return from the front lines. He had given no one the combination.

During the ride to Mayfair, Peregrine could not stop himself from peering into every passing carriage. Though he saw blonde hair aplenty, none had the golden shade he realised he was unconsciously looking for. And the world grew more colourless yet at the thought that he might never get to touch that hair again.

An old, familiar feeling swamped him. A desperate, listless melancholy, that made him question why he was struggling against the tide that wished to lay him low. What was the point of existing at all, when he had nothing but this empty life to sustain him? The society games, the secrets, the schemes—none of it was enough to stop the ennui that had been sinking into his bones day by day, hour by hour.

Not when there was no passion or pleasure. Nothing to moor him to this earth, because he could not care about anything except in the most superficial ways. Because he had put his emotions away like the children's toys he had outgrown.

Right up until she had joined him on that balcony, that first day, and he felt something. A real connection to someone, formed hard and strong. The first time he had felt it in years.

You forgot that all that you have, all that you are—it belongs to me. Your love. Your loyalty. Your very life. Is it any surprise that I cast you out? You snapped my lead on you, and here you are. Your pathetic tendencies to be driven by emotion forged your shackles anew. And now you tie yourself to the daughter of my enemy.

How dare *you offer your love to her instead of me?*

His hands froze on the reins. He had never wanted to name

these dangerous feelings that had been growing between him and Charity. But now that his mother's voice had, a quiver of fear ran along the length of his spine as he realised it to be true.

In a dozen ways, Charity now held the power to deal him a fatal blow. It was even more certain than the night he had put the knife in her palm. But he couldn't bring himself to regret that he had placed himself at her mercy.

He would rather live and die at Charity's hand than be pinned beneath his mother's.

Resolute now, Peregrine gripped the reins tightly in his gloved hands and urged his mount to quicken its pace. To his surprise, the front door of Atholl House opened before he had even dismounted. Pritchard stood waiting, stiff-backed as ever.

"Lord Fitzroy. They are expecting your arrival," the butler said, bowing as he took Peregrine's coat and gloves with professional efficiency.

Peregrine stilled, something in his chest tightening. "*They?*" he asked, his voice sharper than intended.

"Lord Ravenscroft is here, with Viscount Sidmouth and one other gentleman." Pritchard's expression flickered ever so slightly. "They are in the drawing room."

Even from the hall, Peregrine could hear Ravenscroft's voice —sharper than usual, with the clipped edge of his French accent showing through.

Pritchard rapped once on the drawing room door and opened it with quiet ceremony. "Lord Fitzroy," he announced.

Ravenscroft was talking with a guard. Peregrine locked eyes briefly with Sidmouth, who was off to one side of the drawing room. And Perry, walking into the room, nearly missed a step as he recognised the dusky skin of the third man.

Xavier was here.

The guard inclined his head and departed, stepping around Peregrine, as Ravenscroft let out a small noise of irritated relief to

271

see him. "There you are! When no one could find you, I thought you might have gone to drown your sorrows."

"I have been occupied more productively than that," Peregrine said neutrally, flicking his eyes towards the others. "Why is everyone here?"

Ravenscroft ran a hand over the back of his head. "Given what has happened, the Regent and his Queen mother thought it best I establish a headquarters, of sorts, here. In case we received a ransom demand for the duchess."

That might explain the Home Secretary's presence, but— "I know Sidmouth, but I do not believe I have formally met your other acquaintance."

Xavier smiled, white teeth showing against his darker skin, but he played along. "Call me Xavier. I have turned myself in to the Home Secretary as a member of the Order, Lord Fitzroy. I have agreed to help catch the person committing such treasonous offences to prove my innocence."

Peregrine caught the barest emphasis on the word member. Sidmouth was unaware, then, Xavier was part of the inner circle.

Sidmouth crossed his arms. "Indeed, perhaps we can dispense with pretending that none of us are aware of the Order's existence and instead finally trust one another to pool our resources and stop this threat to Parliament. Xavier has exchanged information from the continent with me for years. And I already am keenly aware that *you* are acquainted with Lady Normanby."

"—Who also appears to be missing," Ravenscroft interrupted. "Or at least, she was not found at the house where General Billingham told others at Whitehall he was taking her. Since no one can find the general *either*, we are assuming he has also been corrupted. I swear, Canary, you had the worst timing in your disappearance. It has been utter madness since yesterday afternoon."

Shock snapped Peregrine's head up, causing him to ignore the rest of the magpie's words. "Selina is missing also?"

"Yes." Sidmouth's expression was closed, and Peregrine wondered exactly what sort of relationship had existed between the marchioness and the prickly Home Secretary. An unrequited affection on his part, perhaps? "Focus, Fitzroy. We know nothing about what happened after your trip to the bank, except that the guards say you found Goldbourne dead."

Ravenscroft gave him a telling look. "You came to the palace and immediately left again. Where did you go?"

He had rather lost his head, nearly. "I went to see one of my contacts in the rookeries. The bounty on Duchess Atholl is still unclaimed."

"That's one piece of news, at least," Sidmouth muttered.

"But also, I went to ask him about counterfeiters in London," Peregrine added, pulling the list from his pocket and laying it on the nearby table, pointing to Vesey's name.

"We found this list of names and numbers in a hidden spot in Goldbourne's office. Mr Vesey's brother, the viscount, keeps an account at Goldbourne's bank. Also, conveniently, the bank that he went to, to obtain the funds to repay Mr Vesey's gambling debts."

Sidmouth nodded, sighing. "Eldon said before his death Shedford accused Vesey of falsely paying the debt. It seems it would have been quite easy for Goldbourne to ensure that some funds were bad."

"The only guess I have is that the numbers reference other counterfeit bills." Peregrine said. "Perhaps the final digits."

"It is possible," Sidmouth agreed slowly. "But it seems strange to track the numbers of a few small bills. I would like to copy this. If nothing else, it may give us a list of the politicians being targeted."

As Sidmouth copied out the list, Peregrine stalked closer to

Xavier, who studied Perry just as carefully as Peregrine studied him.

"In my, er, discreet snooping, I discovered some of your mother's correspondence to the Order," Xavier murmured. "I hope you can see why I did not trust you right away, Lord Fitzroy. She has been dangerous to our interests for years, and you were her son."

"And yet," Peregrine said bitterly, sick of being painted as his mother's stooge, "it seems two of your own proved to align more with her than the good of England."

"Sadly, this is true."

"It is done. Nothing matters to me right now except bringing both the duchess and the marchioness home safely. Goldbourne is dead. So who has them? Chandros, or Pembroke?"

"The Duke Chandros." Xavier said. "He rubbed shoulders at Whitehall. It wasn't well known, but he was General Billingham's patron. So he could force or bribe Billingham to put the marchioness elsewhere."

"Perhaps you will excuse my skepticism. You are *absolutely certain* Pembroke is not involved? Because an assassin is performing housekeeping at my mother's behest, and I have learned he is quite expensive to retain."

"Pembroke is currently holed up in his country house, terrified," Ravenscroft said drolly. "It is safe to assume the killer is not in his employ."

Peregrine fought back the urge to pace. "And where is His Grace?"

"We do not know yet, Lord Fitzroy," Sidmouth said slowly, his eyes following Peregrine. "We held off in sending the guard to the duke's properties because we were worried that a knock on the wrong door could have dire consequences."

Peregrine ran his hands through his hair, frustration making his body shake. The need to do something warred with the knowledge of how very little he *could* do.

"But..." Sidmouth continued slowly, worrying his copy of Peregrine's list between his fingers. "When the guards who went with you told us about Goldbourne, we sent people to question the banker's staff. Goldbourne's carriage driver said he often requested to be dropped off at the Archbishop's Horseferry. Where Goldbourne went once he crossed the Thames is unknown. We thought maybe a club, maybe a mistress—"

"—Maybe a counterfeiting operation." Peregrine said, thinking of the industrial buildings near that marshy, riverside area. "I think I will send my *associate's* men to investigate. I should let him know to send further news here, anyway."

Sidmouth stood. "Then Xavier and I will go speak with the men on this list. If we shake enough trees, perhaps we shall knock loose something fruitful."

"If you are looking to question Mr Vesey," Peregrine told them, "he is at my townhouse on Neal Street."

"Then we are left to make a decision." Xavier did not look happy about having to suggest it. "Do we continue waiting, or do we take the risk and send the guard to knock on the doors of the duke's properties and look for the women?"

Peregrine felt sick. "I think we have no choice but to start knocking."

23

"We made each other a promise. Wherever one went, the other would follow. And if aught came between us, we would fight to find our way back."
—Grace Percy, Duchess of Northumberland, in correspondence to Charity

The windows were too high and too dirty to see much through the brownish-yellow scum on them. Standing on the marchioness's back in her stocking feet, Charity scrubbed and scrubbed with a square of the linen she had torn from her shift. But all that she really managed to do was smear the greasy mess around.

"I can make out nothing except daylight and hedgerow," Charity grumbled, still feeling close to a frustrated panic.

"Press your mind to work, Duchess," Selina told her tartly. "Even that much tells us *something*. We are in the country. We can't be too far from London's borders. We may be able to discern what we are likely to encounter when we decide to escape through that bloody coal chute."

Giving a convulsive shudder, Charity nodded, gritting her teeth and hoping that would not be their path. She recognised the command in Selina's voice for what it was—a bannister railing between her and her terrors, with an order to step away from the edge of it.

"You sound very much like *him* when you talk to me in that manner," Charity muttered. Letting herself be baited, sinking into such idle banter, was more comfortable than letting her thoughts wander too far or the silence stretch.

"Peregrine?" the marchioness chuckled throatily. "Who do you think I have been acting the part of, trying to keep you engaged and productively vexed?"

Charity let out a small snort. "He doesn't vex me." The words sounded like a lie, even to her own ears.

"You should want him to. What is the best sort of marriage, anyway, except for finding the one person you want to nettle for the rest of their life?"

"You have a peculiar notion of love matches, Lady Normanby."

"How odd. I do not recall ever saying love was what made the best sort of marriage," she replied mildly. "If one does not find a partner an interesting challenge, what is the point?"

Charity huffed again, scrubbing harder at the window. "And what does that even mean, 'productively vexed?' It sounds like something one would find in a book of medicine."

"You can very well guess, as it has been your motivation to indulge in this most unladylike conduct all morning. And if you are more interested in talking than looking, perhaps it is your turn to be the footstool."

"I am looking! I just can't help but think about how ridiculous we must appear. Can you imagine what the papers would print if they could see us like this?"

"Perry will laugh himself silly, and my maid will faint once she sees my clothes. No hint of a word better otherwise come near the broadsheets, or anyone else, Duchess. Else I will add to the bounty on your head. So for now, look harder."

"There is so little to see," Charity squabbled back. "The shadows I can make out are slanting towards us. We look to the west."

"That is something. Get off of me, then," Selina groaned.

She rose up on her knees once Charity had both feet on the floor, and Charity pulled her to her feet from there. Charity then poured a trickle of their remaining, stale drinking water into the woman's tar-black hands, and Selina scoured as best as she could with the straw and another piece of fabric ripped from Charity's shift.

"It will have to do," Selina said grimly, looking down from her grimy hands to the sorry state of her shift, which was as black as coal in large patches. "I've changed my mind. I will have my maid burn these instead. They should catch fire nicely, don't you think?"

"I think you were wise to take your dress off," Charity said obliquely, playing maid and helping Lady Normanby back into the gown, now that their explorations were complete.

Lady Normanby had offered to be the one to check the coal chute, and Charity had been only too glad to let her. She had flipped their only bucket in order to peer into the chute, rather high off the floor. But she still needed Charity to provide her a boost with her hands to successfully get inside. In addition to being a cramped space, the coal chute was steeply angled, and slippery.

And filthy, Charity thought to herself.

"No reason to let Bellrose know what we were about," Selina

said quietly. "It's best I do it because he's already upset with me for being dirty."

"He wants you to be dirty so he can relish humiliating you for it."

"I know," she murmured. "But there is no sense in him haranguing you for it as well."

Not that Godfrey Bellrose had thus far deigned to notice. He hadn't emptied their chamber pot or brought more water. It was amazing how quickly Charity was resigning herself to their squalid state. And the marchioness need have no fear of her breathing a single word about it because she also didn't want to see her name associated with a headline like *Pearls Before Swine?*

Both lapsed into the silence of thought again, which had been happening more and more frequently as the day wore on and desperation began to chink away at confidence. It didn't help that they were both exhausted and hungry. And rest was difficult with Godfrey Bellrose stomping around on the floor upstairs, but not coming down.

It would be only a matter of time. The coward was clearly building up his confidence.

"What is on your mind, Duchess?" Selina asked her.

Despite how closely Selina had told her she should be keeping all secrets, they had been exchanging the smallest of confidences all day. It was like an affirmation.

"I was wondering if you regretted your choice to join the Order," Charity said wryly. When phrased as a musing and not a direct question, Selina seemed to answer more readily.

"No, I don't regret it," the marchioness said. "In my mind, a game like this has always been the only game worth playing. Given the chance, I would choose it again and again."

Playing with people, her mother hissed, which made Charity want to roll her eyes. All the *ton* games were played with people, just some were better done than others.

279

Not merely playing with people, Mama. Playing a game where the stakes mean something.

Or where the game made a difference to other people, and not just one's own standing. Selina had played the game to try to steer England, to be sure. But she had also used her power to protect Perry.

Such power—to help and protect oneself and others—seemed like the only power really worth grasping.

"What about you, Duchess? Have you regrets about getting mixed up in this?"

Charity picked at her dress. "Oddly enough, no. But perhaps that is because I am not sure I could have avoided the trouble in the end. It was bound to find me sooner or later, like a letter addressed to me."

"The trouble by the name of Marian Fitzroy, you mean. I suppose that's a fair point. I would say the fight between you would practically be fate, except I have some idea of the effort her choices require."

A cramp twisted Charity's stomach, the words about fate reminding her painfully of the words Peregrine hurled on the balcony. *You, not fate.*

With everything that had happened over the years, it would have been easy for the Cresswell and Fitzroy families to part. To let Charity alone. But Marian had steered herself ever deliberately towards an inevitable collision. Peregrine had been right; most people chose the hells that they lived in.

Just as she was choosing her hell now, wandering those memories of their one night's grace. The expression he wore when he looked at her was like a mirror of what she was feeling inside.

This is the opposite of productive vexation, she said acerbically to herself, twisting her hands together. But oh, she missed Peregrine so fiercely. And wasn't that the most ironic thing, that all she could think about was seeing him once more? To know that he was safe?

With nothing else to do, they caught snatches of sleep and waited for the evening, the safest time to attempt escape. But as the light began to wane, Bellrose finally found his courage.

The women sat up as they heard him descend the stair. At the door, the lock rattled. A pause. Then the hinges groaned.

Godfrey Bellrose threw the door open and sneered at them, his nose twitching at the scent. "I could get used to seeing you like this, Marchioness. Scrabbling in the muck that should be your place."

Selina tilted her chin. "If I am soiled with dirt, Bellrose, it is only because of my association with you. *Hardly* the behaviour of a man who would aspire to be a gentleman. But if my current lack of cleanliness repels you, then I am doubly happy for it."

Bellrose let out a snarl and struck her. Not hard, but fast. Charity gasped, but Selina made no sound. She only turned her head back, ignoring the trickle of blood at the corner of her mouth, and waited for Bellrose to speak.

"How *dare* you speak to me like a fishwife, whore."

Charity did not know how Selina could stand there so impassively. But the marchioness did. And then finally, just as Bellrose looked like he was prepared to explode into violence, Selina bowed her head. "My apologies, Mr Bellrose."

His attack was frightening, but Bellrose's response to her capitulation was worse. The marchioness was right. He was a small man who relied on brutality to make himself feel masculine. And a display of meekness was like victory.

But it was a short-lived one. Satisfied he had cowed Selina, his eyes turned towards Charity. "Does the duchess have more respect for her betters than the marchioness, I wonder?"

Charity goggled that this mean, untitled little nobody would consider himself better than a duchess simply because he was a man. Bellrose interpreted her surprise as the barest hint of defiance, and that caused him to round on her.

"You keep trying to tell me that you are better than I am, Bellrose, but then your very next action proves that you were born losing," Selina drawled behind him, forcing him to wheel around.

He hit her again, and this time with enough force to make Selina stagger against the wall. But as he wrapped her braid around his hand, yanking her head around, Selina chuckled.

"Be careful Bellrose," she murmured. "You know Chandros and his lackey have reasons they want you to keep me alive. If you kill me before they can use me, they will make you regret it in ways I don't even have the words for."

Judging by the way he stood ramrod straight, Bellrose knew those words to be true. But then he relaxed with a false insouciance. "I only have to be patient to receive my due, *Lady Normanby*." He shook her once by her braid, then thrust her away, heading back up the stairs in an angry rush.

"Why did you provoke him like that?" Charity hissed at her.

"Because it made him mad enough that he went away." Selina finally wiped the trickle of blood from the corner of her mouth. "In the black cockles of his fearful little heart, he knows I am more important to Chandros than he is."

Then she gave Charity a frank look. "But *your* importance to Chandros is... less established, Duchess. If he stays teetering between his ill desires and fear of what retribution he will bring down on his head if loses his temper and goes against Chandros's wishes, he forgets that fact."

Charity gave her a keen look of worry.

"Never you mind, Duchess. How is... your head?" the marchioness asked her neutrally.

"No more seeing things not there." The large dose of laudanum had plagued Charity occasionally with hallucinations the night before, and some had been terrifying.

"Good. I am hoping we are near enough to London that the lights will show us the way once it is dark."

"That is... a clever thought." It was worthy of one of Grace's escapades, actually. "Perhaps you missed your calling as an adventuress."

"Not at all, Duchess. I expect I shall never complain about a dull party again," Selina smirked at her, her green eyes sparkling briefly. "Are you ready to brave that small space, little dragon?"

Charity clenched her teeth. "If I must."

"Good. It is narrow, yes, but not for a long distance." Selina reassured her. "There is a hatch up top that will have to be pushed open. But I could see sunlight there earlier."

Having to climb and push open a hatch in the darkness sounded terrible. "Are you sure it shouldn't be me playing ladder for you?"

Selina chuckled, pressing a shoulder to Charity's. "Absolutely not. You need to go first, because if you are going to have the vapours, I would rather you do it before we risk alerting Bellrose with any noise from the hatch. Not after. Panic will not be helpful if you have to hurry."

Charity sniffed, stifling pique. But she recognised the truth of Selina's words. "I would like to protest that. But it is a fair concern. I'm glad... that you're here with me," Charity replied. "That sounds awful, because I shouldn't wish this prison on anyone except Lady Fitzroy. But I do not think I would be anything except a huddling pile of skirts without you."

"Courage sometimes takes practice, Duchess." The marchioness grasped Charity's hand then.

Charity held it, realising that Selina was trembling faintly, despite her bold words. And somehow that made Charity feel a little better. Lady Normanby wasn't unafraid. She simply had put her nervous energy to action. That was all.

She could certainly do the same. Fear was acceptable, as long as it didn't keep her from moving. She could use her anger to master her fear, and be a dragon.

"Tonight."

~

They tried to get their rest as they waited for the full measure of darkness to fall. Bellrose, in his fury, did not come back with food or water, or even to sneer at them. But that suited both women just fine.

Harnessing anger, Charity kept her nerves despite having her head stuck inside the steep, dark chute. She could feel air around her legs, and the pressure of Selina's hands below her booted feet. But as Selina shoved her higher, and Charity scrabbled for purchase on the slick bricks, her fortitude quickly began to fail. It was pitch black, and the angle of the chute was disorienting.

"Don't lose your nerve," Selina hissed at her. "It is small, but it isn't like you will get stuck, after all. It's so slippery you will just slide right back out. *Don't* slide back out."

It was strange, the sort of things that could offer reassurance. That she would fall out of a dirty coal chute rather than get stuck was not something Charity ever imagined she would find comforting, but here they were.

Quickly, however, she realised that she had a very different problem. "How do I *not* slide back out?"

"It's narrow enough you should be able to brace yourself against the walls with your knees. Don't worry; I will not tell anyone how unladylike you're being, you hoyden."

Charity snorted, but it was sound advice. It was a challenging thing to master—groping for finger holds on uneven bricks while holding herself steady and shuffling forward inches at a time because of her skirts. She could hear the fabric ripping as it snagged on rough edges, and they sometimes bit into her skin, but she welcomed the distraction of the pain, the ache of her legs from the unfamiliar activity.

"Keep going, Duchess," Selina murmured tauntingly to her when Charity paused to catch her breath. "What would you like to do first when you get back to London? Have a bath, or kiss Perry?"

"For certain, a bath," Charity said grimly, and Selina chuckled.

And then—she was there. Her searching fingers bumped against a metal door. It felt like she had been climbing a mile. But it was probably only a good six feet. Cautiously, Charity pressed against it. The hatch gave slowly, lifting just enough to let in a wisp of fresh air.

"It's not locked," Charity said with relief. "Thank God." But as she pushed the hatch door open wider, she realised that a brick had been keeping it closed against vermin. It slid off the metal noisily, landing with a thud on the ground.

Charity froze, uncertain what to do.

"Bellrose heard you. I can hear him walking around inside. Move, Your Grace!" Selina hissed, and Charity shoved the hatch fully open, whimpering in fear.

Terror gave her wings as she crawled out of the hatch as quick as a wink, then turned around, looking into the dark hole. "Selina! Are you climbing out?"

"No, Charity," she said gently. "I won't get out without a boost. It was never going to be possible for both of us to get out this way."

Peering over the edge, Charity couldn't hear any movement from the marchioness. "Selina! We were supposed to be going together!"

"I lied. Do not waste your chance!" she barked. "Go! Get back, stop them, and help protect Perry."

Charity hesitated only a second longer. Then she turned and

fled, vaulting into the night with her lungs burning and her heart thundering in her ears.

Behind her, the last thing she heard before the coal chute swallowed her escape was the unmistakable sound of Selina's voice raised in furious challenge.

~

Even though she began her flight by crashing into the hedgerow, leaving a long flap of her skirts hanging on the branches, Charity would remember later that fortune smiled on her several times that night.

How ironic it was that she had been kidnapped while wearing the sturdy boots meant to protect her sprained ankle! It would have been impossible to run in slippers, and even walking in them would have been a task.

Second, the half moon and the stars gave her just enough light to make out the track. Charity bolted along it as fast and as long as she could run, only realising once she was too winded to continue that she should get off the road and out of sight. Blessedly, the filth on her made her a wraith amongst the shadows.

But as she stopped to catch her breath, it was then that she remembered she had no idea which way she was going, and frantic, she huddled, shivering in a ditch by the next hedgerow. By dumb luck, her blind flight had been in the right direction. Along the horizon was the faintest wash of light, and Charity blessed Selina's name over and over. She did not know if she would have thought to look for it otherwise.

Lastly, Selina had, by some miracle, kept Bellrose occupied long enough that Charity could do all these things before she heard him finally running down the traces, looking for her.

It was a good thing Charity was too numb to cry. Instead, she burrowed herself into the dirt and branches, cowering for a long, long time as Bellrose snarled, searching. And then, not finding her, he gave up and turned back, going back to the house.

No. He was probably going back to Selina.

Was the woman still alive? She had to be. The marchioness was far too clever and *stubborn* to be laid low by a man-shaped stain like Bellrose.

Charity finally got up again, this time driven by a painful need to keep moving. She had to get to Perry. If she could warn him about Chandros, maybe Perry would know how to fix everything. He could help Selina. She no longer even cared if they stopped the counterfeiting scandal.

But how to make sure she could find her way back to this place? She threw her hands up in the air in frustration. They landed on the edge of her torn skirts, and the rips gaped, exposing the cleaner white shift beneath. The white cloth fairly glowed in the moonlight.

With a curse, Charity pulled back her skirts and ripped a chunk from her shift, leaving two small fluttering strips on her hedgerow. And then she kept on, trotting as fast as she could through the softer dirt on the side of the road, where she could more easily hide if she heard someone moving along the roadway.

She didn't know when it was that she began to pray, but it began as formless yearning. For hope. The safety of Selina and Peregrine. For the distance to close between her and London's streets. She prayed for just a whisper of the strength that had given her best friend the courage to persevere when she had faced down calamity.

It was much later that she realised her supplications were directed not to the heavens, but towards Peregrine. *I am coming back*, she promised. *Wait for me? Please. I am coming.*

It kept her from being afraid in the darkness, leaving pleas and scattered bits of cloth like a trail of breadcrumbs.

She had no idea how long it took—hours, it must have been—before she stumbled out of a wooded glen and into view of a line of gaslit streets. And as she looked around, she realised she was in Hyde Park, not too much farther from Grosvenor Square.

Charity could hardly believe her luck. Bellrose's house must have been in Kensington.

So close, so close. Tears finally began to stream down her cheeks as she kept moving. It felt like a dream when she saw the familiar shape of Atholl House looming ahead, windows lit. Was the night still so young?

Her relief at finding herself finally home was so overwhelming that she collapsed on her knees, right in the front drive, her stamina wholly spent.

Atholl House was as busy as a beehouse, because it was not long before someone saw her shadow through the window. And the front door flung open—her footman shouting out a demand to *get lost, you filthy beggar!*

She couldn't find it in her to respond. But his demand attracted the household's attention, and only a breath after his order did someone issue a short scream. Everything happened at once, then. Or, actually, things began to blur together as she finally began to swoon. Too little sleep, too little food, and too much laudanum.

All she knew for certain was that Peregrine had spotted her. He had come to her house, looking for her? Now he ran across the lawn as the world began to tilt, snatching her into his arms and cradling her to his chest.

And the last thing she heard before darkness claimed her was the sob of her name.

24

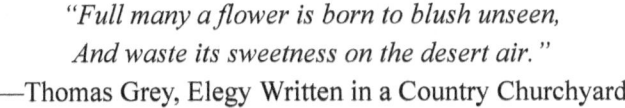

"Full many a flower is born to blush unseen,
And waste its sweetness on the desert air."
—Thomas Grey, Elegy Written in a Country Churchyard

"Take her upstairs!" Charity's housekeeper told Peregrine, rattling orders to nearly everyone who dared to gawk. Her household staff scattered in a flurry of activity, rushing to get water and linens, a sewing kit, and everything else she asked for.

In his arms, Charity regained her senses with a jolt before he had barely crossed the threshold. "I am all right," she said, clutching around his neck. "I was just dizzy with relief for a moment. Oh goodness. Perry, you should put me down."

He tightened his grip, balancing her in his arms as she struggled away. Her voice sounded faint and exhausted. "I absolutely should not," he informed her.

"But I am ruining your clothes," she protested, and Ravenscroft snorted.

"Poetic justice if there ever was any," the magpie muttered.

Perry slanted Ravenscroft a minatory look as he passed by. "You could grind half the coal in London into my coat and I would not care," he told her. *As long as I don't have to put you down.*

As he moved from the doorway towards the stair, it seemed like everyone had found a reason to push into the entrance hall to get a glimpse of Charity—even if only for a moment. It was as though her household wanted to reassure themselves of their mistress's well-being. He couldn't begrudge them. Despite how brief her marriage had been to the duke, the Atholl servants had clearly taken Charity to their bosom.

"Did you flee from a coal mine?" Prinny's wit asked their backs next.

"Perhaps I look like I have climbed out of a coal chute," she blurted out, and then she put a hand to her mouth, her shoulders shaking as she tried to keep slightly hysterical laughter buttoned down.

"For God's sake, Maggie. Do you have to be like this now?" Peregrine said testily as Charity flushed with dismay that others were seeing her like this. Pointedly ignoring the older man, he strode up the stairs. "Nobody cares how you look, Charity. I'm just—" the words stuck in his throat. "We're all just happy you are still alive."

"Get me upstairs, please, Perry," she whispered, no longer fighting to get down.

She was in a dreadful state, white as paper beneath the black marks on her skin. "Easy, Sparkles," he whispered to her, touching his temple to her forehead. "I've got you."

He carried her straight into the bedchamber, the maids and housekeeper hurrying in behind. Charity clung to his coat as he set her down on the edge of the bed, and he lifted her hands in his, seeing the scrapes on the pads of her fingers and the dirt beneath her nails. That, and the rips on the knees and bodice of her skirt suddenly made her comment sound anything like a jest.

"You really *did* climb out of a coal chute," he breathed. She must have been both desperate and terrified.

"Yes. Selina—" her voice broke. "Selina helped me get out."

Ice slipped down his spine. Since Charity had returned alone, he had been afraid to consider what that meant for Lady Normanby. "Then you saw the marchioness? She was with you? Where is she now?"

Charity swallowed several times, her eyes welling with tears, and her chin dropped to her chest. "S-she's still there, in the house in Kensington. The shaft was too high for someone to climb without help." Wet trails began to form on her cheeks, then. "She told me we'd both go. But she knew that would be a lie. She told me to leave without trying to help her. So I could let you know…" Her words faltered again.

"I am sorry. I know you are here to help Her Grace, but we need a moment." Peregrine turned to the fluttering women, pointing them firmly towards Charity's sitting room. "For now, you can guard her reputation from there."

Then without paying the servants any more attention as they filed out, he dropped to a knee in front of her, forcing her to look at him as he examined and kissed the battered tips of her fingers. "This isn't your fault, Charity. The marchioness would reckon the need correctly. I need you to go back. Tell me everything that happened once you left the Palace."

"General Billingham gave us both over."

He nodded, since they had found that part out—too late.

"After I got into his carriage, a man in a hooded cloak entered a few blocks away from Whitehall. He forced me to drink laudanum so I could not see where we were going."

He closed his eyes, gritting his teeth. "Did he harm you? You can tell me. Please tell me if we need to call a physician, Charity, because when I found torn seats and blood in the carriage, I thought I would go mad."

"No—he did not hurt me. Or her. Not *that* man," she said, bitterly. "*He* was a perfect gentleman compared to Bellrose."

She was shaken, and Peregrine struggled to put the pieces in order. He reached for her sprained left foot, relieved when she did not flinch from him. Caressing her calves, he began to unlace one boot, and then the other. "A man with a hooded cloak, you said. With dark hair? Was his cloak brown?"

When Charity nodded, Peregrine cursed. He was certain their attacker had held them alive just to lure him into a trap. "I will destroy Chandros and his lackey for what was done to the both of you."

She clutched at his hands. "You know it's Chandros? That is why Selina wanted to make sure I got away, so I could tell you that Goldbourne isn't working alone—"

"I know," Peregrine interrupted her gently. "We found Goldbourne dead, hidden inside the bank. I am guessing that was also the work of the hooded man. And when the carriage was found empty, we went looking for Billingham. But—who is Bellrose?"

"Godfrey Bellrose. He is a senior clerk from the treasury, Selina said."

"The treasury! Bloody hell," Peregrine swore as his mind put together the scattered pieces of his mother's puzzle. Regretfully, he stood up, letting her hands go. "Charity, I need to talk to Ravenscroft."

"Wait—what have you realised?"

"Goldbourne wasn't creating a scandal with false banknotes, like we thought. He was likely counterfeiting exchequer bills, with help from someone working for the treasury itself."

She blinked at him. "That's... treason, isn't it?"

"Yes. Because exchequer bills are government debt. Forging

them is not merely theft, it is a political crime. It undermines the Crown's credit and strikes the heart of the nation's purse. That is why it is treason."

"But—"

"I will come right back," he told her, tucking some of her loose hair behind her ear. "Ravenscroft is only just downstairs. I have to tell him about the treasury. Also, your servants are likely to kill me if I don't let them assist you out of these clothes."

"Then I need to do this first," she said, struggling to her feet. He caught her around the waist as she slid off the bed, and she balanced herself, resting her palms on his forearms.

Peregrine looked down at her. "What—?"

And she surged upwards on her toes, just far enough to kiss him. It was like the touch of a butterfly wing. Unexpectedly soft. Sweet, chaste, and far too brief, knowing that the door stood open and others were nearby.

He wanted to return it. To crush her to him, banish the servants, and ignore the demands and boundaries that kept blocking the way. But instead, he stared like an idiot, drinking in her face and thinking that he would give nearly anything to have her look at him like this every day. To be able to wake up to her eyes, and her smile, and that unexpected bliss that had somehow snuck into the hardened, broken places of his spirit and taken root.

It was hard to make himself take his hands from her waist. But this was too important to ignore. If they knew the list of bonds that had been duplicated, and the list of their victims, they had a chance of stopping the culmination of his mother's plan: to shake the Bank of England and throw the country into disarray before the talks in Vienna.

This scheme served his mother's need for vengeance, to be sure. But with the leaders of the world about to arrive on England's doorstep, Peregrine had a niggling thought that this might be the very clue that could point the way to where on earth his mother might be hiding with Lark. After they dealt with this, he would have to suggest they examine the invited guest list for who stood to benefit from causing such chaos—and would want to be present to witness it.

Her sad smile turned a little wry when he didn't move. "Ravenscroft? The treasury?"

Oh. Right.

"I missed you so terribly," he whispered. And then because he was an ass, and it was agony to be given hope for a future he never dared to imagine, to be so exposed and raw, he added, "And I will miss you again when I am busy talking to Ravenscroft."

She chuckled, her eyes damp at the corners. "I will be here, waiting."

He could hear the servants filling a tub in the dressing room, so it might be longer than he hoped. "I'll be back—well, as soon as they let me. And then we will figure out what to do next." He peeled his hands away and forced himself to turn on his heel.

Miller, Charity's lady's maid, gave his mouth a keen, knowing look as she passed him in the doorway on the way to help Charity out of her ruined clothes. But her eyes were faintly approving rather than censuring.

You are still steps behind, even if you send Ravenscroft to the treasury and prevent the bonds from being claimed, his mother murmured. *Chandros' assassin has been a very busy man, but he will be returning to the marchioness, to lie in wait for you. The moment he learns Charity has slipped out of the trap to warn you, he will either decide that there will be no purpose in leaving her alive, or he will wait to see if you try to rescue her anyway. And while you decide, Chandros works to escape the arm of justice. What would you like to wager he is already taking his final steps, to ensure that nothing can be traced?*

He would wager nothing against such a sure bet. Peregrine

ignored the fresh ache that took up residence in his chest. The weight as he added another tally mark on his soul.

It devastated him to know that the marchioness had reckoned her odds of surviving, and had chosen to send his heart back to him anyway. Truly, he was a curse upon his own allies.

Lord Ravenscroft had settled in the parlour to wait. He stood when Peregrine strode in, lifting his eyebrow. "How fares the duchess?" he drawled, his voice just a shade above insolence. "I trust you have been busy making her feel better."

"Watch your tongue, Maggie," Peregrine said shortly. "We have other, less inappropriate things to discuss."

"*My* tongue has been exceptionally well behaved all night," Ravenscroft said dryly, pulling a handkerchief from his pocket and offering it to him. "But if you don't want others to guess what *yours* has been up to, perhaps you don't want to walk about looking like you've been behaving lewdly with a fireplace."

Blinking, Peregrine snatched the handkerchief, scrubbing it blindly over his lips and chin. Ravenscroft grinned devilishly, but provoked him no further.

"I have solved the riddle of that list of names and numbers," Peregrine told him, annoyed with himself as he felt colour rise along his cheekbones. "I need you to go rouse the Chancellor of the Exchequer and get to the Treasury. Charity said that she was being held by a treasury clerk. A man by the name of Godfrey Bellrose. I am rather afraid that our list of names and numbers will correspond to numbers of duplicated exchequer bills."

"Bloody hell. The war debts?" Ravenscroft paled. "A rat in the treasury would have been able to steal the paper."

"And if Bellrose is high enough in the Treasury, he wouldn't have had to forge his own signature either. Also, you should find Xavier or Sidmouth, if you can. Someone may want to ride to my townhouse in the Dials and inquire with Mr Vesey as to whether he settled his debt with a transferred exchequer bill. I never thought to ask him how he paid when he said his brother went to Goldbourne's bank—I only assumed it had been regular bills. But the scandal Lord Eldon covered up may have been because Vesey's exchequer bill had already been claimed by whoever held the forged copy."

Ravenscroft nodded, straightening his coat. "I shall go right now. With any luck, that was the only one redeemed. Thank God for this one piece of good news, Canary. We might be able to warn the bank with this list and avert the rest. Stay here and take care of the duchess. And try not to do anything I wouldn't."

"Sorry. I cannot make that promise, since your behaviour ends at acting like a gentleman." Peregrine clapped the man on his shoulder in agreement. "Godspeed, Maggie."

Ravenscroft winked, and Peregrine went to check his face in the mirror. He couldn't care less about the coal on his clothing, but he did not want Charity's servants to whisper more than they already likely were. He would not see Charity driven into another marriage merely to preserve appearances.

A cleared throat at the entrance to the parlour caught his attention, and he turned to find Charity's butler giving him and Ravenscroft a long-suffering look. "Since the house appears to be open to callers this evening," the butler began cuttingly, "I should let you know a lad has arrived looking for you, Lord Fitzroy. I had him wait belowstairs."

"Send him up." Peregrine paced the length of the room while he waited, hardly daring to hope that the youngster brought good news. When a scruffy boy no older than Hodges's nephew appeared, Peregrine braced himself for whatever came next.

The boy gawked at his surroundings, his wide eyes taking in every corner of the room. Peregrine cleared his throat to recall the boy's attention.

"Sorry, guv. Never seen a house this grand before." The boy drew himself up, pretending to be closer to manhood. "Red said to tell you—what you're after's likely near a cooper's yard off Lambeth Walk."

Peregrine froze. "Red found the forgery house in Lambeth?"

Red's messenger lifted one shoulder. "Don't know, my lord. Said it smelled like a print shop."

If Red Hand had indeed found the place, Peregrine was going to owe the criminal man a rather large favour indeed. But that was a worry for another time. "Thank you, lad. Do you want something to eat before you go?"

The boy nodded, looking to Mr Pritchard for permission. Mr Pritchard gave Peregrine another look, but he escorted the boy back out.

Peregrine ran his fingers through his hair, feeling the absence of other assistance keenly. "I never thought I would say this, but if Sidmouth showed up to plague me right this very instant, I would be entirely happy about it."

"I know I am useless in a proper fight, but at least I can help call in the cavalry, such as it is," Ravenscroft sighed. "Right. The Treasury, by way of Whitehall. I trust Prinny will not be upset if I invoke the Crown's business at Horse Guards. Not about this."

Peregrine let his shoulders relax slightly. "Thank you. Take one of Charity's guards with you—at least until you get to Whitehall."

He did not relish trying to argue that Bow Street or the military provide him assistance in this. And he did not want to strip Atholl House of its protection. The assassin could just as easily be waiting right outside as in Lambeth or in Kensington. Until the man was caught, it was dangerous for any one of them to be alone.

Peregrine had to let the duchess know he was leaving. They couldn't let this matter sit any more than they could let the business at the Treasury wait. And he should remember to put boundaries back in place.

Peregrine turned to the footman waiting outside at the drawing room's door. "Could you ask that both my horse and my man's are saddled? Would you also check if Her Grace is sufficiently composed for me to have a word with her?"

He was an ogre. She had spent a day as a prisoner—who knew when she had last eaten or slept?—and now he was interrupting her bath to let her know that he had to leave. But he couldn't force himself to go without taking this moment to say goodbye.

Just… just in case the worst should happen.

Footsteps sounded rather heavily on the stairs, and he rose on his feet to meet the footman. But the person who swung inside the drawing room was not the servant. It was Charity. Peregrine caught his breath as he looked at her. She was tidier than before, but her rushed bath had not lifted all of the heaviest stains from her skin. Now that the worst of the grime had been lifted, he could see the shadows of exhaustion beneath her eyes and the scratches on her face and arms that she sustained in her escape.

His eye twitched.

Charity's wet hair had been bound in a braided bun, and she was again dressed in sturdy boots. But she was wearing a plain cotton gown. "I am ready to go," she said calmly.

"Go? Go where?" he sputtered.

She frowned at him. "You need me if we are going to find Lady Normanby, do you not?"

"Charity." His chest ached to have to disabuse her of this hope. "Selina would have reckoned her odds. Stopping Chandros's plans mattered more than her own safety, and she accepted that when she sent you out first."

Her mouth flattened into a line. Charity knew it too. "I cannot bear the idea that we don't at least try. Oh Perry, Bellrose despises her—he hit her at least twice. I am so worried about what he is doing to her as revenge now that I'm gone!"

"It wasn't a sacrifice made blindly, Sparkles. She will not thank us for going back for her if it means Chandros succeeds or you get caught in a trap. And even if I knew it wasn't so dangerous for you—I would not let you go do this alone. I have to go to Lambeth, right now. Red Hand thinks he has found the printing presses, and now that you have escaped, it is only a matter of time before Chandros learns his plan is about to be foiled. I cannot risk that word gets to him first. We will lose everything."

"No!" she snarled at him, her eyes filling again with unshed tears. "I accept that you have to stop Chandros. But I will not accept that there is nothing we can do for Selina. I will go to the Horse Guards—to the Queen. I cannot accept that we just *leave* her to Bellrose!"

"It's not your fault. Do you hear me? She will not be forgotten." Peregrine let his hand rest on the nape of her neck, bringing his forehead down to hers as he rubbed his hand down her spine. "Call for help, Charity. I won't protest so long as you have enough people to protect you. But... I have to warn you, it has been hours already, and it will be hours more before you can get a contingent to ride there."

"I know." The grief in those two words whispered against his chest broke him. "It is not a perfect solution. But even if the worst has happened... at least we can bring her home. I have to do that much."

Peregrine felt the sting of tears beneath his own lids. "You're right."

Was it selfish to want to deny her? Because he was afraid of letting her go again, without him? With another man from Whitehall who might be corrupted by Chandros? Without any friendly face he would trust to watch her back?

Hodges would be waiting. Ravenscroft would be sending the

guards to meet him. He had to leave the splendorous half of himself behind and tread a path that was full of shadows.

"Your Grace," one of the footmen in the front hallway lifted his voice politely so that they could hear him through the door standing ajar. "Someone else is arriving. I can hear a horse in the drive. Shall I turn him away?"

"No." Charity lifted her head abruptly, wiping at her face. Her eyes were faintly rimmed with red, the tip of her nose pink. But she strove to look composed. "If someone else is here tonight, I am sure it is important. Show him in."

The footman opened the front door to greet him, and a man's voice spoke in a low baritone. "Forgive the hour—I wasn't planning to arrive today, but I had the damnedest feeling I should continue through. Judging by the lights, I wasn't wrong. Is there trouble here?"

Charity's face pinched.

Boots sounded on the wooden floor as the footman brought him to the front parlour. Within moments, the doorway was occupied by a broad-shouldered man with dark hair, and brows that slammed down over his blue eyes the moment they landed on Peregrine.

Perry blinked back at him, for the man seemed oddly familiar, and it was rare that Perry couldn't quickly place a face that clearly knew his. This man almost had the look of the Percy family, but—

"Sir Nathaniel?" Charity's voice was breathless with astonishment and concern. "Whatever are you doing here?"

25

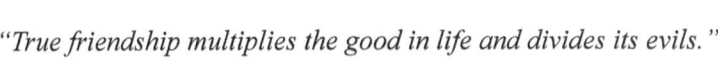

"True friendship multiplies the good in life and divides its evils."
—Baltasar Gracian

C harity was certain that she was imagining things. This was a vision conjured by lingering laudanum and fatigue. There was no way that Sir Nathanial Thorne, the brother-in-law of her best friend, was standing in her front parlour, having made the trip from the very northern edge of the kingdom.

But he had, and was there in the flesh: the elevated bastard brother of Roland Percy, the Duke of Northumberland. A good-hearted man who had loved his brother—and been loved in return. Who had served faithfully as Roland's servant just so they could be near enough to protect one another.

He was one of the men who had helped search the Fitzroy estate the very night she had been kidnapped, two months before that.

Sir Nathaniel was very keenly recalling that fact himself, to judge by the way he raked Charity's appearance before pinning Peregrine with a dangerous look, fists balled at his side.

"What am I doing here?" he repeated Charity's question. "I could ask the same of *Lord* Fitzroy."

"I am welcome here," Peregrine said blandly, crossing his arms. "Are *you*?"

"Of course he is—you both are." Charity cut off the incipient hostility with a wave of her hand, exhausted and confused.

Why was *he here?* Nathaniel looked like he had been travelling long hours for days, to judge by his wrinkled clothes and stiff posture. His face looked drawn. The realisation of when it was, and that he might be there to personally deliver bad news from Northumberland, sent her stomach plummeting to the ground.

"Dear God. Has something gone wrong? Is it Grace? The baby?" Charity asked, putting her hand over her mouth.

It was Thorne's turn to look perplexed. "They are fine, Your Grace," he assured her, before narrowing his eyes on her hands and the scratches marring her arms. "But *you* are not. Might I have a private word?"

Now Peregrine's eyes flared with recognition. "If you have something to say, *Sir Valet*, you may say it in front of me."

Thorne gave Peregrine a brief, cool look. "I find that less of an insult than you might imagine."

"*Stop*," Charity ordered them both, looking from one man to the other. The cracks on Peregrine's soul were showing again. In Nathaniel's fear that she was being mistreated by a man in her house, he had as good as accused Perry of the sins of his mother.

She let her fingers curl around Peregrine's arm to ground him. "Sir Nathaniel, he is not your enemy." She let a corner of her mouth curl wryly. "I did most of this to myself. And Perry—he came to the wrong conclusion. Admittedly, to look at me right now, it would be an easy thing to do."

Peregrine relaxed slightly beneath her touch, and Thorne ran his hand through his forelock in a nervous gesture that looked very much like his brother's. "As Her Grace says," Nathaniel agreed. "I apologise for the misunderstanding, my lord."

Perry gave Nathaniel a long look. "As do I," he admitted. "Given the circumstances of our previous acquaintance, I can see how you might... see cause for concern."

And that was when Charity remembered her last correspondence to Northumberland, warning Grace that Marian Fitzroy was taking actions against the throne—and possibly against her. She let her lashes close for a moment. "My letter to Grace. I suppose you were her response."

The corner of his mouth kicked up in that familiar, boyish grin. "Her husband's, actually. Although I am sure you can imagine how that came about."

Charity shook her head. Grace probably would have suggested coming herself, even if she had been unable to see her feet. "I did not mean for you to become mixed up in our difficulties. I was only warning her to take precautions."

"They have. Roland will not allow anything to happen to them. He has servants enough and Alnwick Castle is an impregnable fortress—or at least it is now. My presence here is as much of a precaution for them as it is to assist you," Nathaniel explained. "The Duke of Northumberland very much feels a debt to you, Your Grace, and right now, if I might be bold, my thoughts are that I am glad that I did not stop for an inn tonight, as I had first intended to. Tell me I am wrong."

"She might demur, but you are not," Peregrine said shortly. "In truth, we are stretched too thin, and have too little time to spare. The bulk of my mother's scheme plays out these next few days, and whether the government survives it depends on our ability to stop each moving part of the plan."

Peregrine's face shuttered, but he looked Sir Nathaniel

303

directly in the eyes. "Charity won't ask you to take the risk, because making yourself an enemy of my mother is as good as asking for a death sentence. But I will ask, as one soldier to another. I have to go stop the evidence of her crimes from being hidden, before they discover Charity fled their custody. But Charity's escape meant our friend was left behind. If you would be willing to help retrieve the Marchioness of Normanby, I will owe you a large debt. And if you also ensure that Charity is protected while I do what I must tonight... I will owe you everything."

Sir Nathaniel's blue eyes widened with each word, and he glanced Charity's way more than once to see whether Peregrine spoke the truth. She nodded, and Nathaniel's eyes hardened to flint.

"If another is in trouble, there is no question. Of course, I am at your service." Thorne said instantly.

Perry nodded distantly. "Thank you. Duchess Atholl can tell you everything else you need to know. Sir Nathaniel—would you please give us the room for a moment?"

Thorne divided a look between them and went back into the hallway without comment. Charity followed just long enough to speak with the footman. "Please get him whatever he needs," she said, closing the door behind him.

And then they were alone.

"Go with him to Kensington," Perry told her simply.

Charity's breath stuttered out. "I admit, I thought I would at least have to argue."

"No. He will need your guidance to find her. With the assassin free to move, I don't know if you'll be safer here at Atholl House than you will be in a carriage. And I would rather entrust your safety to him than another who might be Chandros's creature."

Peregrine looked at her as though committing her features to memory, letting his hand cup her jaw and his thumb trail along her lower lip.

"Don't," she said abruptly. "Do not look at me like we might never see one another again. Because I refuse to envision any other outcome."

He smiled teasingly. "A bold claim from a woman who believes in the whims of fate."

"Maybe we cannot control what is to come. But you were right; we can refuse to let it divide us. I will come back to you, Peregrine. I will choose you. Choose *us*. And if we always look for one another, then nothing can keep us apart. Not this life, or the next."

Peregrine seized her face in both hands, kissing her with all the desperation of a man condemned. And when they both finally parted to catch their breath, he pressed another kiss to her forehead. "It is hard to think about tomorrow when we're always fighting to survive the day. I don't know what the future looks like, Charity—but I know I can't picture any version of it without you in it."

He rested his fingers over the flutter in her chest instead of his. "My heart is here," he said softly. "I'm trusting you to guard it."

Travel weary, Thorne was glad he had washed and changed clothes at the coaching inn. He was gladder still that he had decided to visit the taproom despite the late hour instead of falling directly into bed. Because if he had gone to sleep as he wanted to, he would have missed the furious gossip that the Tory Party was nearly in shambles following the riots and scandal.

He had a feeling then. And as he asked about other gossip from the *ton*, the innkeeper had been too happy to tell him. The

Duchess Atholl had saved the princess from a poisoner, and Atholl House had been sporting Royal guards now for many days, and what did one suppose that was about?

At that point, Thorne had abandoned his luggage at The Angel except for his weapons and purse, searching for someone to rent him a horse. It had taken precious time to wake and placate the grumpy ostler, who had finally, grudgingly, rented him a swaybacked gelding—the only animal he was willing to part with, seeing as Thorne didn't know if he could have it back by the morning.

It was one of the few times he had been glad of the coin Roland had given him for this journey. Thorne thrust more money than the horse and tack was worth at the man just to get him to cooperate. And he set out close to midnight to make the four-mile journey from The Angel to Atholl House, only to find the house ablaze with lights, tense servants, a battered-looking duchess, and Lord Fitzroy.

Not only was there no love lost between his family and Lady Fitzroy, Thorne still had a set-to with the man who had deliberately gotten his brother drunk enough to shame him in front of the *ton* with that stupid wager last year. No matter how that had turned out.

But that grudge could wait for another time. While justice sometimes had a long memory, to look at Lord Fitzroy, it seemed she had decided to call in her due. And even if it hadn't, right now, a lady in trouble had to come before all other considerations.

The son had all but confirmed Roland's worst fear—that the Fitzroy matriarch was settling some unfinished business of her own. Of course, Thorne would help in any way he could.

While the duchess and Fitzroy talked, Her Grace's staff swarmed around Thorne with such efficiency, he would wager they could rival a military encampment. Within minutes, he was given a hearty tray and coffee. A saddlebag was filled with more provisions, and after a quick consultation, they decided to stable the inn's horse and saddle him a hunter. The carriage was hitched and a maid had ensured that a spare cloak had been packed for Lady Normanby.

Thorne felt like he had been swept into a fever dream. He didn't even know the entirety of what had transpired. The bits and pieces he had assembled, pulled from Charity's staff, had shocked him.

When they were ready to set out, the duchess had turned to him, explaining how she had followed London's lights east, through Hyde Park. "I left bits of cloth as markers," she told Thorne, a deep furrow creasing between her brows. "Is it enough? It was all I had."

"You did very well to do that," Thorne told her gently. "If you recall where you came out from the park, we'll know where to start."

He was sure they would be able to find the duchess's bearing. But whether they could follow her trail without the light of the sun? That was… less certain. "Tell me more about what we'll be up against when we arrive."

She told them about Bellrose. And then they were off on their mission. Himself, the carriage and driver with Her Grace inside, and the single horsed guard.

Thorne rode beside the carriage as they made their way to the park, querying her through the window more about her flight east through Kensington, following London's glow. And as the details emerged, Thorne's disbelief warred with anger.

"Here!" called the soldier, lifting the lantern.

Kicking his horse into a trot, Thorne moved forward to join him, seeing the last small piece of knotted white cloth on the branch of the tree she had left behind. Now all they had to do was find the others.

He circled the spot, trying to see if he could spot boot prints.

But between the dark, the dry ground, and the duchess's slight size, there was little to make out. So it was slow, terrible progress, especially through the park, and Thorne and the guard flanked the Town coach widely to the left and right in a shifting pattern, keeping London's fading glow at their back, trying to spot the next shrub or tree Duchess Atholl would have marked.

Things improved some when they found the dirt trace she had followed for a time, but they lost the trail at a crossroads she hadn't seen to mark, having to double back when they went too far with no sign. And when they finally found the right path, Thorne only found a single marker at the edge of the road before the freshly disturbed trail of dirt led him into the field of some pasture.

"I was off the road for a while," she admitted when Thorne dismounted to examine the ground on foot.

He nodded. There was nothing for it. "We will have to walk and look for your path."

"...May I help?" she asked softly.

The more eyes, the better. And perhaps she would recall other landmarks. "Of course, Your Grace," he murmured, opening the door and giving her his hand to help her down.

She squeezed his hand tightly. "Thank you for helping us," she whispered. "I am so sorry—"

"No, don't. It isn't necessary to apologise to me," he cautioned her.

"Then I will say how very glad I am that you are here." She let out the smallest sniff.

Thorne was, too. Especially as Charity began to tell him about what had happened in the last month. Things that she would not have said in front of the soldier, about her escape. It was unimaginable. But the trail they followed in the darkness made a believer out of him.

The carriage followed them as best it could, sticking to the trace. And hours later, as their path wandered back towards another dirt track, Charity finally spotted the double marker that she had left first.

"It's ahead. It should be up ahead from here!" she said, hugging her arms to herself in relief.

"Well done," Thorne told her, resting his hand on her shoulder as he looked around for the coach's lantern, spotting it a few minutes behind them as it negotiated a turn onto the road that would take it past the house, their horses still tied up behind it. "It's time to get you back inside the carriage, Your Grace."

There was enough light in the night sky to see the way from here. He closed his lantern, and the guard with them followed suit. Thorne let the soldier walk the duchess back to the carriage, creeping closer behind the hedgerow to examine the house.

It was entirely dark, now. But this was the place, for certain. He found the spot she had torn her dress, a swatch of it hanging from broken branches, visible in the moonlight.

Thorne brushed his fingers over the torn fabric as he listened for the guard's approach. At this time of night, the whole world was silent, and it made him uneasy. He straightened and turned back toward the house, planning to indicate to the soldier that they check around before forcing entry.

But the soldier never made it that far.

A dark shadow separated itself soundlessly from the hedgerow and struck him hard in the back of the skull with the butt of his knife. The guard collapsed without a cry, tumbling into the grass.

Thorne leapt out of the way, barely evading the hissing blade arcing across his midriff.

The hooded man was already on him.

26

"The best revenge is not to be like your enemy."
—Marcus Aurelius

With all the properties to search, Ravenscroft must have had trouble rousing more help from the Horse Guards, Peregrine thought. Because he and Hodges still managed to arrive before them, despite his delays. And only three members of the mounted cavalry had arrived to see what so desperately required attention at this hour of the night.

A corporal and two troopers. They were further unimpressed by Peregrine enforcing the need for stealth, but this part of Lambeth was as silent as a grave. Perry had heard the clip of the horses' hooves coming from a distance, and had intercepted the men well before they came within sight of their target.

All five of them left their mounts some two blocks away with a wide-eyed stable lad near an inn, approaching on foot to survey the building. The Blues had abandoned the shine and plumage, blending into the shadows with their dark blue coats. And despite their heavy boots, they moved as quietly as they could, dodging rats and the occasional night watchman dozing against a wall.

The two-storey building stood squat and grim near the muddy waterline, where fog clung low to the ground and the stench of tar and river rot drowned out most other scents. A former cooperage or warehouse, by the look of it. Broad-shouldered, soot-stained, and anonymous.

From the front, it looked like just another brick structure with boarded windows and a heavy timber door that bore no signage. And there was no indication of their business sitting out to be discovered, in the alleys or by the doors.

But Red Hand's messenger had been right. Sometimes, when the fitful, fetid wind blew across the water of the Thames, he could catch a bare whiff of ink and oil. There was no doubt that there was some sort of illicit press here.

But what gave him pause was a single light shining in one of the upper windows, a beacon in the darkness. Peregrine didn't trust it. At all.

"Don't know what to make of that. How do you think we best do this? Loud? Or quiet?" the corporal asked him.

Peregrine weighed their options, feeling his skin crawling. Even though he was also filled with misgivings about the light, he did not see how they could avoid checking the building. "We go in quietly—and carefully, if we can."

Beside him, Hodges tightened the cinch on his pistol belt and adjusted the carbine across his back. The three guards checked their sabres and flintlocks.

They approached in a staggered line, careful not to bunch together or let their boots ring too loudly against the cobbles. The warehouse loomed larger the closer they came. It was ugly and inert, but not empty. Not quite. Peregrine had the queerest sense that someone was waiting for them with the light upstairs.

At the door, Hodges crouched to examine the box lock on the

front door, cracking the shutters on his lamp for more light. "It's a new one," he murmured, tracing the edge of the bolt. "Fitted recently." The corporal tapped one of the troopers, indicating he should go around to find whatever back door existed.

"Can you open it without noise?" Peregrine asked Hodges in a low voice.

Hodges peered at it and grunted. "Given a minute."

Peregrine gave him a nod and turned to the others, sweeping the narrow street and the empty windows of the buildings nearby. No movement. But the warehouse gave off the sense of held breath, like something inside it was waiting to happen.

The lock gave a soft click, and Hodges eased the door open with more care than he would typically bother. The air inside rolled out over them. The scent of ink and oil, yes, and paper.

But also of something sharper that Peregrine recognised from hours spent at an easel with a paintbrush. Turpentine.

The corporal bristled at the smell, also knowing what it represented. "Cover this door, Lucas," he murmured to the other trooper. "I don't fancy the idea of someone blocking our way out."

"Aye, sir," the trooper whispered back.

The three of them crept deeper inside, slowed as they checked every corner. The air was close and hot, too warm for the hour. A long workbench stood to one side, cluttered with rags, brass typeset, and sheaves of smeared proofs. In the centre, the printing press itself loomed like some mechanical beast.

Hodges hissed a soft noise, examining a box that sat in a corner. Unprinted paper of a creamy, high-quality kind. But as Hodges held it in front of his lamp, a watermark shone cleanly through. It was stolen paper from the Treasury—the most difficult and necessary part of creating a forgery that would pass inspection. Likely, it had been acquired by the disaffected Godfrey Bellrose.

This was the right building, then. The place where they had created the forged exchequer bills.

Any satisfaction Peregrine had was tempered by the other details that set him on edge: a shattered water barrel in the corner, sand scattered across the floor, a bundle of rags tucked under the stairwell, and many open containers of solvent left dangerously near the lit stove.

They had the right building, but someone had laid the groundwork for a fire, planning to burn the remaining evidence to the ground.

"Corporal," Peregrine muttered. "We are standing in a bonfire waiting to happen."

"Agreed, Lord Fitzroy," the man said through his teeth. "I think I shall check to see if any of the sand or water barrels are still full. And perhaps do what I can to ensure that the turpentine does not light by accident."

Peregrine nodded, tapping Hodges's elbow and pointing with his chin to the stairs that led up to the next level. Hodges nodded and began climbing them, careful to test each step with his weight. Peregrine followed behind.

The closed darkness of the offices on the first storey gave Perry gooseflesh. And above, the U-shaped mezzanine and its light in the darkness beckoned. Peregrine withdrew his own pistol, setting his hand on the rail to go upstairs. Hodges nodded and lifted his lamp to investigate the level they were on.

The gallery overlooked the working floor, and even from the stairs, Peregrine spotted the single lantern perched on a crate atop the dry boards at one end, close enough to the window to attract notice. But there was nothing else there.

Hurrying downstairs as quietly as he could, Peregrine went in search of Hodges and the offices. The first office's door was cracked ajar, but as Peregrine pushed it further open, the copper smell of blood wafted out.

Bodies. Lower class men, by their clothes—the forgers and printers, Peregrine guessed, by the ink on their arms. And lying across the pile of bodies, one other shape that was far more familiar, his hand lax atop his carbine.

Hodges.

Peregrine rushed forward, reaching for the man's neck to check for a pulse. And he found it—slow and steady. But the man's hat was missing, lost when he had been bludgeoned across the back of the skull and left here with the dead.

A footstep broke the silence behind him, and Peregrine surged to his feet. An older man's figure emerged. Tall, composed, and clad in the sort of tailored coat that didn't belong in Lambeth at all, let alone a warehouse at three in the morning. The lamp in his hand shaded his face oddly, but Peregrine saw enough to recognise him.

"Lord Fitzroy," Duke Chandros said, voice calm, as though greeting him at a club. "I was wondering when you would arrive. You took a little longer than I expected."

Peregrine sized up the situation in an instant. He was younger, stronger, and certainly determined enough to overpower the older man. But if that lantern fell in the wrong spot, the building, and those inside, would go up in flames. The guards were too far below to offer any immediate help. And so, Peregrine forced back his urge to repay the man for what he had done to Hodges.

"You will have to forgive my delay, and my surprise. I didn't expect you here at the scene of your villainy, Chandros," Peregrine countered. "Much less standing over bodies."

The duke cocked his head in agreement. "I do not enjoy getting my hands dirty, and the Maker is certainly a dabber hand in killing. But he is busy doing his final parts, as I am doing mine. And I had a feeling you might find your way here after finding Goldbourne. So I waited, and lo! Here you are."

Peregrine remembered that ticking sense of doom that had

plagued him these past two weeks. That sense that his mother's plans marched forwards to some timetable of their own. "I hope that you don't imagine you somehow will survive allying with my mother, Chandros."

The duke smiled softly, an expression which gave Peregrine nearly as much of a chill as watching humanity leave his mother's eyes had. "No, I don't expect to survive it. And neither do I expect you to understand why I am playing this role."

"By all means. Test your logic out on me," Peregrine snarled.

"You are such a tragedy," Chandros murmured, raising his lantern so he could better study Peregrine in the light. "You inherited her intellect and skills of deduction. Her charm, her memory. Everything, really, except that sense of ambition that drives her to such astonishing heights."

He wanted to laugh. "Do not tell me that you *admire* her."

"Of course, I do! Oh, I admit, it took me far too long to overcome my prejudices. A mere woman, after all! I regret it took so long, because I wonder how much more could have been done if I had taken a place at Marian's side while you were still a child."

The statement raised Peregrine's hackles. "I shall remind Your Grace that my mother is a monster. Although judging by the blood currently on your hands, perhaps you consider that a tolerable flaw."

The older duke shook his head. "No, Fitzroy. The flaw is borne in you, and that is why it is so regrettable. In the end, your sentimentality ran too deep to be cut away. To the flock, of course, the wolf must always seem a monster. But I look at your mother and I see the most splendid predator this world has ever seen."

"You are barking mad to countenance her actions," Peregrine hissed. "There is *nothing* to commend her for."

The duke *tsked*. "Here is where we will perhaps

fundamentally diverge in opinion. Given the struggles you have had keeping up, I think even you must agree, she possesses one of the greatest minds of our age. Watching the way her thoughts work, completely untempered by matters of morality—it has been breathtaking to behold. The only thing that would have been more spectacular would have been completely winning over the marchioness and also pressing her clever mind to work. But Selina's a pale star compared to the sun."

"Lady Normanby has a soul. She would never do the things my mother would."

"And more's the pity. *That* was another wretched piece of luck, by the by. Not only did Selina limit herself, she grew attached to the misbegotten son and placed herself on the wrong side as a result of things. We might have broken the back of England before now, the three of us. Perhaps four—but Goldbourne was too concerned with the size of his purse for my liking anyhow."

Peregrine shook his head. "To what end?"

"That would be telling. But you already know the British empire looks down the road towards its end, Fitzroy. Change is in the wind. The colonies grow fractious. The Crown and Parliament are the corrupted legacy that needs to be cleared away, weighted down with small minds who cannot fathom how to build a greater empire. Your mother has shown me what we could build. I am too old a man now to be of much use. But I would see the world burn if it cleared the ground for her foundation."

Peregrine stared at the man. "My mother's empire was built on evil. You can't hide what she's done. And when the truth comes to light—when they finally see her for what she is—they'll cast her down."

"No, they won't. Goldbourne and I have done our part. I know you have seen our efforts. The accounts in your name. The silenced past. I left a letter to be delivered to the press in a few days' time. My shocking confession will ensure the blame for the counterfeiting will fall on my head. The Maker will erase the final few names from the books, and there will be no proof of anything your mother has done, except in the rumours of a few people unable to prove it."

Duke Chandros shuffled backwards from the doorway, holding the lantern high. "The truth will die with us, Fitzroy. And the story I left behind? That is what they will remember."

"Chandros! Stop!" Peregrine shouted.

But the duke's arm was already in motion, and he hurled the lantern over the railing to shatter on the floor below.

27

*"True bravery is shown by performing without witnesses what
one might be capable of doing before all the world."*
—François de La Rochefoucauld

T horne staggered back, boots skidding in the damp grass as
the hooded man's knife swept past his ribs. He hadn't time
to draw breath, let alone his pistol. Taking advantage of Thorne's
surprise, the man in the hood closed with him, pulling his arm
back to strike again.

He was too close. Unarmed, Thorne ducked, twisting
sideways and leaning on his years of pugilistic training with
Roland. He launched a brutal jab to the man's gut to force his
attacker backwards. It landed with satisfying force, breaking the
rhythm of the attack. The hooded figure grunted but didn't falter
for long, pushing forward once more.

Getting his feet firmly beneath him, Thorne launched his
weight into the man, crashing against him, chest to chest, and
knocking him to the ground. He caught himself before he fell with

the man, dancing backwards enough to try to gain the space to finally draw a weapon.

The man rolled towards him, slashing at his legs, and Thorne retreated farther. This wasn't a brawl; it was a hunt. Whoever this man was, he was no treasury clerk, Thorne's brain registered. He was a killer. A man who had been waiting for them to arrive.

Fumbling at his holster for the handle of his pistol, Thorne sought to draw the weapon, and his attacker sprang to his feet, stabbing his knife in a downward arc towards Thorne's exposed neck.

By some miracle, Thorne shifted his focus in time to catch the man's wrist in his left hand, arresting the motion. But the point was still too close to him, and the killer kept the pressure on.

He had healed a great deal since last summer, but his left arm and shoulder was still weaker than before his misadventures in Brighton. Thorne's breath hissed between his teeth, his arm began to shake beneath the strain of keeping the point away.

In desperation, Thorne slammed the knuckles of his empty right fist into the man's eye.

The killer's head snapped back, and he snarled in pain. "You're not Fitzroy," he growled. "Who the hell are you?"

"A friend," Thorne panted, seeing the man's stubbled face peering at him. The hood had fallen back, revealing pale angles and eyes cold with intent. He shoved the man backwards, thrusting his hand into his pocket to grip his own knife.

Thorne barely got his own blade up in time. The attacker slammed into him, and the two went down hard, grappling in the wet grass. Thorne used his greater bulk to flip them, trying to pin the man's arm, but the attacker was fast and wiry. The knife grazed along Thorne's left shoulder, cutting into the cloth and kissing the skin. A trickle of blood spread beneath his collar, barely a scratch.

And then the man hit him, hard, with an elbow to the jaw.

Disoriented, Thorne ended up on his back, and blindly stabbed at the man, catching him in the gut. But it wasn't a fatal wound. Or at least, it wouldn't kill him quickly enough.

Not before this killer managed to end him as well.

As Thorne tried to buck the man atop him off, a shot rang out, nearly deafening him with its nearness. The killer went slack immediately, slumping slowly to one side.

Disgusted by the brief view he caught of what the shot had done to the killer's face, Thorne heaved the corpse off him, rolling onto his hands and knees so he could get up. If anyone else inside wasn't aware of their presence, they certainly would be now.

The guard was sitting up, near the hedgerow, still holding a flintlock. But he dropped it, leaning over to vomit.

"Are you all right?" Thorne rasped.

"Had my brains rattled," he said, spitting into the grass before he lay back down with a groan.

Thorne supposed he should be glad that the man's shaken aim hadn't taken him out. "Glad you still could make that shot," he said as he got to his feet. "Can you mind this door if I leave you here?"

The guard nodded, taking a moment to collect himself. Thorne was happy the soldier was willing, because he really had no choice but to leave the man there.

Thorne picked up the soldier's lantern, since the house was pitch dark, and his had broken when he dropped it after being attacked. There was no chance he was getting caught out a second time. He stepped carefully over the assassin's corpse, lantern casting long, twitching shadows across the grass as he approached the house.

The front door had been left ajar—just enough to let someone slip out silently. Or in. Thorne tested the threshold with his boot, then pushed the door open fully, holding the lantern high.

The air inside was cold and stale. The kind of air that came from hours without a fire. Thorne moved slowly, boards creaking underfoot. To his left, a front room lay in disarray—dust, rat droppings, a pile of old firewood, long since mildewed. Empty.

He turned toward the stairs, listening, and caught a faint scuff. Someone was upstairs.

Thorne crossed to the staircase and began to climb, placing each foot with care. His lantern swung slightly with each step, throwing light and shadow across the cracked plaster walls. He reached the landing and turned, scanning the hall.

He didn't bother whispering warnings or calling out. If they had a weapon, he wasn't giving them a head start. The first door he passed looked like it had been a child's room, abandoned and stripped. The second was locked, but he could hear shifting inside.

With one hard blow, Thorne kicked the rotting door in.

The man inside had been halfway out the window. Godfrey Bellrose—at least, so Thorne assumed—froze, one leg already slung over the sill, the other caught in his coattails. The expression on his face, caught between panic and indignation, might've been comical if Thorne hadn't been so angry at the coward.

What sort of *man* did such things to women like the duchess described?

"Go on, then. Jump," Thorne told him, his voice like dark velvet. "But you'd best be sure you can outrun me. Because when I catch you—and I *will* catch you—I'll see you pay for every hurt you let them suffer. Threefold. With interest."

Bellrose looked down, some twelve feet to the ground. And then he looked back at Thorne.

"What'll it be, Bellrose?" Thorne asked him. "Do you feel like luck is on your side?"

Slowly, Bellrose lifted his hands, and Thorne was almost

disappointed. He crossed the room in three steps and yanked the treasury clerk back from the window, none too gently. Bellrose sagged in his grip, but Thorne wasn't about to trust that display of surrender. He spun the man around with a grunt and yanked his arms behind his back, wrenching free the cravat from around Bellrose's throat. He doubled it over and used it to bind the man's wrists, tight enough to bite.

Bellrose gave a small hiss of pain. "That's unnecessary—"

"Oh, it's the bare minimum," Thorne muttered, checking the knot with a hard jerk. "You're lucky I'm in a mood to walk you out instead of throwing you headfirst."

He shoved him toward the door, one hand gripping the collar of Bellrose's coat like a man hauling a sack of oats. They made an ungainly descent of the stairs, Bellrose stumbling more than once as Thorne gave him no room to dawdle. His boots knocked loudly on each step, the lantern swinging with their movement, casting dizzying shadows across the walls.

Thorne didn't speak again until they reached the entry hall and crossed the threshold of the front door. The guard blinked at the sight of them, still upright.

"Be careful," Thorne said, pushing Bellrose forward at the soldier. "This one squirms."

Then he looked past him, lifting his lantern and waving it, hoping the carriage driver would see. He needed the coachman to come closer to the house, to help deal with Bellrose and the injured soldier.

The duchess had said they had been held in the basement. Thorne uttered a silent prayer that Lady Normanby was still there, imprisoned but alive. Steeling himself, he returned inside, looking for the stairwell below. It was simple enough to find in the end, for the door was barred from the outside. He slid the bar free and turned the handle.

"Lady Normanby!" he lifted his voice as he descended. He

didn't want to frighten her if she was thinking he was Bellrose. "Are you there? I'm coming downstairs. I will help get you out."

There was no answer, and Thorne's stomach turned.

From the top of the basement stairs, he could see a squat, low-ceilinged chamber. When he reached the bottom, all he saw were storage shelves lining the walls, most of them empty. Crates and broken chairs had been shoved into corners.

No sign of the missing woman. But then, he noticed yet another door, held shut by a shiny padlock.

The iron keyring for it was hanging on the doorknob, so confident had Bellrose been in their captivity. "Lady Normanby?" he called again, reaching for the keys. "I'm unlocking the door."

As he pushed open the wooden panel, the smell hit him first. Musty stone, damp coal, and the sharp, sour smell of sweat and fear, mingled with the other unpleasant results of keeping someone imprisoned.

It reminded him far too much of the last time he had found people being held captive, and for a moment he struggled to remain calm, torn between anger and fear that he had arrived too late.

Chandros's lantern arced to the floor and shattered below with a sickening *whuff*. The ink and turpentine caught immediately, and the flames exploded outward like fingers clawing at the air.

Peregrine could hear the shouting from below—the men from the Horse Guards. But he couldn't see, because Duke Chandros now stalked towards the office door, the intent writ clear on his face.

He intended to shut Peregrine in with Hodges, letting the fire take care of the rest.

Snatching Hodges's carbine from next to the man's fallen

body, Peregrine spun and leveled it at the duke's face. "Step. Away. Step away from the door," he intoned as Chandros lifted his empty hands slightly as if in surrender.

The duke cocked his head at him, a mocking smile hovering on his lips. "Do you think that it matters if you point that weapon at me? Dead is dead, Fitzroy, whether it comes by fire or bullet."

Perhaps you should shoot him, his mother suggested.

And put more blood on his hands. Not that he was a stranger, anymore, to ending someone's life. But this felt different. This *was* different, and he knew it—staring an unarmed man in the face while he pulled the trigger. Even if that man was standing between him and the path out, planning to hold him and Hodges here until the fire made it impossible to escape.

Chandros knew it too.

You should know better. Your emotions are why you're going to burn in the first place.

Either way, Chandros and his mother thought they would win this fight. He would continue his slow soul-death, or he would die by their hands. Perhaps in this very building.

But Peregrine was growing mighty tired of people who wished to control him. If others snared him by what they thought were his weaknesses, if they thought that they held a tame animal on the end of their leash... he was prepared to show them how very wrong they were.

If he was damned for this, so be it. Holding Chandros's eyes, he pulled the trigger.

Peregrine had only the briefest satisfaction at the surprise that bloomed on the duke's face. Whether he truly intended to die here or not, clearly he had thought Peregrine didn't have the balls to shoot him.

But he didn't linger on the feeling to gloat. Even before Chandros began to fall, Peregrine was turning, dropping to one knee as he yanked his unconscious driver across his shoulders and spun for the door.

The duke was still alive, though choking—bloody foam at his lips. Peregrine didn't slow to give him mercy. He could feel the hungry fire's rising heat, Hell reaching up to claim him for his myriad sins. But he was not ready to cede to the flame. He ran for the stair, freeing an arm to protect his eyes against the searing blaze of light.

As he drew up to the edge of the mezzanine, he could see the way the cracks of the boards below his feet began to glow. The flames licked around the edge of the stairs in the middle, blackening a growing circle. The press below had already vanished behind a wall of rising smoke, and the first support beam beneath the gallery was glowing at its joints.

"Lord Fitzroy!" the corporal shouted, pointing at one end of the stairs. "Stick to the wall!" The man had tied his neckcloth around his face and was trying to clear a path for him, dumping sand on the fire where it ate at the stairs.

Holding Hodges as he was, Peregrine couldn't cover his face against the choking smoke, and it began to make him cough. Breathing as shallowly as he could, he began to descend the burning stairs, feeling the fabric of his clothes grow hot. He hissed against the singe of it.

And as Peregrine crossed the half-eaten halfway mark safely, where the stairs had groaned beneath his weight, the corporal judged it safe enough to charge forwards, taking Hodges's body. He shouted at one of the others, who threw his shoulder beneath Peregrine's arm, hurrying him to the exit and freer air.

The eastern sky was turning a lighter shade. Dawn was near, and the neighbourhood had already begun to respond to the threat of the burning building. All four of them were dragged further away as the bucket brigade fought to contain the damage to the single building before it could spread.

The trooper, Lucas, knelt beside them, wide-eyed and blackened with soot, patting out a place where Peregrine's sleeve smoked. And then he checked Hodges. "He's still breathing, thanks to you, you madman. You nearly killed yourself to save him."

The man's voice was awed, so Peregrine focused on his own breathing instead of taking offense.

"A real hard case, this one," Lucas continued. "But he's got a lump on his skull."

"He's hard-headed, too," Peregrine coughed, and the trooper laughed.

"Well then, I reckon he'll come around."

The corporal and the others went back to help the brigade. Peregrine leaned against a brick wall and waited beside Hodges's unconscious form in the damp chill of London's morning, watching the plume of smoke rise over the city. Chandros's pyre.

"Fitzroy?"

Peregrine jerked, realising that in his exhaustion, he had fallen into a doze. Sidmouth and Ravenscroft were standing a few steps away. Then he looked over at Hodges, finding the man awake and sitting against the wall beside him. Though he looked nearly as terrible as Perry felt.

"Ah. You're not dead, then. Just doing your best impression," Ravenscroft deadpanned. "You should really expire somewhere less public."

"Call off your dogs, Ravenscroft," Sidmouth told the dandy. "Helping save England has surely earned him a few minutes' respite to die in peace."

"The exchequer bills?" Peregrine asked them, and Sidmouth nodded.

"We managed to catch that end of things, thanks to that list. What happened with Duke Chandros?"

Peregrine dragged himself to his feet, and beside him, Hodges also stood, looking steady despite the soot and blood. Thank God for small favours. "He chose to die in the fire. A martyr for my mother's causes."

"Unfortunate," Sidmouth said. "Although at least we will be able to restore confidence with the news that the mastermind behind the schemes is dead."

"And that's exactly what he wanted," Peregrine said, feeling discouraged. "He and Goldbourne erased my mother's part in everything, from this conspiracy all the way down to her lowest gambling hell and smuggling operation. I lost the little proof that remained of *everything* she has ever done."

"But there's your word, still. And Edmunds," Hodges reminded him.

And Charity—

That he had survived was a miracle within itself. He hardly dared to hope that she and Selina were safe. He had to get back to them.

"What time is it?" Peregrine asked the magpie, no longer willing to spare thoughts for the dead and the things that could not be changed. Not when now his greatest concern was for Charity and the outcome of her quest to save Lady Normanby.

"Is stupid early not enough of an answer, Fitzroy?" Ravenscroft dug around in his pocket for a watch. "It is approaching six. Wait, where are you going? We will have to discuss what to do next—the Crown—"

Peregrine didn't bother turning around, setting a course for the place that he and Hodges left their horses. "Do let me know how those conversations go. I have other important business to attend."

28

*"No man ever steps in the same river twice, for it is not the same
river and he is not the same man."*
—Heraclitus

L ifting the lantern higher to chase away the shadows, that's
when Thorne saw her—crouched low in the corner, her
back against the stone.

The marchioness was filthy, her dark hair tangled, and she
was barely wrapped in the rags that had once been her dress. But
she was awake and aware. Her eyes glittered at him with fierce,
barely restrained hostility. Her right cheek was darkened by a
bruise.

Relief warred with rage. Between him and his brother, Roland
was the one born with a furious temper. But right now, Thorne
had one to rival Roland's worst, and he held onto the urge to go
marching upstairs to give Bellrose a beating that would teach him
never to lay hands on a woman again.

But that could wait. Thorne set the lantern on the floor, lifting his hands in a nonthreatening display. And then he squatted on his haunches. "I am a friend of the Duchess Atholl."

That caught her attention. "Charity?" she finally spoke, her voice cracking. "Charity made it back to London?"

"She did," he said as kindly as he could. "She came with me. She is upstairs, waiting with the carriage."

The marchioness covered her face with her hands, shaking. But almost as quickly as she broke down, she pulled herself back together, wrapping her arms around herself. "I won't believe your lies about Charity. Who *are* you?"

Thorne began shucking his greatcoat, inching forward slowly. After the fight, it wasn't as clean as one could hope, but it would at least cover her. "No lies, Lady Normanby," he spoke to her as he would have to a frightened animal. "My name is Nathaniel Thorne. Brother by blood to Duke Percy, though not by law."

Lady Normanby's scowl faded, and she studied his face warily. "I *know* you. You're Sir Nathaniel?"

"If you do know me, then I'll apologize now, Lady Normanby. I don't remember meeting you."

Carefully, he extended his coat to her, and Lady Normanby's fingers twitched. Then she snatched it from his grip, covering herself, turning her face away in embarrassment. But once her arms were through the sleeves, she looked back at him. "That you do not remember me should be no surprise. I was present at your investiture in Brighton."

He got to his feet, taking a careful step forward to offer the marchioness his hand, and after a long moment, shakily, she took it. But he could tell as he helped her stand, as she straightened, she was hiding deeper hurts than her bruised cheek. And she let go the moment she was on her feet.

"A knight here to rescue the damsel in distress." She made a brief sound of bitter amusement. "Well met, Sir Nathaniel. I hope you had good aim when you fired at dragons."

"Bellrose is still alive and trussed up. He'll rot in the gaol. The other 'dragon' is dead," he admitted.

"A vicious brute in a hooded cloak?" she asked him. When he nodded, she sighed and said simply, "Good."

Thorne held out his hand to her again. "Do you feel equal to walking up the stairs, my lady? If not, I am at your service."

Her eyes flickered slightly, not answering. But she placed her hand in his, stepping towards him and inhaling sharply. Mindful of her hurts and wariness, Thorne lifted her, gently carrying her up from the basement.

"Put me down now, please," she interrupted him as he headed towards the door to the outside. "Those curs carried me in here and I should like to walk out. But… I will lean, if you'll allow it."

Duchess Atholl dashed over from the carriage as Thorne pushed open the door, and Lady Normanby let him go to throw her arms around the duchess. Letting them have their moment, Thorne glanced over their situation. Bellrose had been tied belly-down over the guard's saddle, and the injured guardsman had been helped up to the driver's bench.

What the driver and the soldier had done with the assassin's body, he wasn't certain. It looked as though it may have been dragged behind the house, to judge the mess in the grass.

"Our soldier here is casting up his accounts every ten minutes. Let's get everyone home," the driver said, looking disturbed, and Thorne couldn't blame him in the least. "It's nearly dawn."

Thorne made sure the women got safely inside the carriage, and he shut the door behind them, relieved that things had not gone worse. They set out, Thorne taking the lead of the guard's horse, following the procession back to Atholl House.

The first hint of the sun's rays brightened the horizon by the time the weary group made their way back to the duchess's drive. Footmen and other guards spilled out of the house to assist, getting a cart to take the still-bound Bellrose and concussed soldier to Whitehall for questioning.

Despite the fact that she was falling down with fatigue, the duchess, for her part, managed to act with an authority that impressed the hell out of him, ordering her servants to prepare food, rooms and baths for both him and the marchioness. But he noticed the way her eyes kept turning again and again to a pillar of smoke they had spotted rising to the southeast.

The marchioness refused to let them call for a physician, and sequestered herself in her room with Charity's maid and housekeeper.

Conscious about the effort it would take to heat up so much water, Thorne declined a bath but gratefully accepted a pitcher and soap, and a clean shirt and neckcloth borrowed from a servant.

He found the duchess on the rear terrace, standing just beyond the shelter of the portico, one hand resting on the cool stone balustrade as the dawn broke pale over the garden wall. Thorne still keenly remembered his long vigil in Brighton, and as she watched the southeastern horizon smouldering, he offered what comfort he could.

"It's cool out here, Your Grace. You should at least get a cloak."

She glanced over her shoulder at him, her eyes smoky with fatigue. "I think by now you've more than earned the right to call me Charity, Sir Nathaniel."

The corner of his mouth kicked up wryly. "Only if you dispense with my title. I still feel strange being called anything besides Thorne."

"We have a bargain," she murmured absently. But then she

straightened, as if recalling she had duties. "Are you in need of anything? I have sent to The Angel for your luggage. You can stay here at Atholl House as long as you like."

"That is kind of you, Your—Charity," he corrected himself at her side look. "I actually came here to see if you had need of anything."

"I could use a diversion," she murmured. "How were Grace and Roland, when you left them?"

A spot warmed in his chest as he realised how much news he hadn't had a chance to share, in all the chaos of the evening. "I forgot; I came practically as the mailman. I have letters for you at The Angel. From both of them. And I beg forgiveness for my delay in coming to your assistance. I would have pushed the post chaise harder to make up for the lost time had we had any idea how serious things were."

"It is hardly your fault," she said softly. "At the time I wrote the letter, even I had no idea how serious things were about to become. But why were you delayed starting out?" She suddenly gave him a keen look, as if she was tallying the days. "Did Grace have her baby?"

Thorne laughed. "Yes. Mother and both babes are healthy. I stalled in setting out only long enough to do my duty at church since I did not know when I would be able to return to Northumberland. Roland asked me to be their godfather."

"Both—" Charity's jaw dropped. "She had twins? And you did not tell me this immediately!" He chuckled when she shoved him in friendly pique. "Oh, that is such happy news."

"Aye. Roland, you might imagine, has been utterly beside himself. But Briggs is ecstatic, because if Roland is busy holding the babes, he doesn't have his hands free to disorder his hair or tug at his cravat."

Charity's smile was briefly incandescent. But then, as if feeling the way her cheeks stretched strangely, she let it fall.

"If you don't mind my asking," he ventured gently. "What on earth has transpired here? I confess, seeing a Fitzroy at your side was among the least likely sights I imagined."

"You might find it amusing to know that only a few weeks ago, I would have agreed with you," she admitted. "But everything that has happened... you need to know, he is not his mother. Not at all. As badly as we have been treated by Marian, it does not begin to compare to the things he has endured as her son." And she told him, then, of what had occurred, starting from the poisoning of the prince.

"It isn't my business," he said to her gently, not wishing to pry. "But Grace would have my head if I did not at least ask to make sure Fitzroy was treating you with the respect you deserve."

Another faint smile. "Absolutely, he is not. But... it seems I have become fond of him anyway. Grace will never understand why I want to be with him. No one who knows the truth of what happened last year will."

"I think Grace might take it better than you think," he said drolly. "Besides, if he's won your regard, then that is the only thing that matters."

Charity nodded, tucking her arms around herself as she shivered in the cool morning breeze. "I wish I knew now if he was all right."

He set a hand gently on her shoulder. "If he is half as clever as his mother, he'll do whatever he can to come back to you."

Despite this being one of the busiest times of day for it, the Horseferry wasn't moving because of the fire. Peregrine and Hodges had no choice but to make for the Westminster bridge. It wasn't an onerous detour. In fact, it suited his restless split between the need to get back to Atholl House and see if there was news, and concern that Hodges wasn't fit to ride.

Hodges was even more silent than usual, his face growing more dour every time Peregrine looked over at him to ensure he was still seated. "What is the matter," Peregrine finally barked at him after the third time, unable to understand the man's sour expression.

The man lifted his chin. "You should've left me, damn you. Haulin' me through half a collapsing building like a sack of flour —what were you thinking? It wasn't sensible to risk yourself for the likes of me."

The *sensible* part of his mind pointed out that Hodges would have no way of knowing he had just kicked a hornets' nest. Peregrine had given him only the short version of what had transpired, leaving out the part where Chandros had demeaned him for his sensibilities, just as his mother would have.

That Hodges's bald utterance was an echo too close to what he had told Charity that night, when he told her about Grenville's murder.

It set a spark to the powder keg of his doubt. And his temper. "If you value your position with me, then you shall *never* accuse me again of making a poor choice in saving a life instead of discarding it! Even yours. I am *not* my mother."

"'Course you're not," Hodges said, reining in his horse warily. "I'd be long gone if you were. And I ain't pretendin' I'm not grateful. Fire's a bloody awful way to go. But the marchioness sent me to look after you, not the other way 'round."

Right. Hodges saw his protection as a bloody job, not a question of his integrity. If only Peregrine's head wasn't in such a damned muddle, he might remember that. He rubbed his aching temples.

Hodges didn't kick the horse back into motion, instead giving him a look that cut to the bone.

"You still don't understand why I took the job, do you." It wasn't a question. "Or why I took Lady Normanby's coin the same time I took yours. Fifteen years I was a hired blade—hurting and killing for reasons no better than being paid, Fitzroy. And I was tired. Done with it. I didn't care if I came back from the war. Figured I wouldn't. Figured that was fair. But war didn't end me. And somewhere in all that mess, I found somethin' that made it mean somethin'."

"Protecting my sorry arse, was it?" Peregrine shot at him.

"Working for people who saw what I was—all of it—and still reckoned I was worth somethin' when I followed my conscience, not the coin." The man folded his hands over the reins. "Same way your duchess sees you. And you think I don't look at you and see myself?"

It was more he had heard out of Hodges than in the whole time he had known him, and Peregrine shook his head, speechless.

"You're not yer mother. She came into this world wrong. You didn't. Her sins ain't yours to answer for. And the sooner you believe that, the sooner you'll see takin' care of that duchess of yours might be the one bit o' work that earns back your bloody soul, you great noddy."

Peregrine stared at him. "Well. That was delicately put."

"Don't much feel like apologisin', if I'm honest. Head's pounding like the Grenadiers've set up parade drill behind my eyes, and I've got no patience left for bloody niceties. So the sooner we get to Atholl House, the sooner I can crawl into the stables and die quiet-like. Don't go planning any more heroics 'til tomorrow."

Hodges pushed his mount into a fast trot, and Peregrine's beast followed of its own accord. Which was just as well, because his hands were still lax on the reins. And though there was much still to think about, he pushed it all to one side for later. Like a candle burning at both ends, he was nearly spent.

Finding a quiet place to lay his head sounded rather good to him, too. Even better if it might involve the duchess's lap.

As they made their way to Atholl House, Peregrine decided his driver had nothing to apologise for. Because instead of simply wishing he was a better man, for Charity's sake, Peregrine started asking himself how he could make himself one.

29

"Even so I long—day and night—to return home and see the day of my return."
—The Odyssey, Book 5

The gates of Atholl House stood open. The flicker of candlelight could be seen in nearly every window, defying the early hour. Someone had kept the lamps burning—waiting, perhaps, or unwilling to declare the night over until all of them had returned.

Had he arrived before Charity, then? Peregrine dismounted stiffly, his coat half-burned, boots blackened with soot, and the fire's heat still soaked into the seams of his clothes. Beside him, Hodges grunted as he slid off his own horse, looking more ash than man.

Hodges took their horses and headed around to the side, leaving him at the front door, which opened even before Peregrine reached the steps. Charity's footman gave him a look of relief, stepping back without question. "Welcome back, my lord."

How strange, that Atholl House felt more like home than his own home did. He didn't belong here, not to the house or the name.

Pritchard, standing in the front hall, gave him a thorough raking over, and he answered the question in Peregrine's eyes. "Her Grace is on the terrace."

The butler led him through the morning room, where Peregrine could see her on the other side of the door. She was sitting on a bench, watching the smoke across the Thames, Sir Nathaniel Thorne standing a step behind and to her right like a sentry. And both turned, startled, when Pritchard opened the garden door to the outside.

"*Perry!*" Charity gasped, getting to her feet.

He must look like utter hell. His coat was scorched and stank of smoke and turpentine. A gentleman should have never shown up this disheveled and dirty, bringing such chaos to a fine house. He should have gone back to his house. But it had been utterly unthinkable that his steps would bring him anywhere else. He had to return to her, first.

The relief that she was here was so great, his ears rang with it. And so he didn't hear the words that were spoken at first, as he simply drank in the fact that Charity was alive and safe. Not until both she and Sir Nathaniel pressed closer to him, touching his shoulders as if he were unsteady on his feet.

Maybe he was. But the sensation passed quickly, and he recalled the question sitting on his tongue. "Did you…?"

"We found Lady Normanby, alive," Sir Nathaniel confirmed. "Bellrose has been taken to Whitehall. The man who kidnapped the duchess was also there, waiting to ambush us. He was killed."

Then the biggest threat to both of their lives had also been stopped. That was an unexpected blessing he hadn't counted on receiving. Peregrine closed his eyes in silent gratitude to Roland Percy for sending his brother to London. "You tracked down

Selina. And you kept Charity safe. I owe you and Percy a lot. Perhaps more than I can repay."

Sir Nathaniel's face was a study, looking at him as if he wasn't quite certain his words were genuine. But grudging respect was stamped on his features, even as he brushed off Peregrine's words. "Roland would tell you the same as I would. Blood isn't what makes family. We count the duchess as one of ours in the only way that matters, and protecting her is only proper."

"Thank you for waiting with me. You should get some sleep now," Charity told the man, touching his arm in thanks. Thorne nodded, stepping around them to return inside. And then she reached up, brushing through the soot along Peregrine's jaw. Her fingers were like ice; she had been sitting outside without a shawl for some time. "You came back to me."

"There was never an alternative," Peregrine murmured, wanting to take her hands in his to warm them. But he didn't dare touch her right now, especially in sight of her servants. "You're cold. Let's get you inside."

Charity took his hand anyway, pulling him along the hallway to her rooms, shutting the door behind them. "Your servants will talk," he said reprovingly.

"No. Not if they value their positions, they won't. Pritchard has had a word with everyone, so we can help protect the marchioness. We put her in the adjoining room." Charity reached for the buttons on his coat, undoing them and tossing his singed clothing to one side.

Something about Charity's tone warned Peregrine that Selina had suffered in her captivity. "How bad was it?"

She shook her head, tears forming at the corners of her lids as she unbuttoned the waistcoat next. "She wouldn't speak of it, not even to me. And she wouldn't let us call the physician. But I know that at the least, Bellrose beat her, bruising her cheek and more. Miller wrapped her ribs."

Peregrine clenched his fists. "I will kill that swine."

"You may have to form a line behind Thorne," Charity said wryly. "He was upset enough to truss the man like a boar for slaughter. The driver had trouble getting the knots undone enough to tie him to the horse."

Her hands reached for his cravat next, and Peregrine had only the fleetest thought that he should stop her. But he let her unwind the cloth. "Sparkles," he breathed, suddenly needing to touch her with a ferocity that overwhelmed reason. "If I can't wash this soot off my hands, I am going to ruin another one of your dresses."

Charity's smile turned impish, and she left him to walk to the basin and its towels, dampening one. But she made him hold still instead, while she wiped his face, the sooty part of his hair, and his hands for him. It was a curious torture, this tactile cosseting, and soon he was burning nearly as surely as if he had been caught in the fire itself.

When she finished with his hands, stroking every finger, Peregrine snapped. Dropping the cloth on the floor, he snatched Charity close, backing her towards her bed. "You are a wicked tease," he informed her, breathless with it. "And if you don't mean to make yourself mine, you had better say so now—because I don't think I will have the strength to let you go once I start down this road."

"I am already yours," she told him, lifting her face to his, and he kissed her with a barely restrained tenderness until his desire to claim her completely overtook his control.

He had no idea how long they slept, but it had been long and deep enough that he woke disoriented, confused by the warmth and smell of Charity beside him. She was sprawled just as carelessly as before, this time her arm flung over his stomach, and a corner of his mouth lifted tenderly as he let his hand stroke down the length of her spine.

She shivered a bit, and curled tighter against him, but did not wake.

Dim light peered through the curtains, and his stomach informed him it had been hours and hours since his last meal. But he ignored it. Not only did he not want to disturb Charity, it had been far too long since he had a moment's peace to really think about the future. A luxury he hadn't had much chance to indulge.

But with the Maker and Chandros dead, they finally had a little room to breathe. He was no longer on the back foot, doing what was necessary to survive.

Perhaps the threat against Charity could be lifted. He would have to talk with Red Hand to see what might be done. And until then, he could build up his house. Create a stronghold against future physical threats. A safe place, both for him, and also for Charity.

And maybe also for Edmunds, who had to be kept alive. The old Fitzroy butler might be the only person left who knew—really knew—everything Marian had done. They might need his knowledge; it might be the only proof that remained of her vile deeds. But Peregrine did not relish telling Charity that he was giving protection to the man who had carried out her kidnapping.

At least they did not have to worry about the yoke of the Order. Doubtless, it was in shambles, and the people who were left posed no threat to them. Pembroke—well, that man likely knew a losing battle when he saw one. Between a lack of allies and the threat posed by the Crown, he would either join their cause, or he would quietly vanish.

Hopefully the treatment Selina had endured did not break her spirit and Charity was correct, that her staff would protect the woman's reputation. The marchioness had a fierce will. But it would damage her standing considerably if word got out that

Bellrose had held her for the better part of a week, however unfair that would be.

Peregrine had been soul-sick and twisting less than two weeks ago. But being indentured to the Queen no longer filled him with the grim worry that it had before. Or… perhaps that was Charity who had changed that.

She was the other person who had a tether yet on his life, but somewhere along the way, he had accepted her hand on it, because it meant she was tethered to him, too. And unlike his mother, he trusted her—absolutely, in a way he had never believed he would trust someone again.

Charity would have responsibilities to the Queen, and if he was close to the duchess, he could protect her. And Queen Charlotte was as interested in stopping his mother now as he was. So he could bide his time, as Selina had suggested, especially while his interests and the Queen's aligned.

If nothing else, he had learned how limited Charlotte's power was. She was bound to the throne, unable to act directly, hampered by the fact that information moved slowly, when her enemies moved with speed. She needed them—him, and Charity, and the others, too. And he suspected he would need the Crown's resources for finding his mother and dealing with her once and for all.

And when he had, he would be able to break that leash to the queen. One way or the other. To finally be free—at least, of everyone except the one person he wanted to be bound to forever.

But Peregrine could sense dark crossroads that lay ahead and was afraid. Chandros's gaze held his, in his mind's eye, taunting him. Reminding him that no matter how much he wanted to be a better man, his mother would make it too easy to step a foot wrong, off the precipice, into darkness.

"What troubles you?" Charity murmured against his side, and he startled. "You went very tense."

"Thoughts of my mother," he told her, turning onto his side so he could press his lips to the crown of her head. "I am sorry; I didn't mean to wake you."

"You don't have to try to stop her alone. Not any longer." Charity lifted her blue eyes towards him, and he found himself lost in the colour of the delicate striations.

His fingers itched again to paint, to try to capture that shade. That expression meant just for him.

And for that he was... more grateful than he knew how to express. Because a month ago, the idea of trying to sever himself from this nightmare of his mother's had been crushing him. And that had been even before he had really known what odds to reckon against.

He let his fingers smooth over the wrinkle in her brow and into the glorious golden mass of her hair above her ear, speaking his fear aloud. "Just because we have defeated Chandros does not mean we are safe. She will do what she can to make sure that even if she loses, we will, too."

His mother would do her best to seize a smaller victory from the jaws of her defeat. To ruin him, if she could not have him.

Charity let her palm flatten over the healing gash in his side. "No. She may leave wounds, but they will heal. The only way she can really harm us is if we lose hope. She has no power strong enough to unmake us otherwise."

"There's one other way she can harm us," he said softly, trying to give voice to the notion that had been building in his head since Hodges's shocking speech to him. "I will probably be scouring her from my soul the rest of my life. And sometimes I still hear her words, feel her impulses. My mother ingrained it into my very being that leverage was the only way to ensure loyalty. Secrets that you hold over another are the only way to be *safe*," he said bitterly, thinking of Grenville's death, and how it had bound and gagged him.

343

She waited for him to find what he wanted to say, no judgement on her face, only patient understanding.

"I took a ledger from Goldbourne's office, and I kept it. It possesses all the information we needed to find the exchequer bills. And it holds all the information, still, that I could use to threaten the Crown if they turn against me. Proof that they have covered it up. I should give it over, I know it. It is the right thing to do, and I want to break this pattern. Her hold on me. I don't want to be what she tried to make me anymore."

"You're afraid that if you give it up, you will have nothing left to protect yourself with," she told him gently. "It is a very human thing, to defend oneself with anything at hand. Your mother won't be the first or the last to arm herself with secrets and blackmail.

"But," she continued, "it isn't true that you have nothing. You guarded yourself—both of us—from the Queen and from our enemies without that ledger. With your wits, and with our friends."

"You don't think I would be foolish? To give this away?"

"The real danger in keeping it is the temptation to use that knowledge as a weapon, but that is something I have never seen you do. I understand your impulse to protect yourself, and *I* trust you. Still, others would not say the same. So in the end, Perry—I think it would be a brave thing, to give the ledger up. Trust in yourself that you don't need it. But I will stand with you, either way."

How had he existed before this? He wasn't sure he had ever been living a life at all, unless one counted years of emptiness and self-loathing. Flipping Charity onto her back, he trapped her beneath him, letting his weight rest on his elbows as hovered over her.

He loved her. Even if the word never left his throat, there was no pretending he did not know this feeling for exactly what it was. He loved her in every mood of hers—but especially when he could shatter her poised, untouchable calm.

So he didn't try to articulate the feeling. Peregrine leaned in without warning, letting his lips brush the delicate curve of her ear, breath warm and maddeningly deliberate. Charity shrieked, half a laugh and half outrage, and he lost himself in that feeling a little while longer.

30

"No man is an island,
Entire of itself;
Every man is a piece of the continent,
A part of the main."
—John Donne

Two days later, Peregrine sat perched on the ledge of a window in uncharacteristically high spirits. It was remarkable, really, how much brighter the world looked once one was no longer living beneath the spectre of imminent death.

And also when it was the Duchess Atholl's window he was sneaking into.

The woman of the house sat at her dressing table, her lady's maid twisting the last strands of hair in place. The maid leapt backwards, her hand to her mouth, as a small shriek escaped from her lips.

"Fear not, Miller," Charity said with amusement, laying a

hand on her lady's maid's arm. "This visitor was expected. Will you give us a minute?"

Miller gave him the tiniest *look* and limited herself to an obedient nod before leaving the room.

Peregrine could not imagine Miller ever envisioned another man of his standing climbing in through the window of a woman's bedroom. *Out* of a window, perhaps. But then again, given the past month, Miller likely already thought him rather singular.

He swung a leg over the ledge and ducked his head to avoid the frame before smoothly rising. His polished boots had only the barest hint of dust on them, not enough to warrant a complaint from Charity. Still, he arched an eyebrow at the woman who held his heart. "Expected? What? No argument about me reopening my wound by scaling the trellis?"

She gave him a sly look. "I *expect* you used the ladder I asked my gardener to forget to put away so that you would do no such thing."

He made a face. "Well, that rather takes the fun out of it, now that I know you were issuing an invitation to invade." Peregrine crossed the room and pulled Charity up from her stool. He slid his arms around her waist and gazed upon her perfect face. "Are you hoping for a chance to play the role of damsel in distress?"

"More that of a siren of old," she replied, batting her lashes. She bared her teeth and nipped at the bottom of his chin. "I shall use every one of my wiles to convince you to linger behind after our guests make their departure."

Peregrine tipped her chin up and then sealed his mouth against hers, claiming her as his own. He would have continued his conquest had there not been a knock on her bedroom door.

"Sir Nathaniel has arrived," Charity's butler announced from the other side of the door.

"I suppose I should go down," Peregrine said, turning Charity back to her dressing table. And then he pulled out one of her hairpins on purpose, even though she swatted at him for it. "If Miller is not too scandalised, she can finish pinning your hair up."

"I reckon Miller has your measure. You're in a rare mood tonight. Make sure you play nicely with Thorne," Charity cautioned before letting him leave.

Of course, he was in a mood. He was actually *happy*. "Of course, I will be nice to Thorne. It is Maggie who you should worry will terrify the man into leaving."

Despite his words, Peregrine was looking forward to seeing Lord Ravenscroft, and the others invited to the evening's dinner. He whistled a jaunty tune as he hurried down the stairs to the front drawing room.

Percy's tailor must have been given full licence to dress his brother, because Sir Nathaniel's clothing was as immaculate as any man of the *ton*. Yet the man stood awkwardly in his finery, shifting on his feet near the fireplace. Peregrine resisted the urge to rib him, since the man did not have Ravenscroft's imperviousness to banter. Instead, Peregrine called for the footman's attention and turned to Thorne.

"Well met, Sir Nathaniel. Join me for a drink?"

The other man narrowed his eyes, studying Peregrine as though he expected the offer hid some sort of trick. Peregrine stood tall, feigning nonchalance, until the man's shoulders loosened.

"Port would be welcome." Thorne offered an apologetic smile. "I'm still unused to being a guest at a fancy dinner."

"You look the part, and that is half the effort," Peregrine pointed out, taking a glass from the footman's tray. "Besides, this will be far from the usual society dinner. You're among friends tonight—which means we get to gossip without worrying about who hears. Charity tells me Roland is a father, twice over? That man does nothing by half measures, apparently. How did he take the news when he realised he had found himself with double the trouble?"

"I once saw my brother, unarmed, wade into a line of French troops. I think he'd have preferred to relive that experience." Thorne's mouth twisted into a wider smile. "Still, I envy him for such a happy start for his family."

"Nothing to envy," Peregrine said. "You're a handsome enough man for someone related to Roland Percy. Take a turn around a few ballrooms and you'll be up to your eyeballs in marriage-minded mamas."

Peregrine expected the man to blush, or at least chuckle at the thought, but instead he paled. "No."

It was an uncharacteristically abrupt answer. "No? Why not?"

"I, er—I never learned to dance."

Right. Peregrine could have kicked himself. It was unlikely that someone would have taught an unacknowledged bastard how to dance a quadrille. Fortunately Pritchard helped him remove the foot from his mouth when he gave a polite cough at the drawing room door. "Lord Ravenscroft, my lord."

Ravenscroft gave a nod at the other men. "Where is our host?" His eyes landed on Peregrine and narrowed. "Is that a twig in your boot? Have you been frolicking in the hedgerows or simply fleeing another flaming ruin?"

"Hilarious, truly. You ought to take it on the stage." Peregrine leaned over to pluck the wayward greenery from his shoe. He held it aloft, unsure what to do with it, until the footman strode over and offered his tray.

And then he was possessed of a terrible, wonderful idea. Charity was either going to kiss him or throttle him. Possibly both.

"But! If you are bored and in need of a new project, Maggie, might I suggest Sir Nathaniel?" Peregrine asked, clapping the man on the back. "He has a house in London without servants, a half-empty dressing room in need of Antoine's attention, and an entirely empty social calendar. Not coincidentally, I have *also* been informed by the duchess that the Duke of Northumberland specially requested her assistance in getting him properly introduced to society. Something about a season being an excellent cure for bachelorhood."

"Fitzroy!" Thorne growled, horrified.

"Oh, don't look at me like that. Ravenscroft is, er... Well, if he hasn't exactly got a gift for navigating society, he certainly knows everyone worth knowing and also how to offend them just enough to be remembered."

Ravenscroft ignored his backhanded compliment, already sizing Thorne with the excitement of a child on Christmas morning. Mischief made, assistance rendered, *and* the magpie off his back. Peregrine stifled the urge to rub his hands together in glee.

"Good evening, gentlemen," Charity said, coming through the door. She paused on the threshold, her hands loose by her side, waiting for their appraisal.

Now he saw why she had left out the ladder. He had been outfoxed by his duchess, who had changed gowns since he saw her before, abandoning her rose-coloured confection in favour of delicate, hand-tatted lace in colours that matched his.

His heart picked up speed, part in admiration, the rest in desire.

The creamy silk beneath her gown whispered of skin lit only by candlelight. Peregrine found himself caught between the urge to drape his coat over her shoulders like a gentleman—and the far less noble impulse to forget the dinner entirely and carry her upstairs.

He gave in to neither urge, though it was no easy battle. And she fully knew it.

Ravenscroft beat him to her side, taking her gloved hand and bending over to kiss it. "Our diamond looks spectacular this evening."

"You old flatterer," she huffed. "Stand tall, Lord Ravenscroft, so that I might see what magic Antoine has wrought with your cravat this evening. You must give him my regards."

Charity ignored Peregrine and greeted Thorne, and by the time their final guests arrived, the knight had loosened enough to join Ravenscroft in gently needling Peregrine. So it was with some relief that Perry saw Selina and her partner for the evening come into the room.

"I believe most of you know Mr Xavier," she said, introducing the man at her side.

Thorne's brows raised at the lack of an honorific, but he was quick to offer a warm welcome. If Xavier felt out of place among so many members of the elite, he gave no sign of it. If anything, he kept his own council, nearly fading into the background while the others spoke.

Peregrine made a note to keep a close eye on the man. Anyone that was capable of such discreet observation was not someone to be treated lightly.

Charity had invited her guests for two reasons—first, to spend an evening in gratitude, and second to talk about what came next. Over dinner, talk turned to what Prinny and Lord Sidmouth were doing to diffuse panic over the counterfeited exchequer bills. No one wanted the government to be dissolved, handing Lady Fitzroy exactly the result she intended.

"After a brief conversation with Prinny, Chandros's solicitor was all too happy to hand the duke's written confession over to the Crown rather than to the papers. The Morning Post will run a somewhat revised version as an exclusive on the morrow."

"Might we have a preview?" Selina asked.

"Particularly if our names are anywhere included," Charity added, giving Ravenscroft a hard look.

"It will make for rather tedious reading, I'm afraid," Ravenscroft drawled. "Chandros will take the lion's share of the blame for orchestrating a counterfeit scheme—Bellrose listed, naturally, as his rather sordid accomplice. And thanks to Goldbourne's charming habit of keeping incriminating receipts, Sidmouth managed to recover most of the false bonds before they wandered too far afield."

"And Lord Eldon? Will the Chancellor of the Exchequer survive the scandal of having a rat in his employ?" Xavier asked.

"He'll be credited with uncovering the plot, of course," Ravenscroft said smoothly. "And in a few days' time, when a conveniently placed second article exposes the connection to those so-called protestors, Lord Cavendish's name will be laundered to a high shine. As for Lord Vesey's brother—well. Dueling is illegal, after all, and the law must pretend to care."

"He left for the Americas this morning," Peregrine said from his place near the head of the table, idly swirling the wine in his glass. "Determined to build a fortune of his own. In the meantime, my townhouse is empty again—I've told my solicitor to be rid of it."

His words reminded Charity of the time they had spent there. The horrible memories swam to the forefront of her mind. Of that man pulling a gun. Of the smell of blood in the air, the ringing of the gunshots. She grabbed her glass of wine and took a fortifying sip, forcing her mind elsewhere. The townhouse was also where Perry had taken her after he rescued her from certain death. It was where they had ceased being enemies and began finding common ground.

"Your Grace," Selina said, drawing Charity's attention. "Is aught amiss?"

Charity's gaze drifted to the man across from her, his white-blond hair catching the candlelight like a flare in the dark. "How can anything be amiss when for once we are all in the same room?" She rose gracefully, gathering her shawl. "On that note, I propose we adjourn to the drawing room for coffee and port—if the gentlemen can bear the indignity of being joined by their female counterparts, that is."

"We would be unforgivably foolish to deprive ourselves of your company for even a moment," Ravenscroft replied, the very picture of polished gallantry. Rising with fluid grace, he circled the table and extended his arm to Charity. "If I might have the honour, Your Grace. Lord Fitzroy and Sir Nathaniel may sort themselves out with Lady Normanby. Ideally, without bloodshed."

Charity shook her head at his boldness, amusement dancing in her eyes as she declined the offered arm. "The imbalance is my fault, I'm afraid—a failure in my role as hostess. But then, this was never meant to be a traditional dinner party." She turned toward the marchioness with a warm smile. "I shall offer *you* my arm, and let the gentlemen lead the way for once. We women will excuse ourselves, just for a moment."

Selina nodded her agreement, and Charity latched arms with the other woman, reminded of her debutante days when she and Grace would do the same. Such innocence seemed years behind her. But when she spotted Peregrine striding ahead of them, she found she could not be upset by how all life had worked out.

Charity let the men pull ahead and then guided Selina to the nearby retiring room. "I apologise for the deception, but I wanted to see how you are."

Selina glanced away, her hands running along the satin of her skirt. "Truly? Or in the polite fashion we ask when we have already decided 'I'm well' is the only acceptable answer?"

"If you are not well, I would rather know it."

"There is nothing for it but to rise and meet the morning," the marchioness gave her a brittle smile. "Because I must pretend nothing has happened, and I cannot speak of it to anyone. But... I will say this much, Your Grace. These days, I better sympathise with your fear of small spaces."

"You're wrong," Charity said softly, extending her hand. "You can speak of it to me—if ever you choose to. I didn't, with my dearest friend. Not because I didn't love her, but because I knew she wouldn't understand what it had been like for me. No matter how she tried, she couldn't have. And I would offer you the choice I never had."

Selina eyed Charity with newfound respect. "I appreciate the offer, and perhaps one day I will take you up on it. It seems you have learned a few lessons I could take tutelage from about holding one's own. But not today. Today is for remembering that we have not let our enemies defeat us, and I don't wish to grow maudlin."

And so the women returned to the wide main hall of Atholl House, their fine skirts swishing along the marble floor, walking side by side until they found the men awaiting them in the drawing room.

Soon after, glasses of deep red port wine in hand, they arranged themselves across a seating area in the centre of the room. Peregrine found his way to Charity's side, joining her on an intimate sofa for two. He leaned his leg against hers, and she savoured the warmth of him through her skirt. The comfort to be had in such a simple touch.

Peregrine drew a breath, steadying himself, and began as they'd agreed. "Though this evening has been—remarkably— without incident, I fear our difficulties are far from over. Until my mother is caught, the danger remains, both to us and to the country. I ask for your help."

Ravenscroft leaned toward Selina, eyes wide with theatrical

concern. "Did I hear correctly? Peregrine Fitzroy just asked for help? Did something fall on his head during the fire?"

Perry gave a short laugh. "Fair enough, Maggie—I likely deserve that. But really, what does it say about my desperation that I'm asking you?" His tone was light, but his gaze shifted, landing on Charity as he reached for her hand. "I've been reminded more than once that doing everything alone is the surest way to fail. And now, for the first time... I find I don't want to."

"Where do we begin looking?" Thorne asked.

"We have glimpsed only the edge of whatever my mother is planning," Peregrine said, his tone quiet but grim. "Yes, she means to do England great harm, but I doubt it is merely for her own advancement. Someone, somewhere, is giving her shelter. And given the scale of her ambitions, I very much doubt her benefactor is a man of no consequence. If we can uncover who stands behind her, we may finally have a chance of bringing her down."

"My sources placed her somewhere on the Continent," Xavier said evenly. "There were whispers of her moving through more than one foreign court, though nothing concrete. I haven't heard a word in weeks—which, I suspect, is no accident."

"I'd wager she's being sheltered by the court of one of the foreign delegations due to arrive next month," Peregrine said. "The timing's too convenient to ignore. She undermines the government, disgraces the Crown, and just in time, delegates arrive to witness England's weakened footing."

Charity gave Perry's hand a gentle squeeze. "Marian Fitzroy seeks to eliminate us because she recognises us as a threat. Each of us can be numbered among her enemies, holds particular skills, and more importantly, has access to conversations that rarely leave closed doors. We must use that access wisely and then come together to share what we learn."

"And then what?" Selina asked, her brow arched. "We

uncover her hiding place and hand it off to the Guard, as though that's ever been enough to stop her?"

"Duke Chandros's fanaticism has convinced me that a prison cell would be far too dangerous—for the rest of us," Peregrine said quietly, looking at his lap. "Marian Fitzroy needs to be stripped of every ally, dragged into the light as a traitor and a murderer, and left with no foothold. No name, no influence, no one to take her in again. And no chance to do more harm."

31

"They may suspect. They may whisper. But as long as they cannot prove it, we will remain untouchable."
—Marian Fitzroy

June had arrived fair and mild, fortunate news for the garden parties and parades planned in honour of the visiting sovereigns. London was in such a stir that Queen Charlotte had taken a full two days to respond to Peregrine's request for an audience with her and the Home Secretary. When she finally had, the answer was brisk: he and the Duchess Atholl were to attend her at Buckingham House.

What Peregrine had not expected, however, was the Queen's next move. After they made their formal obeisance, she dismissed her entire entourage with a flick of her fingers, leaving the room empty save for herself, Viscount Sidmouth, Charity, and Peregrine.

Then, at last, the Queen's posture shifted as though she'd allowed herself, for a moment, to feel the weight of the past weeks. "If I have learned anything of late," she said, with a glance toward the now-empty room, "it is that matters concerning Lady Fitzroy have advanced beyond the reach of ceremony—and that trust has become a most rare commodity." She folded her hands loosely. "Without the burden of pomp, I hope we may speak more plainly. Given what so nearly befell Parliament, you may understand why neither Lord Sidmouth nor I have any interest in handing Lady Fitzroy a victory born of miscommunication."

Sidmouth made a moue of agreement.

"I'm gratified to have your support, Your Majesty," Perry said smoothly. "Though I confess, I'm somewhat surprised His Royal Highness is not party to this discussion."

"Regrettably, my son's attentions are rather consumed with both the visiting sovereigns and Princess Charlotte," the Queen replied, her gaze shifting to Charity. "You may have heard, Duchess, that Her Royal Highness has at last consented to the inevitability of a match with the Prince of Orange. The negotiations are progressing swiftly, and we hope to announce the engagement within a fortnight."

"That is wonderful news, ma'am," Charity said politely.

But Peregrine knew Charity too well to be misled by tone alone. Her posture told a different story entirely. *Interesting.*

He had known the princess detested the match, and he had believed Charity had been gently encouraging her to accept it. What he hadn't realised was that Charity's encouragement might have masked a deeper sympathy for the princess's plight.

Queen Charlotte pressed her lips together, as though she too had caught the tension in Charity's response. But she chose not to remark on it. Instead, she turned back to Perry. "I will say, Lord Fitzroy, I am relieved that you requested this meeting rather than forcing me to command it. There is much to be discussed between us, and while I may be your Queen, I suspect we shall fare far better if we proceed in cooperation. And that," she added, her gaze steady, "requires that we are not working at cross purposes."

Peregrine offered a brief, crooked smile. "If we are to speak plainly, ma'am, I confess I am still somewhat astonished to find myself newly admitted to the ranks of the trustworthy."

"You have cheated death, what, six times now this month past?"

"I am afraid I have lost count," he replied dryly.

"Ravenscroft said seven. And if you count the Nive, you're down to the last of your nine lives, Fitzroy," Sidmouth deadpanned, folding his arms over his chest. "Best guard it well."

The Queen let out a breath. "You take my meaning. If *you* are not properly motivated to find your mother, no one will be."

Peregrine inclined his head. "Before I forget, Sidmouth, on the subject of trust—I have a present for you." But Perry made certain that he locked eyes with the Queen before he offered up the book in his hands to the home secretary.

Sidmouth took it from him, frowning as he opened it. "This…"

"It is Goldbourne's ledger. The one I copied the list of names from, that gave us the list of forged bills. I was holding it while looking for some code or clue only I might understand, because of his relationship with my mother."

From the corner of his eye, he caught Charity's smile. It was a small, steady thing, but it cut through the noise in his head like sunlight through smoke.

Giving up the ledger felt oddly relieving, like some great pressure eased off his ribs. But he was wrestling hard with the unsettling vulnerability. It was like being caught out unarmed. Naked, even.

Fear had made a convincing case for keeping Goldbourne's ledger. He'd nearly listened, too. But Charity's promise that the choice was his, that she would support him either way, felt like a burden of trust. It was even more important to make the right decision. And the fearful way was not the right way.

At least, not this time.

The Queen, he saw, immediately understood the gesture he was making, and she nodded almost imperceptibly.

Sidmouth closed his hands over the ledger. "I appreciate you giving us this. We will also be examining it. Perhaps, if we are very lucky, we will find a better tie between Goldbourne and your mother's money."

"I would not hold onto false hope, were I you, Sidmouth." In the days since Chandros' death, Peregrine had scoured the ledger from cover to cover, looking for such a sign. "But of course, you are welcome to try your hand at it."

Sidmouth's expression was regretful, and Peregrine felt a stab of it himself. "That's a pity," the home secretary said. "Because without it, we have not a whisper of evidence with which to convict Marian Fitzroy of any crime at all—much less treason."

Charity looked ill, and Perry guessed she was thinking about how her kidnapping at his ball had been one such piece of proof. Concealed for her own protection. "Nothing at *all*?" she asked. "Not from Sir David's confession, or Grace's word? Half the *ton* has been calling Peregrine the son of a traitor this season."

"Gossip is not proof. You already knew that my hands were bound when you showed up at my door with the wild tale of your kidnapping," Queen Charlotte said, letting her fingers rest against her temples. "Even if you and your companions were prepared to suffer the result of confessing the truth of what had happened, it would have been a pointless sacrifice. Difficult enough to get the House of Lords to put one of their own on trial. They would not be willing to accept your words as proof. Especially for a conviction in absentia."

"But I thought for certain Sir David's confession would have some weight," Charity asked.

Sidmouth disagreed. "A man caught red-handed in a crime? Any competent defender would simply argue that he was attempting to put the blame on a woman, and a woman who was not even there to protect herself, at that."

"And Chandros and Goldbourne scrubbed the slate well enough that we wouldn't even be able to tie her to owning the Scarlet Jack, much less a high offence," Peregrine added.

Charity let out a small, disbelieving laugh, putting her hands to her cheeks. "So not only do we have to find your mother, we have to gather irrefutable proof that she is a criminal."

Perry gave her a faint smile meant to reassure, though he felt the weight of it just as keenly. What lay ahead pressed heavy on them both. "One problem at a time, Sparkles," he whispered, low enough for her alone.

"Does that mean what I hope it means?" Queen Charlotte's gaze flicked between them. "That even without a royal command, you still intend to pursue Lady Fitzroy's whereabouts? Because I see no reason to believe she intends to live out her days quietly on the Continent."

"It would seem, ma'am, that my hopes of dying in old age may rather depend on it," Peregrine said, cynicism twisting his mouth. "And not mine alone. Mother's black list is growing longer by the day."

The Queen shifted, her expression tightening. "It unsettles me deeply to think she would shake Parliament itself. To aid a foreign power while undermining her homeland. Treachery of the most chilling kind."

"An exchange with whomever is sheltering her," Sidmouth suggested, steepling his fingers. "They may think twice if the alternative is being branded an enemy of England. But I doubt they'd consider it for anything less, especially with the conferences looming, and the temptation to gain an advantage there."

Disorientation caught Perry, enough to stir that old, unsteady sense of shifting sand beneath his feet. The creeping feeling that he was a few steps behind. He thought of how his mother never moved without purpose and never wasted a gesture that didn't serve her ambition.

His mother, who had been so silent in his head these past few days, chuckled softly, in agreement.

Queen Charlotte regarded him, her face expressionless. "First things first," she said calmly. "I want that woman found so we may know precisely what we are dealing with. Only then can we decide what must come next. Tell me, Lord Fitzroy, what can I do to assist your search?"

"Whoever is harbouring my mother will arrive with the other sovereigns," Peregrine said evenly. "These scandals were crafted as public humiliations. My mother's vanity would insist on an audience capable of appreciating her genius. There's little satisfaction for a benefactor in hearing of one's triumph weeks later by letter when they might witness the calamity firsthand."

He glanced at Charity, who was looking down at the floor, her brows furrowed.

Feeling his gaze, she lifted her head and addressed the Queen. "We need access to the delegations, Your Majesty. Not just the sovereigns, but all their ilk. With all of us working together, we can cast a wider net."

Charlotte's eyes flickered in thought. "I take your meaning. Courts can be fractious things. If she has been given shelter by a sovereign, someone's discontent might tell us what we need to know. Am I to assume you will have the marchioness's assistance?"

"Hers, and others." Peregrine spread his hands. "Sir Nathaniel Thorne has pledged his aid. Lord Ravenscroft, I believe, has a vested interest. And Mr Xavier—but he will not be able to pass as one of the aristocracy."

"How is the marchioness?" the Queen asked, her inquiry as close to regret as Peregrine had ever heard. "I am sorry that I did not decide to keep her as a guest for longer. And you, Duchess Atholl?"

"She is—we are well, Your Majesty," Charity said, giving the polite lie. But her head turned towards Perry. Her soft gaze told him that though the words might not be entirely truthful now, she believed it would be. Someday.

Queen Charlotte's brow drew down, and she gave Peregrine a look with the barest lift of her eyebrow.

What would the future look like for the falcon and the diamond? Charlotte could keep wondering, because Peregrine didn't know how to answer her. Not beyond that he fully intended to keep Charity as close as she would let him.

They would not be able to pretend they were courting indefinitely, and he would not shame her by making her into a mistress. But as for something more permanent, they had discussed nothing.

"You need access to the events, to the delegations," the Queen summarized, when no one said anything further. "What of the Duchess Atholl's guards?"

Peregrine shook his head. This part they *had* discussed. "Her Grace will not be able to move easily or attend events with guards in tow. Fortunately, I believe we have put an end to the threat against her, so you may reclaim them, Your Majesty."

"You lifted the bounty on the duchess's head!" Sidmouth exclaimed. "I did not hear that part. How?"

"It proved rather easier than expected. Chandros had used a middleman to sign the contract. As soon as the papers reported the duke's death, rendering his agent quite unable to dispute whether the terms had been honoured, the bookkeeper was content to act as though the funds had simply fallen into his pocket by accident, never to be spoken of again."

"What a happy accident," the Queen said acridly. Peregrine huffed in reluctant agreement.

"Then perhaps our tasks are not quite so impossible as they seem," she continued. "I shall see that you have as many eyes as you require to greet our guests at St James's. As for the matter of what to *do* with your mother..." Her lips pressed into a thin line. "That may wait for another day."

Sidmouth shifted position, as though weighing whether to speak up or hold his tongue. In the end, his words won out. "It will certainly be something to think about. Even if we knew where Lady Fitzroy currently resided—even if we did not have to convince a court of her peers that she was guilty—it will be nearly impossible to pull her from the grasp of her benefactor. You may find that the only way we can dispense *any* semblance of justice to your mother... would be to take a page from her own book."

Peregrine could feel the weight of their eyes on him. As if everyone wanted to see how he would react to the suggestion that assassination might be the only way to stop her.

He swallowed the lump in his throat. "I hope you are not asking me to play that part, Sidmouth. If it ends up coming to that."

"No, Fitzroy," Sidmouth said, his voice muted. "I would not ask that of you. But I did want to point out that it might be a... necessary evil."

"Necessary evils have a tendency to crawl up from the forgotten places you have boxed them in, Sidmouth," Perry told him. "Be careful."

The home secretary nodded, and Queen Charlotte gave them leave to go. Peregrine's stomach was churning as he stepped back out into the hallway.

Charity followed him. "Perry," she said, reaching out to set her hands on his arms. "Perry, I am so sorry Sidmouth brought it up like that."

"Don't be sorry, Sparkles. I daresay my mother has earned such an end. Irony and all."

She stepped closer, and Peregrine closed his eyes, inhaling her perfume. It brought him some measure of calm. "That doesn't mean that it wasn't cruel."

He cupped her jaw briefly. "Truth can be cruel."

"Perhaps," she said softly, her next words coming out in a rush. "But there is something else I wanted to ask you, before you go. The welcome reception. I—I know we have not had a chance to look forward beyond tomorrow, but… I would like you to stand beside me."

His lips parted in surprise. "Are you quite certain, Charity?"

The Duchess Atholl, given her rank, would be standing near the royal family. To put him beside her at such a public event, by her own choice, was a very bold statement indeed.

Charity's eyes crinkled slightly. "I am not particularly interested in abandoning our courtship or concealing it, Lord Fitzroy. I am ready to declare it before all… if you would like to have me."

Peregrine was too speechless to find an answer for her. But the brilliance of his smile seemed to speak well enough.

32

"The moment I heard, your father sent for the smelling salts. My own daughter, promenading through Vauxhall with Lord Fitzroy. Have you entirely lost your reason?"
—Lady Cresswell, in the unread letter to her daughter

I t was the seventh of June, and London was aflutter with news of the arrival of the foreign guests. By early afternoon, the city's residents lined the streets along the carriage route, beginning at Hyde Park and continuing through to the gates of St James's Palace.

Behind the palace gates, footmen in livery and hurried maids darted through the corridors in a flurry of movement. Garlands adorned the entrance, and the air inside was thick with the scent of fresh roses. Excitement thrummed through the halls—an electric undercurrent that seemed to hum along the marble floors and rise straight up the spine.

Inside, Prinny's only child paced restlessly, pulling a handkerchief through her fingers. She had appeared composed enough at luncheon, smiling at the guests and delicately picking at her food. But the moment she'd made her escape with Charity, the mask had slipped.

"What if he means to make the announcement today?" she cried, spinning around to face Charity. "Someone will ask and he will forget that I have not yet agreed to the engagement, and then—"

"Your Highness," Charity said gently, cutting into the histrionics. "The announcement of your engagement will be an occasion in its own right—not a footnote to a royal welcome. You've nothing to fear." She paused, then added with a pointed look, "Unless, of course, you're not planning to accept the match after all?"

"I—I mean—" The princess faltered long enough that Charity began to fear the worst. But at last, she gathered herself. "I'm almost certain, Your Grace. It's all just dreadfully overwhelming. Everyone speaks as though it's already settled." Her voice grew more agitated. "I know Papa and Grandmama want what's best for me, truly, but Prince William is so dull. And what if I hate living in the Netherlands? The Grand Duchess called it quaint. *Quaint!*"

Charity's and Lord Ravenscroft's recent visit to the Grand Duchess of Oldenburg had not tempered the woman's mission to drive the Prince Regent to an early grave. Her brother was due to arrive within the hour, and Charity had little hope the Grand Duchess would be better behaved instead of turning towards the worse.

Frustration bubbled up in Charity's throat, causing her to voice words she would have otherwise bitten back. "However well she means, you do yourself and your family a disservice by allowing her to be the arbitrator of your future happiness. Life's unpredictability is its only certainty, Your Highness."

The princess flopped onto a settee, wrinkling her skirt, and laid a wrist over her brow. "How am I meant to make the right decision?" She sighed heavily, but set about straightening herself up before Charity could intervene. "Ignore me, Your Grace. I slept poorly last night. I will do as my father expects. But please, promise me you will stand near my side in the receiving line."

"It would be my honour," Charity assured her, holding out her hands to help the princess back onto her feet. "You barely touched your luncheon; it is no wonder your head is spinning. I will ring for tea and sandwiches. Fortify yourself and I will see you again in the throne room."

The princess blinked back tears, managing a fragile smile before granting Charity leave to go. Charity pulled the door closed behind her and leaned against it for a moment, ignoring the guard stationed just beside. Today, of all days, the girl had to get cold feet *again*. And the fate of the nation *quite literally* rested on paying attention to the foreigners in the hopes they could unearth Marian Fitzroy's hiding place.

How could the princess imagine coming second to anything else when she has been told that it is her own decision which will have the greatest impact on England's future?

The voice of reason was, unfortunately, correct. Charity smoothed her skirts, taking a moment to settle her emotions. Yes, much rested on the outcome of the next few days, but Charity did not have to face it alone. And while she stood at the young woman's side, she would be well-placed to gather hints of where Perry's mother had gone to ground.

Peregrine was likely waiting for her in the throne room, keeping half an eye on the door while he circulated amongst the members of the *ton*. Desire to see him again urged her feet into motion. She was nearly at the throne room doors when she heard her mama's voice ringing sharply in her ears.

Slow your pace, darling!

Charity's feet slowed of their own accord at the order.

It allowed the woman walking behind her to close the distance between them. "That is much more appropriate, Charity dear. A duchess glides, not runs."

Charity's head swung around and she rocked to an abrupt halt when her gaze landed upon her mother's countenance.

"*Mama*?" she asked, too dumbfounded to say anything else.

"You are surprised to see me?" Lady Cresswell hissed. "Have you read any of my letters? I see you have not, else you would have known to expect me."

The letters Charity had allowed to pile up on the sideboard of her study, unopened and unread. Less urgent than the other matters occupying her attention.

"Is Papa here?" Charity blurted, leaning sideways to see past her mother's golden hair.

Her mother gave her arm a sharp rap with her fan. "He is in the throne room, where we ought to be. I gave thanks not to see you there and immediately set out to find you. Here, at least, we might speak without interruption. I have questions."

Questions which would require more time to answer than Charity could spare. "You can come over tonight, or tomorrow. I must check my diary, but I am certain I can find a window when I am free."

"I will do no such thing," Lady Cresswell muttered, seizing her daughter's arm and steering her firmly toward the nearest retiring room. "If I am to endure society's scrutiny, you will first address my concerns. The whispers are appalling, Charity— scandalous beyond comprehension!"

"The princess's attempted poisoning?" she asked hopefully.

"*Lord Fitzroy,*" Lady Cresswell hissed, her cheeks blotched with fury. "Unchaperoned carriage rides. Waltzing at Vauxhall. *And* if the rumours are to be believed, far worse."

All that and more, Mama—and I intend to do it again, Charity thought, almost giddy with defiance. She had entered into her entanglement with Peregrine knowing her family would disapprove. That they would never understand. It was one thing to accept that truth in the quiet certainty of her own room. It was quite another to face her mother's livid expression in the corridor of St James's Palace.

"Mama, it is not so simple—" she began.

This was not the time nor the place. Not that Charity had any hope her family would understand, but surely they would not deny her love after all she had faced.

"Not simple?" Her mother's gasp turned heads from those waiting in line to enter the room. "Have you given him permission to court you?"

"I—"

A fanfare of trumpets rang through the air, cutting off Charity's words. Lady Cresswell dug her nails into her daughter's gloved arm, but Charity shook her free.

"I must get inside. I am to stand beside the princess, Mama."

Lady Cresswell narrowed her gaze, searching her daughter's face for any hint of a lie.

Charity forced another false smile on her face, hating that her mama's disapproval could reduce her to a feeling like a child. "All will be fine. You will see. I am still, as ever, in the Queen's good graces."

With that, Charity pivoted and hurried to the open doorway, wielding her title and position at court like a knife to cut through the people waiting to get in. They stepped aside, allowing her to go ahead, and then closed ranks again, blocking Lady Cresswell from following.

Flames flickered in the chandeliers hanging overhead, making the precious jewels sparkle at the necks, wrists, and ears of the women of court. But none dazzled so much as the crown atop the head of Queen Charlotte. She sat upon her throne, beside her son, her bearing betraying none of her advancing years.

The floor in front of the thrones was clearing, the guests forming two lines of reception on either side. Charity caught the Queen's eye and bowed her head in obeisance. Then Charlotte's gaze slipped sideways, in a pointed reminder of where Charity was supposed to be standing.

There was no time to search out Perry, to tell him her parents were there. Or perhaps he had already spotted her father across the room, and was looking for her even now. The whispers carried on the air, speeding her steps. Only when she stood at what would be next to the princess's left hand did Charity properly search the room.

Peregrine stood on the far side of the crowd, his shoulders feigning ease. But Charity saw the truth in the line of his jaw, clenched just a shade too tightly. He must have felt her gaze on him, for he turned—and their eyes met across the distance, the din of the room fading for just a moment.

He lifted one brow in silent question. Did she still want him to go through with their plan?

It was the height of foolishness, expecting him to flout society. To expect him to abandon his station and come to her side. She had asked, but neither of them had known her parents would arrive today. It would be far simpler to shake her head. To tell him to stay where he was. To delay the inevitable reckoning.

But she loved him. To retreat now would extinguish the light she had fought so hard to kindle in Peregrine's eyes. That, she would not do. Not for her parents. Not for anyone.

So she smiled, steady and sure, and gave him the smallest nod.

The princess joined her, entering the room through a side door. Charity did not turn her way. Instead, her eyes never left Perry's as he excused himself, cutting between the people jostling for a place at the front, and crossed the empty space in the middle of the room.

He did not touch or speak to her. He did not need to in order to state his claim. All he did was pivot into place on her left, standing in a space his title alone did not warrant. From the side of her eye, Charity watched to see how Queen Charlotte would react. The woman stared studiously ahead, not remarking on the breach of protocol and thereby giving tacit approval.

And Charity ignored the rising whispers from the rest of the *ton*.

Epilogue

"Surprises are foolish things. The pleasure is not enhanced, and the inconvenience is often considerable."
—Jane Austen, Sense and Sensibility

From the corners of his eyes, Peregrine watched the expressions of people who were busier watching him and Charity than they were the visiting delegation. There was going to be a firestorm of gossip to rival their Vauxhall appearance tomorrow. And down the line, he could see that her parents could barely hide their dismay.

The Royal Chamberlain rapped his wooden staff on the floor, shushing the crowd, and announced in a ringing tone, "His Imperial Majesty, Alexander the First, Emperor and Autocrat of All the Russias!"

Tsar Alexander strode into the room, tall and striking beneath the chandeliers' gleam, his pale blue uniform ablaze with medals. His eyes swept the chamber before alighting upon England's ruling regent and queen, cooly assessing both people and the opulence of the room.

Charity and Peregrine bobbed their heads as he passed before them, and then turned their attention back to the door.

A second fanfare, more restrained, heralded the entrance of Frederick William III, the King of Prussia. Where the Tsar's stride had been commanding, Frederick's was more hesitant.

One by one the chamberlain proceeded, working his way through princes, military generals, political leaders, and aides. Peregrine could almost hear Charity make note of each person's appearance as they passed, particularly those with whom she would be expected to speak. He, however, was paying less attention to the names and faces, and more to the unspoken language their bodies conveyed.

Tsar Alexander was making jealous comparisons between his possessions and England's. The King of Prussia was trying to make himself look like he was the equal of Russia and England, but his posture showed the truth. And so on.

Charity was hoping someone would reveal their alliance with Marian Fitzroy practically the moment they presented themselves to the Crown. But if his mother was in hiding, it would never be so easy.

He watched the woman beside him as much as he observed the others. Charity kept her gaze forward, marking the Queen's expression with each sovereign. Whom did Queen Charlotte respect? Who elicited faint frowns? She studied them to avoid looking in the direction of her parents at all.

And as the ladies of the courts began to filter in, his interest in watching anyone besides Charity began to wane. His attention drifted until Charity stiffened beside him, causing him to look up.

Pale blonde hair, twisted into an elaborate knot, and held in place with pearl encrusted combs. A young face. A familiar face.

Lark?

His sister walked past the pair of them, her head held high, with the ladies of the Russian court.

It was so unexpected, he was frozen stiff and didn't notice the woman stepping out of line to approach them. Not until she was already upon them, with a false smile on her lips and the monster watching from behind her eyes.

"Peregrine, love, how well you're looking!" Marian murmured, pressing a cold kiss to his unresisting cheek. "How fortunate we arrived in time to wish you a happy birthday."

Dear Gentle Reader - do not despair! This story continues in Radiance and Revenge, book 3 of the Diamond of the Ton Regency Mysteries.

A royal threat. A dangerous love. A feud that refuses to die.

After enduring the court's suspicion, Lord Peregrine Fitzroy has finally earned back his standing, and Charity's heart. But the arrival of her family in London threatens to reopen old wounds and reignite a bitter feud that once made their love impossible.

Charity, Duchess Atholl, is ready to stand beside the man who was once her enemy. Yet just as they begin to build a future together, foreign royals descend on London with secrets, schemes, and ties to a powerful adversary thought to be in hiding. Determined to uncover who is harbouring their most dangerous enemy, the couple is drawn into a tangled web of espionage, revenge, and political sabotage..

As whispers swirl of a plot to upend the royal succession, Peregrine and Charity must outwit an opponent who knows exactly how to strike where it hurts most. Loyalties will be tested.

One misstep could cost them their love, their lives… or the crown itself.

Find out in **Radiance and Revenge**. Order now on Amazon.

Radiance and Revenge
A Diamond of the Ton Regency Mystery

A royal threat. A dangerous love. A feud that refuses to die.

After enduring the court's suspicion, Lord Peregrine Fitzroy has finally earned back his standing, and Charity's heart. But the arrival of her family in London threatens to reopen old wounds and reignite a bitter feud that once made their love impossible.

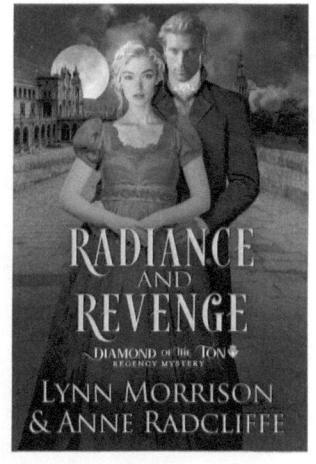

Charity, Duchess Atholl, is ready to stand beside the man who was once her enemy. Yet just as they begin to build a future together, foreign royals descend on London with secrets, schemes, and ties to a powerful adversary thought to be in hiding. Determined to uncover who is harbouring their most dangerous enemy, the couple is drawn into a tangled web of espionage, revenge, and political sabotage..

As whispers swirl of a plot to upend the royal succession,

Peregrine and Charity must outwit an opponent who knows exactly how to strike where it hurts most. Loyalties will be tested. One misstep could cost them their love, their lives… or the crown itself.

Find out in **Radiance and Revenge**. Order now on Amazon.

Historical Notes

We had a hard end date for this book, knowing we were having Lady Fitzroy make her grand return as part of the Russian entourage. Given she had already attempted to foil the royal wedding plans, we thought hard about her next step. It did not take us long to land on destabilising the government.

In 1814, the Tories had tight control over the House of Commons. Though we may play fast and loose at times with the historical record, toppling a major political party was a step too far. We needed something big enough to cause a major scandal, but small enough that it could conceivably be foiled. Counterfeiting rose to the top of our list.

Counterfeit bank notes were a significant problem in 19th century England. Privately owned banks had the right to print and issue their own currency, so long as they held an equivalent amount of official currency in their vaults. The Bank of England did not take control over the printing and issuance of bank notes until 1844, as part of the Bank Charter Act of 1844.

Anyone with a printing press and a capable forger could copy standard bank notes. While such an operation certainly would have made our life simpler, spending counterfeit funds wouldn't be enough to achieve Marian Fitzroy's aims. We had to think bigger.

That's how we landed on the idea of counterfeiting exchequer bills. The British government used these as a primary vehicle to fund the Napoleonic Wars. They were more difficult to counterfeit, as they required the official paper and ink, and potentially ownership registration in the government ledger. If Marian Fitzroy wanted to accomplish something of this magnitude, she would require a friendly banker and a connection in the Treasury Department.

We chose to put the counterfeit funds into the hands of various Tory grandees as a means of drawing negative public attention to the party. Had such a scandal actually taken place, it would not have been impossible for the Prime Minister to resign, and to call for new elections.

We want to touch on a few of the real historical figures, places, and newspapers we mentioned in the book:

Beau Brummel and his bow window at White's - We have to thank fellow author Candice Hern for making us aware about White's Club's introduction of a bow window to its famous facade in 1811. Beau Brummel, regency arbiter of fashion, was a fast friend of young Prinny, until the two had a falling out in 1813. In 1811, Brummel immediately staked out the new bow window as his throne in miniature, a place where he could sit in judgment on members' cravats. By 1814, his reputation was in fast decline following Prinny breaking off their friendship. It suited our purposes to have Perry lay claim to his infamous power seat at the start of the book.

The party at Burlington House - for the riot scene, we needed a host who was highly placed enough to warrant having the royals as his guest, but also independent enough to have friends on both sides of the political aisle. Lord George Cavendish captured our attention. Although he did not officially purchase Burlington

House from his nephew, the Duke of Devonshire, until 1815, he did make use of it earlier. We took some liberties with making him the host a full year before his purchase of the house, but we hope you will forgive us.

Burlington House guests - in addition to the usual Who's Who, we included some more unusual personages on the guestlist. Nathan Rothschild provided us with early inspiration for Goldbourne, so we put him there as a nod. John Scott - then Baron Eldon - was indeed the Lord Chancellor of the Exchequer during this time period. Elizabeth Vassall Fox, Baroness Holland, was the wife of Henry Vassall-Fox, 3rd Baron Holland. She was a famous political hostess of the day, with her husband a leading Whig, and well-placed to help someone like Charity make sense of the events. The last guest we needed was someone brave enough to stop the rioters from getting violent. Anne chose Thomas Graham, 1st Baron Lynedoch, a man with a storied military and political career.

Moving on to the Grand Duchess - sometimes we stumble across a real person with such an incredible history that they all but demand to be included. This was the case with Catherine Pavlovna of Russia, Grand Duchess of Oldenburg. We could spend days recounting her antics during her visit to England in 1814, but it was much more fun to incorporate our favourites into this book. When you have some free time, we strongly encourage you to learn more about her.

We mentioned two newspapers in this story - the Morning Post and the Morning Chronicle. The former was a conservative daily newspaper in circulation from 1772 to 1937 when it was purchased by The Daily Telegraph. The Chronicle, instead, took a radical position, one that landed its publisher in jail for libel on more than one occasion. It was also home to Charles Dickens, a few decades later.

The last historical place we want to highlight is the brief

mention of The Angel at Islington. It was there that we had Thorne leave his luggage after he learned of the gossip surrounding Charity and Peregrine. The Angel was a major coaching house on the road into London, and also where Thomas Paine is believed to have sat down to pen his Rights of Men in 1790. It was exactly the type of place a tired traveler would choose to stay for a night, and where he might learn the latest news of London before arriving in the city.

This book ends on June 7, 1814, with the arrival of the royal visitors in St James. We have plenty more to say about the guests and the events, but we hope you will understand why we'll hold off on telling more until this historical notes in book three - Radiance and Revenge.

Acknowledgments

We'll start by thanking Kim Killion at The Killion Group for the amazing cover design. We are also super grateful for the editorial guidance Zoe Burton provided.

As always, our brave beta reader team of Ken Morrison, Brenda Timmons Chapman, and Lois King provided immeasurable support and feedback on the early drafts of this book.

From Lynn - I owe a debt of gratitude to Anne for putting up with me while writing this book. I scheduled surgery halfway through our writing time, and foolishly assumed I'd be back to work within a few days. Suffice it to say, it was definitely longer than that. Nonetheless, Anne refrained from killing me and picked up all the slack. Thank you for being the best book wife in the world!

Our final thanks go to you, our readers, for cheering us on, reading our books, leaving reviews, and helping us get out the word.

About Anne Radcliffe

As an American Expat living in Ontario with a husband and teen son, Anne Radcliffe spends a lot of time editing or writing in order to avoid having to become a Maple Leafs fan. Anne loves a great story no matter the genre or medium - books, graphic novels, TV, movies or video games. You can find out more about Anne on her website at AnneRadcliffe.com.

BB bookbub.com/authors/anne-radcliffe

g goodreads.com/anneradcliffe

a amazon.com/stores/author/B0D1VMVDZ1

About Lynn Morrison

Lynn Morrison lives in Oxford, England along with her husband, two daughters and two cats. Born and raised in Mississippi, her wanderlust attitude has led her to live in California, Italy, France, the UK, and the Netherlands. Despite having rubbed shoulders with presidential candidates and members of parliament, night-clubbed in Geneva and Prague, explored Japanese temples and scrambled through Roman ruins, Lynn's real life adventures can't compete with the stories in her mind.

She is as passionate about reading as she is writing, and can almost always be found with a book in hand. You can find out more about her on her website LynnMorrisonWriter.com.

You can chat with her directly in her Facebook group - Lynn Morrison's Not a Book Club - where she talks about books, life and anything else that crosses her mind.

facebook.com/nomadmomdiary

instagram.com/nomadmomdiary

bookbub.com/authors/lynn-morrison

goodreads.com/nomadmomdiary

amazon.com/Lynn-Morrison/e/B00IKC1LVW

Also by Lynn & Anne

www.ingramcontent.com/pod-product-compliance
Lightning Source LLC
Chambersburg PA
CBHW031742180726
48283CB00005B/1629